MR. AND MRS. DOCTOR

MR.
AND MRS.
DOCTOR

A NOVEL

JULIE IROMUANYA

COFFEE HOUSE PRESS
MINNEAPOLIS
2015

Coffee House Press books are available to the trade through our primary distributor, Consortium Book Sales & Distribution, cbsd.com or (800) 283-3572. For personal orders, catalogs, or other information, write to: info@coffeehousepress.org.

Coffee House Press is a nonprofit literary publishing house. Support from private foundations, corporate giving programs, government programs, and generous individuals helps make the publication of our books possible. We gratefully acknowledge their support in detail in the back of this book.

Visit us at coffeehousepress.org.

LIBRARY OF CONGRESS CIP INFORMATION

Iromuanya, Julie.
Mr. and Mrs. Doctor : a novel / by Julie Iromuanya.
pages cm
ISBN 978-1-56689-397-8
I. Title.
PS3609.R63M7 2015
813'.54—dc23

2014033362

PRINTED IN THE UNITED STATES

FIRST EDITION | FIRST PRINTING

For my mother

1.

CHAPTER 1

EVERYTHING JOB OGBONNAYA KNEW ABOUT SEX HE LEARNED FROM American pornography. So on their first unchaperoned meeting, Job rushed his new wife, splitting her thin body against the papered wall of their lavish honeymoon suite at the Presidential Hotel in Port Harcourt, Nigeria. Job tore at her lacy pink panties and only released his lips from her face to haltingly shout, "You-are-the-dirty-slut-girl!"

Ifi punched his gut with the sharp heel of her sandal. He crumpled. Together they landed on the floor in a tangled heap, legs splayed in every direction.

"You are ugly," she said, glaring at him. Potato-sack head. Stout shoulders. Hog's gut. Bushy, curling eyebrows. Thick glasses pushed into the lips of his nose. "Eh? And now a beast? I married a beast. Hey!" She wound up her fist and struck him squarely on an ear.

Job clutched his throbbing ear. For a moment, he struggled to unwind the underwear from his wrists before handing them back to her.

When Ifi attempted to put them on, the ripped elastic band left the underwear lopsided on her hips. "You see what you have done, oh?" She thought of the time and care she and Aunty had put into her appearance for this day—the matching underwear set, the hours cooking her hair in an egg-smelling relaxer and then curling it; her lipstick and eyeliner were now a streaky veneer finish on her face.

A solid fist banged at the door. Ifi disappeared into the bathroom, clutching at the panties. When Job opened the door, a man in a too-tight suit stared up at him with liquid eyes.

"Is everything fine, sah?" The man took in Job's appearance—his trousers with the zipper open and belt dangling, his face prickling with beads of sweat, his slack, bare chest. A smile gradually spread over his face.

Job cleared his throat and heard his father's voice in his ears. "What is this? You have come to disturb me on the day of my honeymoon with this nonsense?"

"No, sah, my apologies, sah," the man said.

Job and the man stood in the doorway, awaiting the next line in the script. Finally Job gently let the door close on the man's teasing grin.

He turned back to Ifi, who now sat on the bed with her legs crossed, her face turned away from him. He positioned himself so that his body was turned away from hers too, then gradually he made his way toward her. Still she remained unmoved. His hand snaked toward her bare, brown thigh. Her skin gleamed, shiny. Just before he touched her, his hand dropped short. He thought of her words. She had looked prettier in the photographs, even light skinned—not this tall, skinny thing with no buttocks. She was lucky a man like Job Ogbonnaya would even consider her appropriate for marriage. Although Job's life had been bare in America, he had never convinced himself that what he felt was loneliness.

She looked tossed apart to him, like the two legs of the goat his grandparents had butchered in honor of the engagement. On the day of the celebration, Job had stood back warily as the butcher knocked the goat unconscious before they pulled its insides apart and prepared it for roasting. He'd always loved goat meat, so much so that as a child he'd earned the nickname onye ohi, thief, from his mother and sisters, because he would always let his hand slip into the large pot and steal bits of meat as it cooked. Still, he'd wanted no part of the killing.

"I can give you back to your people," Job said.

Ifi turned a furious glare on him, one eye widening. Aunty and Uncle would be angry with her. After all, they had found her a doctor husband who lived in America. He had even promised to send her to an American university, so that she could be a nurse in his clinic. Aunty would say, *How can you, an orphan, be so ungrateful?* Aunty would say that all their hard work in raising her since her parents died had been in vain. Still, Ifi could not take this. She was nearly thirty, almost a decade older than he believed, not a child.

She would find her own way to her dreams without him. "I will go," she said. Their bags were open on the floor of the hotel room. Ifi began, indiscriminately, to dump article after article of clothing into her suitcase. Job saw his tan slacks disappearing into the bag. "That belongs to me," he said.

As if in rewind, Ifi flung clothes out of the bag. "It belongs to you!" she said. "It belongs to you!" Job ducked, barely missing the flying clothes.

"Ifi," he started. Then, clumsily, he added, "Darling." Although she didn't turn back, she stopped flinging objects from the bag. He thought of his virgin wife tensed against the wall and wondered. Surely she had been schooled in the responsibilities that came with marriage. But perhaps she hadn't. No one had explained it to him. He had been a boy of nineteen when he first came to America all those years ago.

Job sifted through his bags until, from far beneath the clothes and shoes, he produced a faded, well-worn magazine. He slid the magazine across the bed to Ifi and flipped it open.

It was a simple enough story. Page one: the doctor and the patient. The caption read, "Doctor, it hurts here," followed by, "Let me examine you."

Ifi flipped the page. The doctor's milky buttocks stared back at her. The patient had her arms and head back and was chortling wildly.

"What is this?" Ifi exclaimed. Was this how Americans paid for medicine? She covered her eyes, but couldn't help peeking through her fingers. She had been with one man before, but it was over in seconds, and she'd never actually seen him completely disrobed.

Suddenly there was a flickering of lights, a gasp, and the room filled with darkness. They waited for the generator to click on, Ifi curious to turn the page, and Job expecting to consummate the marriage without further complication. When the generator did not turn on, Job instead suggested that they leave the room for a meal.

They ate at an outdoor restaurant, partially shaded from the elements by skinny, frayed umbrellas. Fela Kuti roared from a radio. A big man in khaki pants and a loud printed shirt owned the restaurant. He wrapped Job in a thundering embrace. "Oga! Doctor!" he said, "Mr. Doctor, how long are you staying with us?" Job told him he was with his wife on honeymoon, and the man proceeded to rattle off all the years he had known Job and his family.

"This man's father is my father's cousin. I have known him since before he could stand."

Job ordered two Coronas. When the bottles arrived, sweating cool, wet pearls down the sides, he paid in U.S. dollars. Ifi and Job sat silently across from one another as he swallowed his Corona and then hers. Job sucked the layers of slippery flesh free of the fish bone as Ifi nibbled. She sat quietly— thinking of the magazine—and wondered, *Is this how Americans pay my doctor husband?* Light streamed in diagonally, cutting his face into odd patterns. His features seemed to surrender to his surroundings. *Is this what America does to a man?*

Finally she spoke, her voice low. "Are Americans so poor that they must . . ." She couldn't finish her question without thinking of the naked doctor and patient.

Job sipped the beer and told her, "Money is time in America." Then he launched into telling her about the shops, the ladies' clothes, the shoes, and Ifi was no longer listening.

A beggar boy of perhaps nine moved from table to table with a pan full of peanuts. His lean, meatless face was filled with long lashes, and his sinewy limbs were shiny and exposed through the holes in his wrinkled Michael Jackson T-shirt.

Many of the dining couples flagged him away in annoyance or simply ignored him. But he refused to go unnoticed. He leaned into a table where a large woman and a thin man took up the seats. They were dressed well. He winked flirtatiously and clicked his teeth at the lady. "Mah," he said, smiling. "Mah."

"I will buy you a fur coat," Job said to Ifi. He would have to get one of fake fur.

"Mah," the boy said again.

"I am not your mama," the woman said, drawing her wobbly chin back. "I am not old enough to be your mama." Shifting her wig back, she turned away from him.

"This foolish boy," the man said. Still, with his knees pulled close together, he smiled and hunched forward, scraping the floor with a cane. He was old enough to be the woman's grandfather, much older than Job.

Ifi wondered how this man and woman had met. Ifi had met Job only once before their honeymoon. Even during the wedding, Job's junior brother had stood in while he was in America. All Ifi had remembered from her one meeting with Job was that his face was nothing more than a jagged relief etched on the dark. He'd sat across from Ifi, Aunty, and Uncle, all squeezed together on the smaller couch so that he could have the large one. Aunty and Uncle had unsuccessfully tried to borrow a generator for the occasion and had been forced to settle on kerosene, so they stiffly argued about Nepa, the oil truck drivers' strike, corrupt politicians, and the ongoing teachers' strike in abashed explanation. The kerosene had scrubbed roughly at Ifi's nostrils and throat. Outside, she'd heard the sounds of church services going on despite the dark along the length of their street. Children had been play-ing outside, chasing the rooster and dirtying their bony knees in the muddy roadway. She'd thought of how the ankles of the man who sat before her would, in light, appear like the children's: bloodied from the wet, dirt road.

Before they met, there were packages of gifts. At the time, Ifi knew noth-ing of the letters, pictures, and conversations with the people who would become her in-laws. All her life, Ifi had been instructed to tell neighbors, friends, agemates, that her father was *away,* whether they believed it or not. So she fooled herself into believing that the packages were from him—that he really did live in America or London or Germany, that he had never been arrested for suspicion of fraud, that he had never been investigated and then murdered before his arraignment. As her cousins paraded through the pot-holed streets of their neighborhood in blue jeans and sweaters that were too big for their slight frames and too bulky for the thick Nigerian heat, Ifi had imagined her father sitting behind a large desk in London, papers stacked neatly around him awaiting his signature.

Of the sweaters, blue jeans, and jewelry, Ifi kept nothing except for a red, gold-chained handbag that she took out only for church—and today. Only after the package's contents had been spread across the couches did Aunty and Uncle inform her that a man was coming to visit her. Aunty had watched her closely that day. "You see all the good things we've done for you? You, a skinny girl with nothing. No parents, sef. And now you will see America."

Ifi needed to ask Job about this America. Before leaving her cousins' laughter, Aunty's gossip, and Uncle's stories, she needed to know everything. But the skinny beggar boy was standing at their table now. Ifi began to shoo him away, but Job stopped him. The boy dumped the peanuts into his palms, tumbling his hands in such a way that he magically released the shells. He was grinning, proud of his work, but how could he be so pleased in his condition? She imagined him curled into a tight ball underneath a bridge near the hotel. The ground would be muddy, a deep red where the rain had softened the earth. If he slept deeply, he might not notice how close his face was to the water; the shit; the dead, malarial mosquitoes. Ifi shuddered. Instead of sitting at a fancy table alongside her doctor husband, she would have been an under-the-bridge girl, had it not been for Aunty and Uncle.

The little boy before her. Too small for his shirt. The shirt with all its holes. He would have gnats and lice in his hair. His skin, his lips, chalky from the residue of dusty dirt.

Job was still smiling in distracted amusement at the boy when Ifi thrust forward the bowl of peanuts. "Ngwa, go!" The peanuts splattered across the table and the floor. The boy's eyes met Ifi's in desperation, just for a second, before he averted his gaze to the ground in deference.

The restaurant owner was on them in seconds. He knocked the boy's head with the back of his hand. "Why must you disturb my customer? He is a doctor, here from America for only a short time. I will beat you today!" To Ifi and Job he said, "I am so sorry." The boy tried to run, but the man shoved him to the ground with his foot and began to beat him.

The boy whimpered and heaved tearless cries. "No, sah!" He turned to Ifi. "Sorry, Aunty!" he said. On his knees he begged, his thin, quivering frame on the floor before her.

Ifi's voice was small as she spoke. "Leave him." Everything stopped. A chill rose through her body. This was what it meant to be a big woman.

Half-bowing, half-filling the bowl, the boy attempted to sweep up the mess as he left. He would go hungry for the rest of the day, maybe the rest of the week, without the money he would have earned from the peanuts. "Leave him," Ifi said again, with force. "Ego," she said to Job. "We will pay for the nuts."

Job retrieved a few naira. He tossed them on the ground.

"Go," Ifi said. "Go!" The boy collected the money and ran as fast as his bony legs allowed.

When he was gone, the fat lady laughed into the skinny man's ears. The bartender brought Ifi and Job two more bottles of Corona. On the house. And Job said to no one in particular, "In America, boys like that are in school."

By the time they started back to the hotel, a steel gray had enveloped the orange sun as night began its descent. All around, the breeze interrupted the calm of long-necked palm trees. With their wares balanced on their heads, hawkers darted across the streets. Job's driver swerved through the gaps in the roadway with practiced turns that knocked Job and Ifi into one another. Each time they touched, Job felt the softness of her skin against his. He tried to reconcile this gentle touch with her harsh way with the boy, telling himself that he had been in America too long. Even the boy, with his tearless cries, had walked with his head erect. He would likely brag to the boys in his gang about how his crocodile tears had earned him double what they had earned. Now, more than ever, Job was glad to be home.

When they reached the hotel, they did not immediately return to their room. Instead, they made their way across the marble lobby floor that Job explained was imported from Spain, France, somewhere like that. A dull light glowed from the gift shop across the lobby. The gift shop was a boxed-in room with shiny glass walls. From the outside, the glass walls, illuminated by shocks of overhanging lights, gave the illusion that the cramped space was larger than it actually was. Nearly every inch of its shelves was loaded with trinkets: jewelry, clay figurines, wood-carved masks. Paintings of women with baskets on their heads were hanging or leaned against the walls, filling every available space. As Ifi gazed at the objects, her eyes stilled on a painting of a couple in an amorous embrace.

"Do you like?" Job asked.

"No." A necklace of shiny shells and beads was the first item within Ifi's reach. She grabbed it.

For the first time, the storekeeper pulled away from the cash register and gave her attention to the pair. "Ah, lady of fashion," she said. Up until then, she had been curtained behind paintings across the room, her eyes idly following the couple as she leafed through a magazine. "You must buy the earrings and bracelet too, or it will not be complete."

Without complaint, Job purchased the jewelry and handed it to Ifi, mentally subtracting the cost from the wad of bills tucked away in his brief-case. When they left the gift shop, both knew that they would be heading to the empty room, the large bed tauntingly illustrating its sole purpose.

❖

Ifi followed Job inside. Hot, stale air had settled for too long. Their bed had been remade, each pillow set delicately. The clothes Ifi had thrown about the room were neatly folded in their suitcases. Even the magazine was packed away as if the morning had never happened, as if Job and Ifi were entering for the first time.

Ifi set her handbag down and sat on the bed, the tiny package in her hands. "Will you not try them?" Job asked.

Ifi wordlessly unraveled the necklace, earrings, and bracelet. She slipped the earrings and bracelet on without trouble, but when it came to the neck-lace, she struggled. Her back and shoulders relaxed under Job's hands as he tried his fingers over the clasp. Finally he managed to connect it. He stepped back, swollen with the small success. It was beautiful.

When Ifi rose to make her way to the bathroom mirror, she could not move her neck. The clasp had caught on her hair. Job tried to pull it free, but Ifi swung her arms wildly as if swatting a mosquito. "Leave me!" she yelled. "Leave me, oh!"

Job yanked harder at the clasp. Suddenly the necklace exploded, shells flying in every direction.

Ifi collapsed to her knees and began to pick up the shells. Impossible. She would be on her knees all night, like the boy in the restaurant.

"Leave it," Job said. "I will buy another." Ifi ignored him, silent tears spreading down her cheeks.

When the lights went out again with a sudden whoosh, Job was relieved. In the darkness, Ifi continued to feel her way to each shell. Job opened and shut drawers in search of matches or a lighter. In the bottom drawer of the bathroom sink, his fingers finally closed over a box of matches, slightly damp with the scent of cleaning fluids. He tried each match until he finally found one that worked and struck it. From there, he could just make out a raw, half-eaten candle, which he lit.

With a backwards swipe, Job erased the perspiration from his face. He decided that he would return her to her people and go back to America alone. His family could begin the process again, inquiring into the reputation of each prospective family, sending him snapshots of stoic women, their heads draped in wigs, coolly gazing past the flash of the camera.

She should have been prettier, he told himself. After all, his family had made a point of forgiving her poverty; her good name would do. She was tall by his family's standards. Lean in a way that made wrappers and dresses appear ill fitting and silly. Still, her thinness was ideal for the blue jeans that American women wore. His father, who had never visited America but had watched every videocassette he had mailed him, had reminded Job of this. His grandmother had insisted her small buttocks would grow with the birth of their first child. *She is still just a child herself,* she had explained. Ifi's legs were bony and ridged at the knees, her face taut with strain around her eyes, as if she squinted furiously at everything. She was also not as light skinned as his mother would have preferred, and her hair was not ideal. But, Job reminded himself, she wasn't ugly.

Job sank down onto the toilet, striking his foot against Ifi's bag and knocking the few articles of clothing, makeup, perfume, and jewelry loose. He began to place each item back in the bag, using the flickering light of the candle as a guide. Women with all their tools. Men didn't have it as easy. If a woman was fat, thin, too dark, too light, too short, too tall, there was always something she could do about it. His sisters, Jenny and Florence, had used lightening creams for years, wearing tall heels to compensate for their short frames and even slipping cotton balls into their bras. When they went to their rooms at night, they were his plain sisters with ashy skin and acne, but when they reemerged, they were something new.

His fingers ran along a pearl necklace in Ifi's bag. He'd sent it to her many months before. He remembered the awkwardness of picking it out at Wal-Mart, the saleslady watching him closely as he gazed into the glass case. Now, he lifted it against his hairy chest and clasped the ends behind his neck. Success. Why hadn't he been able to get it right when it mattered?

With the pearls around his neck, he remembered the feeling he had the first time he wore a stethoscope. Strangely, it was just like this, the same satisfaction. A small smile grew on his face as he listened for his heartbeat once more. He was a boy the first time he'd heard this sound—the wonder, the amazement at a device that could track the rapid sound of his own music. His brother, Samuel, had smiled when Job asked if a small ear was in the tool.

After the funeral, when Job was going through his brother's things in the room they'd shared, he found the stethoscope again. Job fingered and played with it, listening to the sound for a long time, enthralled. His mother came in then and saw him on his knees with his dead brother's things scattered around him on the floor. She beat him, asking what he was thinking, playing with his brother's belongings. "Samuel will be angry. Hurry, put it away!" she had said, as if Samuel was among the living, as if he was still fighting for Biafra.

After the beating was over, and Job wept silently at his sister's side, his father called him over. Job's mother was turned away, her face set in a frown. His father had the box of Samuel's things. "Choose what you like," he said to Job, "and then I must never see you playing in this box, you hear?"

At first, Job didn't know what to do. He saw his mother with the look she made when she tasted something spoiled, so he waited, but he heard nothing. After a while, she turned to face him. Only then did he take the box. He went through it, lifting each object out slowly, examining it, deciding on its weight, its smell, its usefulness. Since the stethoscope was the start of all the trouble, he wanted nothing to do with it. Instead, he took a jazz record. He had never heard it play, but he knew one day he would have the money to buy a music machine of his own. He also took a cricket ball and mallet. He would practice until he was better than all of his agemates. Samuel's trousers were too long, but he took them anyway, and his brother's hat, which he tipped forward on his head, like his brother had. The brim dangled over his eyes. A smile twitched on his mother's lips, loosening the scowl, so he put on his brother's pants, adjusting his hips so that the waist gapped around his narrow body. Like the trunk of an elephant, the trouser legs bagged at his feet. His mother laughed and pulled him into her arms for a tight hug, her eyes wet with tears when she released him.

"He is not finished," his father had said. He pushed the box back toward Job. All that remained was the stethoscope. Job wanted nothing to do with it. "Take it," his father had said. Job shook his head furiously. His father reached for him and put it around Job's neck. He put the ear tips in Job's ears and then, kneeling before him, he placed the chestpiece to his own chest. Job heard no sound, so he adjusted the chest piece until he found the sound of his father's heartbeat, a dull, raspy thudding.

Standing in the hotel bathroom on the night of his honeymoon, Job no longer replayed his memory of the stethoscope. Instead, he remembered his mother's laughter at the sight of his small frame in his brother's oversized clothes. She had gone from tears to anger to laughter, just like that. But what had made her laugh? Was it merely the sight of him in his brother's clothes? It had to have been more than that.

Job picked up Ifi's perfume, sprayed it into the air, and sniffed. It smelled good. He twirled his fingertip in her rouge, absentmindedly dragging a deep red line across the sink. Then, still staring at the streak, he began to spread the rouge on his cheeks, then his eyelids, and finally his lips. Laughing, he reached for her bra, thinking of his flat-chested sisters standing before the mirror as small girls. He put it on, filling each cup with toilet tissue. Ballooning his chest, he made motions like a woman, then a gorilla, then the Incredible Hulk. The little cups barely jiggled on his chest. He chuckled— how silly this was! But maybe, like his mother did, Ifi would laugh; perhaps like his father did, Ifi would hope.

He didn't see himself in the mirror. Instead, he saw his reflection in Ifi's horrified expression as she leaned in the doorway: potbellied, tangled curly hairs escaping the bra, straps crookedly balanced on his broad shoulders, smudged red rouge covering his mouth, as much on his teeth as on his lips. She wasn't laughing, not even a hint of a smile. Ifi was paralyzed and Job was too, his mind flashing to the kind of humiliation her scorn could bring. He simply could not survive it. He had failed badly. Job struggled to peel off the bra. *Pretend this never happened. Send her home with the driver. Return to America. Alone.*

Suddenly, she let out a burst of laughter. She raised her hand, stopping him. Her eyes formed a question, then her lips followed: "Americans do this, too?"

"Nothing is too strange for Americans," he admitted.

Ifi motioned to her dress, heaped on the floor. With a toe, she gently kicked it to him. *Go on,* her look said, *don't let me interrupt you.*

Is she trying to make a fool of me? He couldn't. He wouldn't.

And suddenly he realized, understood, that something had been fixed, and would be broken if he did not proceed. Just not while she watched. Twirling his finger, he motioned for her to look the other way. She obliged. Carefully, he stepped into her dress, yellow with daisies along the bottom, fitted around the waist. It was a struggle, but eventually he secured the straps in the back. There he stood, ashy feet and unclipped toenails peeking out from under the hem. "Turn around," he said.

When she saw him, something like hiccups began to erupt from her chest—a laugh.

He sighed. He could do nothing but blow her a kiss.

As she backed through the open doorway, falling onto the bed, she continued to laugh. He turned his hips this way and that, standing on his toes as if in his sisters' heels. She laughed harder, nearly choking.

"No, no! Like this." Standing before him, Ifi began to stir her buttocks in slow, deliberate strokes. She spun as if she were unwinding. Once thin and featureless, her body was now defined only by the movement in her hips.

Jerking his hips, knees, and buttocks, Job imitated her. Uproarious laughter rose through Ifi, exaggerating the movement in her hips until she could dance no more. There was a freshness in her face. It made Job laugh as he hadn't in years.

It was only natural that gradually the clothes began to fall away. The dress refused to come off peacefully; it caught on the bra strap. He squeezed each buttock muscle individually as he lowered the bra to step out of it. It didn't occur to him that he could simply turn the bra around and unclasp it. One after another, he fought each article of clothing before tossing it to her.

With nothing but the makeup on, Job came toward his wife. Propped on the bathroom sink, the dancing flames peeked through the open doorway and illuminated Job just enough so that the contours of his heavily painted face were accented. Ifi ran her fingers across her husband's face, tenderly wiping away the rouge with his sweat. "This is only for your lips," she said. "And for your eyes, there is something called eye shadow and mascara. Did your mother not teach you anything?"

Then, in a blast, the light returned.

In the blinding light, their gazes split apart.

She could not look at him. He could not look at her.

CHAPTER 2

JOB OGBONNAYA'S FIRST WIFE HAD, LIKE IFI, ARRIVED IN A STACK OF photographs before they were ever married. To be exact, the photographs were postcards. Cheryl's was the third. On one side, stock photography of sandhill cranes dotting an amber Nebraska landscape with a blazing sunset misting around the birds. On the other side, no photograph; instead, her particulars: American, white, twice divorced. She was thirty-two. She owned two dogs and lived with her only sibling, a deaf-mute, in the home their dead parents had left them. His name was Luther. He was on disability. Cheryl was out of work. These were the things Job must know. The rest could be lies.

It was 1982, and he had only been in America for five years. He was just twenty-four, with less than a year left on his visa since he had flunked out of college. His father had given him money for tuition, but he was using it to pay for the arrangement. Half now and half after the business was done. His father didn't need to know. There would be too many questions. Job could talk to the proper people; he could take the proper tests; he could go back to school, later.

Job arrived that day wearing a tan corduroy suit, a tie, and cracked leather shoes that he had coaxed to a shine with vegetable oil. He had even barbered his hair. As agreed, they met by a Volkswagen across the street from the county clerk's office, a tall limestone building with dark windows like gapped teeth. An American flag clapped in the breeze, and the sprinkler chopped the bronze placard on the front of the building with a wet streak.

Emeka had said to marry quick-quick, and then *irreconcilable differences.* Emeka had said his was nineteen, a model. Emeka had said his was getting a degree in literature, but her parents wanted her to study home economics, so she was doing this to pay for her tuition. Anyway, she had said, it's a free country.

Instead of the American model studying Shakespeare, Job got a short woman, slender with loose, pale skin, red hair, and a freckled face full of teeth, like a small boy. Her stonewashed jean skirt exposed knobby, raw knees. Surely, she was older than the thirty-two on the postcard.

In an hour they would stop processing applications for the day. There were two men waiting upstairs, the broker told them, the witnesses. Once the money had been exchanged, the broker left them on their own. After, the broker would return and they would exchange the second half. In a few months they would be divorced, and it would be like the marriage had never happened.

As soon as they met, without even looking at him, Cheryl said, "I don't usually do this."

They always say they have never done this before, Emeka had said. *It is a mistake to believe them.*

"Of course," Job said to her with a curt smile. "Of course. You will change your dress and we will go."

"What do you mean?" Cheryl asked.

"This is not what you will wear."

"What's wrong with what I have on?"

Could she really have intended to appear without properly dressing? Real or not, this was a wedding and should be observed accordingly. Job eyed her closely.

They will ask you to spend more money than you have agreed, Emeka had said. *Do not fall into this trapdoor.*

"I will not buy you anything more. You understand."

"Wait a minute," she said. "You think I want *you* to buy me clothes? *You?*" She spoke as if conversing with a diseased goat.

Job shook his head. He would have to tell the broker that this one was not good for the price.

"First of all, this is not Africa, o.k.? This is America. It's a free country. We can wear whatever we want here. Second of all, I don't need your money. I don't need to take anything from you. And third of all—" she took a deep breath. "Do you have a light?"

Just as Job reached into his pocket for his lighter, she produced a packet of cigarettes. He stopped himself. It was one thing for her to dress so foolishly on such a day. It was yet another for her to smoke like a man in his presence, America or not. "No, I am sorry," he said.

Across the parking lot, there was a strip of faded brick buildings and linked to those, a gas station convenience store. "I'm gonna run down the street to the gas station and get a lighter," she said.

"Come now," Job said. "You can smoke your cigars after. One hour is remaining. They are waiting."

"Just back off, man. I need to relax." She kneaded her fingers into her face. "I need a cigarette."

Slowly, he lifted the lighter out of his pocket. Fixing his gaze on her, he spoke coolly. "You need to smoke." When she sucked her teeth in surprise, he did not bother to feign an apology.

She poked out her lips and put the cigarette between them anyway. Again and again she clicked the lighter on, but there was no flame. She flung the lighter into the street. "You did that on purpose." Her fingers pressed into her temples so hard that they left red prints along her hairline. "Fuck, I can't do this."

"Okie," Job said, frowning. "Okie, we will buy you a cigarette lighter."

They stood along the doors of the gas station. Cigarettes were a part of the job, she said. So he was paying for that now, or it would be added to everything else in the end. *Fine,* Job had said. Fine. She hadn't eaten, and when they entered the gas station she wanted food too. But he drew the line at the cigarette lighter.

Once outside, she wouldn't light the cigarette until he turned away. He was making her "antsy." But he would only go as far as the end of the build-ing. From a payphone, Job dialed Emeka's number.

"Emeka," he said, "how are you, my friend?"

"I am living on top of the Chrysler Building. And you?"

"My man, I am preparing to become an American citizen." Job laughed into the phone. He turned away from the receiver and faced Cheryl, who was still sucking on the cigarette. She twisted the frayed ends of her skirt with her other hand.

"Excellent," Emeka said, "and after, you will come and we will celebrate."

"Of course, my man," Job said, "but I am wondering: are some American women more prepared in these arrangements than others?"

"Abeg, Job. Have you not listened to me? I hope you are not wining and dining for this American." Emeka sighed into the phone. "Do not make a fool of yourself. Americans are way-o."

"What are you talking about? Do I look like a fool?" Job asked. "Ah-ah! She is long legged and blonde, like a model."

Cheryl pinched the cigarette with the heel of her shoe, gathered her worn-out purse straps, and started for the county clerk's office.

"I have to go. I will call you back." Before Emeka had a chance to respond, he hung up.

This time, Cheryl entered the county clerk's office before he did. All the way down the dark, airless halls, her sandals left a hollow thud while his scuffed soles creaked.

Two men in tan slacks and tucked shirts leaned against a tall wooden door with the number 113 stenciled on it. One of the men was white with tufts of hair sprouting from around a faded baseball cap, and the other was a Native American with a greased ponytail. When Cheryl saw the men, she stopped.

"I need to eat," she said. "I feel sick to my stomach."

"Let us finish this, oh," Job said in exasperation.

"We need to eat now," Cheryl said.

"You want chips? You want Coca-Cola? We will buy you Coca-Cola when we are finished."

"Look," Cheryl said. She was beginning to shake. "I am not some whore, o.k.? I barely know you."

Down the hall, the men glanced in their direction.

"Lower your voice," Job said.

Cheryl's lips had whitened. "You think just because you come to this country and we give you a job and you make a little money, you can do whatever you want. It ain't fair." She was near tears. "I mean, I was raised Catholic." Her voice lowered. "Marriage is forever."

Job thought her words over. Cheryl had been married and divorced twice. That was not the problem.

She gripped the edges of her skirt. "My parents, they would be turning in their graves over this. *You.*" Again, there was that peculiar note of disgust.

Sweat dampened Job's brow. "What is the problem?"

"I'll be sick. I ain't some actor, you know. If I go in there feeling like this, I'll give it all away. My brother has the liar's face, not me."

Her brother. Job remembered the name on the card. Luther. He thought of his own brother, Samuel—older, taller, stronger, smarter—the first son, the one meant for America. "Luther," he said, gently. "What is his age?"

"He's a year older—that makes him thirty-three," Cheryl said. "But he's no good. A prime-time bastard."

Again, Job thought of Samuel. Sharp in a way his father had glowingly called wit, tact. But was it really that?

She clenched her fists at her sides. "I lose my job and everything goes to shit. We lose the house and then there's nothing."

"Everything will be okie," Job said. "We will finish and you will receive the second half of the money."

"No!" Cheryl said. She started to walk away. "Fuck it. I don't need this. Fuck you and fuck Luther."

Job grabbed her by the wrist. "I paid you." Glancing up, he met the eyes of the white man. The man untucked his shirt and started toward them.

"It ain't even enough money," Cheryl said.

"You will get the second half when we are finished." Job's voice was a whimper.

"You can't speak English? I said it ain't enough."

"You want chips? You want Coca-Cola?" Job asked. "Fine. But I will not take you to eat in a restaurant."

"Is there a problem?" the man asked.

"No problem," Job said. Cheryl pushed out her lips.

The man rushed toward Job and turned up the collar of his shirt. "Are you trying to run a scam?" The man looked to Cheryl for an answer, but she was suddenly still. He turned from her to Job and back to Cheryl again. "Silas said be here at four and you two don't show up and it's almost five. What's going on?"

"There is no problem," Job said through gritted teeth. "I am paying the woman." Without counting, Job reached into his pocket and produced the remainder of cash in his pocket. The man loosened his grip. Job adjusted his collar and flicked it where the man's filthy hands had touched him. Only after he handed her the money did the man back away. Cheryl stuffed it into her purse.

"And after we're done, he's gonna pay the other half, right?" she asked.

The man looked from Job to Cheryl. Job's fists tightened. He met the eyes of the other man, who gave him a long, tired look. It was as if he met this scene once a day. It was as if he was saying, *You Africans fall for this every time.* Job felt the blood rush to his face. He nodded slowly. Then, once again, he flicked away at the filth of the white man's farmer hands from his neckline.

Job sat licking the remnants of spicy pepper soup from his fingertips as he told Emeka about the blonde, tall-legged American model he had married earlier that afternoon. King Sunny Adé's *Explosion* rumbled in the background, and Job shouted to be heard over the lyrics. "I am not lying," he said. "She even offered to blow job me."

"You are lying, my friend," Emeka said with a clap.

A door swung open and closed. It was Emeka's wife, Gladys, wrapper bound tightly at her armpits and stomach ballooning, pregnant even in shadow. In the five years that Job had known Emeka, he had watched him graduate from bachelor to married man. He had begun, like Job, as a student studying for a bachelor's degree. Emeka studied engineering. Job studied molecular biology, the degree that was supposed to get him into medical school. Emeka, like Job, had worn wrinkled suits with high collars and wide legs even on the hottest of days.

Five years later, Emeka was in graduate school, the civil engineering program at the University of Nebraska Omaha; Job had failed out of his undergraduate program and was employed as a nurse's assistant at a local hospital. With his medical background, he earned the certificate quickly. All that mattered was that he worked in a hospital. The experience would help him in medical school, because eventually, he assured himself, he would make it there.

Annually, when his father sent him tuition money, Job stored it in a savings bond. Even as his father's businesses in Nigeria began their decline, somehow, faithfully, he managed to send Job the money to educate him abroad. His father even bragged to his friends that it was the duty of the old to care for the young, so the young could care for the old one day.

At first Job thought about returning the money. After all, his family needed it. His father would never admit it, but his mother wore less jewelry with every annual visit. But there would be too many questions. What had he been doing in America all this time? How could he possibly have failed his classes? His father's face would be hard, the look Job saw when Samuel disappointed them all by dying.

There was also no sense in giving Emeka fodder for gossip or his unrelenting, unsolicited advice—*You know, my friend, there are three things a man must do in his native land: marry, bury, and retire. America is the stepping-stone. If you cannot make it here, then go home a joke*—and so they spent most free evenings in airless rooms, sweating into the yellowed armpits of old linen shirts as they discussed their favorite topic.

"A-ah! A-mer-eeka!"

"A-ah! A-mer-eeka!" Emeka clapped again.

Gladys arched an eyebrow in the direction of the television, where Tom Brokaw spoke in measured syllables. Usually Brokaw elicited their exclamations. She dumped one of the children in Emeka's lap, a girl, all legs with large wet eyes and a charcoal cotton ball of hair.

But for the globe that Emeka carried for a stomach, he had changed little over the previous five years. The greatest change Job had noticed was in Gladys. In the beginning she wore her hair in neat plaits, a concentric design of endless circles woven together into tight bunches at her nape. Her nails were always a bright red, and her lips were painted to match. She was one of the big-bottomed women whom Job and his school friends would sing at as teenage boys as they hung from the limbs of the trees leading into town. They would promise the women that they would marry them and build them a palace of gold. They would line the streets with American dollars. They would dress the women in diamonds. *There she is, Miss America,* they would sing.

Gladys would emerge from the wings of any room with two dripping mugs of Sapporo. When Job would lean to sip from his mug, Emeka would always smack Gladys's bottom swiftly. Huffing at him, she would exclaim and straighten up just as Job looked in their direction. Always there was a look in her eyes that complemented that of Emeka's, a look that said, *This is the American Dream.*

That day, Gladys smelled of onions, Similac, and sweat. She swatted an errant fly and turned a fierce look at the girl. "Stay with your father!" Only then could Job make out another child, a baby girl jiggling against Gladys's backside where she was bound tightly with cloth. Job could never keep count of the multiplying children, all girls. Gladys never joined Job and Emeka like she used to, balanced on one end of the sofa, her voice shrill as she interjected on behalf of one cause or the other.

"Chai! I do not believe it," Emeka said. His entire body shifted, and the child sprawled from his lap where she had just begun to nod to sleep. At that, the girl howled. Emeka pressed her face to his neck. Her cries were muffled, and his neck slickened with her saliva and mucous. Her cries went unabated. He jostled her, his shoulder jutting in an uneven rhythm.

"I cannot believe it, my friend," he repeated.

"I am not lying," Job said with satisfaction.

Suddenly a fan clicked on, and the chopped sound of another daughter's voice joined it, following the fan as it turned a short arc. Like her father, she was all legs and stomach.

"Turn that off! Can't you see your father speaking?" Emeka bellowed in disgust. "Go help your mother." The girl bounded to the kitchen, squealing as she thundered across the room.

"The next one will be a boy," Job assured him, knowing full well that Gladys and Emeka would never have a boy. In a small way, he relished that certainty.

Just for a second, Emeka glared. Job rested his head on the wooden ridge of the La-Z-Boy in satisfaction.

Emeka's scorn was quickly replaced with amusement. "Tell me, now, what would I want with a boy?" He lifted the sniffling child's face to his and blew a wet, airy kiss at her cheek. She shrieked. "Boys, they grow up and leave their fathers. They chase ugly American whores." He met Job's eyes with a wink. "These ones will all marry Nigerians. This one will marry a lawyer. You see how she cries and cries? She will win any argument. And that one—" he indicated the door. "That one will marry an engineer. You see how she looks at the fan? She is interested in the way machines work." He stroked the puff of his daughter's hair, wet with his sweat and her saliva. He looked into her watery eyes. "Your baby sister will marry a doctor." He looked back at Job with an avuncular smile. "One day, maybe you will be so fortunate."

Job frowned, faltering for a moment. "I am a bachelor." Mustering all the dignity he had, he added, "I am a free man."

"Yes, you are a free man, a bachelor," Emeka conceded. "But you are free in the way of Americans." He twisted his thumb at the storm of rioters on the television. The camera returned to Brokaw, who spoke in his gravelly voice about the scene. The Americans were in New York City's Central Park, rallying against nuclear weapons. "The Americans are happy with nothing."

Bruce Springsteen and Linda Ronstadt were among the attendees. "Look at this nonsense," Emeka said. "The Americans fight against the nuclear weapons they have made and given to other nations." He jerked a thumb at Springsteen. "This one—I have heard his music, singing of crashing on the highway. What does he know of nuclear weapons? And this one, she should return to her husband and children. She has married the California governor, you know."

Under his breath, Job retorted, "When you make the rules, you do as you please. That is the golden rule."

"Ah, yes, the words of a Mobutu. A man like you would say such a thing."

Job thought of his brother, the one his father had lost in the war, the one they had all lost in the war because of his weakness, the arrogance of a small man. "What kind of nation can be ruled by a small man? Any man can tell you this."

Gladys returned just then, elbowing her way through the room with one child strapped to her back and another wrapped around her leg. The baby in Emeka's lap was asleep now. "Good," Gladys said. She began to reach for the girl, but Emeka stopped her.

"Let me help, dear."

Job watched in silent disgust as Emeka carefully rose, making a show of his gentleness with his precious daughter. He kissed her forehead and cheeks multiple times, twirled his fingers through the tangles of her hair, and smoothed out the creases of her shrunken onesie. Emeka and Gladys marched toward the back room, where Job could already imagine the scene: Emeka laying the girl on the bed, the mother placing a kiss on her forehead. Just as they reentered the room, Emeka forcefully smacked Gladys's rear. She feigned protest, a chuckle caught in an exclamation. Then she told him she needed milk. Like a soldier ready for battle, Emeka, armed with his shoes in one hand and his wallet in the other, headed for the door. Job followed.

Night overtook them. Normally, they fought over who would drive. That day, Job didn't have it in him. Walking to the car, Job dreaded the over-stuffed seats piled with the children's toys. After a short series of protests, the Audi started. It climbed the curb, toeing the pavement in a way that reminded Job of the way Emeka walked: forcefully, with all the weight bearing as far down as possible on his heels. They started through the night, hot wind blowing through the windows like stale breath, stopping once they reached a gas station.

In the curt, overenunciated English Emeka used with Americans, he ordered the attendant to fill his car with plus unleaded fuel. "I do not want any of the impurities," he explained. Then he burst forward in his long strides. Emeka bought the milk, a small bunch of lollipops for his daughters, and a pack of mints for Gladys. Job bought two bottles of Heineken.

Just as they returned to the car, they could see the attendant slouched in his seat against the poles. A messy streak of dirty water still cut across the windshield, and the gas meter on the pump showed that he had fueled the car with regular unleaded. Emeka's jaw tightened. In unrepentant disdain, the attendant turned his nose up and watched them. His mouth widened into a smile, revealing clean, straight teeth. It was a surprise hidden in his dirt-streaked, sun-browned face. Where the collar of his blue work shirt pulled away from his neck, a pink band of skin was exposed. He was the same trash that Job had recognized in Cheryl that morning. It filled him with disgust that inched toward rage.

"This is not what my friend ordered." Surely there would be no charge for the fuel. "This is not plus unleaded."

"Excuse me?" the attendant asked.

"Do you not speak English?" Job asked, his voice rising.

"Come again?"

There was no crowd, just the three men, surrounded only by the rusted pillars that held the tarp over the gas pumps. Inside the convenience store, another man leaned heavily against his palm, staring blankly into the television screen.

"Thank you, my good man," Emeka said to the attendant. He stood between the two. "This is exactly what I ordered."

"No, this is regular unleaded."

"What are you talking about? I ordered regular unleaded. The man is correct."

The attendant nodded warily as Emeka's declamations grew in gusto.

"Job, my friend, you are not hearing well."

Job understood. He said no more.

Emeka paid the attendant the money. Then, like an afterthought, he gave him a hefty tip. "Thank you, my good man," Emeka said again.

In the car, Emeka sat up straight in the driver's seat, as proud as if he had won some war. Bright spots of headlights left a dazzling glare on the windshield.

Job fumed with rage. "Way-o Americans. There was no need to give him a tip."

"Job, must you shame yourself wherever you go?" Emeka turned on the radio. A scratchy horn announced the beginning of a jazz song.

They turned onto a narrow road. Weeds snapped across the beams of light. Job gazed out the window. He did not want to play Emeka's games of diplomacy. He had been an accomplice many times, but today needed to be different. It was the arrogance in the man's action. How easy it would have been for him to simply fill the tank properly, just as it would have been easy for those men to expose Cheryl for the fraud she was.

And Job knew Emeka. He was just the way Job imagined Samuel would have been, if he had lived, if he had reached America instead of Job, like their father had planned. Perhaps it was Samuel's arrogance that had killed him in the end, not any bullet. Perhaps in some strange way this was why Job had remained friends with Emeka all these years. After all, he reminded himself, he had not, in nearly a year, been able to admit to Emeka that he had flunked out of school. He could not be Emeka's joke to Gladys over dinner. He could not be the joke of his hometown in Nigeria. He could not be his mother's pity and his father's failure. Because of this, Job and Emeka still met in the student union lounge several times a month to discuss their classes. "You have made your point."

Emeka whistled with the song's horn section and tapped his palm on the steering wheel in time with the drums. "So, you say this American woman asked to blow job you?" Emeka asked.

A small smile widened on Job's lips. "I'm not lying."

Emeka pulled a finger along his mustache. "Hey! American woman!" The familiar joviality had returned. "What did you say when she offered?"

Job laughed heartily. "You know the answer."

Emeka turned to him. "You said yes, no?"

Job fell back in his seat. "I am a man." After a pause, he added, "Of course I said yes."

"Where did you take her?"

Job had not thought so far ahead. "I took her behind the car." He paused. "She insisted."

"Hmm." Emeka sighed. "Me, no thanks." He turned his head swiftly from side to side.

It was Job's turn to react with shock. "What is wrong with your head?" Job asked. "An American, tall-legged blonde."

"Only a fool would combine his business with his pleasures." Emeka spat out the side of the window. "Have I not taught you well? America is for business. Marry, bury, and retire in Nigeria." They had just pulled into his driveway, the gravel crunching under the car's tires.

Inside, the house was silent and still, each child asleep and King Sunny Adé at rest. Gladys received the milk. "What has taken you so long, oh?"

"My wife, Job has been looking for trouble," he said. With a small wink in Job's direction, he added, "First he begins by harassing the store clerk. You see, if it had not been for me, World War III would begin today."

Job sulked. "Your husband is a United Nations peacekeeper."

Gladys smirked but said nothing. Instead, she poured some milk into a pot and set it to boil on the stove.

When he had her full attention, Emeka continued. "My dear, you will never imagine the disgusting ideas in this man's head."

Gladys drained a tin of Ovaltine into the boiling pot. She stirred slowly.

"Imagine, sleeping with an American whore," Emeka said.

"Eh?" Gladys turned a startled gaze in Job's direction that sank into deeper and deeper levels of disgust.

"Yes, Job," Emeka said. He spoke evenly, like Brokaw reporting the news. "Tell my wife about how you took the *whore* behind a car."

It was as if Gladys was staring into a pot of urine and feces. Job withered under her glare. He could not call Emeka a liar in front of his own wife, yet he had no words for himself. What could he say in his defense?

"Gladys," Job said, "abeg, don't listen to your husband's foolish jokes."

Emeka chuckled and nuzzled into Gladys's chin, gracing her with a kiss. "Don't mind him, my dear. It is because he is alone. One day, my friend, you will find a jewel like this one. One day. And then you will not waste your time with whores."

Imbecile. Only in America could a man like Emeka rise to something. In Nigeria, he was nothing more than a pauper's son, unlike Job. Most of all, he hated the imaginary American woman, the tall-legged model, and the red-haired Cheryl, with her small boy's face.

Nineteen years later, it was the fall of 2001, the year the United States was attacked. Just days before Ifi was to arrive in America, it was the small boy's face, the mouth full of teeth, and the red hair that Job remembered when he heard the voice on the other end of the phone. He went cold and set down the paintbrush in his hand.

"Job, it's Cheryl," she said. And then, as if it was an afterthought, she added, "your wife."

Remembering the paint on his hands, Job stopped the fingers that ran through his hair. It was under his fingernails and even on his bare feet, this eggshell white that the fools at the hardware store had lied about to him and said was as white as the notebook paper he had brought in for them to sample for the walls of his apartment.

"You are not my wife. You are a liar," Job said. His voice choked with emotion. The marriage was done with, he told himself. He had been a citizen for nearly nineteen years. There was nothing more to say about it now.

"Don't hang up. Please, Job," she said. "I'm sorry. I was a stupid kid. And well, it was Luther. It wasn't even my idea. The whole idea was Luther's. I didn't want to have anything to do with it, but he made me. I'm an honest woman. I keep to myself and go to work and file my taxes. That's what I do. And I bet you don't even pay taxes. But me, I always pay mine. And I never cheat or lie on them like most people." Her voice was liquid with tears and snot.

"I am hanging up the phone now," Job said.

"Wait! You can't hang up," she said. "Please. There's something you gotta know."

Job waited.

"After we got married, I needed more money. You didn't give me enough for the house."

"What?"

"Don't be mad at me," she said. As if they were old friends. As if this was just a small disagreement. "There're some things I applied for using your name and mine."

"What are you talking about?"

"Anyway, we were married. It's totally legal. I didn't break any laws."

"That's fraud," Job said, heat rising to his face. "Won-der-ful. I have met Satan."

"No, no, no!" Her voice rose like a siren. "I never stole any of it from you. I paid it all. You probably got better credit because of me."

"Tell me, what is this?" His volume met hers.

"I couldn't open a line all by myself after Danny—my ex, the first one. That's it. Anyway, Luther, that bastard, he says he'll turn me in to the police, knowing full well it was his idea to use your name. Job, you can thank me," she said. "You have good credit because of me. I paid the bills every month. I did what I had to do to pay them."

"Luther."

"Your brother-in-law. My bastard brother." She gulped, and the wail started again. "He says we should take the loss and sell the house. He calls it dead weight. But I won't, Job. I can't. My daddy built this house for my mother. He had nothing, put everything in it. And me too. I don't have a single good thing. All I got is the house. I got nothing, and the house has everything. And Luther never did anything to help, even though he's getting those disability checks."

"What do you want?" Job asked. "Again, you ask for money."

"No, no money. I wouldn't ask for a dime, I promise."

"You want a cigarette lighter?" The laugh began deep in Job's chest and spilled out sideways.

Cheryl joined in his laughter, an uncertain, nonsensical laugh that built in pitch. "No, no, of course not," she said. "I'm just a little behind right now, you know? I been paying the bills real good all this time. I work in a florist shop. I wait tables. I do landscaping. I walk dogs. I wash dishes. I do it all to make those payments. Only now . . ."

"You are asking for money. Like last time."

"This time is different. I'll pay you back. It's a loan."

"No," he said. How simple.

"It's not like that, Job," she said. Her voice floundered between mean and desperate. She hadn't decided. "We're together. We're in this together, whether you like it or not. We were married. I'm within my legal rights."

Together. The first time she said the word, it sounded foreign to Job. Imagine, the ugly, redheaded American with a small boy's face. The second time, it filled him with rage. Thinking of Ifi, thinking of her smile on the night of their arranged honeymoon as he danced for her, he said, "Cheryl, there is no together." The dissolution of marriage papers had been signed years before, submitted to the county clerk with no contestation from her. In fact, she hadn't even bothered to show up to the hearing. On the line labeled *Reason,* he had written *Irreconcilable differences.* What an understatement. She was ugly, crude, a liar, way-o.

Now he was a citizen. An American. He had no need to even hear her voice. He would return to painting this room for his wife, his real wife. "There is Job. There is Cheryl," he said calmly. "No together business. I will help this Luther send you to jail. And you will never call this number again." He left room for one final word before he pounded the phone into the receiver. "Thief."

CHAPTER 3

A T THE AIRPORT, IFI WAS SUDDENLY AFRAID. WITHOUT THE YELLOW DRESS and lopsided bra, Job was unfamiliar to her. He wore a white lab coat over a flat black suit. Protruding from his right pocket was a stethoscope.

They did the dance: their eyes met, separated, reconnected, and separated a final time before Job collected her bags. "Kedu?" he asked.

"Ọ dị mma." Fine, Ifi said.

"Welcome."

She gazed curiously at his stethoscope. "You have just come from hospital."

"Yes," and he added importantly, "a patient, a most troubling one. This man's dementia has left him nearly crippled. He needs extra care. Many nights, I'll be away." He paused and continued carefully. "He was an important man once. All the nurses—*my* nurses—call him Captain."

Ifi nodded. "Captain. He is important. Will I meet him?"

"No." And suddenly, he laughed. "Of course not. No need to worry yourself over patients. This is my business." He paused, and she felt him drawing his eyes over her coat. "You are wearing it. Good. You will need it this winter."

Carrying the fur coat from Port Harcourt, to Lagos, to London, to Minneapolis, and finally to Omaha, Nebraska, had been a struggle. It was much heavier than she had expected. But each time Ifi removed the coat— to slide it through conveyor belts for each security screening—she reminded herself that she was a big woman now, a doctor's wife, Mrs. Doctor, no longer the skinny housegirl in Aunty's home. So she held her head up high. Even when a customs agent asked if she was on her way to Russia. A joke. Ifi had laughed with the poor woman and turned up her nose. *Somewhere better,* she thought to herself. "America," she had said.

"How is everyone?" Job asked.

"Ọ dị mma," she said.

"Speak in English. The ones who do well in America learn to adapt." Ifi nodded and he suddenly clapped, a broad grin filling his face. "Now then, Florence and Jenny, they have taken care of you?"

"Yes," Ifi said carefully, smoothing her face into a smile. Florence and Jenny had taken care of her, if it could be called that. After the honeymoon, Ifi had been summoned to stay with Job's family, at least until the immigration papers were processed. Ifi had known no brothers or sisters while growing up, though she had tended to her young cousins since she had been sent to live with her aunt, so the thought of her in-laws becoming her sisters had filled her with joy—until she arrived. Florence and Jenny had regarded her with impassive politeness, nothing more. When Ifi entered a room, their laughter stilled, and they took on cold airs. Once she even tried to help the housegirls prepare a meal, and the next day, when she returned, they barred her from entering the kitchen, shakily insisting that the sisters didn't approve.

Still, gazing into Job's expectant face, Ifi took a deep breath and reminded herself that perhaps his sisters had meant well. She was not lying when she replied, "They watched me very carefully."

"Good." He beamed. "Have you eaten?"

"No."

"Come now. We'll drop your baggage at the house, and then we will meet other Nigerians at a restaurant. Emeka and Gladys. You'll like them." He paused for a moment, as if choosing his words with care. "You will like Gladys immediately. She is a classical lady. But Emeka, you must become acquainted with him before you can understand his foolish humor."

A pale-blue skyline rimmed with ash gray guided the Audi along the interstate. Job drove in silence until they reached a junction and turned off onto a two-lane road. Zonta, the town that would be Ifi's new home, was twenty or thirty miles south of the Red Cloud reservation, and south of Zonta was Omaha, where Job said he went to medical school. They would meet Gladys and Emeka in Omaha for dinner. This was also where Job commuted to for work each night. Zonta, Nebraska, was a town whose name meant "trusted flat waters." The Indians had named it that. Job told her this as they sped over concrete roads surrounded by flats ankle deep in snow. One year, he said, in the middle of winter, there were several hot days, and it all melted. "River drained into street," Job said, thrusting one finger along the skyline. He had finally understood what the name meant.

All the way to town they passed trees, skinny, brown, and gnarled like old hands. Snow wetted the fingers. Overnight, there would be such a freeze that from a distance the trees would look silver. Later, this was the feature that pleased Ifi most when she stared out the window at night while Job was away at the hospital.

Dusk melted into a chalk white that floated and exploded into the sky. Job clicked the wipers, and they flipped back and forth at a frenetic pace, splitting the flakes. In defiance, they grew fatter and rimmed the windshield with dust that scattered on the wind.

"Snow," Ifi said as it slowly dawned on her. She had only read of it in books. This was snow, flaking on the car, the same as the blanket laid on the grass. *This is America,* she said to herself. She would scoop it into an envelope and mail it to Aunty. No, she would not do that. She laughed. Instead, she would take a picture for her little cousins. Without thinking, Ifi reached for the door handle.

Job swerved the car. "What are you doing? Are you crazy?"

Save for a pickup truck that had passed many miles before, there was no one else on the road. "Let's stop. I would like to touch it."

He gave her a strange look. "We cannot be late to dinner."

"Darling," Ifi said, settling on the word she had heard Aunty and Uncle use in the middle of quarrels.

"Okie, okie," he said. "We will stop. We are not far from home."

They pulled off the road and parked in a clearing surrounded by twisted metal piping for a fence. Clapboard sheds were spread across the fields. These were the county fairgrounds, where twice a year, during the fair and on Independence Day, everything was lit up. Farther still was just the outline of a string of corrugated-iron warehouses.

Ifi opened her palms and let snow fall into them. She scooped it into her hands, pressed them together. She placed it in her mouth and tasted. It was cold and wet, like rain. That was all. She felt foolish.

At first he sat in the car, wiping away the fog on the inside of the windshield. Then he came out, his back against the car, as she rose from the snow.

She looked to him like he imagined himself at nineteen, walking the curious, ginger walk of feet unfamiliar with snow. She shivered. When her eyes met his, he said softly, "I did that as well."

Snow was in her hands. It melted and ran along her palms and evaporated into the white at her feet. Again she looked at him, and it suddenly occurred to her. "I can do anything here," she said, her eyes large and bright. When he looked at her again with a queer expression, she elaborated. "I can be anything. Like you," she said. "I can be a doctor in America if I like."

Job watched her face. After a moment, he cleared his throat. "You can be a nurse. I am the doctor."

She thought it over. "Yes. And we will build a hospital here and in Nigeria. Together." An infection took her mother, even though it supposedly had a simple cure. It didn't even cost a lot of money. Her father had had the money, but she died anyway. All they'd needed was a clinic, a good one, equipped with the right medicines and a real doctor. Her mother would have survived. Ifi was sure of it. After a moment, Ifi added, "Jesus brings people together for good reason. Don't you agree?"

"Yes," he said absently, a nod.

"That's why I am here with you. Is that not it?"

Job said nothing.

She looked away. "My mother could have lived, if she had been in a real hospital. And if she had lived, my father would surely live."

"Allow me time," he said. "You will be trained as a nurse, and we will build a clinic in Nigeria. I promise."

She believed him.

And he believed himself. It was all very simple. The tuition money was there in the savings bond, two thousand for every semester his father sent him money. Job hadn't touched a cent. He would reapply, take the proper classes, and go back to school—all this without her knowing. Even at his age, he could do it. Americans did it all the time.

He pointed out the warehouses in the distance. "The house is on the other side," he said. They lived on the fringes of a town where industry came and went. What were left were the meatpackers, and with them came the Somalis, the Mexicans, the Ethiopians, and everyone else. They couldn't even wear proper clothes. They couldn't even wash off the smell. It was a job for those with nothing, not even shame, he explained. "Can you smell it?" he asked.

Ifi sniffed deeply and was startled by the taste of meat in the back of her throat.

"In summer," he said as they walked to the car, "the scent will be raw and angry." At noon, the workers would trudge home bloody with flesh and lard up their arms where the gloves pulled away from their elbows. "You will get used to it," he said. "What you will not get used to are the young men." They camped out on the fairgrounds and drank in shifts. They bayed at the moon like wild dogs. They stank of blood and guts, and they were hungry for trouble. "You must avoid them. They are useless men," Job added. As if to prove his point, he thrust a finger at the twisted metal fence surrounding the fairgrounds, where a row of broken beer bottles and squished cans rested along it.

Huber Lane was a cavalcade of faded brick apartments alongside fall-apart houses, their faces a study in patchwork—shattered windows patched over with tape, peeling siding, missing tiles on the roof, and cracked concrete for steps. Of the houses, most of the porches were empty, except for one, populated only by a mossy living room couch. Job stopped before this one.

This was the fourth of the residences Job had occupied since his arrival in the United States at nineteen years of age. Before this, a basement apartment with a separate entrance. At every month's end, the old man had cornered Job to make sure he paid the rent on time: *We're all living under the foot of the Man, right, man?* He'd also lived in a closet of a room in a dormitory-style men's residence hall, complete with communal showers. It was a place where walls were so thin that he was troubled by the most intimate of sounds: tears, passionless sex, and yes, farts. One of his homes had been on the topmost floor of a building scarred by the scents of mingled garlic, curry, and stockfish, regarded with collective disgust by guests of this nation, international students like himself, unlucky in their ability to smell American.

All of these places had been available to Job then. When he found the advertisements tacked to bulletin boards in campus buildings or in the *American Classifieds,* he needed only to tell them that he was a medical student who commuted to UNMC three times per week for his studies. The thin voice on the other end of the telephone would dismiss the accent. He needed only to arrive for the interview in scrubs, and the eyes would forgive the dark skin. But that was long ago.

He took Ifi's two bags from the trunk. Snow so high it reached her ankles filled Ifi's sandals with dampness. Neighbors did not welcome Ifi as she had expected. When she stopped to look over her new home, Job, with her bags in each hand, nudged her forward.

Only the light that filtered through the cracked door windows led the way. Spirals of dust flaked down and around. On Job, the potbelly, Ifi discovered, was merely a disguise. After three flights of narrow stairs, Ifi was winded while Job fumbled through his pockets for the keys.

The phone was ringing as they entered. Almost immediately he dumped her bags on the floor and disappeared into a bedroom, leaving Ifi undisturbed in her assessment of her new home.

"Hello?" she could hear him asking. "Who is this?"

Well, it was not exactly *The Cosby Show*. One small room with a kitchen to one side and a doorway leading to the bathroom. One more door could lead to a closet or a bedroom; from the size of the room, one could not be sure. Warped laminate floors creaked underfoot. Grayish walls were riddled with holes and splatters of paint. From the scent alone, it was obvious that someone—perhaps Job—had attempted to paint the room before Ifi's arrival. Along the walls was a line of overfilled boxes of newspapers, a bicycle even. A couple of plants hung from the center of the ceiling.

"I have said you are not to call again," he was saying.

Set imperiously alongside the couch was the only new object in the room: a baby's carriage. Ifi redirected her eyes. He must have known then, she realized. She had, after all, spent the past few months in his family's care as they waited for her papers to be processed. In alarm, she suspected now that her private moments had ended long ago.

He concluded, "If I see your face this time, I promise I will pepper you. You will never see the light of day. You understand?" Ifi heard the phone slam into the receiver.

At just that moment, Job stood in the doorway, sweating. Before she could say a word, he stammered, "That was a telemarketer trying to sell me nonsense. You must be forceful with them."

"Oh." But she was not concerned about the phone call. Without lifting her gaze from the carriage, she asked, "You knew?"

His gaze followed hers. He said nothing.

In the months she had spent with his family in Port Harcourt, almost daily, she had vomited. Still, she continued to collect Kotex, to carefully wrap them in tissue and deposit them in the rubbish bin. She had hoped, in some small way, to pretend that it wasn't true, so she could go forward with her plans. Having this child would only get in the way. "You knew."

He laughed. "Of course. You are my wife."

"Jenny spoke to you."

"Florence."

Ifi took a step toward the carriage. She rolled it forward, then back. Lush, green tendrils spiraled from the stems of one of the plants, reaching for the one window where light poured in through its gaps. In awe, Ifi wondered, *Is it true that a man can grow something with such care?* She decided that perhaps it would be okay. She would be a nurse, and they would open their clinic. Only it wouldn't happen overnight. She would raise this baby in America with this man, her husband. She had nothing to fear. As a doctor, he could make her dreams real. She would be his nurse, and one day they would return to Nigeria, to Aunty, to her cousins, and open the clinic.

"Come now," he said. "Put your box here." He leaned one suitcase against the wall alongside some of the newspapers and stacked the second suitcase atop it. Unpacking was finished.

He did not lead her around the apartment, showing her the ins and outs: how to light the gas stove; how to turn the showerhead to one angle if she wanted a steady, uninterrupted stream; how to set the mousetraps and plug the holes in the walls; how to arrange the pots in such a way that on rainy days the incessant drips from the leaky roof would not keep her awake. These Ifi learned on her own.

She was wearing the yellow dress from their honeymoon night, but it was all wrong. He had stretched it out with his broad back and hairy belly when he'd put it on and done the strip tease that night.

Or she didn't have the body for it and never had.

Job didn't say anything at first, but Ifi realized almost immediately that he didn't approve. When he was younger, he might've said something right away. But he was older now, nearly forty. And anyway, there wasn't time. Dinner would have begun already. He put off his explanation about the merits of time, something he would share with her later. Instead, he said, "Wear it like this."

After all, it was not the dress. He hadn't even noticed the dress. It was the fur coat. Job stood before her. Like a mother with her child, he carefully fitted each button into place and finished by jerking the furry collar so that it sat upright around her neck. Ifi lifted her jaw, threw out her chin. Already she felt taller, composed, like a woman of consequence, a big woman.

Just before starting the car and pulling away, he decided that she would have to hear the speech after all. "You people come to America and still believe you are living in the village. Time is money in America."

Reservations were hard to come by at Divine Davinci's. A low brick building trimmed with a striped green awning was surrounded by an empty patio space, its newly shoveled walkways gleaming. Gladys and Emeka were already waiting outside with four girls in a row like goats with their kids. Her first glance at Gladys, wearing a printed ichafu headscarf and regally positioned alongside Emeka, her pregnant belly held before her like a bouquet of flowers, made Ifi realize why Job disapproved of her. Gladys was wearing a fur coat, but not just any coat. It was exactly the coat that Ifi was wearing, and the collar was pulled to her jaw.

"Mommy," one of the girls said, "she has one like yours."

When Gladys didn't reply, the girl tried again. This time Gladys gave her a firm jab to the side, but not without a small smirk that settled into the corners of her mouth.

"Ah-ah, you have gone for a second trip to Nigeria this year," Emeka said by way of greeting. "Are you still living in the bush, my friend? Time is money in America."

"I'm delivering a precious box," Job said, looking at Ifi, then Emeka. "I had to drive carefully." He both embraced Ifi and thrust her forward, to be devoured by the hungry eyes of the four girls. They varied in age from toddler to teenager. Job had told her the two oldest were away at university. The girls wore dresses under wool peacoats. All of them were adorned in braids and silk ribbons. Only the youngest wore thick cotton tights, covered with clinging balls of lint from the fabric of their coats.

Maybe if she had said something about their lateness, like Emeka, Ifi might have felt differently about Gladys, but Gladys only said, "Welcome." Then she hugged Ifi far from her body, with the warmth that one would give a venomous snake. It was then that Ifi realized the single difference in the two coats: Gladys's coat was real; Ifi's was not.

Inside the restaurant candles glowed, revealing the silhouettes of masticating jaws, forkfuls of linguini, and wine glasses wet with the imprint of lips. A line awaited them, mostly older white couples, women in pearls and blue wigs, men in jackets and ties. As they made their way into the vestibule and stood at the end of the long line, their party began, one by one, to remove their coats and jackets, dusting off the fine layer of snow. Only Gladys and Ifi remained with theirs on.

Their voices joined the shrill chatter of the room. "Now, my friend, you are almost a man." Emeka sent another glance Ifi's way.

She smiled.

"Almost, you say?" Job grinned. "We are expecting our first son."

"Son. You are so certain, eh?" Despite his smile, there was a hard edge to Emeka's voice. He turned to Ifi and his smile broadened. "Well then, congratulations are in order. Dinner is on me."

"No." Job cut his eyes at him. "Not today. I will pay."

"Thank you," Ifi said quickly to Emeka. Again, she thought of the months she had spent with Job's family. They had known that she no longer bled every month. They had known the subtle changes in her body because they had been looking for them. In a flash, Ifi saw her dreams begin to blur.

To Job, Emeka said, "Well now, perhaps your son will grow up to be a doctor, like his father." Then suddenly, there was a private exchange between Emeka and Gladys. Had Ifi not been staring at the lining of Gladys's coat she might have missed it, that small, discreet exchange of glances, just a whisper.

"Yes, Job, tell me," Emeka said. "My wife has had a pain in her side during the entire pregnancy. She complains every morning when she rises. What can it be?"

Job stopped then. With a serious expression on his face, he made his way to Gladys. Ifi watched with pride as her doctor husband produced a stethoscope from his deep coat pocket, but she was still troubled by that secret exchange between husband and wife.

"Don't mind him," Gladys said. "It's nothing."

"No, she is only being modest," Ifi said. Whether or not anything was wrong with Gladys, the fact was that Job was the only one among them who could do anything about it. She was not about to allow Gladys to spoil that.

Emeka agreed. "Gladys, allow him."

"Not here," she hissed.

"No, no. The obstetrician we see is a joke. I do not trust that woman, any woman doctor for that matter." He beckoned to Job. "We have time. Look at this line. We are not going anywhere fast. And no one is paying attention." Then he pointed to her side, smooth and elongated under the coat.

Job unbuttoned the coat, and Ifi watched in delight as Gladys shrank back in embarrassment. While he tapped along her side, she repeated, "I am fine." Finally, he raised the stethoscope to her chest and listened to her heartbeat. After a moment, he pulled away.

"You have a heart murmur?"

"No."

"You have a heart murmur." It was no longer a question.

"How do you know?"

"It's there, in your heart, a sound like a slow hammer."

"Is that the cause of her pain?" Emeka asked.

"Of course."

"Whatever can we do about it?"

"Acid-o-mana-phin."

"Acetaminophen?"

"Yes."

"Tylenol, you mean?"

"No, acidomanaphin."

"Of course."

"Yes, twice a day. Twice a day with a glass of orange juice each time. Or you can crush it into your fufu." He paused. "Less time on your feet. Allow your husband to chase the children."

"Will do." Emeka nodded dutifully. "What would we do without you, my friend? Heh? Free medical treatment in a country where nothing is free." He laughed, a jolly sound. Then Gladys joined in, and suddenly each of their daughters was joining in and laughing. Before long, the only one who was not laughing was Ifi. Even Job was laughing. There was a joke there, but perhaps she was too new to America to understand it. Slowly, uncertainly, Ifi joined their laughter.

"Now we eat," Job said, swinging forward in the line.

Gladys hung back. "My, you are moving fast." Instead of looking at Ifi, she turned up the jaw of her smallest and wiped away at a runny nose. There was a triangle of saliva on the front of the girl's dress. "If you spoiled the picture, I will beat you, oh," she said to her.

The girl shook a fierce no.

Emeka explained, "We have just come from our family photo."

"You have no plans for yourself?" Gladys asked Ifi.

"Eh?" But Ifi knew exactly what she meant. Indeed, her words brought up the very fear that had been on Ifi's mind since that morning months earlier, when it first occurred to her that she had stopped menstruating.

"Now that you have started, they will come." Gladys's eyes fell on each daughter. "One after the other."

Ifi said nothing. It wasn't true. Job had promised. After all, in spite of his wealth and success, he had chosen to return to Nigeria to find her. She stubbornly shook off the image of the shabby apartment, reminding herself that as a man, he surely had no taste for the finer things. He was practical. Her life would require a series of small adjustments, but they would all pay off in good time. She would follow through on every one of her dreams. She would be a nurse, and, just like Job had promised, they would build a clinic together at home.

"Never mind, oh. You have time. I am finishing my second master's degree. If you work hard, Jesus will deliver."

Again Ifi felt a hardness in her gut. She did not like this woman.

Emeka drew back to stand by Ifi. Following the line, the rest of the group moved in a swift procession. Job led the way. Eventually, just two couples remained ahead of them.

"Job tells me this is your first American meal."

"Is this not Italian?" Ifi asked. She glanced at the inscription above the podium: *Authentic Tuscan Cuisine.*

"Ifi, my dear," Emeka said, "when you have lived in America long enough, you will know that Americans have nothing and everything all at once."

Ifi couldn't help but think of her coat, heavy with its false weight. She felt ridiculous, like a small, hairy beast. Right then, she decided to slip out of it. When she did, Emeka smiled and sent her a knowing glance. She pretended not to notice.

"I am telling you, there are two choices one must make when ordering at this restaurant. Every fool who makes the mistake of ordering the wrong dish reveals something of himself."

"Oh?" Ifi asked.

"For example," he continued, "those who order lobster and crab are fools."

"Why?" Ifi asked.

"We are in the middle of the country, and there is no ocean. You are eating the remains of a dog and its feces."

"Tell me now, you are joking," Ifi said. Could this be the humor Job had warned her about?

"I am quite serious." Job was ahead with Gladys and the girls. Emeka bellowed to him, "What will you order tonight, my friend?"

Job thought it over, fingered through the menu plastered on the wall, and finally reached a conclusion. "Lobster."

"Yes, a wise choice," Emeka said. "You have chosen the most expensive item on the menu."

"Only the best," Job called back.

First Ifi laughed, but in an instant she was shamed by the look of delight on Emeka's face. "What of this?" She pointed indiscriminately to the menu: spaghetti.

"No, no. You can prepare spaghetti in a can. You'll enjoy the lobster. I eat it every time we come to this restaurant."

Ifi walked ahead and leaned into Job. Just loudly enough so he alone could hear, she said, "You will not eat dog feces."

Job gave her a quizzical look. Gladys interrupted just as Ifi was about to speak again. "Come now," she said calmly. "Let us go." She leaned heavily to one side, the girls heaped around her like wilted flowers.

"Why?" Emeka asked. "What of the reservation?"

Gladys did not bother to respond. Instead she led the way toward the door, and the trail of girls followed behind her, their litany of whines a chorus.

Job sent Ifi an irritated glance. They must have been late. She thought of the snow and the fur coat. They had missed their reservation because of her.

"Wait now," Job said. "Allow me to talk to the woman." He moved to the front of the line, and Ifi released a deep breath.

"Excuse me, missus. What is the problem?" he asked.

With a thick coat of red lipstick and glossy curls bunched in a ponytail at her nape, the woman before them was young enough to be Job's daughter. "You missed your reservation. We've already seated someone in your place. I'm sorry, sir."

"Our car stopped us on the way." He glanced back at Emeka, then Gladys.

"It's company policy to cancel reservations after fifteen minutes," she said.

"I know this," Job said, "but it is my wife's first day in this country, and I would like her to enjoy a meal at the finest restaurant in America." He beamed.

People waited behind Job in line, and the girl's gaze drifted past him. It was as if he hadn't spoken. Ifi remembered the small boy on their honeymoon night, the way he had cowered before them. She thought of the ringing tone of the barman as he threw Job into a thunderous hug and ordered their drinks on the house. This girl, with her bold lipstick and silly earrings. This child spoke to her doctor husband as if he were nothing. Ifi shuddered.

The hostess's tone didn't change. "Everyone in line has a reservation. We can't change the rules just to accommodate *you*."

Ifi hesitated behind Job. Perhaps she should say something, interject on his behalf. After all, she reminded herself, this was her fault.

Just as she was about to speak, Job turned to Ifi and smiled in a calm, placating way. "Call your manager. I would like to speak to him," he said to the hostess. As the girl turned to go, Job nodded confidently. "Ask to speak to the manager and he will give you what you want. That is the first rule of America."

Moments later, the hostess returned with the manager. *She* wore a buttoned-up black suit and tie, and her face was set in a deep frown.

Emeka stepped forward, dusting his hands together in front of him. He thrust a jovial palm on Job's shoulder. "That is not necessary. My friend has wasted time curling his hair and applying his lipstick, and because of this we are late. We will eat at another restaurant."

Job frowned. "We cannot eat at another restaurant at this time." It was nearly nine.

By now the smallest of the girls was squirming at Gladys's side. "Mommy, I have to pee," she said.

"Why didn't you come in and save our seats?" Job whispered.

Emeka's voice was intentionally loud. "Come now, you are not going to insult yourself in front of your wife by saying we should have eaten before you came."

Ifi shrank at the sound of "wife" from Emeka's mouth. She thought again of Job's cautionary words about Emeka's humor, and she decided that Emeka was not funny at all.

Before Job could respond, Gladys turned a tired eye to Emeka. "We will go to the house, and I will prepare our dinner."

A look of horror clouded Job's face. "No, no. That's not necessary. We will find another restaurant."

For the first time, Gladys looked squarely at Ifi. "Your wife has not eaten. And it's late. Let us go."

In desperation, Job turned to Ifi. His look sent a chill down her spine. He couldn't argue with Gladys's expression, but Ifi, as a woman, could. All she could think of was the lobster of dog. And the venomous woman before her. And her coat, which was draped around her broad backside like a cape, while Ifi's hung limply on her arm. Suddenly it became clear to her that, like the coats, Gladys's home would not have mousetraps, holes in the walls, and splatters of paint. Instead of the real thing, Ifi's was a poor man's imitation. But she refused to submit herself to scorn. She would do anything not to go to Gladys's home. "We will do this another night," Ifi said.

"Nonsense, you'll not inconvenience us. I will expect the same from you when you have the means."

Ifi met Gladys's eye, woman to woman, a knowing glance. "I have not seen my husband in many months. It is not lobster that I am hungry for."

Gladys shriveled under Ifi's gaze, and Emeka thundered into laughter.

Gladys immediately turned on her heel, her fur coat sweeping the air in a smooth arc. At the hostess's podium, all they could hear of her voice was the honey-silk tone. And then it was done. In a matter of minutes, both families occupied two tables pushed together at the rear of the restaurant, where glowing candles rippled against the hot breaths of each of Emeka and Gladys's daughters.

Ifi couldn't help feeling annoyed by Gladys's haughtiness as she responded to Job's gushing compliments, which he delivered through bites of dripping lobster meat. He had all but forgotten Ifi. "Tell me now, how did you do that?" he asked.

"Never mind, oh." Gladys waved her hand at Job. "It takes nothing to speak to another human being in a civilized manner."

"No, that was medicine." He chuckled. "Eh? How do you do it?" He beamed, turning from Gladys to Ifi. "Ifi, my dear, you must follow Gladys. Learn her ways. If you do, success will find you in America."

Ifi leaned back in her chair and crossed her arms. The only reply she could muster was "Yes, of course." She had not seen Job so animated since the night of their honeymoon when he danced before her, when he had forced a smile to her lips, though she had resisted it. He had, for that moment, shrouded in the flicker of shadow and light, taken over the muscles of her face and pressed her lips into a smile purely through his actions. That thought had sustained her and insisted that life with him would be something more, even on her loneliest nights with his family in Port Harcourt.

Now, he swept one palm across his face, coating his mouth in butter sauce as he recounted Gladys's many successes. In the course of an hour, Ifi learned that Gladys was a CPA, had a master's in actuarial science and another in theology, was the leader of a women's society at home in Nigeria, had sponsored two local businesses in her native town, and had begun second renovations—elaborate designs, imported furniture, marble—on their retirement home. Throughout the conversation, Job had not once mentioned any of Ifi's achievements—her impressive JAMB scores, her proper soup, her skill with difficult stitching techniques, all praised during their courtship— but then, she admitted to herself, who could compete with Gladys?

"I tell you, Ifi. You see this? You see this? Watch this woman and learn how to become a queen of Africa *and* America."

"Now, if my wife is the queen, I am assuming that makes me the king, no?" Emeka chimed in. Gladys nodded in approval. "And that, my friend, must make you—the man of humor tonight—court jester." He laughed uproariously, and his daughters, linked together at the end of the table, smearing their fries with ketchup, joined in, the rush of their voices like that of bleating sheep. "Daddy, then we are princesses!"

Job smiled uneasily, and Ifi struggled once again to grasp the intent of Emeka's humor. The image of a bumbling court jackal, remembered from books she'd read as a child, filled her mind, and she was immediately shamed. Why hadn't Job said a word in his own defense? "I have not heard of a doctor who is a fool," she said.

"No, no, of course not. Me, I am only teasing." Emeka paused. "Though not everything is as it seems."

Ifi frowned. Perhaps she had misunderstood. But once again she caught a shared glance between Gladys and Emeka. "What is it you mean by court fool then?"

Gladys lifted her face away, smothering a haughty chuckle. "Don't mind him. My husband, he suffers me, oh."

"Yes, listen to my wife," Emeka said curtly. "Don't mind me at all."

Job chuckled. "Ifi, dear, I warned you about this one, did I not? Don't find trouble with him."

"Find trouble?" Why was he defending Emeka? Ifi wondered what it was that Job liked about these people, particularly Gladys; unfortunately, Job went on to explain.

"Do you remember the first time I met you?" He nodded at Gladys, who was carefully trimming away the fat surrounding her overcooked cut of steak. "When I first came to this country, Nigerians were few. Only Sundays playing soccer—football—did I meet the other Nigerians. Among them was this toothpick of a man with a fufu pregnancy." He gestured toward Emeka's protruding belly, and Ifi had no trouble imagining him nearly twenty years earlier. "We were playing one evening and we collided. Well, I am strong and younger, so I rose first, and when I looked, my friend was still asleep on the ground. All the women surrounded him, you know, and among the women was a tall, beautiful queen." He paused. "As soon as this woman touched his face, his eyes opened," Job continued, softly. "You see, he had been faking the entire time."

Emeka gave a winsome smile. "Yes, and imagine, my friend, if you had not been in such a rush to show your strength, perhaps Gladys would have come to *your* aid."

Ifi frowned as her gaze caught Gladys's deliberate chuckle.

"Yes, it is strange. I saw her first," Job admitted. "I saw her that day, sitting with her legs crossed on the far bench with a book propped in front of her, pretending not to pay any attention to foolish men pretending to be boys."

Emeka smiled and pinched Gladys's side. She feigned protest, hastily slapping his fingers away. Their daughters' eyes lit up as they watched him. In spite of her irritation, Ifi felt a flash of tenderness. Were there any words to describe what she had witnessed other than love? She turned to Job, whose face was shiny with butter sauce. Emeka and Gladys were one and the same, but she and Job were cut from two different cloths.

"Yes," Job ceded, "perhaps things would be different."

In a way, his life in America was smaller than Ifi's at home. There were no cousins or neighbors, no festivals or celebrations, no hawkers in the streets or church services blaring from megaphones. The streets were silent, and only occasionally did Ifi hear music buzzing from passing cars. His only friends, Emeka and Gladys—he had mentioned no others—and his hours at the hospital collided with the visions in Ifi's imagination. She had pictured dinner parties with diplomats, doctors, and American businessmen, not eating in the shadow of Gladys's arrogant laughter and Emeka's churlish remarks. She had imagined a house with a white fence, jeweled chandeliers, marble floors—the house that the first dinner had confirmed belonged to Gladys and Emeka.

Nonetheless, over the next few months, Ifi would endure many tedious dinners, where Job and Emeka mocked one another for their boyish amusement as she and Gladys coldly sipped from the tops of their glasses of imported beer. They would invariably return to Divine Davinci's, Applebee's, and various other restaurants, flanked by Gladys's daughters and the shrill squawk of their voices as they fought over their menus.

But that first night, as Ifi and Job prepared for bed, they did not know what awaited them. From the darkened corner of the room, where he was awake, Job imagined Ifi's movements mimicking his on the night of their honeymoon, but in reverse. Rather than putting the jewelry and makeup on, she was removing the dangling baubles from her ears, neck, and wrist with ease. She wiped the makeup away with a damp washcloth. Rather than shining with beads of sweat running down the creases of her face, the flesh along her face, arms, and neck rippled with shivers. While Job had stripped slowly and clumsily on the night of their honeymoon, Ifi now undressed with economic precision, knowing how the surfaces of her body, its valleys and crags, responded to the dress; there was no battle with bra straps.

On both sides of the closed door, they were painfully embarrassed by the screaming silence. While Ifi urinated, she ran water in the sink. Job listened for the drunken sounds of the meatpackers on the other side of the fairgrounds, baying at the moon. Then, for several seconds, they lay in the dark, afraid to move, afraid to repeat the mistakes of their first night alone.

Although they completed the task, they got it all wrong by taking opposite approaches. Unlike that first night, Job was gentle, almost cautious. He fumbled through a kiss, pressing his tongue into the back of her throat. But Ifi choked him between her thighs. Her movements were furious, forced. His fingers were ensnared in her weave. Her eyes remained fixed in concentration through each thrust.

He even said to her, "I love you" and "You are beautiful." Because right then, even more than on the night of their honeymoon, he believed it. In the silence, she should have replied. But what could she say? "Thank you."

After, she flipped over. Because the bed was so large, or the room was so small, Ifi landed with her face inches from the wall.

Job was pleased that she enjoyed it; he was surprised that he did not.

One thought had troubled Ifi since dinner: the moment when he had paused and said that things could have been different, had he only risen first. Surprisingly, she had no difficulty reversing the images: Job alongside Gladys—one boastful remark after another—and Ifi alongside Emeka, with his mean-spirited humor. Still, she couldn't see herself haughtily chuckling after his boorish humor like the "classical" Gladys. In spite of his simpler ways, Job was sincere; Emeka was a cunning schemer. Imagine the kind of man who could con a woman into loving him. Perhaps, in this way, Gladys and Emeka made the perfect pair. At least whatever Ifi needed to know of

Job was direct. *But what of his feelings for me?* she thought. Ifi couldn't help but ask, "So, you would be the one married to Gladys had you risen first?"

Job's voice entered the dark. "Don't mind Emeka. He is silly. I married you."

His last words stayed with her—*I married you.* In spite of this, they slept with their backs pressed together. Ifi, with her naked arms wrapped around her head as if to protect herself from a fall; Ifi, with the silent picture of Gladys and her fur and her girls and her husband. All that was real.

And snow fell outside, a dressed-up rain.

CHAPTER 4

THE TROUBLE BEGAN WITH A LETTER.

Every night since the day of Ifi's arrival, Job Ogbonnaya dressed in his white lab coat and black slacks and tucked his stethoscope into his pocket. In his other pocket, he took the mail. He sipped coffee from a Thermos and carried an empty briefcase to the door, the way he imagined a doctor would. He kissed Ifi good-night and from his car watched as the lights flickered off inside the apartment. Just like the night of Ifi's arrival, a block before he reached the St. Ignatius Rehabilitation Hospital, Job turned into a parking lot abandoned to the night. Under the cover of darkness, he changed out of his lab coat and slacks and carefully folded each into a plastic grocery bag that he placed underneath the seat. Then he changed into pale blue scrubs and pinned himself with the nametag that read, *Job Ogbonnaya, Certified Nursing Assistant.*

As he made his rounds that night, he told his patients the familiar story: he came from kings. It meant more to them than if he were to explain the truth: that his father was a chief and his father before him. Job told them he came from kings as he crouched to bathe them over the pot, to empty their bedpans, to wipe the caked spittle from around their mouths, to re-dress their wounds—the work that shamed him. Patients young and old listened to his stories: the little girl who lay in a coma for nine months, the woman with gums so bloodied and swollen she could only hum, the old man who forgot that he must remove his pants before relieving himself.

Job was there now, kneeling before the old man. All the nurses and patients on the hall called the old man Captain. Long ago, he was a lawyer or an investment banker, something important like that. Perhaps, once, he was surrounded by important legal briefs and framed plaques on the walls. Today, a soiled heap of clothes lay on the tiled floor between them. "I come from kings," Job was saying to him. "And I am a prince."

He waited for a reaction, an exclamation, something, but Captain said nothing.

Job set him on the toilet seat. He placed Captain's palms on each thigh, a reminder that the old man must remain sitting as he relieved himself. Captain scratched his head. Already his business was done, but Job had to make him remember. Captain's eyes roamed the room, locked on the door. He began to rise.

"Hakeem Olajuwon, you know him," Job said, hurriedly. Captain stopped and listened. "I used to play basketball with him." Each time Job told the man the story, he listened as if hearing it for the first time.

"You don't say?" he said.

"Oh yes, it's true."

"You mean that basketball player, the one from Africa, the one who played with Michael Jordan?"

"Yes, that's the one. He is from Nigeria, you know, like me," Job said.

"Ni-ger-i-a. That's in Africa," Captain said.

"Oh yes, Olajuwon went to primary school with me."

"Primary school."

"Olajuwon was skinny, with legs as tall as a giraffe's. But he was not always so good. I taught him to play. Every day, I explained to him the fundamentals of basketball," Job said. "I taught him how to slam dunk and shoot a free throw from his ankles."

Job helped Captain off the toilet and wiped him. Like the first time, it brought him shame. He thought of his father. What disgrace his father would feel watching his "doctor" son at this. He looked away, but his eyes couldn't escape the reflection in the mirror: the old man kneeling forward, his thin, sandy legs covered in sparse gray hairs, his withered testicles shamelessly dangling before him, and Job bent before the man like a beggar.

"I explained everything he knows to him," Job said quietly.

"Doctor," Captain said.

"Yes?" He told him he was an African prince from an ancient empire. He told him he was a friend of Olajuwon. But each time he returned to this room, the one thing Captain remembered was that Job was a doctor. Of all his patients, Captain was the only one who called him Doctor, and for this Job believed they shared a secret kinship. He set a palm on the old man's shoulder, kindly.

"Did you marry that African queen?"

"Yes." Job beamed.

"Good. Tell me about her. What's her name?"

"Gladys." Job frowned, flustered. He corrected himself. "Ifi, I mean."

"Well, which is it?"

"Ifi," Job said. "My wife is Ifi. She is beautiful, tall, classical, a nurse. She is the woman I have made queen of my kingdom." A mistake; nothing behind it. Still, best to be careful not to repeat such an error in front of Ifi or—dare he think it—Emeka. Admittedly, Job had felt something for Gladys, *but that was long ago,* he told himself. He was a mere boy then. Anything he felt now, a twinge here, a flurry there, was a bit of nostalgia and indigestion. He had grown old. Now he was a man, and a man was a decider. He had thumbed through the photographs and settled on Ifi's picture, deciding on a future they would eventually share in America. *He* had chosen her. He hadn't run around after Ifi like Emeka had for Gladys, sweating and stumbling over himself. He hadn't deceived Ifi into loving him—not exactly. He had told Ifi he must care for patients each night. He just hadn't clarified that he was here as their nurse, not their doctor.

Half truths were of no consequence; he would become a doctor one day, and they would open a clinic together. Only not today. Job faced Captain, glaring into his heavy-lidded eyes. "She will make a fine mother. We are expecting our first child."

"Oh, I don't like children."

"I don't like them either," Job admitted. "But it's time. Some men have had six children by now, sef," he said, thinking of Emeka. "Me, I have none. And what is a man without children to carry forward his name?"

"Yeah, I guess so," he said. "We're not getting any younger."

"But we're getting prettier." Job laughed at his joke. "You know, it was my junior brother who sat for the wedding in my place, so I could be here with my patients." It must have confused Captain. Job wondered how to explain the way the arrangement happened, how he told his relatives that he couldn't get away from the hospital, when it was really that he couldn't possibly afford to miss so many shifts; how his junior brother took his place in the traditional ceremony; how they had agreed that once everything was settled, once Ifi came to America, he would marry her in a church and send the family photographs. There was the civil ceremony in Port Harcourt on the day of the honeymoon, but the church wedding in America hadn't happened after all. It would be far too expensive and extravagant. But his family would never know.

There were staged photographs instead, taken at the studio where Emeka took his family for photos on the day of Ifi's arrival. Job had rented a tuxedo, and Ifi had worn a lacy white dress that Job found at a thrift store. In the photograph, she stared into the camera, hard, fierce, but beautiful, a bouquet of flowers hiding her protruding belly, a picture his family now hung with pride in their parlor. *None of the small details matter,* Job reminded himself. What mattered was that he had done something that made his father proud. "In a few months' time," he said to Captain, "my father will receive the photos of my first son."

"Well, that's kind of you. You're kind. My son doesn't take care of me, but you take care of your father," he said. "Just like a good son should."

"Yes."

"I've written him letters, and the boy still won't reply."

"That's terrible." Job helped him back into his slacks and slippers.

"I should never have left home. Doctor, when am I going home? I want to go home."

"We are going home right now," Job said calmly. Just like that, he guided him through the bathroom doorway into his hospital room. "We are home, Captain," Job said, and the old man began softly weeping, shaking his thin fists in front of him.

A mute television, a bed surrounded by an aluminum railing, pictures scattered across a windowsill of people whose faces were cloudy to the old man—a daughter, tall and sturdy, pretty at just the right angle; the little boy whom she wrapped her arms around, the one Captain believed was his son, the one the old man wrote his letters to. The son he'd never had.

Job thought of the child that was growing inside Ifi. He knew nothing of children, how to feed them, how to dress them, how to stop their tears. In spite of this, he had always understood that children must come. Having a child was part of the natural progression of things. For a man his age it was time, yet the thought brought nothing to him. He felt nothing.

"My letters," Captain said.

Job handed Captain his notepad and pen.

"I'm writing him another letter. He's been a bad boy, but I forgive him."

"Good," Job said. "Fathers should always forgive their sons." He helped Captain into the bed. "But first, it's time to sleep."

Captain looked at him with watery, reddened eyes. "It's time."

After his rounds, Job found his way to the break room. Except for the hum of the refrigerator, it was empty and silent. It was a solitude he savored. Glancing one way and then the other, Job opened a foil-covered bowl of soup and warmed it in the microwave. In the past, he'd opened short plastic containers of tasteless Campbell's soup. Now that Ifi was with him, each night he ate garri and pepper soup. Job quickly lapped the soup up in satisfaction, hoping to finish before a coworker arrived with the questions and complaints about the acrid scent.

During his breaks, away from Ifi's prying eyes, he would thumb his way through their mail. Each envelope presented a dilemma: how certain was he that his paycheck would make it to his checking account before his payments reached the bill collectors? Until now, it had never been his practice to write out checks at work, but Ifi was at home, and she didn't need to know about their expenses, or the savings bond with his father's money.

As always, Ifi's letter was in the pile, a weekly note to her aunty. Normally, Job stamped the letter and added it to his collection of outgoing checks. But today, he thought of Captain and his unanswered letters, a neat stack in the bottom of one of his drawers. For the first time, he wondered what each short note contained, and why Ifi had chosen not to share their contents with him.

In Job's absence, Ifi had taken to writing letters, licking and sealing them, and then waiting for Job to return with the stamps that would deliver them to Aunty. It was their regular routine for Ifi to check the mailbox in the afternoons and arrange its contents, along with her letters, on the kitchen counter for Job to collect.

In her first letters, Ifi described the clean streets and the water that did not need to be boiled. *Light does not go. Snow is just as it appears in the books,* she explained, *but only on the first day. And then it soils the legs of your trousers, like the muddy streets in Port Harcourt on wet days. Americans are healthy, so healthy that their bodies do not stop growing. And I am such a queen that my husband will not allow me to lift a finger.*

In the next letters, Ifi decided it was best to explain herself. *Job has hired a maid—it is even Oyibo woman, an American—because he is so cautious with the baby. Fat red roses fill my garden. In fact, my yard alone is larger than your entire street in Port Harcourt.* Instead of the warped walls, riddled with holes; instead of the splatters of paint; instead of the mousetraps and cockroaches, she told Aunty about a big-screen television with one thousand channels, a stereo with a five-CD changer, a three-car garage—all the things she had seen in magazines.

It had started on a flat, gray afternoon as Job and Ifi shrugged their way through the grocery checkout lane. Ifi had seen the glossy magazines: celebrity tabloids with George Clooney and Julia Roberts on the covers, stories about babies born on Mars, and a couple of covers with shiny basketball players, their biceps dancing on the pages. Job picked one up, glanced at it, and murmured something about Hakeem Olajuwon. A misplaced *Good Housekeeping* magazine was behind it, which Ifi took.

A beautiful home graced the cover, with a manicured lawn, artful shrubbery, and lights that glowed all the way to the arched doorway with Ionic columns on each side. Inside, the pages were filled with cherubic men and women spread on sleeper sofas, attractive and healthy, with mouths flexed into smiles. Every item matched. There was nothing extra, nothing used or soiled. No sandy red grains from the outdoor walkways in Port Harcourt. No mousetraps like the ones that lined the walls of Job's apartment—because, although she had lived in it for two months, Ifi still considered the apartment his home, not her own. As she glanced at the pictures that afternoon, she knew that one day she would have a beautiful home like the ones in the magazines, and she would do with it as she pleased. A real home. Not an imitation like her fur coat.

She became a regular subscriber to three different interior design catalogs, picking them up from the newsstand during their weekly outings to the grocery store. As her body grew larger each month, the intricacies in the design of her imaginary palace grew bolder. There were low-swinging chandeliers, crown molding, bay windows, and bougainvillea wrapped all along the red brick exterior.

Yes, Ifi wrote in another letter, *there are already four bedrooms, but because my husband is considering the inclusion of a home library to store all of his medical diagrams and journals, we are discussing with contractors the possibility of adding a fifth room.*

Aunty, she concluded, *you would not recognize me for the skinny girl who left home.*

Leaning into his open locker, Job folded the letter into squares. As the doors clanked shut around him, he collapsed on the hard wooden bench, stunned, puzzling over the descriptions of a home he didn't recognize. He folded each square into successive squares until the letter was as small as a business card. Then he unfolded it and stared at the broken lines of Ifi's longhand against the seams of the folds. What could she mean? They did not have four bedrooms—but perhaps she was counting the kitchen, the living room, and the bathroom. They did not have maids, but perhaps she had a difficult time explaining to her aunt that in America, one relied on machines for help instead of the poor. She had also described a music system, and indeed they had one, a small portable radio with bent wires that worked as well as a brand-new machine. But what puzzled him was the television. Job did not own a television, nothing like it. There must have been a mistake.

At first the sound of his name was a faraway echo, until suddenly the charge nurse was peering into Job's face. "Job, it's a phone call, for you," she said. "But I hope you keep in mind our policy about personal calls. In case you've forgotten, this is a place of business. I'm not picking on you, so don't get that idea. I'm only saying that you can't make personal calls to friends. You understand? And if it's long distance, we'll have to send you a notice."

Grinning dumbly, he nodded furiously. Still clutching the letter, Job stumbled into the reception area, his hands shaking, his mind attuned to the new problem at hand. Ifi did not have the number to his workplace. He had made sure of it. No one knew where he worked, not even Emeka and

Gladys, and for good reason. What would they say? Panic swelled in his chest as it occurred to him how easily his supervisor could have answered the phone and given away his secret. As he glared at the glowing switchboard, his hand paused over the phone. How could he explain? *A miscommunication,* he would say, *a jealous attendant.* He was not a nurse's aide. He was the doctor. *And the television,* he thought, remembering the letter. *That I can buy if I want, but there is no need. It is a foolish waste of money.* He repeated these words to himself, the whisper in his head faltering as it rose in fervor.

"Job?" The voice was soft and airy. He was so caught up in his worry that at first he didn't realize the voice belonged to Cheryl. He was only immediately grateful that it was not Ifi or Gladys or Emeka. It must have been this note of gratitude in his tone that she registered as his pleasure, because her words sounded light with relief. "It's me," she said.

Job swallowed, regaining his composure. "How did you get this number?"

"I have my ways."

He moved the phone away from his ear.

"You hang up, Job, and I'll just call you back again and again until you speak to me."

He peered around the bend of the reception desk, hearing the clatter of voices and footsteps down the hall. He softened his voice. "Leave me alone."

"You don't answer my calls, my letters—what am I supposed to do?" A pause. "Just hear me out."

"I cannot speak to you now. I am at work."

"Then I'll meet you somewhere."

Now a sound cut into the call, another call illuminated on the switchboard. He glanced at the clock. Soon the day shift would arrive, and he would have to stand among the other nurses as the charge nurse gave a report of the night's activities. He had to end the call fast, or there would be too many questions. Of all the secret places to go, Job could only think of his abandoned parking lot, where nightly he changed from suit to scrubs as he passed from the world of his imagination into the world of reality. He gave her the directions.

By the time Job arrived, Cheryl was already balanced along the side of the building, her back hunched over a cigarette. Illuminated by the dusted clouds,

Cheryl seemed much smaller to him than he remembered all those years ago. Instead of the denim skirt with the frayed ends, she wore tight jeans and a heavy overcoat. He gazed about the lot looking for a second or third helper, like the day of the marriage. But there was no one, just Cheryl quickly putting out her cigarette on the back of her snow boot. As he edged the car to her and climbed out, his throat smarting from the cold, she straightened up. Losing his footing on the snow, he caught himself just before he reached her. She greeted him with a smile.

"You've changed," she said.

"You are the same," he said, though it wasn't true. She was smaller, thinner; that much was true. But there was something else about her that was different. He just couldn't put his finger on it. The hair was still red, mostly, except for the silver lines that reached along the contours of her forehead, where her hair was neatly parted. As she grinned at him, the smile still revealed the small boy's teeth. *What is it that has changed about her?* he wondered. And then it dawned on him: She was wearing rouge. Her pale cheeks were accented by powder. There was a flip to her otherwise limp hair. She was even wearing earrings, shiny pieces that caught the morning light. Cheryl had tried to make herself presentable for him. Indeed, much had changed since the morning of their courthouse wedding. What she had now that she didn't have for him then, Job realized, was respect. Recognizing this calmed the nervous shake of his hands, and he loosened his grip on Ifi's letter in his pocket. "Hurry now. What is it you want?" he asked with confidence.

"All right, you're here. You're finally here," she said, taking a deep breath. "And now I'm nervous." Her smile dropped as Job backed away from her in his impatience. "But you're leaving. All right, out with it, Cheryl," she said to herself. "I've called you here to ask for a loan."

He waited for the tears, the wails, the moans, the big show. But there was none. Instead, Cheryl lifted her eyes and said, "I will pay you back, every cent, when I get caught up. I mean this as business, an arrangement. I'll pay it back. No games. Here." She knifed through a big tote bag, pulling up papers. "This is the deed for the house. This is the letter from the mortgage lenders. I will gladly give you whatever you need as collateral. Your name is on it too, see? As soon as I make the next payment, your name will come off. You hold the papers until I give you a return."

"You have used my name to steal?"

"Christ, I thought I told you on the phone." The papers in her hands scattered, fluttering to the snowy lot. "Shit." She reached for the papers and stumbled, losing her grip on the tote bag. Without thinking, Job reached to catch the bag before it hit the snowy pavement. In doing so, Ifi's letter left his hand and ended up among Cheryl's belongings on the moist concrete. Now Cheryl had his letter and he had her bag. Their hands awkwardly met in an exchange.

"My ex—the first one—ruined my credit. I was dumb and seventeen when I first met him. I let him take advantage of me, and I was stupid enough to let him do it again. Then my brother, Luther, he says we should refi the house. He says we should use your name to get the money, since my credit was so bad. Then, soon's we get the money, he takes it and bails." Cheryl sighed. This time when she looked at him, her eyes were wet. "You know what it's like to have your own family do that to you? You know how *stupid* it feels?"

Job had no words. His own siblings would never do such a thing to him. But then he thought of his father and the money that he had put into the savings bond, all the years of his father's earnings thrust in earnest at Job's education. For a moment he floundered, guilt rising in his chest. But he shook it off. With the marriage and now the baby, the thought of going back to school just then was impossible. He would go back in good time. Joking around as a boy, not understanding America, that was what had prevented him from becoming a doctor. But now he was a man. His thoughts turned to Ifi's letter and the description of the television set. What did one need with a thousand channels anyway? With resolve, he repeated the mantra that had kept him afloat over the years. He would use his father's money as intended and become a doctor. Only now was not the time.

"I tell Luther I'll call the police," she continued, "and he says he'll tell them about me and you, our arrangement." She squinted at Job, and suddenly he felt complicit in her thievery. "Me and you," she said again, slowly, "that we frauded the government with our marriage."

"Won-der-ful!" Job sighed.

"I know, that's what I said. But I tell him I can't make the payments, it's too much. He says, 'The money's gone'—he lost it on a score—'so sell the house. Be done with it.' But I can't." She stopped and looked at him. "Job, I can't. I can't sell the house. It's all I got. And I'm sorry that I dragged you into this, but now I'm trying to do it the right way, so I'm asking you for a small loan so I don't default. I promise I'll pay it back."

"How should I help a thief like yourself? Are you sick? What is wrong with your head?" Job backed away again, the words leaving his voice in a splutter. *What am I doing here?* he wondered. *Why have I agreed to speak with this charlatan?* Was it fear? Perhaps. After all, she was an American. He remembered that day, standing in the hallway of the county clerk's office with Cheryl's two accomplices making their way toward him. Job looked around again, catching nothing but the ripple of a cold wind off the façade of the brick office buildings. *She is only a woman,* he reminded himself.

"I'm not a thief," Cheryl said firmly. She sucked in a deep breath. "Besides, you, you're the only person I know who is capable." At the conclusion of her words, her eyes trembled.

"Capable." Job frowned. He didn't understand.

"Yeah. I mean, you're a doctor. You can afford a small loan, right?"

He stopped backing away for a moment and took in the word: *capable.* How could someone like her, born and raised in this rich land of opportunity, her father's land, have nothing, be nothing? It was strange to him, an American in her homeland, appealing to him, a foreigner, for help. Yes, he agreed with her words. He *was* capable. Perhaps, in a strange way, it had taken her words to remind him of this. He *was* a man after all. He could do anything. It was only a matter of his desire at the moment. *Anything,* he said to himself, thinking of Ifi's letter and the television set. If he wanted to, he could buy a television set with one thousand channels.

Job frowned at Cheryl—her shoulders were bowed, her papers a clumsy sheaf. With grit he murmured, first to himself, "I am capable." Then he repeated himself for Cheryl to hear. "I am capable," he said carefully, "but why must a man like myself help a crook like you?" Still, even as he said the words, he remembered the savings bond, his father's money, and he knew that he would help her.

Not long before Job was to arrive home from work that morning, there was a knock at the door. It was Mrs. Janik, standing in the entryway, its wide window overlooking the patches of frost outside. With ragged curls in her hair and a few missed rollers still dangling, she clasped her hands together and apart in excitement. She had no children, no husband, and lived alone next door, an American life that would shame a Nigerian woman. Perhaps it was with pity that Ifi received her, or perhaps it was simply loneliness. Either way, one thing was certain: In Nigeria, a doctor's wife would never associate with such a woman. It would shame her. Still, every afternoon, when it was Mrs. Janik's ritual to hurry outside just as Ifi checked the mail, Ifi would wait every time Mrs. Janik hurried down the steps to purse her lips together and shout a breathy, "Hiya!"

And then:

That Chinese lady, the one with three teenage boys across the street. They have filthy character. They invite prostitutes into their home. With their mother right there, they sleep with all of them at once. But is it any surprise? The apple don't fall far from the tree.

And the black girl over there. C level of Apartment 3. Yeah, over there. She's a drug addict, a prostitute to support her habit.

And the Mexican with the toolbox—a liar, a thief, an illegal. And his wife is a prostitute too. None of them nine kids is even his.

Ifi didn't exactly believe Mrs. Janik. But she didn't exactly disbelieve her, and so when Job returned from work most mornings, as he furiously chewed chunks of meat or swallowed balls of garri, she repeated these stories with the certainty of a firsthand witness.

"We's the only two civilized ladies in this neighborhood," Mrs. Janik said, concluding her monologue for the day.

"Yes," Ifi said.

She started to let the door close between the two of them. There were dishes to wash, a soup to prepare. But Mrs. Janik stopped her with a single envelope.

"Someone put it in my mailbox, but it's addressed to your husband."

"Is it?" Ifi snatched the letter from her. It had already been opened.

"Some kinda mistake, huh?" Mrs. Janik laughed in her horsey way. "I mind my own business, but I just wasn't looking. I usually assume a letter in *my* mailbox is addressed to *me*."

"Yes, I know you did not open it intentionally," Ifi said.

"What kind of news do you suppose would be delivered by hand?" Mrs. Janik asked. She stabbed the space missing a stamp with a bony finger. "And whyn't she just go up to your door and hand it to you like a real woman?"

"It's a patient," Ifi said, but the uncertainty in her voice gave itself away immediately. "And why must it be from a woman?"

"Named Cheryl."

"Cheryl."

"Maybe she's a prostitute." The look of horror on Ifi's face only gave Mrs. Janik a slight pause. Ifi could only think of Job's magazine on the night of their honeymoon. "Well, maybe not a prostitute," Mrs. Janik continued. "Maybe just a woman who does things with men for money."

"A prostitute," Ifi said.

"You tell me, honey." Mrs. Janik rifled through the two letters in her own hands. "I wouldn't worry about it. All men are dirtbags," Mrs. Janik said. "That's why I didn't get married. What would I want with one? I say you kick him to the curb."

Ifi put the letter in her pocket. "I am not worrisome."

"Ain't you going to read it?" Mrs. Janik asked.

As she prepared the meal for the day, Ifi meant to forget about the letter. While slicing greens and spinach, the letter remained off to the side on the countertop. "He will find the letter," she told herself. "He'll look at it, and whatever he says will make sense." But then, just when she heard Job's key in the door, she slipped the letter into the tie of her wrapper.

Immediately Ifi could tell that he was in a stormy mood; she was too. Just like most mornings he returned, stripping down to his underwear and splaying each article—from the white lab coat to his socks and his briefcase— on the living room couch. Today, he did it all with his face creased into a frown. There were no chairs, so they ate the slightly scalded soup standing over opposite sides of the countertop, Job with his hairy belly sagging over his underwear. As they ate, Ifi imagined every possible scenario of sliding the letter to him and watching as he read it carefully, listening as he offered an explanation. But she would not; therefore, he did not.

Later, in the bathroom, Ifi crouched on the toilet, silently reading the letter.

Dear Job,
Whether you like it or not, we did get married. And that means I'm
entitled to some help. I don't ask for help from anyone. But this is a big
deal. Just talk to me. Please.
Love,
Cheryl

Ifi punched the wall, upsetting a mousetrap and staining the wall with peanut butter. Suddenly she remembered. Just after she had arrived, there had been that phone call. Why hadn't she questioned him about it? What a fool she had been. Nothing more than an ignorant housegirl in a big man's house. She cried. There had never been plans for her to be educated, to become a nurse. He was shifting his money to each of his mistresses. *He has brought me to America for this?*

He was still asleep on the couch. Her hands fumbled with the buttons of the phone dial. Aunty would advise her well. Ifi had never placed a long-distance call from America. Job had explained that the cost was far too expensive. And if Aunty were to receive such an expensive call, at such an hour, the only explanation would be a death. She set the phone back in its cradle. She would handle this on her own. After all, she was no longer a young girl. Ifi placed the letter on his slack chest, went to their bedroom, and began to pack her belongings: the jeans, the Nebraska sweatshirts, the yellow dress.

There was a knock at the door. It was Mrs. Janik. "I just came to offer you my support," Mrs. Janik said. "We women just can't put up with the abuses men give us. He can go back to his prostitute. He can keep her diseases to himself." She leaned in. "You know there's an AIDS epidemic. And it's because of men like him."

Job turned on the couch.

"You just tell him you don't want to have anything to do with him. You pack your things, and you can come over to my place."

Job turned again, slowly.

"Yes," Ifi said.

Mrs. Janik waited expectantly. She tried to glance around Ifi into the room.

"I will do it when he wakes," Ifi said.

Mrs. Janik arched an eyebrow. "Listen, you tell him this isn't Africa. I was reading about them men. Twenty wives! Well, he can't do that here. He can't own a woman in America. We got our own minds and our own money to do what we want."

Ifi nodded. "When he goes to work," she said.

"I'll come over and get you," Mrs. Janik said. She leaned in farther and whispered to Ifi, "It's probably better that way. We don't want him to get violent or anything. If there's one thing I won't tolerate, it's a wife beater."

Ifi nodded and let the door close on Mrs. Janik. When she turned around, Job was sitting up. The letter was on the floor. Mrs. Janik was right. Who knew what such a man was capable of? In three quick strides, she walked to him and stepped on the letter, hiding it.

"Which man beats his wives?" Job asked. He yawned and stretched.

"The Mexican."

"With the nine children? The wife that's a prostitute?"

"Yes."

He laughed. Ifi's laugh was an imitation of his.

"Imagine what that crazy old lady has to say about us," he said.

"What do you think she says about us?"

"Never mind her. She is a useless woman." Job said these last words with a yawn as he rolled over.

But Ifi wanted to know, and it made her angry that he hadn't bothered to answer her question. It bothered her that he could so easily dismiss Mrs. Janik. Mrs. Janik was right; Ifi would not be deceived. She wondered what he would do when he woke to find that she was gone.

For the first time, she slipped on her shoes and coat and went next door to Mrs. Janik's place. Like Ifi's building, the concrete was broken, and the front door hung on its hinges with a torn-out screen. There were three buttons, and Ifi found the one labeled Janik. She punched the button several times, but there was no answer. Just as she was beginning to lose her resolve, Mrs. Janik stuck her head out her window at the top of the building.

"Hiya!" she said. "It doesn't work. I'll let you up. Gimmie a second." She arrived at the door in moments, breathing heavily, her rear stooped out behind her. "Come on in, sweetie." She threw the door open and Ifi followed.

"Where's your stuff?"

"I'll get it later, when he goes to work," Ifi said. But she dreaded going back. She never wanted to see him or that dump again.

"Well darling, you don't have to worry. I wouldn't let that dog lay a hand on you."

"Darling," Ifi said softly. She cringed. It was a word she could only understand in the context of lovers, lovers who were quarreling.

They proceeded up the steps, three tall wooden flights of stairs that wound up the old building. The hallways smelled musty. As they passed each landing, Ifi could see used, dirty newspapers.

Mrs. Janik lived on the top floor, even at her age. It occurred to Ifi that she wasn't exactly sure how old Mrs. Janik was. She hadn't yet learned how to tell the age of a white person. Before Mrs. Janik opened the door, Ifi could immediately smell the strong scent of cats. Once inside, she glanced around, looking for the offending animals. But she couldn't find them. Instead what she saw was an orderly, windowless room with a harsh overhanging light that illuminated row upon row of dusty porcelain figurines along shelves pushed against every inch of wall space. Small porcelain children, dogs, birds, cats. Ifi leaned in and sniffed one of the cats.

"I can't ever seem to keep the dust from coming in," Mrs. Janik said. She picked up a duster from a drawer and proceeded to swat at each figurine, succeeding only in stirring and rearranging the dust with each whisk. It was no use.

Mrs. Janik showed Ifi around, pointing out the kitchen, the bathroom, her bedroom, and a small closet with a sewing machine. It was the same story in each room: shelves lined with tiny porcelain figurines with matte finishes from the fine layer of dust. "You can sleep in the guest room," Mrs. Janik said once they stood outside the sewing room. "You can have it as long as you like. I'll even pull in a cot for you to sleep on." Then, for good measure, she happily added, "We women have to stick together."

Mrs. Janik poured them cold tea in small cups from the back of her cabinet. They sat around a wooden table in uncomfortable wicker chairs. It reminded Ifi of staying with Job's family for those three months. Tea after church on Sundays, the white wicker chairs, and the way Job's sister, Jenny, and his mother would regard her with a look that was a mere shrug between disgust and acquiescence. The Ogbonnayas were of the haves who no longer had, those who had once lived in wealth and then found a way to lose it all. Even then, Ifi knew that they were settling on her, a girl without even a first degree. The only thing she had was her good name.

"Ifi," Mrs. Janik said now, "you haven't had your tea. Drink up. It'll get cold."

Ifi sipped the cold tea.

"You'll like it here." Mrs. Janik pointed to a spread of home decorating magazines, selecting one. "I noticed you reading one the other day," she said. "I read them too." Then she looked around the room and beamed. "See? I'm the queen in my home. Tomorrow we'll go and get you whatever it is you want to eat at the grocery. And you don't even have to cook it."

How could she be queen of such a place? This could not be Ifi's home. Her eyes rested on the magazine cover, the gloriously furnished room with its skylights and sleek leather furniture. This was the home she would make for herself. This was the place she left Nigeria for.

"Don't worry. You can stay as long as you like," Mrs. Janik said. "I know you're not like them."

Ifi nodded as Mrs. Janik made her way to the kitchen. She'd heard her reasoning before. Mrs. Janik had explained that the black woman across the street was a prostitute. *After all, there is no way a girl her age could afford to live on her own, and so many men come in and out of her home.* Ifi had seen the men before, all tall and narrow, like the woman. For the first time, she realized that they could merely be her brothers and uncles. She felt ridiculous. Surely there was a logical explanation for Job's letter. Suddenly, all Ifi wanted was to leave. Soon Job would wake for work. She would start another letter to Aunty tonight. It would ease her mind. Already Ifi was crafting the letter in her mind, imagining the details of the magazine, describing the skylights and the finish of the wooden furniture. She gazed anxiously at the magazine. There were so many that Mrs. Janik would not notice. She slipped it under her wrapper.

"I have to go," she said when Mrs. Janik returned.

"What?" Mrs. Janik frowned.

"After he leaves, I'll return."

"Okay," Mrs. Janik said. "I guess it makes sense. We don't want to make a scene when he gets violent. God knows I can't stand gossip."

Job was still asleep when Ifi made it back to the apartment. She returned to the bedroom and sat staring at the suitcase with the clothes in it. Nothing was hers. Not the yellow dress, not the Nebraska sweatshirts or jeans. He'd bought them all. After a while, she put the clothes back and sat gazing out the window. A thin veneer of frost outlined the panes. The colors outside were muted, ash gray. She hated this place.

Job's snores rose from deep within his belly. Ifi stared into his face, watching as his nostrils widened with each inhalation. She picked up the letter from the floor and placed it in her pocket. She fixed their food.

At mealtime, they ate silently. After hesitating, Job asked, "What do you write about to Aunty?"

"I tell her," Ifi said truthfully, "whatever it is that she would like to know."

Job left for work. Twenty minutes later, Mrs. Janik knocked at the door. Ifi didn't answer it. She put the light out, switched off the radio, and crawled into bed. She reminded herself of how a simple explanation from Job would suffice. Any explanation. When the knocks finally stopped, she rose one last time and set the letter on the couch, where Job would place his briefcase on his return.

CHAPTER 5

WHEN JOB ARRIVED HOME FROM WORK THE NEXT MORNING, THE phone was ringing. He cringed at its sound, hoping it wasn't Cheryl. It was only Emeka. Emeka's breath caught on the phone. Gladys was in the delivery room. "My boy is coming," Emeka said with triumph. "He is here."

Although they left in the same car, it was as if Job and Ifi arrived separately. By the time they made it to the maternity ward, the contractions had stopped, and the baby had been delivered: he was dead. His body was cold and colorless in the incubator. His features were immovable, like a waxy ball of clay carved with a fine needle. A patch of wet, dark curls was splayed across his crown, as if someone had pressed a palm onto his head.

Each of Emeka's daughters waited in a line, and one by one they peeked over the glass at the lifeless baby. The room was respectfully somber. And there was Gladys. To one side of her bed was a photograph recently taken, the one Job imagined them sitting for the evening he had collected Ifi from the airport. Emeka and Gladys were surrounded by their daughters, all striking in their likeness to both parents, the youngest in ribbons and hair baubles. Even the eldest daughters stood in the picture, women who in their silly youth could not yet embody Gladys's grace.

Today, Gladys was drowning in hospital sheets, her face turned toward the sunlight that poured in through the windows. She looked bloated, like flayed dough. Yet somewhere, hidden, was her effortless beauty. Seeing her there, exhausted yet beautiful, Job felt the familiar tug to his chest.

One of Emeka's daughters was peering at the baby, her gaze incredulous. Her smallest finger darted forward and hooked into the baby's nostril. She wiggled it around. No one noticed right away, except for Job.

Thinking about it after the fact, Job was struck by how quickly everything happened. How immediately after, Emeka had pulled the little girl to his body and embraced her tightly, and gently said, "Your brother." How suddenly, almost thoughtlessly, Emeka's arm had sliced through the air and thwacked the back of her head, hard, like he was catching a falling pebble. Her chin had butted forward, connecting with the rim of the incubator. Her lip had split open. Blood seeped through the crack into the space between her teeth, and a pink film washed over them. Her shrieks filled the room.

For a moment, no one knew what to do except for Emeka, whose arms were tightly wound around her body. He kissed her forehead. "Come now," he said. "Stop this crying. Stop this."

In answer, the girl shrieked, "Mommy!" She flung her body at her mother.

Several nurses entered the room. They saw the split lip, now an angry lump. Their gazes were a collection of fury, but they didn't know where to look or how it happened. Maybe the girl fell. Maybe it was one of her sisters. Or maybe it was *him*.

Gladys kneaded her fingers into her forehead. A haggard, insistent sound from deep inside her chest hissed, "Go." She turned to Emeka. "Ngwa, get out!"

At first, no one left the room. Then, gradually, each made their way toward the door. One of the nurses attempted to pry the daughter loose from Gladys, but she was unrelenting. The nurse looked at Ifi. "Go with your aunt," she said.

For the first time, the little girl stopped crying. "That's not my aunt," she said through hiccups. "Mommy says to call her Aunty, but she's not my real aunty."

"Well, you don't have to call her Aunty if you don't want to," the nurse said.

"Good," the girl said. Then after a moment, she reconsidered. "But I want to." The nurse finally had her hand, but the girl took it back. She glared accusingly at the woman and took Ifi's hand instead. They walked out of the room together, her cries softened to a just-audible hum.

Job was already waiting with the line of girls in their jeans, denim skirts, and cotton tights, when Emeka finally emerged from the room. He stalked past the row and Job followed. Emeka had made a bad impression, and Job couldn't help but feel vindicated. After a look at the open doorway, he imagined Gladys on the other side of it, swallowed by grief. He was immediately ashamed.

A circuitous route of glowing corridors and elevators took them outside to the parking lot. Emeka climbed into his car, a shiny SUV with panels of glowing lights on the dash. At first Job waited outside, thinking that once Emeka straightened up and collected himself, he'd go back to the room, to his wife, to his life. Instead he started the car, and Job was forced to occupy the passenger seat.

"Where are you going?" Job asked.

"We are blessed to have the sun on such a day," Emeka said with cheer.

It infuriated Job. Why must he pretend now? Better to apologize and beg for mercy. "You be careful, my friend," he said. "Those nurses will call police for what you did to that child."

Emeka laughed, tightly.

"And what of Gladys?" Job asked.

"Oh, she'll be fine." He nodded vigorously. "They'll be fine."

After the second circle around the parking lot, it was obvious they had nowhere to go.

"Let us get a drink," Job said. "It will calm you."

"You think so," Emeka said. A look of spite was on his face, a look that Job recognized almost immediately from the little girl. He glared at Job, but turned out of the parking lot. They made their way up tree-lined streets until they approached the cluster of buildings that was Omaha's downtown. All the bars were closed at that early hour, so they drove until they hit Highway 6. The roads were mostly empty, occupied by scattered fence posts and morose-looking cows with shining marble eyes peering out onto the road.

A billboard alerted them to the only building for miles, the Cattle Crawl. It was a stout brick building surrounded by a ring of rusted cars and trucks. After a moment, they climbed out of the car. The light was on, a flickering pink neon sign that said *Come Right In*. A man was just putting his cigarette out when he saw them. He shifted his considerable heft to hold the door open and let the two pass.

The lights inside were a misty fog that spread through the room, illuminating stools and tables streaked from wet rags and a scuffed, empty stage. A howling country song murmured through the room. Men sat hunched over the bar. One woman with an old, sour face and puckered lips was among them, sucking a murky drink through a straw.

After looking the woman over for a long time, Emeka leaned into Job, but his voice was loud and delighted. "Disgusting!"

They ordered whiskeys straight up, and the bartender brought them out in cloudy glasses packed with ice. Emeka picked up his glass, inspected the smudges along the rim, and shook his head. At the top of the cluster of ice cubes, a small fleck floated. Job was equally disgusted. If he were with anyone else in the world, he would ask the bartender to bring another glass.

They sipped silently. After a moment, Emeka spoke. "She tells me it was juju." He smirked. "That's why she has not had a son for all these years."

Job smirked along with him. He didn't believe in such a thing, the thought that a witch could put a hex on Gladys to bring her misfortune, let alone deny her a son. It was the kind of story his grandparents and generations before them had repeated to him as a small child, the kind of story his parents respectfully nodded at, then quietly chuckled over.

"Her sisters." Emeka rolled his eyes. "They are sending an emissary to the village for a native doctor. Can you believe this nonsense? I have had to pay three thousand dollars to take care of this matter." He looked gravely at Job, and Job could see in Emeka's eyes that he really did believe it. "I have an enemy. Someone is jealous of me, my friend."

"Come now."

"It is true. I am a man with the fortune of marrying a beautiful, intelligent wife. I have six beautiful daughters, two at university. I own a palace. I have the top position at the university. I tell you, a jealous man is watching."

"You don't believe such nonsense," Job said.

"Of course not," Emeka snapped at him and crossed his arms on the bar. "Of course not."

They ordered a second round. And then a third. By the time they had lost count, the men and the sole woman had turned away from the bar and faced the stage at the back of the room. A string of scantily clad women with knobby knees and bruised thighs stood on the stage in various poses. At twenty, they were destined for a cruel middle age. Emeka glowered. He called them ugly harlots, cows. He said, "See that one, and that one. Ashawo!" He waved dismissively at their stretch marks, at the downward dip of their nipples. "They already have children. What kind of mother dances naked? Shameless. Ah-ah! A-mer-eeka." But his eyes did not leave them.

Job nodded in assent, his eyes shamefully dodging those of the women on the stage. He told Emeka about the phone calls, about Cheryl—"She has called three times, oh, begging me for my money"—but he left out the fact that he had given it to her.

Without his eyes leaving the stage, Emeka wagged his head. After a moment, he reconsidered. "Wait, wait, wait. Is this the woman who gave you a blow job so many years ago? This one?"

Job nodded carefully.

Emeka laughed. "You mean to tell me that this woman has used your name to pay her bills? And you have done nothing?"

Job thought it over. "It is a business arrangement."

"You are being taken for a long ride, my friend." He shook his head at Job. "What does she want?"

"Money. All the time, begging me for money. You see, I am the most successful man she knows. Of all her American friends, I am the only one who is *capable* to provide the investment income," Job said. "But I have refused to hear her nonsense."

"Americans are way-o. I would not be the fool in this business," Emeka said. He clucked softly.

"I would not know this thief if it had not been for you." Job's voice rose. "You said it would be easy. You said, 'Marry quick-quick, divorce quick-quick, and citizen.'"

"Job, my friend," Emeka said, "I have known you since you were still suckling your mother's breast from here in America." He sighed. "Have I not taught you anything? You do not know how to make your voice heard."

"What are you talking about?" Job shrugged. "I have washed my hands of this woman until I see a profit margin increase."

"Then she wants to blow job you again. Is this the profit margin that you will be increasing?" Emeka laughed throatily. "Why are you complaining to me?" Emeka drunkenly swatted at Job. "Eh, why are you wasting my time?"

"Heh." Job fumed. Why must he turn to Emeka for help when the man couldn't even control his own home? Clearly it was Emeka's fault about the baby. What kind of man forced his wife to work in that condition anyway? Ifi did not have to work, though Gladys did. Job thought about Ifi's letter, about the palace she had described to her aunty: *Ionic columns, crown molding, curtains of lace, a big-screen television.* What did they need such non-sense for? None of it made sense to him. Lies. She had seen him leave for work each night. She must have known that he was not a lazy man. He had provided her with all the comforts a man could: a home, a comfortable bed, a fur coat, necklaces, and a designer dress. She had not suffered like Gladys. He turned to Emeka. "Gladys was still working, eh?" His voice rose in that warning note, the same note Emeka had used when he said Americans were way-o.

"Fuck you," Emeka said. His mouth was full of spit, and his words salted the air with saliva. Then, almost guiltily, he straightened up, regained his composure, and turned to the bartender. "Drinks for everyone."

The bartender lined up several of the stout, cloudy glasses on the bar and filled them all with ice and whiskey. Everyone nodded his or her thanks. One fellow patted Emeka on the back and called him "buddy." Again, he was the hero. And once again, Job hated him for it. Why must everyone honor Emeka? Couldn't they see that he was nothing more than a crook? He did not even come from a good family like Job.

The lone woman at the bar blew Emeka a kiss. She made her way over to them. Pale pink lipstick stained a row of yellowed teeth. Wrinkles lined her powdered face. "Listen, buddy," she said, "I just want you to know, I appreciate your fellowship. So what do you do?" she asked.

Job answered for them. "He is an engineer and I am a doctor."

She pulled out a card from her pocket and handed it to Emeka. Her name was Sheryl. Job laughed. He couldn't help it. She was a boutique owner. She told Emeka to come by anytime. "Anytime at all."

Emeka placed the card in his pocket without looking at the lady or the card.

Job gazed at Emeka. His eyes had begun to glaze over as he watched the gyrating strippers. Beads of sweat ran down their faces. The lipstick smudged. Dark raccoon makeup encircled the eyes of one of the strippers, and it matched the bruises on her bowed legs.

Job reached into his pocket for Ifi's letter. He hadn't yet decided what to do with it. He glanced at the envelope, but instead of Ifi's careful longhand, he saw a typeface with Cheryl's name and address. He shrank back in horror. Could he have accidentally posted Ifi's letter with the bills for the day? For the first time, he wondered how many of these letters had made it to Aunty. And who else had seen them. It was not even what was contained in the letters that bothered him. Everyone had done it, he supposed. To some degree, they had all told their little lies. Uncomfortably he thought of his stethoscope and briefcase, and his nightly trips to the parking lot. But why must Ifi tell the little lies? Her life was uncomplicated, and when the baby arrived, it would be complete. Never would she have to endure the insults that he faced nightly—working long nights with little sleep, being chastised like a child by coworkers who had come from nothing, wiping feces from patients' anuses. Never would she face these humiliations. He would make sure she lived the unsullied life of a big man's wife if it killed him.

Job started to take the letter out of his pocket to show it to Emeka, to complain or to find a way to make Ifi, like Gladys, a woman dignified and content with life. He wasn't sure which. Maybe Emeka would have an answer for this, as he had an answer for everything, as Samuel had.

Before Samuel left for the war, there were long talks with Job at age seven, his chin resting in his palm as Samuel strutted back and forth in front of his bed, instructing him about his civic duty as an Igbo. Samuel was one of the first to go, a rascally nineteen-year-old with jagged teeth and too much confidence. While others were dodging conscription, he enlisted. He so heartily believed in the cause. All those secret meetings he went to; for their father, the idea of an Igbo secessionist state was merely hushed, angry whispers in living rooms. Even so, Job worried that his brother was mixing with troublesome people: tall men in khakis who patted his shoulder and allowed him sips from their beers during the one meeting he followed Samuel to.

Everyone was so foolish with pride when they saw Samuel in that uniform. They had even thrown him a big party before he left for military training, convinced it would be over in a matter of days. They were fooled, all of them. But most of all Samuel, whose body came back in a bruised wooden crate, damaged from its bumpy ride home in a street lorry.

Glaring at the dingy stage, Job's memory set on the image of the battered crate, and he was filled with such a surge of simultaneous rage and remorse that he ordered bourbon and drank it so fast that it choked the words that were in danger of escaping him. Bourbon drowned the accusations in his heart—against Samuel, the one meant to be the doctor, meant for America; against Ifi and her malcontent.

After some time, the bartender slid the bill across the damp bar. While he half waited, half slept, Job and Emeka argued over who would pay the bill, until Job stumbled and told Emeka that his practice was growing larger and he didn't need help from anyone to pay any of his bills. And his wife was just fine and happy with it. Emeka gave him a strange look, but allowed him to pay. Job paid with a MasterCard, signed the bill, crumpled it, and placed it in his pocket without looking. Still, no one surrounded Job gleefully to pat him on the back and call him "buddy," and, as a result, he scowled as they made their way to the car.

It wasn't until they were on their way down the long stretch of highway that Job realized that in the past, he had told Emeka and Gladys that he was not in private practice quite yet, that instead he worked for a regional hospital. It surprised Job that Emeka hadn't caught his mistake. And then it pleased him. *Emeka is the fool,* he thought, and the ride back was liquid; Job's face relaxed into a tranquil smile and Emeka's a complement.

On the way into town, they took a different route, skipping across Highway 6 and cutting to Interstate 80. It was a longer ride, but Job said nothing until they'd pulled onto a service road. A string of glass storefronts faced the main road, and they stopped in front of one with miniature bears and helium-filled balloons in the window. Emeka selected two stuffed bears with candy canes in their mouths. At the register, he plunged his hand into a barrel of candy canes and dumped the heap into a plastic bag. A pot of plastic lilies sat on the countertop, the kind with little faces meant to be filled with photographs. Without words, Job already knew. This one would be for Gladys. Emeka paid and collected his peace offering.

Not until they were out the door did it occur to Job that perhaps he should purchase a gift for Ifi. By then, something had caught his eye: an electronics warehouse at the end of the storefronts, with a faded billboard and a banner with markdowns indicated by slashed-through numbers. "There," he said, and the two went into the warehouse.

A red-faced salesman in a collared blue shirt greeted them. Almost immediately Job saw the one he wanted. He marched past the salesman.

"Thirty-two inches," the salesman said, following them too closely. It was the same size as Emeka's. "Crystal-clear picture—"

"No, no," Job said suddenly. He swiveled away and pointed at an even bigger television. "This one."

"You are drunk, my friend," Emeka said, his eyes growing large.

The salesman gulped. Job could see him retracing his steps, going through his script a second time to find where he had left off. "It has a crystal-clear picture and excellent sound. It's compatible with the latest digital technologies. Your own home theater."

"I'll buy it," Job said.

"What do you need that for?" Emeka asked, his voice tight. "What are you trying to prove?"

Both Job and the salesman ignored him. The salesman beamed. "In-store credit. No interest for the first twelve months. Free delivery."

"Good," Job said, "I want it now."

"Not a problem, my good man. We'll have two fellows get it on a truck ASAP."

At the register, Job filled out the application form. The clerk ran his credit, approved him, and Job left with a small plastic yellow bag full of receipts and warranty information.

On the way back to the hospital, as Job grinned with satisfaction, Emeka glared at the road ahead. His hands wobbled on the steering wheel. He complained that Americans watched too much television. He said it was bad for the eyes and for the brain. He said his daughters were university educated because he had restricted their television use. He said he didn't care for any of the nonsense that came from television. To illustrate his point, he took the card out of his pocket with Sheryl's phone number on it. He tore it in two and tossed it aside. It landed in the plastic bag on Job's lap.

Cheryl clutched Ifi's letter, still folded into a tight square, when Job arrived at the lot in the early hours of the morning. His stomach grumbled. He shivered and felt exhausted from his overnight shift, another night of Captain's howling complaints about his "son," an angry night spent lashing out at the nurses as they entered his room. Job was the only aide who could comfort him, and as such he was left to attend to Captain's rages, his bloodcurdling shrieks, brutal curses, and gummy blows. Still, Captain's wrath was a reprieve from his sorrow. Tomorrow would be a sad one. Tomorrow Captain would curl in a ball on his bed, his body wracked with unanswered grief, and that, for some reason, was the hardest to bear.

Job snatched the letter from Cheryl's hands, feigning disgust to disguise his relief. His in-laws would never see another one of Ifi's letters again. He would make sure of that. Only after he had crumpled the letter and allowed it to drift into the snow did Job notice Cheryl closely observing him.

With a shivery laugh, she said, "Good riddance. I'd have done it myself if you'd just asked."

"It's nothing. Just some nonsense." After a moment, reluctantly, he added, "Thank you."

Snow had begun to fall, light flecks that coated her eyelashes. An awkward moment passed as Job pried open his door, heavy with ice. He said good-bye, thanked her again, and started the car. Only after he'd circled the lot to make his way to the street did he glance back and notice Cheryl pulling the lip of her coat up past her chin to her nose before steadily bearing her weight through the snow. He wondered how far away she lived, and, begrudgingly, he admitted to himself that when he had arrived at work that night, it had been Cheryl who had called to let him know that she had Ifi's letter. She could just as easily have kept it for herself or read its contents. As far as he could tell, she had done neither. He'd be late arriving home, but he was filled with a sudden rush of relief at the certainty that the letter would never make it into the hands of his in-laws. He turned the car one last time and opened the door for her.

Cheryl climbed in, shivering. "Thanks. I mean it," she said. "My car's in the shop. Piece of crap has a broken muffler."

Heat from their breaths clouded the windows as they drove through the calm streets. Every few minutes Job dragged his forearm in a circle along the windshield so that he could see out. His woolly coat left a jagged streak across the window. When they arrived in front of the tall wooden house, with its peeling siding and lopsided gateposts, they sat for a moment in mutual stillness. In the early morning hours, the street was quiet, a fading streetlight lazily flickering. One lone bird, abandoned for the season, waded across the street before clumsily tottering away. This was Cheryl's home, the source of their strange encounter. Had it not been for such a place, they might never have met all those years ago for a marriage of convenience. They might never have met this time. This was what she was willing to fight for.

She seemed to hear him, because suddenly she spoke, but she didn't say what he expected to hear. "I never had all of those nice things," she said softly. "I been working my whole life, and there's nothing to show for it. Just the house, and I can barely even keep it up. You just got here, but you, you've made yourself a success. How is it possible?"

Job burned with shame. "You read the letter."

"I thought it was one of my letters." She bit her bottom lip, but instead of guilt, a pained expression crossed her face. "I've never been the type to bring that kind of treatment out in any man, just lies." When she said this, with the strange note of jealousy in her voice, Job's fists relaxed. She had believed every word of it. With all of Ifi's bragging, all of her exaggeration, it was as if she had entered the car and interceded on his behalf. Cheryl offered a dry laugh, and only because he felt it was the polite thing to do, Job laughed along with her.

A deep frown set on her face. "She must be the happiest woman in the world. I can't even fix that stupid piece of shit for a car. A hundred dollars left, and the jerk mechanic holds it hostage. Complete asshole. I'm not a thief. I always pay when I get the money." She paused and grunted. "Your wife must have it made."

"She does," Job said with sudden pride. "My wife has enjoyed many blessings in her life because of me. She no longer has to work. She will go to university in America. I have decided that she will be trained to be a nurse in my clinic. It is I who brought water and electricity to my in-laws in Nigeria, sef. I have provided for her cousins' education. Just yesterday, I bought her a new television. It is a surprise, but I am sure she will be pleased."

"Shit," she said in awe. "What are you, a messiah?"

"Ah, yes, messiah." Then, he couldn't help but add, "It is not in my nature to brag, so I will only say that this television has crystal-clear picture and digital technologies." Job looked out onto the street. He felt, strangely, as if he owned all of it. He was a big man. Then, as Cheryl's eyes grew in alarm, Job found himself unfolding five twenty-dollar bills and casually tossing them at her. For just a second, a flicker of worry rose on the crest of his brow, but then he quickly dismissed it. His next paycheck was only a week away, and if they needed groceries or gas for the week, he would pay with his MasterCard. "Fix your car," he said easily.

She lunged toward him for a hug. "Thank you." Tears started forming in her eyes.

He shrugged her off, faked a sigh of annoyance. She smelled of cigarettes and strawberries. Up close, he could make out the whiskers around her eyes, the chapped lips. "Just take it and fix your vehicle."

After Cheryl entered her house, Job returned to his car lot, and sitting there, it occurred to him that he had never seen his hideaway during the day. In early morning light, the outlines of a warehouse and two adjacent suite-style offices—tall brick buildings—were nothing but stark shadows. Now, in daylight, men arrived in black suits, swinging briefcases at their sides as they purposefully marched through the snow to their office buildings. Job pulled up to the spot where he and Cheryl had met earlier that morning in the graying light, and he retrieved Ifi's crumpled letter. With the same jealous note in their voices as Cheryl, his in-laws would read another of Ifi's letters. They would nod triumphantly. They would brag about his successes in a land far away. Because it was so early in the day, the letter was only damp. He smoothed out the wrinkles, affixed postage to the envelope, and placed it in a blue postal drop box before heading home.

Between two uniformed men and a dolly, the television made it up the creaky flight of wooden stairs, only getting dropped twice. After much struggle, the deliverymen had realized that the television couldn't fit through the frame of the doorway, so they charged Job extra to take the frame off the door. And then they charged him again to put it back on.

Finally, the television squeezed through the door sideways. One of the men held his shoulder where it hit the doorway. Circles of sweat were in the other man's armpits. They were both skinny, one tall and one short, and when they had first arrived at the door with their clipboard, Ifi had thought they were the fumigators coming to spray the apartment for roaches again—since, she had learned, landlords did this sort of thing all the time in America. Since the fumigation hadn't worked very well to begin with, she had signed their papers without really looking. And because she had thought it was the fumigators again, she hadn't even bothered to wake Job. They were supposed to leave the apartment whenever the fumigators came, but they never did, and so she left Job sprawled across the couch in his underwear, snoring loudly, only draping his naked chest with a blanket.

That is, until the uniformed men appeared at the door again, covered in sweat, with a turned-sideways box big enough to fit three small children. Mrs. Janik was with them. Even after the two men left with the delivery tip, Mrs. Janik remained, scrutinizing the television from her position on the couch between Ifi and Job, who now had the blanket tied at his waist like a wrapper.

After a lengthy silence, Mrs. Janik was the first to speak. "I never seen one that big before."

Simultaneously, the three gulped. They'd had to move a few items around to make room for the television. Now the couch backed the kitchen, and the television was anchored against the back wall, blocking out part of the window. Two long, winding plants sat atop the television on either end, with their leaves dangling down the sides of the screen. Only a foot of space was left between the couch and the center table. It leaned against the base of the television.

Job stood in front of it, gathering the blanket around his waist. He swept his fingers across the screen and instructed Ifi and Mrs. Janik to do so too; they obliged. Ifi felt the spark and crackle of the static on her fingers. For a moment, it filled her with delight.

"You people see this?" he said. "Crystal-clear picture and compatible with the latest digital technologies. My own home theater."

Exactly what he meant wasn't clear to Ifi, but Mrs. Janik nodded vigorously, so Ifi nodded her assent. Carefully, she repeated his words: "Crystal-clear picture and digital technology."

On, the television was less of a miracle. Static rained down, and a permanent crack in the image, received during the television's wobbly ascent up the steps, would always remain. That day, however, Job didn't seem to notice.

Ifi took the remote control and flipped to one channel and then another. Each channel lent a different texture to the warbled images and snow. On most channels, there wasn't even any sound but a roar. "What is wrong with this?" Ifi asked. She handed the remote back to Job. "Chineke, they have damaged it."

"You gotta order the cable now," Mrs. Janik said. Her eyes were somber moons.

"Yes," Job said, slowly. "Soon." Then he harped on all the channels they'd be able to watch. They'd even be able to watch Nollywood movies. "It is my own home theater," he said again.

When he finally left to shower and dress, Mrs. Janik leaned in and whispered to Ifi in a shrill voice, "I knew what he was up to as soon as I saw the deliverymen outside. I just knew it."

Ifi nodded. Admittedly, she hadn't understood any of it. She still didn't. When Ifi had asked about where he had purchased the television, why, the cost, Job had said, "You people think you are still living in the bush. This is America."

Mrs. Janik blinked. "He's trying to make you forget about his mistress. He thinks this is all it takes. Like you're some cheap prostitute he can purchase and take back when he's through." She worked herself up into her own rage.

"I'm fine," Ifi said. A path of muddy track marks led from the doorway into the room, from the deliverymen. She wetted a rag and started to wipe at the stains.

Mrs. Janik sat back on the couch. With much effort, she lifted her two legs onto the center table, pushed the magazines aside, and picked one up. It was the interior design magazine that Ifi had taken from her apartment. Ifi felt a sudden chill.

Mrs. Janik thumbed through the magazine, settling on the well-worn pages like Ifi had. Ifi had memorized the pictures by now: the all-white living room on page twenty-five, with the shiny black contemporary furniture, the Chinese tapestries draped along the walls, and the Berber rugs on the gleaming hardwood floors. Ifi had already begun to compose a new letter for Aunty, describing the texture of the rug in precise detail. Now, she felt cold and ashamed, like a common beggar. But it wasn't stealing. "My dear," she said in her calmest voice, "thank you for dashing me your magazine. You see, I planned to bring it back to you tonight."

Mrs. Janik didn't seem to hear her explanation. "So what happened to you that night?" Then she answered her own question. "Listen, you got nothing to be afraid of. We're in this together. I won't let nothing happen to you."

Ifi put the rag down. "It was a mistake," she said. Wasn't it? Surely she had jumped to conclusions. Yet, she couldn't bring herself to present Job with the letter. In fact, the letter was once again in her pocket.

"Do you still have it?" Mrs. Janik asked.

"What?"

"The letter of course!"

"No, I threw it away."

But it was not true. The letter had driven with Ifi and Job to the hospital. It had been in her pocket when Gladys's little girl had taken her hand. And it had also been there as she gently rocked the girl in her lap until her sobs subsided. It had even been there when the baby in Ifi's stomach had begun to kick for the first time. Although she knew immediately what it was, it had felt like a rumble inside her belly. She hadn't expected it to feel like that. Ifi had taken the little girl's small palm in her hand and pressed it into her belly. The little girl had looked at her with dark eyes and said, "My brother did that too."

Ifi pulled her closer and kissed her forehead then, thinking of the colorless body in the incubator. Emeka and Gladys had agreed with the nurses that the girls ought to have a chance to say good-bye to their little brother. And then, while everyone had waited outside, their angry raised voices had argued that they had done it all wrong, and the girls should never have seen the dead baby. But Ifi had silently disagreed. Had she seen her mother and later her father when they passed away, it might have made more sense that they were never coming back. Perhaps her nights wouldn't have been filled with silly fantasies. Ifi had kissed the little girl's fingertips and pressed them to the lump on her lip. She had told the little girl that her baby brother was in heaven with Jesus. Since that time, Ifi hadn't been able to think about anything but protecting the baby inside her. It astounded her that she could feel such love for someone she had never met. She thought of Job.

Mrs. Janik flipped through the pages of the magazine so quickly that she ripped one of them. "Don't you even wonder what the woman looks like? Aren't you even a little curious?"

Ifi scrubbed harder at the spot on the floor.

Mrs. Janik had the rag in her hand before Ifi realized it. She glared into Ifi's face. "If I were you, I wouldn't take this lightly. You think this is the last you've seen of this prostitute? Well, you're wrong. You're wrong. Do you understand? That prostitute is coming back. And if I were you, I'd want to be on the offensive." She dropped the rag in front of Ifi, straightened up, and headed for the door, letting it slam behind her.

Ifi shook her head. What an ugly woman. Useless, just like Job had said. No husband, no children, no family, sef. There was a sister somewhere, but Ifi had never seen her, probably because she didn't want the woman's bad luck to spoil her. Ifi shivered at the thought of the cat smell in Mrs. Janik's apartment and the dusty porcelain figurines all along the walls, like a mausoleum of animal corpses. Again, Ifi thought of the lifeless baby boy in the incubator.

She rinsed out the rag in the sink and spread it to dry. Balancing her hand at the base of her back where the weight of her belly seemed to rest, she struggled to squeeze through the small space between the center table and the couch. Ifi rearranged the items in the living room, shifting the plants on top of the television and stacking Job's boxes on the floor in an orderly arrangement. Wobbling lines greeted her when she turned on the television. Ifi glared into the screen, trying to piece the warped images together into one.

And then she felt the baby kick again. A yell rose in the back of her throat. Job, wrapped in a towel, rushed in, dripping and warm from his shower.

"He's kicking." Ifi guided Job's hand to her belly.

He could only murmur again and again, "Je-sus Christ. Je-sus Christ."

They both realized that the shower was still running, and he rushed back to turn it off. It was then, with Ifi low on the couch, straightening the items on the floor, that she stumbled on the plastic yellow bag from the electronics store. Receipts were stapled together in a cluster. Her eyes widened at the number of nines behind the dollar sign. But she pushed it back into the bag. There, she found half of a torn business card, one half that read: Sheryl.

CHAPTER 6

ONCE MRS. JANIK WAS SEATED NEXT TO HER IN THE TAXI, IFI REACHED into her handbag and set the interior design magazine on the slope between them. Mrs. Janik didn't even look at it. Instead she pulled the shaggy brim of her snow hat so that it rested just above her eyebrows. "Let me see it here again," she said. She meant the business card, but Ifi pushed the magazine into her lap anyway. It stayed there unopened and untouched for the remainder of the drive, and when they made it to their destination, Mrs. Janik left it behind.

They stood before a large empty lot backed by a line of squat storefronts; the one on the end was hers, Beacon Boutique, a shabby affair. Most of the stenciled letters on the façade had begun to fade and crack. Dead cigarettes were scattered along the pavement. Ifi thought it must be a mistake; the driver said it was not. To prove himself, he pushed the torn halves of the business card together. The numbers on the building matched. He didn't bother to ask them what they were doing there, a pregnant African woman and an old white lady. And this—and this alone—was what frightened Ifi the most. With little more than a cluck, he dropped them off and drove away, taking the crumpled bills from Mrs. Janik. The abandoned magazine shrunk the farther the cab drove away.

To come to this place had been Mrs. Janik's idea, although, to be honest, Ifi had helped in forming it. After she had seen the business card, Ifi had pounded on Mrs. Janik's door. She was right. She had been right all along. They had a problem. She needed to be a woman and take care of it. And it had only taken that for Mrs. Janik to insist that *the prostitute* had gone *just too far,* buying the peace offering with *her man.*

Now the two stood outside the dark, empty building, their hands frozen in their pockets, uncertain of their next move. Nearby a stooped streetlight illuminated a row of bus stop benches with a dull orange glow. Spread across the lot, there were two abandoned cars, newer models, big, boxy cars. But it was such a desolate scene that Ifi couldn't imagine the cars having ever belonged to anyone. It was nearly seven, so early that the sky was nothing more than a dark strip shrouded by pale fluff. Job would be home soon, and, Ifi supposed, in their haste, they hadn't exactly come up with a plan; they hadn't figured out how it would be done, or, for that matter, what would be done.

In turn, they peeked into the storefront window, clouding the glass with their heat. After a while, Mrs. Janik said, "We'll just wait out here in the cold until she shows up? That's what we'll do?" She indicated the faded timetable on the door. "We'll wait here until nine for her to open?"

"Yes, that's what we'll do." Ifi glared through the windows at the shelves. She could just make out the books and toys, the clothes hanging on skinny wire hangers in the back. The longer they waited, the colder she felt, and the angrier Ifi found herself. She thought of the magazine riding through the dark city streets. In her next letter to Aunty, she would have to describe the details of the furniture and the rug from memory. *Will Aunty doubt me?* she wondered.

"Let's go," Mrs. Janik said. "We can come back tomorrow."

"No."

"She's not here."

"She will come."

"And your husband. He'll be home soon. What's he gonna think?"

"That will be for him and his maker."

"Maybe we were mistaken." Mrs. Janik shoved her hands farther into her pockets. "We'll just wait out here until she shows up?" She nodded her head assertively, as if convincing herself of this logic. "That's what we'll do." She yanked at the brim of her snow hat. "You know who this prostitute is and what she's doing with your man." Short concrete slabs circled the perimeter of the parking lot. Mrs. Janik dragged her narrow legs along one. "We should make her pay." She gave the slab a swift kick, stronger than Ifi expected of a woman her age. The concrete crumbled into smaller pieces. Mrs. Janik glared with pride. "You know, these prostitutes, they think they can mess with me. But they can't." Another kick and a block of concrete spiraled through the air, striking the storefront window. It wasn't even Beacon Boutique. Webs spread out along the glass. "Oh goodness!" Mrs. Janik clasped her palms together. "Oh goodness gracious!"

A dull light blinked on in the rear of Beacon Boutique. Mrs. Janik backed away from the building. With the baby acting as a barrier, Ifi tried to reach out to Mrs. Janik, but to no avail. Almost immediately, Mrs. Janik stumbled over backwards on one of the parking slabs and landed flat on her rear. She started to cry. Mean old lady tears.

When Ifi saw the flash of Emeka's eyes, she started to run away, waddle really. *What will he say to Job? Surely he will say something to his good friend. How can I explain myself?* But it was strange. He said nothing to her, as if meeting Ifi in the parking lot of a strip mall so early in the morning was the most ordinary event of his day. He lifted Mrs. Janik off the ground. Her pantyhose were torn. Pebbles were caked into the backs of her doughy legs. "Are you all right, madam?" he asked.

Again, those old lady tears. Mrs. Janik bent to examine her leg and whimpered. She looked so small and pitiful, so old as Emeka took her by the arm, led her to the side of the building, and helped her sit. Ifi thought of the twelve dollars Mrs. Janik had paid for the taxicab, and she wondered why she hadn't done this alone. *Would I have needed such a woman in Nigeria?*

"Everything okay?" This second voice belonged to a woman with a withered face, white with powder. She wore a shiny silver jacket, hastily thrown on.

Ifi's eyes trained on the woman. She nodded slowly. This couldn't be his woman. Her stare hardened as she looked the lady up and down—so old and withered—until the woman turned to face the glass storefront. "Sheesh." She gazed at Ifi. "You did this?"

"What is your name?" Ifi asked.

Mrs. Janik made fresh tears. "I didn't mean it. It was an accident."

"Well, I don't like the jerk that owns that one," the lady said after a pause. "Puts his cigarettes out. Never picks up after himself. You get out of here real fast and no one will know." She nodded to Emeka.

Emeka started his car. Mrs. Janik followed, but Ifi waited.

"You own this store?" Ifi asked.

"Yes, Beacon Boutique." She thrust out a hand. Without thinking, Ifi took it. When she pulled her hand away, Ifi found a cold, hard piece of cardboard identical to the one in her pocket with the name Sheryl. "Whatever you need in fellowship, I have it."

Ifi glanced back at the store. Now that it was illuminated, she saw the miniature ark and stuffed giraffes, elephants, and tigers. A train of crucifixes followed a Mother Mary doll. *What kind of prostitute owns such a store?*

After a moment, Sheryl narrowed her eyes at Ifi. "He's waiting for you."

Heat rose from the grille of Emeka's SUV. Before entering the car, Ifi gazed at Sheryl one last time. She was propped up against the side of the building. She lit a cigarette and waved her hands in front of her face, fanning the fumes in all directions. She took two long, stirring sips, and then the cigarette met the others on the pavement. All the cigarette butts were hers, so why had she lied? Ifi frowned.

"Where do you two ladies live," Emeka said. It wasn't a question.

Ifi hesitated, but she played along with him. They would be strangers to one another. Perhaps he would not say anything to Job. She wondered why, but decided it wasn't worth pursuing. She gave him the address. The whole ride home, Mrs. Janik moaned about the pains in her legs. She said nothing about Sheryl or prostitutes or *her man.* Ifi waited for Emeka to ask her what she had been doing there, but he said nothing. Then it suddenly occurred to her that he hadn't said what *he* had been doing there.

They stopped in front of the apartment building. "Well, ladies, we are here safe and sound, no?" Emeka gave them a tight smile.

With an overpronounced limp, Mrs. Janik thrust out her hip and made her wobbly way toward her building. "Too much excitement for a lady my age."

Emeka laughed heartily.

Ifi's eyes met his.

He grinned. "So this is it." He surveyed the big old building that housed their flat. "You know, your husband has never allowed me to follow him home."

Ifi thought of Gladys's fur coats and the palace of Ifi's imagination drawn up from her interior design magazines: mansions of marble, tapestries, and archways. In spite of her anger with Job she felt guilty, understanding now, as she had the night of their dinner, that whatever Emeka and Gladys possessed was real.

"A very comfortable home," she said defensively. Immediately she felt anger. *How can I defend him, even now?* But the smug look on Emeka's face infuriated her. She couldn't let him go without saying something. What of Gladys? She felt her anger shifting from Job to Gladys and finally to Emeka. *What of his six girls and the little boy in the incubator? What of Gladys?* Ifi remembered the look of Gladys's vacant eyes staring out the window, but at what? Nothing more than a parking lot and short houses all along the road. *This is the America we have all come to? For this?*

"Chai! Is this what our men are doing in America?" Ifi shook her head.

Emeka's grin tightened. His forehead was shiny. "Little mama, you are tired."

"Both of you?"

Emeka frowned for the first time.

"What is this Sheryl?" *Can such a woman tempt both Job and Emeka?*

Emeka suddenly laughed. Hard. "Little mama, go to sleep now. Your husband will be home soon."

"I have no husband," Ifi said.

"No?" Again, Emeka laughed. "Well, I believe your husband will disagree." He was teasing. Ifi didn't like it.

"Go home now and sleep. He will be home soon. Today is an uneasy day for all of us." He rested a palm on one of Ifi's shoulders. Gradually, the pressure hardened until he was pushing her toward the door. But Ifi didn't budge.

"She is an ugly prostitute."

"What is this talk of prostitutes, eh?" Again, he laughed heartily. "I have just taken you home. Now if you hurry, you will go inside before your husband returns. He will never know that you have left."

Ifi reached into her pocket and thrust the letter at Emeka. He read slowly. At first he looked confused. Then he laughed suddenly, so hard and long that tears started in the corners of his eyes. Spittle filled the corners of his mouth, and he wiped at his face with his dry, crackling palms. "This is nonsense! A crackerpot. The American Job married for papers many years ago."

"Papers?"

Emeka nodded slowly. "You see, in America it is easy to marry quick-quick and then *irreconcilable differences*." After a pause, he explained. "Divorce. The American way." He patted Ifi's shoulder. "You people forget you are in

America, oh." After a moment, he gazed at her carefully and soberly added, "Your husband has not paid his full debt. But I am his friend, and so I go and meet her, so she will leave him."

"Eh?"

Emeka nodded. "Now, it is not wise for you to tell him about this. He is a man. He will be ashamed to see another man paying his debt, even his brother."

What he said made sense. Men and women married for papers. It was true. Had it not been for such an arrangement, Ifi's only course to come to America would have been the lottery. In her lifetime, Ifi had only heard of one person who had received papers that way.

Suddenly, Ifi couldn't meet his eyes. Instead, she gazed down at her belly. With nothing to do with her hands, she rubbed, willing the baby to remind her with a kick that she wasn't alone, that he had seen it all. *What a fool I have been.* She laughed to herself. She would never make such a mistake again. Of course Emeka had gone to meet the woman in the early hours of the morning. Of course they had exchanged the money quietly. Of course her insecurities had taken the place of common wisdom. Hadn't Aunty called her jealous and ungrateful as a child? Well, perhaps Aunty had always been right. How would they ever pay such a debt back to Emeka? Job would need to take more patients. Work more hours.

"And the old lady?" Emeka asked.

"Mrs. Janik. Our neighbor."

"Hmm. She must not speak."

"Don't mind her." A pause. "And how is Gladys?"

For a moment, his expression clouded. Then, like a sun breaking through clouds, his grin resurfaced. "My dear, Gladys is a champion."

"And what of the boy?"

"Marry, *bury,* and retire in your native land." He smiled. "His burial is set for two weeks from today. We will go and return in three weeks' time."

"I am so sorry."

"Don't worry yourself," Emeka said softly. "We have talked. Gladys is strong. In fact," he gazed at Ifi almost tenderly, "she has decided that it's time. We have six children. That is enough. Healthy children, all beautiful, all intelligent. What of if they are all girls? We have been blessed enough, and Gladys is not so young anymore, like you." He smiled at her. "I have spoken to her, and she has agreed to dash you the boy's crib." He grinned triumphantly.

"What?"

"I will drop it before we leave for Nigeria."

Ifi didn't know how to respond. "That is kind of you."

"Don't say anything to your husband. Just accept the gift. I know him. He will appreciate it once he sees it, not before. And it will be good for my wife if it is gone. She will be reminded that our family is already complete."

Outside, whiteness spread across the clouds. Ifi tried to remember her first night in America. Was this the first sign of a heavy snowfall, like cool, dusty Harmattan winds in Nigeria? Was this the sign of an ending and a new beginning? "Do you believe Gladys? Is she finally done?"

Emeka's face shined. He looked away out the window, up at the clouds. "We will move forward. The sun will rise tomorrow as it rose today."

"And how are you?"

His laugh was thick, from a place in the back of his throat. "I will tell you this, little mama: you must always look around you, because your enemies are watching."

What must he mean? Ifi started to ask, but Emeka stopped her with a gaze up to the apartment window. "How are you enjoying your television?"

When Job returned to Captain's room for the last time during morning rounds, the old man was so knotted together under his sheets that Job panicked and believed he was dead and rigor mortis had set in. Many times he had seen it before: the blinkless, lifeless eyes of the dead, the turning of the flesh. At age seven, Job had seen those eyes on his brother when he peered down into his face in the open casket and lifted away the buttons that had been placed over each eye. To look and to be looked at by such eyes. At the time, Job had believed that Samuel died from fright, not the bullet. He had been a coward. His arrogance had been a cover.

Before he reached Captain's bed, the smell told a different story. Today it was only a thick paste that made it as far as the fitted sheet. Job's jaw tightened. *Right at the end of my shift. If I don't clean him, the morning shift will accuse me of leaving him filthy on purpose.* Job would be written up and reprimanded in front of everyone by the charge nurse, a woman ugly and mean enough to be a boy's uncle. She had done it before.

Shivers rose on Captain's scrawny, hairy legs as Job, with a wipe, followed the path of the feces along Captain's leg. He pretended the old man felt as ashamed as he did. He pretended he was the doctor and Captain was the patient, and that he was examining him, and that he could hear the slow drum of the old man's heartbeat through his stethoscope. Like Ifi. Ifi's stomach had been a steel drum, and the baby's foot had felt like the flutter of a heartbeat. As he worked quietly, Job didn't tell Captain about what he felt when his boy kicked through Ifi's stomach. Instead, he told Captain about his television.

He spoke quietly. "It has the latest digital technologies." When Captain didn't reply, Job continued, describing the detail of its make, its size, the color saturation, the reception—all that he had learned from reading the manual during his meal break.

As he spoke, Job unwound the soiled sheets and pulled them loose from their corners. He wrapped a new sheet over the edge and did the same for the other end, smoothing and flattening it out with the back of his gloved hand. He gagged as he dumped the soiled sheets into the laundry basket. All the while, Job recounted the television in detail. Captain was so silent and still that Job no longer listened to his own voice. True, he had spent the night debating if he should return the television or keep it, tell Ifi something was wrong with the color tube, something as simple as that. He had wondered if instead he should pay for it with his father's money. It was money he couldn't afford on his own. But finally he had settled it, reminding himself that if he paid the minimum every month for the next eighteen months, he would finish the payments. *Ifi's next letter to Aunty will describe the television,* he thought to himself, *and for once it will be truth.*

Job parked his car one block away from St. Ignatius Rehabilitation Hospital. In the dark, he peeled off the scrubs and their stink. Gagging, he balled the clothes up and placed them in the plastic grocery bag he tucked underneath his driver's seat every morning on his return home, a secret place Ifi would surely never find. Even without the clothes on, he thought to himself, *I smell*

JULIE IROMUANYA

of nshi. Captain's shit. Its stink would never leave his body. Rocking back and forth, naked except for his underwear, he shivered. Then, before he knew it, he was sobbing.

I can't do this anymore. Today, he decided. *Today will be the day. I will try again.* After all, it had been a long time. Nineteen years. He would go to the bank and take out the money, minus what he had given to Cheryl. Forget their faces, all those years ago, when he had arrived at the admissions office and told them it was a mistake. Yes, he had seen the academic probation notices, but wasn't there someone he could speak to? Where was the chair, the dean, the provost, someone important, not the silly secretary? And so he had gone to see the bald-headed dean, sitting there in his suit and tie. An important man. The man his father was. The man Job would be one day, if he only had the chance. A man who could make things happen. He had heard of it being done in Nigeria quite easily. Although he had never admitted it to himself, he wondered now if his father had done just that for him, had spoken to the right man, negotiated in the right way for him to easily pass his JAMB, the highest standard, and then the TOEFL.

Standing before the dean, Job reached into his pocket and slid a hundred-dollar bill to the man. The dean took the money and stared. *Not enough?* Job slid another hundred-dollar bill to him, then another. As it dawned on the dean what was happening, he shifted back into his rolling chair behind the desk. Then he bellowed, "You lazy, immigrant bastard! Go back to Africa."

Forget all of this, Job said to himself. *Now is the time. Many years have passed.* The money was still in the account. This morning. He would not even sleep. He would go directly to the bank and then the admissions office. He would finish his classes before Ifi knew it. Before long, he would be making real money. And then he wouldn't suffer each time he sent his family a check, nor would they ache in their silent poverty. They would rise to the station they once had when Job began his life in America. He pulled on his trousers and lab coat. His body trembled. He released a long, drawn-out breath. *What have I been so afraid of? What is keeping me from following my dreams?* Job smoothed out his stethoscope. He placed an eartip in each ear and listened to the beat of his own heart.

❖

Job's thudding heartbeat was still on his mind as he filled his car with gas. It was there, in the palm of his free hand, that he saw the first signs of the great snowfall that would come that night. He released the pump and met the eyes of the stars that descended on him, tiny and moist. The ash-gray sky was pierced only by the wavering glow of the headlights he had forgotten to turn off. He tried to think of his child, but all he could think of was the childlike look in Ifi's eyes during her first snowfall.

Bank. Admissions office. *Today will be the day.* Elated, he smiled. He dried his palms across the thighs of his dark pants and brought them to his face. The scent was strong, like kerosene. It reminded him of his grand-mother's kerosene lamp back in the village. It reminded him of the darkened home he had visited on that humid summer day, with the lamp flames cast-ing shadows on the walls, the girl with the slim hips and pointed breasts sit-ting on the couch between her guardians.

In the gas station, he stalked back and forth between the aisles, his back straight, an important man making a decision, letting his fingers rest on bags of potato chips that he knew he'd never had a taste for. He stopped only after the clerk, a boy in dark frames, sent him a sidelong glance.

"You got gas on two?" the clerk asked.

"Yeah," Job said, in his best imitation of an American.

Just then, three tall black Americans came bursting into the store. They were young and loud, wearing baggy pants, their hair in plaits or hidden under pantyhose covers. They were boys, no more than seventeen in age. Job had been in America long enough to know of this type. They took off in dif-ferent directions. One disappeared into the cooled Spirits section, another shuffled through the potato chips Job had just grazed. As Job hurried to the register, the third broke for the register as well. They arrived at the same time, and there was a tense moment as Job shifted from one leg to the other. The boy had calm, sleepy eyes. He was small, the youngest of the gang, likely no older than twelve or thirteen. He nodded to Job, and Job paid the clerk before hurrying out the door, away from trouble. On his way, he bumped into another boy. They were just feet from Job's car.

"Motherfucker, get the fuck out of my way," the boy said to him.

He was nothing. A boy of such a young age and low education would not speak to Job like this anywhere else. *Only in America.* It angered and humiliated him. He should have hurried away, but he didn't. Not this time.

"Why he looking at you like that?" one of the other boys said, egging him on. "Like he want to kill you." Foil crunched in his hands as he opened his bag of chips. A chip crunched loudly in his mouth. Flakes drifted from his face. His cheeks were slick from its grease. "Want one?" He held a chip out to Job and grinned. "They tasty. Smell it."

When Job didn't respond, the boy put it so close to his face that he could smell its salt. His mouth watered. Between them, the potato chip hovered, a bullet in slow motion.

The filth. The filth on his hands, on his body, the stink of Captain, the stink of gasoline. It filled Job with rage, and the rage tasted like shit in his throat.

"I ain't playing. They good," the boy said, laughing. As he pulled the chip back, it fell from his hand, landing in a puddle of shrinking snow. "Aw, man, you made me drop my chip." He reached into his bag, found another, and chomped loudly, his mouth open.

Now all of the boys were there. "He should say sorry," the first boy said. Initially it sounded like he was joking. One or two even laughed. But Job knew better.

The skinny attendant was bolting the door. He didn't say, "I don't want any trouble." He didn't say, "I'll call the police." He simply clicked the door locked and returned to his post at the register.

"Motherfucker," the boy said, getting close to Job, so close he could smell cigarette ash on his breath, "say you're sorry."

Sleepy Eyes shrugged.

"Naw," the boy said in reply. "I want this motherfucker to say it. And then he gonna eat that chip he knocked down with his funky breath."

In the back of his throat, Job heard the word forming. By the time it left his mouth, he was stunned by it. He'd never said it, except to make fun of the kind of boys who were in front of him now. "Motherfucker," Job said.

A pause.

Then Potato Chips laughed. Sleepy Eyes joined in. Finally Apology laughed, hard, a revolving laughter that didn't stop, but only grew.

"Say it again," one said, and the others chimed in, imitating his accent. "Mudd-ah-fock-ah!"

As the impotent word shrank in the folds of their laughter, Job burned with humiliation. *These boys, nothing but riffraff who know nothing, who cannot even speak their first language correctly, have shamed me.* They should fear him. They should respect him. In his mind, Job rehashed a million scenarios that ended with the boy's face cracked on the pavement, the jeering faces of his friends frozen in fear. Job, still carrying the stink of Captain on his hands, still pinned with the badge that read *Job Ogbonnaya, Certified Nurse's Assistant,* thought to himself, *They will fear me.*

Seconds before the door opened, Ifi heard his footsteps as he made his way up the stairs. Only then did she drag herself to the kitchen, giving the pot of soup one final turn before shutting it off and filling two bowls deep with meat, mushrooms, and greens. She had made his favorite soup, an apology of sorts. Emeka had cleared things up for her. How could she ever forgive herself for not believing in her husband? He was right about everything. Things would happen. In time. After the baby.

"Kedu, how are you?" she asked.

His voice was a muffle. He headed straight to the bathroom. Water burst from the showerhead.

"You will not eat first?" She made her way to the bathroom. "Your food will be cold," she said to him in exasperation. *And then you will complain without words,* she thought to herself. He would sigh and chew with demonstrative difficulty, giving his bowl vigorous stirs with his spoon after each bite. Then, *This is not the village. You people come to America . . .* he would begin. Ifi laughed to herself as she stepped into the bathroom.

Inside, the sink was splattered with droplets of watered-down red. Job's clothes were crumpled in a soiled heap on the tile floor.

Her hands felt gummy and thick at her sides. "What has happened, oh?" She swiped the shower curtain back. Water came down in sheets, blurring Job's features.

She shouted into the rain, "What is this?"

With force, he shut off the water. He yanked a towel from the metal bar. She grabbed another. Together, the two dried his body in struggling turns. She couldn't see any scrapes or cuts on his body. "What did you do?" Ifi asked.

Finally he turned to her, and she gasped. Gashes were spelled out across his face.

"Chineke!" she said. "Are you all right?"

Job tried to push past her, but she blocked his way with her girth. She had never been a woman of size, but now here she was, large the way mothers and women were supposed to be. Naked, he balanced on the edge of the tub, his belly drooped at his waist like a gunnysack. When she pressed the pale-blue towel to his face, it came away dark with his blood.

Without thinking she guarded her belly, the baby. "I will call hospital."

"No!" Knotting the towel at his waist, he righted himself and stalked past her to the kitchen, to the pot, to the heaping bowls.

"What happened? Tell me, now," she said. "We must call police."

"I am fine," he said. "It's done." One cut was set deeply into the side of his face, near his lip. Ifi tried to touch it with the towel. Job's expression turned into a scowl. He snatched the towel from her hand and flung it across the kitchen. He returned to the pot and added a heaping spoonful to his bowl before sidestepping the kitchen table for the living room couch. Clumps missed his mouth as he swallowed. Ifi took her bowl and stood in the doorway gazing at him, unable to eat.

That afternoon, the storms began. Snow rushed past the window in flakes that grew in size, hour after hour. By night, the falling snow outside reminded her of the staticky television she had grown to hate. It talked, it gurgled like a live, breathing person, witnessing and judging their every misstep in America. From the living room, Ifi could hear the sounds of its babble, and eventually Job's gurgling snores. Snowstorms were silent, but Ifi expected lightning, thunder, something dramatic to account for the snow that would meet her knees the next morning, something to account for the day ahead of her.

CHAPTER 7

HE MUST FILE THE POLICE REPORT IN PERSON. THIS WAS WHAT THE NASAL voice on the telephone said to Job. Slowly, loudly, for his immigrant benefit, the man pronounced the charge. Not only must he file in person, he must be examined, thoroughly, from head to toe, for a proper report of his injuries. None of this sat well with Job. But then, they had told him that a vehicle had been impounded, that it might be his, and so he must go. If the matter was handled correctly, he would have his car and the scrubs and nametag that were balled underneath the seat. He would warm his car, scrape it clear of snow, go to work, and Ifi would never know a thing. She couldn't know a thing. *How can a woman respect a man who has been treated in such a way by mere boys?*

Standing in the doorway, her hands wet and red from the dishes, Ifi wore the frown of a child when he told her about the car. "They have asked me only to identify and sign. You see, this is why I drive the old car," he joked. "A silly thief who suspected a doctor like myself is a millionaire is incorrect."

She didn't believe him. But never mind that.

"I will come with you." Ifi grabbed a bra from the laundry heap, lowered her wrapper, and began to snap the hooks into place.

"Stop this, now. You are nearly eight months pregnant," he said. "There's no need. I'll collect the car and go to work from there. You are delaying me." He glanced at the clock. In an hour his shift would begin.

His body was an open sore. It hurt merely to breathe. But he righted his legs and moved as swiftly as possible to disguise the pain. In the living room, he found his pants and his lab coat clean and ironed on the couch, the same place she laid his clothes out every day. Faded bloodstains marked the shame of the night before. She had no doubt scrubbed while he slept through the day and evening. Job gazed at the coat for a long, hard moment.

"You will have to buy a new one," she said, softly. "No patient should see you this way."

All but the jacket was on him now.

"It's not clean," she said, taking three unbalanced strides across the room. For a brief moment, the jacket was in both of their hands and they fought with it. Her will was stronger than Job's, or perhaps he feared that his only white jacket would be split into two. He laughed. "Solomon's judgment."

She glared at him. A small orange container of baking soda was in the refrigerator. She dumped nearly the entire contents on the scarred cloth. Under the sink, she found a brush. She wet it and furiously scrubbed at the stain.

Nothing but the scratch of the brush fibers could be heard. The sound was like chalk on a board in Job's ears. He snatched the jacket from her grasp.

"Give me time, now! No patient should see a doctor like this," she protested.

"You have done good work," he said. "In the proper light, no one will notice." Indeed, obscured by the shadows of the room, it was barely noticeable.

"And your face. You're so ugly." An accusing finger jabbed at his raw wounds. "Who will see a doctor as ugly as you? Eh?"

"My junior brother received the looks in the family. This, I'm afraid, is improvement, plastic surgery."

"You're so funny. But you will not be so funny when they come back."

"They won't be back," he said calmly. "They've taken my wallet, what good thieves are always after." For good measure, he added, "You stay inside. Don't make any foolish trips. Let my injury warn you of the dangers in America." Even as he joked, Job felt his body rippling with the fear that he had felt that night, the moment when he had realized that he was trapped.

"Don't patronize me. What type of clinic do you work where you will be attacked like this? I will have the baby, I will find work, and you will find a clinic elsewhere." Gripping her wrapper, she faced him. "We'll leave this place and go back to Nigeria. I will not die in this country."

"What is this?"

"I don't like this America," Ifi said. "The food tastes of rubbish. Every day is cold, and there is no one, not even one person outside, except that nonsense old lady," she said with a shudder.

Job saw the pain in her eyes, and he felt a twitch in his belly. But he hid his hesitation with a broad smile. "I believe the nonsense old lady is your friend, no?"

"You're so funny," she said again.

But suddenly, he felt himself giving in to the feeling and agreeing. "Let's go back."

"When?" After a moment, she said, "You are mocking your wife."

"I'm not joking. Tomorrow. No, no, not soon enough. Today." Ifi was frowning, but Job couldn't stop himself, and suddenly he meant it. Such an outrageous idea, but why must they stay? *Why must we stay in America to do humiliating work, to live among riffraff, far from our families?* "Yes, that's right. Instead of going to the police station, I will go to the airport and buy two airplane tickets. By tomorrow night, we will be home."

Ifi was silent. Softly, she said, "You promised. We'll open a hospital. I will be the nurse, and you will be the doctor."

As he drifted back to reality, Job felt the air let out of his balloon. "We will," he said, a whisper.

"But not today," she said with finality.

"Not today."

Naked from the waist up, Job straddled a white wall. The camera bulb flashed, capturing the bruises all along his body. A black whorl spewed from his chest, another near his ribs, where the boys had kicked him. Several swollen knots rose on his back. Each time the bulb flashed, Job flinched. He was humiliated. Not because of the cameras, but because of the cold, clinical gaze of the eyes inspecting each part of his body, as if he were a lab rat. He couldn't be here feeling this, so in his mind, he retreated to an image of him standing before a patient, dressed in his lab coat, recording numbers on a chart.

This would not have happened in Nigeria. I am respected. I am Mr. Doctor. Again, his stomach went rigid with anger. *They will pay,* he decided. Job imagined the three boys in a lineup. He saw himself identifying them as he'd seen it done in many movies. From behind a glass screen, he eyed their hardened glares. He pointed to the first, the boy with sleepy eyes, then the mouth flaky with potato chips, then the boy with cigarette ash for breath. *They will never make me afraid,* he decided. He would have them locked up for the rest of their natural lives. He would say whatever he needed to say to make sure they never saw the light of day. They would sit on the bottom of a cold cell, and he would spit on them from above. He decided on a sum for the distress that he would claim at the time of his civil lawsuit, because surely he would sue the three boys and their families for everything they were worth.

And then he would take their money and resume his classes, somewhere expensive and prestigious like Harvard or Yale. He could see himself presiding over the groundbreaking ceremony for his clinic in his father's village. He could see himself with Ifi, his assistant, standing alongside him in her nurse's uniform, their three children, all boys, alongside them. He could see himself in black pants, a white lab coat, a tie, a briefcase, a stethoscope. *This will all be worth it in the end,* he assured himself. *After all, this is America.*

"I took your photographs and filed the report," Job said to the photographer, a frail man with bulging eyes. "Where is my car? I'll be late for work."

"Listen, call them and tell them you'll be a little late. You need to be treated first."

A physician's assistant began the process, a younger woman with a doughy face fixed in place by thick glasses. "Ice on and off for twenty minutes," she said of the bruises and bumps. "Most of these lacerations are superficial, except this one. This one needs stitches, but you've waited too long." With her gloved hand, she rubbed an antiseptic ointment across the gash and applied butterfly bandages to it. "Keep it clean and dry. You'll have an ugly scar, but you'll live."

Job slipped his shirt, tie, and jacket back on. A knock at the door jolted him to attention. A wide-bottomed officer with square teeth split by a gap waddled in and spoke to him. "We just need you to clarify a few details."

"Where are you taking me? I gave you my report."

Panting and wobbling the whole way, he hurried Job down the hall to an airless room. Two hard plastic chairs were angled around a table. Only after Job sat did the officer take a seat across from him, and in that moment Job had just enough time to take in the man's massive rear, his unzipped fly, and the sweat stains at his armpits. Not exactly the image Job had in mind of the long arm of the law. Instantly, he recognized that any chance he had for justice would not happen today, not in the hands of such a man. Job's sense of righteousness turned to disappointment, and finally anxiety.

His words tumbled out of him. "Three black Americans attacked me. I was not finding any trouble, and these three black Americans beat me." Before the man had a chance to say a word, Job began with his description. "They had cornrows and women's hose like this covering their hair. They walked like this." He began to ape their swinging steps. "They wore trousers like this." Job pulled his down just low enough so that the top of his underpants was exposed. "But you see, they wore boxer pants and big coats, like thieves."

"So they were African American, like you?"

"Yes. I mean no. Not African American. I am not African American. I am from Africa. I am a citizen. I am an American, but I am no African American."

"I see." In apparent confusion, the officer frowned. "But they were black, though. Black like you?"

"No. Not like me."

"Were they *my* color then?"

"No." Job glared at the officer's pale pinkish flesh. Then his. He stared for a long time. "They were this color. One maybe a little lighter. Two maybe the same."

"Black, like you."

After a moment, Job gulped. His eyes fixed on the officer's open fly. He wanted badly to reach forward and yank the zipper up, to teach this insolent man something about what it meant to be a professional, to walk like a man. But there was nothing. He couldn't think of a single word to describe the boys, other than *akatta,* a word the officer would never understand. "Yes, they were my color, but no, not like me."

"I see." The officer scrawled some things on his pad. "There's just one thing I'm unclear about. You said earlier that they didn't take your money. They didn't even take your wallet. But they took your car."

Job thought it over. With anger, he decided, once again, *I will make them pay.* "They didn't take my wallet," he paused, and the lie tumbled out. "But they took my money."

"Now they took your money. An hour ago they only took your car."

Sweat built on Job's brow, and it stung against his raw face. "I said they took my money, my car, and they beat my face."

"So they took your money and your car and *then* they assaulted you, Mr. Og-ban-ooya? In that order?"

"Yes."

"Why?"

"I don't know."

"Tell me, does this make any sense even to you? Again: they took your money, your car, and then they just suddenly decided to return and attack?"

Job felt it slipping away. A deep breath steadied him. "They beat me. Then they took my money and car. They did not want my wallet. They threw it at me."

"I see, Mr. Og-ban-ooya. And how much money did you have on you? Ten dollars? Twenty?"

Job's voice was suddenly low. "Are you accusing me of lying?"

For a long, silent moment, the officer looked him over. "I'm gonna ask you one final thing. Just answer as completely and honestly as you can, and we'll let you go."

"Let me go? Am I the victim or the assailant?"

"Mr. Og-ban-ooya."

"Doctor."

"*Doctor.*" There was a sardonic ring to his tone.

"Yes, Doctor."

"*Dr.* Og-ban-ooya. Did you have any drugs or paraphernalia in your possession at the time of the . . ." He paused. "Assault."

"You are asking if I am a drug dealer?"

The officer's eyes remained unmoved. "Did you know the assailants?"

Job quivered. "You do not believe." He swallowed. Words were a tumble in his mind. He started from the beginning. He started from the beginning of what the boys looked like; he started way in the beginning, when he had no more years than the boys who attacked him, when he came here on his own with nothing but his father's tuition money and two suitcases. Then he started at the beginning of that night. He needed to tell the man about arriving at the gas station, about the ball of clothes under the seat of his car, but to tell the officer that, he must tell him about his clandestine retreats to the parking lot, where he changed his clothes each night and every morning so that his wife would not know, so that the world would not know. And to say this, he must describe the failure he suddenly felt, realizing for the first time that he would never be a doctor.

So he said none of these words. His tongue was in knots. He did not tell the officer about the potato chip, or about the way he swore at the boys. He did not even tell the man that they were boys. *Were they even old enough to purchase alcohol in this country?* He did not tell the officer about the things they had said to him.

Instead, Job heard himself repeating, "I am a doctor, and I find no trouble from these black Americans. I am not illegal like the Mexicans. I am a citizen." He dug into his pocket and retrieved his wallet, showing him the card.

After a long sigh, the officer scrawled a number onto a card and handed it to Job. "That's your case number. I'm Officer Peete. Right there. That's my number here at the station. You call if you can provide any other information."

"That's it? What of my car?"

"On the report, you gave a description of your car being a blue-gray, two-door Audi, dent on the driver side, cracked taillight."

"Yes."

"That's not your car in the impound."

"Yes it is."

"And I believe you."

Job was stunned, silent.

"And because I believe you, I suggest that you file a report with your insurance."

"No, no, no! You said you have my car."

"Mr.—*Dr.* Og-ban-ooya. The vehicle we have is suspected in a botched narcotics transfer."

"No, you have my car. Allow me to see it!"

"We'll do our best to recover it, but I can tell you now, it's a long shot. By now, they've probably stripped it for parts that are on their way to South Dakota. Your best bet is to call your insurance and report the loss."

Job swallowed. "What of the thieves? Won't you arrest them?"

"We'll call you if we apprehend the suspects."

"You will just let them go free?"

"Like I said, if you can give us any other information you think will help, call the number on the card."

"But my car . . ." Job felt a shake beginning low in his body. "How will I go to work? I am late already."

"There's a phone in the lobby. Call someone. Your wife? A friend?"

"No," Job said, grimacing as he imagined Emeka's smirk.

❖

Large fluorescent overhead lights cast deep orange pools on the tiled floors of the lobby. Little else was in the room except for two flags that hung limply from their pedestals over a carrel of hard-backed plastic chairs. Job flipped through the phonebook and found the number for a taxicab company. But when the cab arrived with a "Cash Only" sign glaring through the back panel, remembering that he had given all of his cash to Cheryl for her car repairs, Job abashedly admitted that he could only pay with credit card or check. He tried to explain that he had been the victim of an assault; they stole his cash, beat his face—he was not a criminal—but even dressed in his crisp doctor's suit with his stethoscope dangling from the front pocket of his jacket, the driver cursed him, shouting that Job was supposed to request a cab with a credit card machine, and he had wasted his time and cost him his gas and a fare, and for that Job was a motherfucker. The driver spat out the window and squealed around the corner, leaving Job to stand limply in the cold.

One last time, he reentered the police station and braced himself before dialing Emeka's number. But when he heard Emeka's arrogant voice, Job couldn't bear the thought of his friend's admonishments: *Have I not taught you anything?* Job slammed the phone down. Reluctantly, he dialed the only number he could think of: Cheryl's. After all, she did not know Emeka, Gladys, or Ifi. He had even given her money to repair her car.

As he waited, the entire scene reminded him of the day they had married: a room cold with the thud of empty footprints across the tile floor, flags hanging limply against one wall, a potted plastic tree on another end, and the sound of telephones ringing from distant rooms. Like then, everything had a fakeness to it. Important business could not possibly happen here. For a moment, he locked eyes with a janitor who brusquely swept the floor.

The man whistled and shrank back at the sight of Job's face. "Sonny, it looks like you were doing business from the wrong angle." He set the mop aside. "Look-a here. Put a pack of tenderloin on that, press it in real good, and it'll be gone in no time." Setting the mop aside, the man encouragingly motioned where Job should place the meat on his face. Of course he had nothing to do with the attack, but instead of the wrinkled face, chin ashen with gray hairs, and body stooped with age, all Job could see and hear was the man's skin color and the voice carrying the rhythm that sounded so similar to the young boys' voices. A fresh chill of fear climbed up his spine. Long ago, this old man had been one of those young boys, wearing women's hose over his plaits and trousers so low they exposed his underpants. *Akatta,* he said to himself. A black American. *Riffraff,* Job decided with such bitterness and anger that it turned to hate, *just like those criminals.*

"Those bastards!" Cheryl exclaimed as Job climbed into her 1980 Ford Thunderbird, a rusted red, the pieces of its frame fitted together like Legos. As they pulled away, the Thunderbird let out a metallic screech. When he had called, Cheryl had answered after three rings. At the time, he had oscillated between how to ask a favor of her, a woman he had been married to but still considered a stranger. *Should I order her?* he thought to himself—after all, he wouldn't have needed her help if he hadn't provided her with the last cash remaining in his wallet. Should he try to gain her sympathy by explaining that he had been brutally beaten by three black men? Surely she would empathize with his fear. *Or should I treat the whole affair with nonchalance?* She must remember that they had at one time shared a reluctant, though lawful, mutual union.

In the end, he hadn't needed to say any of those things. When Job mentioned that he was at the police station and that his car had been stolen, Cheryl arrived within twenty minutes. She knew the police station well. Luther, her brother, had been arrested on a number of frivolous charges over the years, and she had been forced to pick him up and bail him out on many occasions.

One time in particular stood out in her mind, and as they headed for the hospital, Cheryl lit a cigarette out the window and stuttered the first words to the story. "He had too much to drink. He was having a hard time dealing with our mom's passing. Anyway, the police, they pull him over, he gets out. They tell him to put his hands up and all that. He does. And they're asking all these stupid questions. And he can't say anything." Her hands shook as they gripped the steering wheel. "So they beat him, you know? They beat him up because he wouldn't talk," she said. "He tried to show them his wallet, to explain that he couldn't talk, you know? He's mute, so they almost killed him. When I arrived, he was still unconscious. Said they thought he was reaching for a weapon, the bastards." She paused at a red light. "That was the day something changed in him. He didn't give a shit about anything after that. He didn't give a shit about me, about the house, about our parents. That was it."

Job let the weight of her confession sink in. A white man born and raised in this country had faced such a fate. *What are the chances of me, a Nigerian, receiving justice if a white man receives such treatment?* It stunned Job. They passed his hideaway lot on the way, and he glanced out the window, glaring at the muted brick façade of the office buildings.

When they arrived at the hospital, Cheryl gazed at him with somber eyes. "They did that to you too, didn't they? Some bastards steal your car, and they find *you* guilty of that shit. I hate those fuckers. I hate them."

She thinks the police have beaten me! Job thought in alarm. Admittedly, he felt relief. He preferred not to rehash the story, not to tell her how children, mere beggars, had pushed his face into the snow, stepped on his back, and beaten him. *Enough,* he decided, remembering the probing eye of the camera and the officer's accusatory questions. *They treated me as if I was the criminal—me, Job Ogbonnaya, whose father is a chief.* Suddenly, he realized that the officers might well have beaten him the way they had beaten Cheryl's brother. One thing Job understood that made him feel strangely akin to Luther, a man he had never laid eyes on in his life, was that, like Luther, he would never again look at a uniformed officer in the same way. "Yes," he lied, "the officers beat me for no reason."

"You know, Job." Cheryl flicked the cigarette out the window, and they watched as the orange light flickered through the dark sky and then died. "Just because me and you are . . ." She paused, then continued with care. "Different, it doesn't mean the world hasn't flung some shit in my direction."

Rolling back her coat sleeve, she revealed her luminescent skin, dotted only by the occasional winter freckle. "They always prejudiced me because of my red hair and pale skin. That's kinda like being black, don't you think?"

Job nodded uncomfortably. It seemed to satisfy her.

In quiet awe, she gazed at him. "What I can't understand is how you can sit here so dignified after they did all that to your face, after they treated you like a dog." She shrugged. "But what do I know? You're the doctor." She turned up her finger as if drinking from a teacup.

She still believes I am a doctor. Job looked over his uniform: the white lab coat, the dark pants, the stethoscope. He sat up higher in his seat and silently agreed with a confident nod.

As if struggling to piece his world together, she continued. "My mother always said I didn't have the manners of a lady—I'd be hauling ass, I'd be cussing someone out. But I can't help it. When something isn't fair, my emotions just take control, and all the logic runs away from me. I lost it when they beat my brother. They probably would have hauled me off to jail if I hadn't told them I'd sue their asses off."

"Did you?" Job asked with fresh curiosity.

"Nah, no money. I looked in the Yellow Pages and everything. I called a few places, but nah. Besides, Luther wouldn't have it. He just wanted to be home. He wanted the whole thing behind him."

Job nodded slowly as he climbed out of the car, once again surprised by how the woes of Cheryl's life had somehow made her more real to him, someone more than the freckle-faced liar with knobby knees, maybe even someone to take seriously. Knowing Cheryl was still watching, perhaps in awe, as she pulled away, he straightened his jacket and walked purposefully, his briefcase swinging at his side like the men in the suits outside his hideaway.

Because he was dressed only in his black pants and white lab coat, with the stethoscope dangling from his pocket, the nurses on the station didn't recognize Job at first as he hurried from room to room doing rounds. Balled together in his bag and squeezed under the front seat of his car, his clothes were, as the officer had said, likely on their way to South Dakota. At that thought, he hurried through his rounds: A young girl in the south end of the station who had a fever—he administered Tylenol and listened to her rabbit heartbeat with a stethoscope. A man down the hall, a diabetic—he needed new dressings around the sores at the base of the stump where his leg had recently been amputated. Job dumped the urine-filled bedpan of yet another patient.

Near the end of the night, Captain's light came on. Job hesitated, shivering at the memory of the strong scent of his feces, before reluctantly pushing the door open. Captain was asleep, a letter torn to shreds at his side, another one directed to his "son." Job picked up the pieces and put them together, but the words were nothing more than scribbles. Gazing at the prone man, Job shook his head. *Growing old is without dignity in America.* Not the way he remembered it back home: the old men, tall in robes; old men smoking and chewing kola nut; old men surrounded by wives and children meant to bring them soup, porridge, and palm wine. *Here, it is withering under twisted sheets,* a man of pimpled flesh.

Job shook his head. He shouldn't be seeing any of this. This was the work of the poor. Not someone like him. *This is the work for illiterate savages, like the three black boys who will amount to nothing when they grow old, nothing at all,* he told himself. *They will be janitors, like the man at the police station.* Feeling the anger rise in his gut, he left the room.

None of the other nurses on the station looked him directly in the face, and Job thought, with relief, that the night would continue in the same manner, with his head bent forward, his charts clipped together, his stethoscope in his pocket—until a nurse passing by asked, "Doctor?" Recognition crossed her face as her eyes ran from Job's face to the white lab coat and stethoscope. He tried to pass, but she grabbed his shoulder, spinning him around. "What on earth?"

And then a second, a third, and a fourth nurse were surrounding him. Now they saw his face, raw with the young men's work, a congealing scar. Each drew in a sharp gasp. At first, he couldn't decide which they would respond to first: the fact that he was out of uniform or the look of his fresh scars.

"What happened, Job?" one asked.

"It's nothing," he said.

"Are you in some kind of trouble?" a second asked.

"I was assaulted, but I am okie now."

"Oh my God. But you're o.k.?" a third asked. "Did you file a police report?"

"I was assaulted," Job said. *What good did filing the police report do?* He was still without his vehicle, and his body had been searched. *They treated me like a criminal, a drug dealer.* Cheryl's brother had been a drunk alcoholic; it made sense that they would arrest him. But Job had done nothing. *Why must they find me trouble, oh?*

"Did. You. File. A. Police. Report." All the voices blended into one. All he could hear was the menacing arch in the officer's voice, a question that sounded more like an order than a request, a question that sounded like an accusation. "Job, I think it's a good idea for you to go home tonight. Call personnel tomorrow morning, and we'll try to straighten this out."

"I did nothing." Sweat prickled down Job's face. His heart beat wildly, and his chest tightened. The room went black. He shouted over the flurry of flashing camera bulbs, "I am not a drug dealer!"

Then, a nurse's voice: "No one said you're a drug dealer."

A second nurse: "Why are you suggesting that?"

A third nurse: "Are you hiding something?"

He was suddenly back in the nurse's station surrounded by the crowd of his coworkers. *Won-der-ful!* he thought in panic. *Now they will inventory all the medications in the supply closet.* He didn't even own a key to the supply closet, because he didn't have the certification to distribute medications. But never mind that.

"Job, I need to ask you to leave." His charge nurse.

"I call the police, but because of my color, I am a drug dealer. Is that it?"

"Job, come on, don't play the race card. Nobody's picking on you. Have we ever treated you differently?"

"No," Job said with resolve. "No, I will not leave."

"If you don't leave now, I'll have to call security."

Job collected his things. He shuffled out the door.

When the cab pulled up to the curb of his apartment, Job froze in awe. *Could this all have been a dream?* he thought to himself. Parked on the street in front of his building, as if it had never been moved, was his Audi. All of it, even the dent in its side, even its cracked taillight. Without his eyes leaving the sight before him, he hastily threw a few bills to the driver. As the cab screeched away, his brow furrowed in bewilderment. Maybe there had never been any troublemaking youngsters. Maybe there had never been a police station.

He shook his head. Of course it had all happened. The officer, Officer Widebottom, had proven to be competent after all. He must have tracked down the assailants and returned Job's car to him. Job would have to thank him—and he would have to stop thinking of him as Widebottom. At that, he rushed to the windows and peeped in, taking in the cracked leather interior. A loud creak answered as he swung the door open. Everything was just as he had left it. Even the old tape deck was still in place. A deep breath of relief escaped his lungs. Every tight knot, every ache in his body melted away. Feeling more alive than he had in months, Job started for the apartment. *My wife,* he could hear himself saying, *yesterday's matter has been resolved.*

But when he reached the steps to the building he froze. There was one thing he had forgotten. He swallowed, turning slowly to face his car once more. Feeling the cold snow rush past his ankles, up his thighs, he crouched to the ground and slipped his hand into his secret place under the driver's seat. Nothing. He gulped deeply and felt again, pushing farther. *Surely there has been a mistake,* he told himself. Still nothing. *It is here,* he insisted. But after searching all the seats, he was finally forced to give up. *Won-der-ful!* he thought as the horror began to set in. Of all the things, his plastic bag with his scrubs and nametag had to be missing.

Kneeling before the old car, he whispered a prayer: "Take the car, but please do not take the bag." One last time, he splayed his hands and reached as far as he could under the seats in search of the bag. But his hands only met the cold metal surface of the seat rails. Someone knew his secret. *But perhaps it is only this Officer Peete!* Perhaps he had swept the car for the drugs that he had accused Job of taking, and after finding nothing, he had sheepishly returned Job's vehicle to him. *Yes, that's it.* As he made his way to the apartment, Job found himself smiling.

Old Mrs. Janik glared at him from her porch, the only witness to his frantic search. Still wrapped in her bathrobe, with a shawl drawn across her shoulders, her curlers half-undone, she looked like a madwoman. Job shuddered, wondering yet again how someone with his father's name could have ever ended up in such a place with such people. *Only in America.*

"I wouldn't trust them. They're criminals. And prostitutes. All of them. Don't believe a word they say," she called out to him.

Nodding, he called back, "Yes, that's right," as he hurried to his building.

Mrs. Janik hobbled down the steps, cut across the snow, and blocked his path. "Oh, you think I'm crazy, but I'm telling you, that wife of yours is a fool dealing with those types. They're corrupting her. You're good folks. Not like them," she said. "My folks were immigrant types, like you. Nobody gave us what we have. We worked for it. We didn't take no handouts. Not like them."

"Not like them," Job repeated her words. He sighed, giving in, and settled his lips into a patronizing smile. "Not like whom, Mrs. Janik?"

"I waited right there on my stoop until I saw you pull up, because I knew they were up to no good. Niggers, that's what *they* are."

Job jerked at the sound of the word. She had said *that*. The old madwoman had said that. Unable to find the words to respond to her, once more he hastily started for the building.

Only she followed. "Trouble. Every one of them. I don't blame her. She's not been in this country long enough to know like you and me."

She is speaking of them, not me. Bright, flashing camera bulbs flickered in his eyes. A cold, clinical glare hardened on Job's features. Officer Peete's voice boomed above the clicking camera shutters. *Black like you.* "No," Job protested. "Not like *them.*"

"That's right," Mrs. Janik said, her voice filling with gusto. "It's them and the Mexicans. Prostitutes. Drug dealers. Rapists. But you, you're not like them. You're like me. We're good people. Good immigrant stock."

"Yes," he said slowly, sadly. Because *that* was not him. *That* could never be him.

All he could hear was the sound of those words, echoing in his ears as he took the stairs two at a time. *Black like you. Not like them.* At the top of the landing, he found his apartment door unlocked. He would have to warn Ifi to lock the doors at all times. Because of *them.* He yanked the door open and thrust it closed behind him, unknowingly putting the door between him and Mrs. Janik.

Like a floating beach ball, Ifi's belly rose and fell with each breath. A plastic bag was on her lap. *My bag!* he thought in horror. His plastic bag, with his scrubs, with his uniform, with his nametag. Heat seared Job's face, but there was no time to think, no time to explain himself, for there, squeezed on the couch alongside Ifi, were two figures: a tall black woman and one of his attackers, Sleepy Eyes. Job drew in a sharp breath. His eyes met the wrinkled plastic bag, rising and falling with each of Ifi's breaths.

"You!" He charged across the room, lifted the boy by his shoulders, and dragged him to the door. It took everything in his power to keep him from tightening his hands around the boy's flailing neck. *I could kill him,* Job thought to himself, *and no police will come. I have seen how the law operates in America.* All it would take was a small movement, and he could cut off the boy's airway, and the boy would crumble to the floor before him. "You are not so strong without your friends, eh?"

"Let me go." Tears dampened the boy's lashes. "I'm sorry."

"You see what you have done to my face? You see your work?"

Balancing her weight on a palm at the small of her back, Ifi stood up. "Job, release him."

Job loosened his grip but remained within inches of the boy's face, a boy who, in the strange light, looked like a skinny cat. Once again, Job eyed the bag. It was still tied in his careful knot. *Maybe,* he thought to himself. *Maybe she has not even opened it.* When he had his chance, he would take the bag. He would tell her it was rubbish, pretend to take it out to the dump, and instead slip it back into the car. He would find another hiding place.

"This is our neighbor, Mary, from across the street, and her nephew, Jamal."

"My brother's son," Mary offered. She was tall, shaped like a pear, with lips red from lipstick. Her hair was flattened where the curls had rested against the wall behind her. Eyes filled with fear, she made no movement toward Job. As if wading in deep waters, her hands wavered out in front of her. "Tell him," she said to the boy. "Go on, tell him."

Sleepy Eyes—Jamal—straightened up, his feet together. "I'm sorry, Doctor . . ." His voice trailed off. "I brought it back the way it was."

Mary spoke up again. "I knew it was yours when I saw it parked in the street. I recognized it, and I told him to turn it in and turn hisself in." Job made a motion to speak, but the rest of her words came out in a rush. "I told him it's up to you to decide what you do with him. You can turn him in to the police if you like; God only knows he deserves it. But I'm telling you,

JULIE IROMUANYA

Doctor, he's not a bad kid. He's just—" she hesitated as if struggling for the right word. "He's stupid. Dumb as rocks."

Jamal squirmed.

"He wants to fit in with these knuckleheads. He wants to be one of them, but he's not. He's smart. Just started junior high, and the dumb kid drops out. I'm taking him back tomorrow, if they'll have him. But it's not his fault. His daddy, my brother, Jake, he's in jail." She glared at Jamal, as if a thought had suddenly dawned on her. "You think if you lie and steal and beat people up you'll be there with your daddy? Is that what you want? You think he wants that for you?" She turned her pleading eyes back to Ifi. "And his mother, she don't know nothing. He could steal her blind, and she wouldn't know."

"You give me excuses," Ifi hurled at her. "My mother and my father— both dead. Do you see me attacking people? Eh? Do you see me stealing from people?"

"You're right," Mary said. "You have every reason to be angry. That's why I told him he could work for it. He fixes stuff—cracks in your windows, tiles. If you give him the materials, he can mend anything. He can even sew. He taught hisself. He's a smart boy. You got a baby coming—he can put your crib together. He's even good with kids." Eyes pleading with Ifi and then Job, she added, "We're black people, right? It's the same for all of us here. We gotta help each other out. We're brothers and sisters."

"You are not my brother," Job said, spitting the words into the boy's face. His grip tightened as he remembered the blows to his face. "'Go back to Africa,' is it?"

"I didn't mean that." Jamal looked away.

"Yes, go back to Africa."

"No," Jamal said.

"What did you mean then, boy?"

"I didn't mean nothing." Very faintly, he spoke again. "She's right. I'm dumb. I'm stupid. I said it 'cause *they* said it." As if resigned to his fate, he closed his eyes. His eyes slanted, his tense features relaxed, he looked like a sleeping cat.

With his fingers pressed into the boy's throat, once more Job thought to himself, *I could kill him.* A beat pulsed under his thumb where the boy gulped in raspy breaths. *Police will not stop me. They will thank me for removing him from the streets.* The boy's breaths had grown raspy and loud, so loud that it was the only sound Job could hear in the room. *And then my wife will feel safe in this country once more. And then I will be a man again.*

But suddenly a thought occurred to him: *There are more.*

"Okie," Job said softly, removing his fingers from the boy's neck. "He will work."

"Wait, now." As the others waited in the living room, Ifi pulled Job into their bedroom. She pushed her weight against the door, and it slammed shut behind her. "I asked them to wait until you returned so that *you* could call police."

"No," Job said sadly, waving his hand.

"Should I have called?"

"Let them go their way."

"The boy attacked you, and he will go to jail!"

Rather than the flashing bulbs directed at him, Ifi shimmered under the lights. Her clothes torn, her skin ravaged, she wailed as Officer Peete presided. All three of the attackers stood with the cool look of absconding thieves. At this image, something broke inside Job, and the words began to plunk out one by one like raindrops. "Ifi, my dear," he said, his voice cracking, "there were three. They beat me. They spit on me. They took my wallet and spit on that too. I said to them, 'We are all black, no? You are my brothers.' They said, 'You are not my brother. Go back to Africa.' Do you see what they did to my face?" He punched a finger at the butterfly bandage.

Ifi gasped.

"Do you think I am trying to help them? I *hate* him. All of them. God punish them. But I went to police. And you know what police say? They say, 'They are black like you.' Like you and me."

"What?"

"Police, they called me a drug dealer. If he goes to jail, he will be released by tomorrow morning, and he and his gangsters will prowl the streets. Eh? And maybe there will be six next time. And they will come for you."

"My husband," she said softly, "why didn't you tell me about them? Yesterday." Then her eyes met his, and something in them changed. "Why must you keep secrets from me, oh? I am your wife."

She knows, he thought to himself. She knew that his real uniform was in the plastic bag. She knew that his real uniform stank of feces and urine. She

knew about the nametag that read *Job Ogbonnaya, Certified Nurse's Assistant.*
She knew that he was not a doctor. She knew that he was nothing. *How small
I must look to her,* he thought. Spat on, beaten by illiterate boys, like the riffraff who shined his shoes in Nigeria. *They have taken my car, my house, and
now my wife.* He felt himself slipping, drowning. All the renewed hope that
he had witnessed on Ifi's first day in America as she stood in the snow was
slipping away. Even her boastful letters to Aunty were dissolving, like the
potato chip, into nothing.

Flinging his promises into the air, he struggled to rebuild what he realized was on the verge of being lost. "You will go to school, and I will train you
to be a nurse, and then we will open a hospital in Nigeria. All in good time."
Clasping her hands in his, he added, "We will buy a house, a big house, for me
and you and the baby. We will build a mansion for our retirement in Nigeria."
His head felt light, like a balloon rising. The more he spoke, the bigger the
promises, the larger he felt. How could he forget? People rose all the time—
Rockefeller, Ford, Hearst, Horatio Alger—but they all started out with
dreams, dreams that seemed silly to the rest of the world. But dreams nonetheless. *Every journeyman begins with one step.* His chuckles made a strange
sound, like tears. "This is only temporary," he said to her through his laughter. "To save money. After this month, we will be out of this ghetto." Even
as Ifi stood silent, her look doubtful, he continued to speak, his hands shaking from the sheer velocity of his dreams, dreams that would seem wild and
unrestrained in Nigeria. *It will happen,* he told himself, *because this is America.*

2.

CHAPTER 8

THIS WAS THE FIRST OF MANY PLEASURES THAT HE TOOK FROM HER. ON her back, the water to her chest, Ifi allowed her breath to rise through her body in its slow way. Her feet were red, red as they had been back then, after she mixed the boiling water with the cold. She remembered her body sinking lower and lower into the water until it filled the space between her legs, her navel, her breasts. Now, each part was taken over by the baby. Back then, sweat beaded her brow. She tasted it in her lips. Salt stung in her eyes. All after a long day.

Her days began like this:

As the dust-tinged morning light rose, filtering out the dusk, Ifi sat up in her bed. The grit of scattered sand tangled into her sheets, and she felt the familiar scratch against her thighs, her calves, her feet. Before the people of the house rose, goats, chickens, and roosters let out their chatter, rummaging about through the potholed alleyway, shifting through the broken, discarded bits of sandstone that jutted in and out of the streets. Church services blared through megaphones, and the women who heralded the cry ululated ecstatically in response. Sometimes their neighbors simply sat on their narrow stoops, swinging their feet along the heavy, misshapen stones that led the way to their storefront homes.

The man who arrived with the water each day, filling a large drum, had a face stretched thin from the many smiles he offered to Ifi every morning. Each day he would propose to her, stooping so low that his knees nearly touched the ground, offering his hand in marriage.

"You are old enough to be my father's father," Ifi would chastise, and the old man would swing his head in dismay, knocking his chest and proclaiming the strength in his powerful legs. Then, gingerly, he would right himself, the pain shooting up the backs of his legs and his spine until it registered in his face. But he would sift his stretched-thin face into a serious gaze, only broken by the flirtatious wink that filled his eyes with lashes.

After he left each morning, Ifi filled a pot with water and set it on the stove. And when it was warm, she poured some into a bucket and the rest into an old oversized coffee flask to keep it warm for the rest of the family.

But her day only truly began in the moments that would follow, as she sank into the bathtub, alone. Before the morning had passed, Ifi would have cleared the sticks and twigs surrounding the house. After, she soaped away the lime and rust-colored mold along the walkway. Inside, she swept the red sand all along the tile floors, scattering the debris out into the street. Next, breakfast was to be prepared, the family fed, dishes washed. Darkness or light. Nepa did not discriminate. Light could be taken at any moment of the day or night. By the dancing flame of kerosene, Ifi would finish her chores in earnest.

On the day the motley crew arrived, boys and men—some lanky, some stocky, some dark, some pallid—Ifi watched from her window in dismay. Ashy, red, bare feet and jeans rolled to their ankles were the only features they shared in common. They were loud, raucous, rapping quickly in pidgin. And they worked from dusk till dawn each day, arriving just as Ifi rose every morning to do her chores and leaving as Ifi, finally, exhausted and spent, sank to sleep.

No one told Ifi what they came to do, or whom they came to work for. But through the curtains in her window, she could see the progress of their task, beginning with the deep hole they bored into the ground with a loud sandblasting drill that pierced the hard, stony earth. Then came the pipes: long metal structures fitted deep inside the hole.

One day they did not arrive, and Ifi knew their task was complete.

Ifi's uncle stood in the kitchen over the sink and turned the old, rusted tap, and water came spewing out into his palm. He slapped his thigh and Aunty danced. Ifi's cousins spilled into the doorway, watching with big eyes until their mother's shrill cheer and gyrations gave their cue. Then suddenly they were all dancing their way to the sink, cupping their hands below the tepid water released from the tap.

After that, the entire neighborhood no longer called her Ifi; she became "Mrs. Doctor."

Ifi's mornings changed. No flirtation from the old man delivering the water barrel. The tepid water did not need to be heated when it came from the showerhead. Instead, Ifi stood angling her head forward into the burst of water at the strongest part of the stream.

Thousands of miles from her past, Ifi lay in the tub, her large belly separating the curtain of water, when there was a knock at the door. Quickly she dried her body, tied the wrapper to her chest, and checked the small peephole. The criminal, Jamal. Ifi jerked with a start, and then she fumed. *What can he want?* she thought. She returned to the bathroom and finished dressing, but the knocking continued. Exasperated, she stumbled back to the door. Chain still in place, she opened the door a crack, just enough for her lips to make an audible sound through the door. "What do you want? Get away."

"Ma'am, I come to fix your crib."

"What crib? It's fine," she said.

"But I got to," Jamal said.

"No, it's fine. No trouble."

"Yeah, but he told me. And my aunty did too."

"My husband will not call police. Go."

"Please, I got to," he said again. "I got to do it." His voice stammered.

Dumb, calculated, Ifi thought to herself.

"You think I am a fool?" she asked. A cold gust of breeze slipped through the doorway. All Ifi could see of the hallway was his tall, lanky frame, but she felt certain that his friends were hiding in the hall, waiting. "You think I am an idiot, because I am a woman. Because I am from Africa. I will come and open this door for you to steal again and beat me?" Ifi slammed the door, and when the knocks began again, she turned on the television, loud. Still, it did not block out the noise.

"I will call police," she yelled.

Finally the knocks stopped.

Suddenly cold, she sank into the couch, drawing her wrapper tightly around her body. And then she paced. Ifi dumped the hardened leftover fufu in the kitchen drain and flipped the switch for the disposal. Job had not been eating. Night and day he was gone, and when he came home, he stank of pig. Often, he disappeared into the shower for what seemed like hours and reemerged with his skin pruney from the water. Later, Ifi would find pig remains in the shower's drain. When she asked questions, he always explained that he had taken on more patients at the hospital. *Why must my husband keep secrets?* In spite of the fact that she knew about the contents in his bag, he had begun, once more, to leave each night in the white coat, carrying the briefcase and stethoscope. *What can I say?* she had thought to herself. Reluctantly Ifi had resumed the task of laundering the lab coat and pants before setting them out for him each day.

As she paced in the kitchen, Ifi scrambled to unfurl the truth in his words to no avail. *Lies, boldfaced lies.* What troubled her the most was the certainty of the words as they tumbled from Job's mouth. *Everything he has told me,* she realized, *is a lie.* He had stood before her, one lie after another escaping him, as the criminal and his aunt sat only feet away in the other room. Now, she wondered, *How can he do it so effortlessly? How can he speak with such certainty about what we both know to be false?*

For a moment, her mind slipped to her letters to Aunty, letters that described, with great facility, her imaginary mansion. Ifi pushed the guilt from her mind, reminding herself that Job's lies were much more insidious. His lies could determine the outcome of their future, while she was only shielding Aunty from the ugly reality of life in America. In a way, she was also protecting Aunty's dream, defending her from the humiliation of finding out that she had failed at securing Ifi a suitable marriage. With this certainty, Ifi's thoughts returned to Job's lies. *There will be no nurse, no clinic, no doctor,* she said to herself, *and we will always live in this apartment of holes.*

Akra soup had congealed into a green paste with a yellowed edge, a nauseating smell that nearly brought her to her knees. Ifi flipped the entire pot over the garbage disposal, letting the chunks of meat fill the drain. With a crimson palm she smacked the pot's bottom until the remains filled the sink. The garbage disposal chewed and swallowed the soup with a satisfied gurgle. Suddenly, Ifi fell forward, emptying her stomach of its contents. She was alone, cold, and miserable; the pregnancy had been hard on her. In silent agony, Ifi cradled the base of her stomach.

Once this boy enters the world, everything will change. She had to believe it. Somehow she had to shake off the feelings of self-pity. After all, she had been lucky to come to America. Rinsing her mouth with water, she thought, *When this child comes, we will be a family.* There would be voices, warmth, friends, laughter, stories, *And then, I will finally be Mrs. Doctor.*

A hard thought forced Ifi to her haunches. She gasped with the weight of it. *He could have died.* Lies and all, criminals could have killed Job, and then there would have been no one. *To be alone in this place, of all places. Without friends, sef.* Without her own people, only Gladys and Emeka, *Chai!* For the first time, Ifi imagined the years that Job had spent alone in America. His odd mannerisms—the way he adjusted his glasses simply by jerking the features of his face; the grinding of his teeth; his cleanliness, even as they lived in such a sty—all suddenly had a source of explanation. Looking around the room, she mused, *Anyone could become silly in such a place, alone.*

She couldn't stay there, she determined. Not in such a place, where food was left to rot in the refrigerator overnight; where neighbors were thieves; where there was no one, no friends, neighbors, or family to ask after her. Still, how humiliating it would have been to return to Aunty and Uncle, a widow, with nothing but the suitcases she had left with months earlier. *Who would marry such a woman?* Ifi decided that she must speak the truth to them. She began a letter to Aunty.

Dear Aunty,
I have truth to tell you. It has all been a lie. We do not live in a mansion. We live like rats. Worse than rats. In a shack, surrounded by gangsters, akatta. They have attacked Job, stolen his car. He is no doctor. I married a pretender. I am afraid here.

After signing the letter, Ifi sealed it and rummaged through the kitchen drawers until she found a stamp. She stamped the letter and pulled on her boots.

Just steps from the front door, the weight in her body suddenly dropped. So swift was the movement that it took all of Ifi's effort to remain standing. Stirring the air as it dropped, the letter fell away to the scuffed floors. Ifi reached for the telephone. Balanced on the kitchen countertop, near the emptied pot, it was beyond her reach. Pain pulsed through her back and thighs. *Can it be happening now? So early. Too early. I haven't even spilled water.* A strangled whimper reverberated, a peculiar gasp and moan that Ifi had never heard before. The voice belonged to her. She tried to shape the sound into words. Nothing but a damp moan escaped her body, like that of a grunting dog.

In a hapless countermelody, the phone rang out, filling the room and punctuating each of her moans. Pain pounded through Ifi's body, and her eyes began to flicker. She hefted her weight to one side and struggled to rise. A few more pushes between each burst of pain, and she would be on her two feet. Her eyes flickered and she groaned.

A heavy thud forced the door forward, and then a second, and then a third. Under the weight of each thrust, the room rattled and hissed in protest. Ifi's whimpers turned to small cries. *Is it happening? Have they come to beat me?* Had she willed this to happen to her with her unforgiving thoughts of Job? As she lay on the floor bracing for the attack, Ifi imagined another scenario: Job all alone in this country, once again. Perhaps he would go on as if they had never met. Perhaps he would start over with a new wife. Unlike Ifi, his new wife would be beautiful and young, and she would trust in him completely, like a good wife.

A strong urge, something like jealousy, growled inside of her. Ifi dragged her weight with her forearms. Slowly, gradually, her body began to slide across the floor, away from the noise of her attackers.

Wood along the door's frame splintered, and the door thrust open. Jamal. For a moment, he stood in the doorway, glaring at Ifi. A wild look took over his face. Daring him to attack her, as he had attacked her husband, Ifi growled rabidly.

Jamal took the room in three steps, but he didn't come near her.

There's nothing to take, she had the urge to tell him, but the anger, fear, and pain were all coming from one place, and they forced their way through her back, her belly, and her legs. *I will have this baby, oh,* she thought to herself, *on this floor, with this teenage boy as witness.*

"The phone, lady, the phone," he said to her.

Will he take it and throw it away? But the pain was too terrible. All Ifi could feel was her hand, obeying his command with a motion to the countertop.

He placed the call.

"My aunty's at work," he said.

He'll call 9-1-1, she thought in relief. Giving in to the pain, she began to calm. Soon she would be in a hospital bed, and the baby would be out of her.

He disappeared. When he reappeared, he was holding the blanket from the bed and a towel from the bathroom, the very towel that was still stained with Job's blood from the night of the attack. Jamal swaddled the blankets around her, and she felt as if she was drowning under the weight of the sheets. Sweat rinsed down the sides of her face before she realized that she was hot and thirsty. She fought to pull the sheets apart from her body. In answer, he brought her a cup of warm tap water in a dirty cup. Seeing the pieces floating in the cup, she hesitated.

"Drink it," he said.

Another contraction rattled through her body. She obeyed.

They were still, the two, for fifteen minutes or more. Ifi couldn't be sure. Then suddenly, she was gazing up at another tall brown boy who stood in the doorway, another boy like Jamal, but without his softness; older, at least sixteen or seventeen. Ifi tensed. *What can they want with a pregnant woman in labor?* But then, as she wheezed, struggling to breathe, she reminded herself, *This is America.* Anything was possible. Maybe Mrs. Janik had called the police. For once, Ifi prayed that the old woman would put her gossip to good use.

"Oh shit," the older boy said. "What the fuck? She having a baby."

"Yeah," Jamal said.

"You didn't tell me."

"We need your car," he said.

"No way, man," the older boy said, but his eyes never left Ifi.

"You want me to call 9-1-1?" Jamal asked. "You want them to have police come here and pick the lady up while we here?"

The boy backed into the doorway. "Naw, man. You wouldn't."

"We just go and drop her off at the hospital. They won't even see us. If we don't, we'll be in deep shit. Something could happen to her and the baby."

"No way, man," the boy said again.

"Yeah, we gonna use your car," Jamal said with an urgency tinged with anger. Though he was smaller, he thrust the taller boy into the broken door. Another large splinter sounded as the door bumped the back wall.

"Fuck you, man," the boy said. "I ain't part of this."

"Naw, you are," Jamal said back, and as their eyes met, it was suddenly clear to Ifi that she was face to face with yet another of Job's attackers. It filled her with rage. "Give me your keys," Jamal said. Another quick shake to his partner, but the boy wouldn't budge.

The other boy shook his head furiously. "Naw, fuck you. You on your own." And just like that, he shoved Jamal one time, just hard enough for him to sprawl on the floor next to Ifi, and he disappeared out the door in a crash of footsteps.

Jamal swung his gaze in all directions. For the first time, he looked frightened. "I can't call the police," he said, more to himself than to Ifi. He picked up the phone. He began to dial some numbers and then hung up.

"Call my husband," Ifi said. Her voice was strangled and low, but the words produced sounds.

"No way," Jamal said. "No way."

"Call Mrs. Janik," Ifi said.

"Who?"

"The old lady."

He made as if he would do just that. Then he stopped in the doorway and returned to Ifi, where she was writhing beneath the sheets. "I can call my aunty at work. She'll pick you up. Mrs. Janik is crazy. Everybody knows that."

"Call Janik," Ifi said again, through gritted teeth.

He grabbed the phone and dialed some numbers, but even from her place on the floor, Ifi could hear the ringing.

Jamal hung up. He dialed another series of numbers. He said Ifi's address into the phone. He told the voice to hurry, but nothing more.

"You called hospital?" Ifi asked.

"Yeah, sure," he said, grimly. "Now let's get ready." He helped her to her feet and wrapped the blanket around her. Her boots were thankfully still on her feet.

They stood at the top of the landing, Ifi leaning against Jamal's broad, skinny shoulders, and it looked impossible. He sighed and then half lifted her against his body. One step at a time, they made their way down the three flights of stairs. Twice Ifi thought they'd stumble and fall the whole way, so she clung to him more tightly. At one point, she felt his skin break underneath her fingernails, but she couldn't let go. Even the tiniest release would surely send the baby spilling out of her insides and onto the steps.

On the bottom stair, Jamal leaned her sideways against the wall. He stood in the doorway, peering out into the street.

After Ifi had begun to lose hope that the ambulance would arrive, Jamal suddenly thrust the door open. A cool shock of air breathed on Ifi's face. It felt good. Somehow it calmed the pulsing in her back to a mere ripple. Jamal grasped Ifi and lifted her, gasping in sharp, jagged breaths from the effort. They plunged out into the whiteness of the snow to a yellow cab.

"Where is the ambulance?" Ifi asked in confusion.

"We'll get there," he said.

He hefted her across the snowy walkway, and again Ifi was forced to half submit as they made their way to the cab.

The driver, an ashen-faced man, gazed at them in bewilderment. "I don't want no mess on my seat," he protested. "I don't want no trouble."

Jamal offered the driver a steely expression, the one Ifi imagined that he had shared with Job the day he and his gang had attacked her husband. He started to open the door, but the cabdriver hit the gas. Back door flapping like a bird's broken wing, the car careened down the street and around the corner.

Both Ifi and Jamal stood in the abandoned street, their mouths open in a stupor until the cold overtook Ifi's body in shivers, and the waves in her back buckled her knees.

"Shit, damn motherfucker," Jamal said. The sharp edges of his teeth bore through his clenched jaw. He led Ifi back into the building.

"Please, Jamal," she said, using his name aloud for the first time.

Without a word, he loped up the stairs. A moment later, he returned with a grave expression on his face. He had another glass of water in his hands, but before he handed it to Ifi, he started talking quickly. "I can't stay with you. I gotta go. I told them you're here, the address and everything, so they'll find you. I can get the crazy lady to wait here with you until they come. Just don't say nothing about me. I can't go to jail. I promised my daddy."

When his words began to make sense to Ifi, she was surprised by her tears. "You are not leaving me, oh," she wailed. "I won't tell. He won't tell," she said of Job. "He has not. I will promise you."

A pained expression crossed Jamal's face. He hesitated, then collapsed on the floor next to her with his face in his hands, his back turned to Ifi. She ventured to reach for him, but he knocked her hand away. Sirens wailed as the ambulance and police arrived. His body flexed and tensed like a cat ready to pounce. Jamal burst out the door, leaving it swinging behind him. Just moments later, flustered attendants propped Ifi onto a gurney and carried her out to the ambulance. Her last backwards glance reached Mrs. Janik, cup of tea in hand, peering out of the window of her apartment.

❖

The angry and puckered face staring back at Job belonged to his son. His first son, *because there will be many more,* he decided. *Tall, sturdy-backed boys whose nameplates will be followed by MD, JD, PhD.* Before setting the boy back in the incubator with his own swollen, trembling hands, Job stared into the wrinkled face for one long moment.

When he had received the telephone call, he was on the line at the meat-packing factory, white gloves to his elbows, drenched in the blood and fluids of an animal. In his white jacket, white gloves, facemask, and hat, Job felt, in a peculiar way, like a surgeon. Instead of an electric knife that buzzed and whirred as it sliced through frozen flesh, bone, and fluids, he wielded a scalpel, neatly slicing through the layers of fat and cartilage of a patient.

Strange how quickly he had taken to the work when his supervisor first introduced him to the line. But Job had a secret system that he hadn't shared with anyone. It was simple: he told himself that he was a machine. Nothing but bits of iron held together each of his joints, and the muscles and tendons were really hardened bits of twisted wire. This is what he told himself, and he moved like it, staring at the broken cow in front of him, sawing, breaking apart each bit with a sudden swift turn of his wrists, thinking of his life in America, thinking that finally he would raise the money for a better home, a place where a doctor and his wife could live.

Supervisors circulated among the rows of identical lines, shouting for the workers to keep things moving, to pick up the pace. Each time they stopped at Job, they nodded with approval. Once, a tall, willowy Somali woman, complained that she needed to urinate, but the supervisor yelled obscenities into her face until she whimpered back to her place on the line.

Secretly, Job sided with the supervisor. She had no business here among men if she couldn't handle the work. When a portly Mexican man, angered by the woman's treatment, had spoken up on her behalf, he had been fired on the spot. A surprise it was that the man had spoken on her behalf anyway. It was the Mexicans who complained that the Somalis used their prayers as an excuse to break the line. And the Somalis complained that the Mexicans used their cigarettes as an excuse to break the line. Job had sided with the Mexicans on that one.

During his interview, as his tie-and-jacketed supervisor had questioned him, Job had to clarify that he was Nigerian, and from the south, and so he wouldn't be wasting the factory owners' money on prayer breaks throughout the day. After the Mexican man was fired, he returned three days later, begging for his place on the line back, the position to which Job had promptly been promoted, the fastest line with the highest pay. While the man descended to Job's former position at the bottom of the line, Job switched stations and resumed work, his fingers cutting and flashing with efficiency. Wet floors, the noise of whirring knives, the cold of the room meant nothing to him. He simply moved, keeping up with the line, cutting and sorting the pieces of flesh as he had been instructed in the orientation video, blindly imagining the life he would live in the palace Ifi had described to her aunty.

Only when he reached home each night did he stare down at his large, swollen digits. In the shower, he would turn his palms up to his face and let the warm water run down them, rinsing them clean, thawing his talons until they became human and he could hold a fork again.

Because they would never understand, because they would consider the work beneath him, Job couldn't explain to anyone, least of all Ifi or Emeka, the strange pride he took in his work, cutting and scoring cow parts that would be distributed to restaurants and grocery stores all over the nation. Each time he took a bite of seasoned beef in pepper soup, he was secretly reminded that once he had held those precious pieces in his hands.

His first laceration. It had happened fast—on the day he received the call about Ifi and the boy. Job had been slicing, panting, with quick turns of his frozen hands and wrists, when he heard the click over the intercom, a grainy voice interrupting the rhythm of his movements on the floor to say he had a call. Just that bit of distraction broke the wires of Job's machine, and he was human again, looking at his hands and looking at the lump of flesh on the table. His hands were cold, ice cold, and his joints were sore and pink from curving around the knife handle. Where they weren't sore, his fingers and palms were numb with tingles that ran up the length of his wrists.

Regaining his composure required all of his attention, and so Job pressed on, ignoring the urgent call over the speaker until a supervisor tapped his shoulder, after first, according to the man, calling Job's name over and over. Then it happened. One turn, too fast, and Job sliced a tear that landed through the thick, rubbery protective gloves.

Not until he was standing in the office overlooking the floor with the phone cupped to his ear did he notice. As he listened to the voice, he stared out at the teeming swarm of workers spread across the floor, albino cockroaches with quick, precise movements. Looking out, trying to make out the faces of the Somalis, the Mexicans, the Vietnamese, the Sudanese, the Bosnians, they all looked the same, faceless behind the masks and underneath the white jackets and white hairnets. Without the sound of the whirring knives, the cold, the slickness of the floors, he saw how the floor looked to him from the ground when he was a machine, just those moments before the intercom took him out of his dream. It was peculiar, as if Job was watching himself on the floor, working the knife one way and the other, dropping the bits into the sorting bins. He didn't know what to make of it all—*Do I feel insignificant? Do I feel like a giant?* As he gazed out, a nurse was saying that Ifi was giving birth. "That's wrong," Job had said, and he explained that it was too soon. "No, no," the nurse had said in excitement. "The baby is premature. God help us, we can't tell them when to come. Some babies come when they're good and ready." And Job knew that she didn't understand. She couldn't understand.

He hadn't had time to put the pieces of his life together in the right order. He hadn't saved money for a new home. He hadn't restarted classes at the university. He hadn't obtained a degree. Instead he was alternating shifts at a meatpacking plant and at the hospital as a nurse's aide. He lived in a home infested with roaches, with a wife swollen and fast approaching the permanent middle-aged frown he had seen on too many women.

When he put the phone down, he sucked in a deep breath, his face pitted with such a scowl that when the secretary said, "Oh, Job," she thought he was grimacing from the wound in his hand. Only then did he notice the smear of blood filling the opening in the glove. When he peeled back his gloves, he found the blood had traveled up to his elbow. A spot of blood dribbled down the body of the telephone. After, as the medic cleaned and stitched his tingling hand, he watched maintenance wipe away his bloody print with a few sprays from a clear, bleach-smelling agent.

Cleaning and stitching hadn't taken long. What took a while was the succession of workman's compensation forms. Job had to report the "incident," and they wouldn't allow him to leave, even for Ifi's delivery, until the forms were signed with the appropriate signatures. Each of Job's urgent protests was pacified with the stubborn politeness that Midwesterners seemed so expert at when a situation required contention. They could make the most humiliating and painful information sound so pleasant. Then it was all done, and Job looked at the neat square bandage on his hand.

He was released into the cold air, a flat, starless night, and told to report to work as usual the next day. Air, sweet with the antiseptic smeared on his chapped hands, filled his nose. He drove through the night, his hand throbbing from the cold. Along the stretch of highway, Job felt the residue of the glare on his face. He felt the grooves of his face deepening into resentment. *Too early,* he repeated to himself. *An impatient child!* He hoped it was a girl— if it was a girl, he would at least have the time to make things right before his boy entered the world. A girl could survive on watery, tasteless soup and dry biscuits, but not a boy; a boy who was to be a success needed the proper ingredients.

Now, in the hospital room, as he looked into his son's angry face, Job felt the ice in his chest thaw, the grooves in his face fill. His hardened features softened under the boy's bleary eyes. When he opened his tiny mouth to yawn, Job peered into his son's throat, at his soft, slippery tongue. Job swallowed back the tears that began to form in his throat. *I am a father,* he thought to himself, sore, exhausted, but suddenly exhilarated. In the old days, it was thought that you hadn't reached full adulthood until you had created the life of another, until you had extended the cycle of your name through another. Well, Job had finally reached his manhood. *What now?* He needed a name for this, the greatest achievement of his life. The child needed a name to reflect the enormity of his birth to a father who loved him so completely that it hurt. *His name,* Job though triumphantly, *will be Victorious Ezeaku Ogbonnaya, the victorious king.*

❖

Three days later, Gladys and Emeka arrived. Job was away at work. Their youngest daughter dumped a crumpled heap of flowers on the nightstand and promptly disappeared, her hand in her father's in search of crackers and lemonade. Gladys stopped them in the hall, and Ifi could hear the tops of their voices. She could imagine the girl with her hand pressed into her father's, forgotten. Their voices swelled in and out of the waves of Ifi's fatigue. They spoke in Igbo.

"Where are you going?" Gladys.

"You heard the girl," Emeka.

"Aheh, you are leaving without saying good morning to the woman?"

"Dear, let's not quarrel like this. In front of the Americans."

"We are not quarreling."

Ifi ran her hands over her belly, a sagging paunch now. She glared out past the sun into the clear sky, over the tops of cars. In spite of the noise, the boy slept soundly. Right now, at home, Ifi thought, Aunty probably stood over a pot in the kitchen, instructing the housegirl in a halting whisper, telling her to hold the knife in her palm at this angle, not that, when cutting the onions. Her words would be wet, like the sprays of onion that watered the girl's eyes. Ifi hated the smell of the onions in the girl's hands. She knew that no amount of washing would rid her of the scent for the rest of the day. If she had any imagination at all, the girl would rub her hands with dirt and leaves. She would sprinkle lemon juice on them, with the hopes that the smell would be gone by the time she took her lover late that night.

Immediately after delivering the baby, Ifi had phoned Aunty. Every third word the connection broke, and Ifi found herself repeating, again and again, "boy," "tall," until they eventually lost the connection all together. She cried until her eyes were swollen. Had Ifi lived in Nigeria, Aunty would not stand over a pot instructing the housegirl. She would be by Ifi's side. She would be holding the boy, pressing her lips to his forehead, cupping his small head in her palms. There would be uncles, cousins, neighbors, all surrounding Ifi and the boy. Each one would shout their praises about the delicacy of his skin, the pinkness of his cheeks, the tufts of charcoal hair, the size and shape of his large nose. Noise, laughter, and admonishments would fill the air.

Outside the room, Emeka's and Gladys's voices had shrunken almost to a whisper. "Why must you worry me, my queen?" he said, teasingly. "How can I fight with such a face, such a bright face, Miss America?" They sounded like lovers at the end of a rendezvous. Silent, caught in the middle, their daughter had ridden the high tide of their anger and watched it resolve to a tremulous wave. Something about the girl's calm, childish hum suggested to Ifi that she had been privy to such arguments and resolutions her entire short life. Gladys's objections had faded to a watered-down silence.

Alone, Gladys returned to the room, sucking her teeth in shallow, sullen protest. He had won. Emeka's and the little girl's footsteps vanished down the hallway. Remembering his voice, Ifi knew that she too could not have said no to him, not to his gentle pleas and his flirtatious chuckles. *Why can't Job be like that?*

At first, she sympathized with Gladys—the woman with the husband whom she couldn't even rejoice in feeling anger toward when he was wrong—until Gladys strolled past Ifi's bed, smoothing out the front of her skirt, inspecting her painted fingernails, refusing to even glare in her direction. For several long, silent seconds Gladys hunched over the incubator, pressing her lips together sternly, watching the sleeping boy.

"You had better feed this boy, oh," Gladys said. "You didn't eat well during your pregnancy, heh. He is too small."

Heat filled Ifi's cheeks. She searched for a response.

"Trying to be skinny like the Americans." Gladys turned to Ifi for the first time. Once more, she examined her cuticles. "Your breasts resemble uncooked dough. How will you feed him? What kind of woman does not know how to prepare for a child? I don't blame you, sha. You had no one to teach you."

Biting back her anger, Ifi turned away. That morning, she hadn't expected anyone. *Once his shift ends, Job will come,* she told herself. Tired, sore, and stitched between her legs, she hadn't bothered with a bra or even a comb. Now, imagining her own heavy, ashy breasts, etched with stretch marks, her eyes couldn't leave Gladys's well-formed shape. At her age, after six children, surely a Band-Aid of Spanx, bra, and hose held her body together. Straightened hair, smoothed curls, glossed and shiny from Blue Magic. Fingernails, long arcs, painted red. Face bleached by powder and cream. Ifi tried to imagine Gladys before all of it, when she was nothing but a schoolgirl in Nigeria with low, kinky hair, sandals, and a starched linen uniform. No more or less than any of the other girls in her level. *All that is real,* Ifi scoffed to herself, remembering that first night at Divine Davinci's. Gladys's fur was now draped across the back of a chair, like the one hanging limply in Ifi's closet at home. Summoning energy, Ifi shouted, "Don't insult me. Get out!"

Gladys turned up her nose. Nothing but calm resided in her voice. "You are too good for sisterly teasing?"

When their eyes met at Gladys's shaking hands, Gladys spun away. Ifi suddenly remembered Gladys behaving the same way just a month ago, looking away from her dead son in his incubator. *She's in pain,* Ifi thought, a wave of pity overwhelming her. Maybe she could understand this woman after all. Maybe there was nothing more to her than bones and a soft heart in a fragile case. Like Ifi, Gladys was just a woman. They were both mothers. No better. No worse. "Will you hold him?" she asked.

"No," Gladys said, her voice rising, almost in derision.

Emeka and the daughter returned. The girl sipped juice from a small white cup. Crumbs powdered her cheeks. He crowded the door, and Ifi caught Gladys's gaze trained on him. Guilt etched into the fine lines of his face, he shrank in the doorway. Ifi suddenly couldn't remember the guile of his voice just moments earlier. Instead, he had the look of a boy prepared for a scolding.

"Hold the boy, now," he said to Gladys gently, with a hint of irritation.

"No," she said, backing away.

Roughly, Emeka pushed past her to the incubator. He lifted the boy up, his back and shoulders squared to Ifi and Gladys.

"Put him down," Gladys said after a moment. Her eyes still contained their hard, scolding expression. "What is wrong with you? Have you forgotten how to hold a child properly?"

But he just stood there, holding the boy in his arms, staring into his eyes. Their daughter placed the cup on the nightstand and slipped her fingers into Gladys's. Limp, forgotten, her hand dangled. All of a sudden, Ifi understood. *The girl will never be the son that her mother needs.*

Before they left the room, Ifi knew that as she slept later that night, Gladys's and Emeka's bodies would be tied together in a confused embrace. They would be rigid with frustrated desire, with the hopes that another boy would begin to grow in Gladys's womb. Perhaps they would even hang a watery charm from one of the posts on their bed to ensure that it would happen this time—the thing that had happened so effortlessly for Ifi, the thing that Ifi began to understand had already changed her life in innumerable ways. She would not go to school and train to be a nurse as Job had promised, and they would not open the clinic together. But her son would train to be a doctor. Her son would train and marry the nurse. Her son would open the clinic in Nigeria. Having a child had made her a mother.

CHAPTER 9

HIS CRYING AND SHOUTING WAS SO LOUD, SO ANGRY, THAT IT NEARLY escaped Job that the front door was slightly ajar. With the boy drooping in Ifi's arms, Job pushed her back into the hallway, and she waited while he surveyed the apartment. Everything seemed just as it had been when he left that afternoon to check Ifi out of the hospital. Several emptied cans, coated to the rim with the congealing juices of pinto beans, straddled the countertops and the cool stovetop burners. Job swept the cans into the trash bin. A crumpled heap of newspapers, turned to the finance section, was spread over the living room couch and floor. His towels, still damp from his shower, hung from the bar in the bathroom. Then he let out a sharp gasp.

A crib. Gladys and Emeka's. He'd seen it before in their nursery, a room whose walls had changed from blue to pink so many times that Job had lost count. *What is it doing here? Why is it assembled?* he thought. Perfectly assembled, erected, and squeezed into the tight space between the back wall and the bed that Ifi and Job shared. Clean sheets were spread over the bed. Even the mobile of plastic and glittering stars hung over the bed. For a moment, Job surveyed the bed, his mouth agape. *How can it be?*

Calmly, he ran his fingers over the dark chestnut frame. Nicks caught against his fingertips. He engaged and disengaged the side rail, and it moved up and down smoothly. *Who could have done such a thing?* He tried to play the events of his featureless day in his mind. Arriving home from his night shift at the hospital exhausted, showering, eating the tins of beans before leaving for his shift at the meatpacking plant. From there, like he had on the day of his son's birth, Job had made his way directly to the hospital, this time to pick up Ifi and the boy.

"Chineke!" Oh my God, Ifi said, now standing next to him.

All of a sudden, saliva and mucous erupted from each orifice of their son's little red face. His balled fists punched awkwardly at the air just ahead of his nose. Job gazed at the boy. *An ugly baby.* But never mind it. *After all, he will one day be a man.*

"I told you to wait outside," Job said. Then he changed his mind. Over the boy's shouts, he explained, "I left the door open. I'll have to remember next time." No sense in frightening Ifi. No sense in letting her know that Emeka had a hand in this, because surely he did—always flashing his money around, always acting like he was Job's chief.

Just slightly, Job turned away from Ifi and the boy, who dangled precariously from Ifi's grasping arms. Weaving in and out, the boy flexed his back in abrupt spastic motions. Like a fish trying to jump free of its bowl.

Cocking his head to the side, with his shoulder thrust to the crib, Job blinked away his fears and the shame of Emeka's hand in his home. He shrugged casually, the way he'd seen Americans do it. He had to pretend. *She cannot know about Emeka.* "How do you like it?"

"You did this? Yes, it's good," she said slowly. Ifi placed the baby into Job's arms. Back and forth Job weaved, gripping the boy at his sides as he tried to slip away. She fingered the wooden railing. She punched the buttons on the mobile, and the intimate chime of bells sounded as it slowly rotated. Job pushed the boy up over his shoulder, and the boy wet it with his saliva and furious sucks. A sprinkle of lights—soft oranges, blues, and pinks—swirled overhead. Job lifted the boy's face to the eddying lights. At first, the boy offered nothing but hasty, shrill shouts mixed with a choking cough. Then he stopped. Amazed, silent, they watched together, father and son. Job breathed a sigh of relief.

Somehow Emeka had managed to find their address. Probably at the hospital while Job was away. Maybe it was on an intake form. Emeka had come over, that sly fellow, and put the crib together. Then he left the door wide open to show Job that he could come and go as he pleased in Job's home, and he could not stop him. He would have to pay Emeka for assembling the crib and thank him, act like it was his own idea, to rob Emeka of whatever satisfaction he had felt as a result of his intrusion into his home. Job fumed.

Ifi placed the boy in the crib. His large wet eyes continued to stare at the mobile. Curling to his side, he shoved a plump finger into his mouth. Furiously, he sucked.

"He's hungry," Job said.

"Yes, he is." A smile. Cocking his head, she fed him, overlooking the crib with continued awe. In minutes he was asleep, a reservoir of breast milk captured in his pitted cheeks. Job ran his fingers along the boy's mouth, and the saliva shined against his finger. For the first time, it seemed, Ifi noticed Job's hand. After setting the boy in the crib, she placed Job's hand in hers. Carefully, she examined the warped flesh, oozing with pus that was held together by frayed stitching.

"What happened to you?"

"On the day he was born," he said simply. "It happened then."

"What happened?"

"It will scar and heal, and each time I look at it, I will remember the day my son was born." He knew that he wasn't answering her questions, but she mustn't know about the factory.

In acquiescence, she said, "It's infected." By now she understood that if he did not answer her question immediately, he never would.

Holding his damaged hand, she led him to the bathroom. While their son slept for the first time in his new home, Ifi and Job retreated to the sink, where she cleaned his wound.

When he arrived at Emeka's that night, the pockets of Job's white lab coat were filled with twenty-dollar bills. His shift at the hospital would begin in exactly one hour, at eleven. By his estimation, the business would be done quickly and efficiently, with plenty of time for Job to get to work. Emeka and Gladys lived on a suburban cul-de-sac, a street that curved just beyond the entrance, with skinny ash trees lightly salted with snow. As Job pulled up, he could make out a stooped figure, with a flat shovel in hand, scooping snow to the sides of the wide driveway. Working only from old-fashioned incandescent street lamps overhead, it was Emeka. Only then did Job realize that Emeka's was the single home on the entire block without cleared sidewalks. Footprints of various sizes were scattered along the walkway. When Job parked and stepped out of the car, he placed his feet in footsteps large enough to hold his own.

Before Job had a chance to speak, Emeka said, "Exercise is good for the soul, my man." Wind had chapped his large lips. Aside from a shaggy, lop-sided hat and a pair of down mittens, Emeka wore khakis and sneakers filled with the snow that he had beaten into the shovel. Splitting into laughter, he tugged at his shirt and revealed his hard, round gut. "This is all muscle and fufu. My six-pack." He threw a glance back at the house, a mischievous one. "I need all the exercise I can get to keep up with activities at home, you know?" Heaving a second shovel at Job, he added, "Take it."

Both Job and Emeka peered up just then; Gladys had stopped in an upstairs window. Her figure checked the glare that was just beginning on Job's face. Before she disappeared from view, her eyes met Job's and then steadied on Emeka. After a moment, another face appeared in the window: Emeka's youngest daughter. With her mother's petulance, she eyed them.

Job leaned the shovel against one shoe. "I see," he said with false joviality. When Emeka didn't greet him properly, when he didn't ask why Job was visiting at such an hour, he finally spoke again. "I did not come for this." Still, he couldn't find the words to accuse his friend of breaking into his home and erecting the crib, like a dog urinating on his territory. Snow patched beneath his shovel as if he had not even shoveled. Shiny concrete glowed under Emeka's hand. No matter how hard Job shoveled, he found the same patches of snow caught underneath his shovel. Hot lights left Job's lips tart with the taste of sweat. He peeled back his winter coat, standing in his white lab coat. With vigor, he pushed the shovel harder, swinging his freed arms. His shovel was scooped. *I have the wrong type of shovel,* he thought.

Free of his winter coat, Job reached into the pockets of his lab coat. Casually, one hand still directing the shovel, he dumped the wad of twenty-dollar bills on the snow between them. Each bill refused to separate; they landed in a clump. Wind and snow stirred the bent bills.

"I like to make my hands dirty," Emeka said, ignoring the money. "You know, the Americans have this one right. In Nigeria, I would pay a small boy to do this chore for me. But here, I am using my muscles." He let in a deep gasp of breath, and from the side, Job could make out a slight twitch as Emeka's jaw tightened.

Remembering the glossy Sears and Roebuck ads folded in with his morning newspaper, Job said, "Buy a snowblower." He beamed. "I'm thinking of replacing my own this year."

When Emeka didn't reply, Job looked up. Instead of meeting Emeka's eyes, he spread his gaze all along the dead lane. His eyes escaped to the hulking houses, the manicured lawns, the exaggerated outlines of fresh-cut Christmas trees in the dimly lit windows. For the first time, Job noticed that Emeka's was the smallest house on the street, boxed in between two large, gleaming mansions.

Emeka's front door opened. A long-legged girl with crooked braids burst out, her hands precariously grasping two large, steaming mugs. Each mug heaved one way and the other, and the liquid stained the white snow a dirty yellow as she descended the stairs two at a time. Just before she made it to them, the girl let out a squeal. "Money!" she shrieked. The mugs slipped from her grasp and tumbled into the snow.

"Stop it. Don't you touch it," Emeka bellowed.

She frowned at him.

"Your uncle has dropped his wallet."

"Oh," she said softly. After a moment, she smiled. "Can I have some money, Uncle?" She knelt and began to scoop the bills.

Again, Emeka yelled, "Remove your hands."

"Take it," Job said, a challenge in his tone.

"Leave it." At her father's words, her frown slipped away and was replaced by incredulity. Looking from one man to the other, her father and the man she must call Uncle, she refused to move.

"You spilled our drinks, clumsy girl," Emeka said softly. "Go on, get us two more." Both men watched the top of her head as she collected the snow-covered mugs in her shaky grasp and returned to the house.

After she was gone from their view, Emeka spun on Job. "What is the meaning of this?"

"Take the money and buy a snowblower," Job said again.

"I don't need a damn snowblower." He ground his shovel into the snow.

"My boy likes the crib," Job said casually. "So take it."

Emeka's face softened. Thoughtfully, he stared past the windows out into the distance. "She gave you the crib. I hoped it meant she would be happy, that this 'boy' nonsense would be done. We have all we need. We are a great success." He sighed. "Nothing pleases her these days. Ah, this boy of yours has started it all over again." Emeka threw back his shoulders in a shudder. His shudder turned into a chuckle, and before long, the chuckle morphed into a great laugh. "Women."

At first Job couldn't understand. Then he thought of that night, he and Emeka at the bar, faces upturned to strippers slippery with sweat. He remembered Emeka complaining about juju and native doctors, all commissioned in hopes of producing a son. Gladys again. *Was it Gladys who sent Emeka to my house to put the crib together?* Perhaps. Knowing this changed everything. This whole situation was nothing more than Emeka giving up and acknowledging that Job had bested him in the most significant manner, producing a son. He chuckled softly. "Why not take the money?"

He thought of Ifi at home, asleep on the bed next to their son in his crib. She had touched Job's hand. *We are a family,* he thought to himself. *Finally.* The piece that had cemented their lives was the boy—with his beautiful, ugly, red, angry little face. "Buy your wife something nice, Emeka."

"We both know that you need it more than me, my friend," Emeka said.

His tone. His haughty tone. At that, Job pounced on Emeka. His movement was so sudden, so unrestrained, that for days afterwards, he struggled to pinpoint the place it came from within his body. What had he hoped to accomplish? Whites of his lab coat trailing on both sides, he was on Emeka, feeling his hard gut against his own, tasting Emeka's powerful breath in his, soaked with the snow on his legs, hating Emeka with all his anger and might. "Take it!" he shouted into Emeka's bewildered face. "Take the money!" He snatched a handful of bills and thrust them into Emeka's face.

Emeka resisted. His jaw tightened, so Job bore down with his weight, pinning Emeka farther into the snow. He forgot about the street and the houses and the garages. In that moment, it was just the sounds of their breaths, the scent and taste of beer and crayfish from Emeka's mouth. Surely Emeka would call him crazy. *Perhaps I am crazy,* Job thought. But he didn't care.

Both men looked up at the sound of a creak. Balancing the same mugs glistening with melting snow, once again his daughter stood in the doorway. Silently, she regarded them, a look like her mother's, a look too grown for her five-year-old legs, the rounded belly like her father's, and the messy braids piled on top of her head. *Stupid girl,* Job thought. He was glad to have a son, a boy.

Like a drunken man, Emeka burst into laughter. Playfully, he jabbed at Job's sides. *Ah, he wants us to appear that way,* Job realized, like two drunks wrestling in the snow. Like two rusty men who will be scolded by their wives for a late night and juvenile antics. *Well,* Job decided, *I won't have it that way.* After all, he had come to make a point. "Stop it." He shook Emeka. "Stop this laughing."

But Emeka's laughter only rose in pitch. Job took both sides of his shoulders and pressed him into the snow. "Stop this laughing! I am not fooling!" Emeka's body flailed like a rag doll. He laughed and laughed and laughed.

His daughter descended the steps one more time, trying to decide if she should join the play or simply observe the two men. She settled for the latter and placed the drinks on the snow within their reach. In his distraction, Job loosened his grip on Emeka's shoulders, and Emeka rolled free. He grasped one of the mugs and drank deeply, staining his mustache with foam. Exhausted, Job joined Emeka, draining his mug in one gulp, watching his life from outside of the ring, his hands red and dripping from the snow.

"Come and take this money your uncle has brought for you and your sisters," Emeka said to the girl. Happily, she clambered down the stairs and claimed each of the twenty-dollar bills, folding them into the pockets of her jeans.

"Thank you, thank you, Uncle!" she said. She danced up the stairs, all two hundred dollars in her possession.

"That one will not share. She'll spend it all on candy," Emeka said proudly. "Three cavities the last time we saw her dentist. Three cavities, I tell you. But she's stubborn. Like her mother."

The thought of the five-year-old consuming streams of bubblegum and licorice with the money infuriated Job. "Do not enter my house ever again, you hear?"

Emeka glanced up, startled. "Your house. Heh?"

"Yes," Job said evenly. "Spend the money on lollipops if you like, but never, under my dead body, never come into my home uninvited again."

"What are you saying?" Emeka began a strange laugh.

"I mean this."

"Is this why you have come to me here? You think I have broken into your house to steal your money? You think a man like me would need anything from you? Come now, you cannot be serious."

"I am not silly."

"You have lost your mind, my man." Emeka stood and dusted off the rear of his pants. Snow rained around him and then rose again with the wind. He took a long, deep swallow from his mug.

Job felt cold. But his winter coat was sprawled somewhere in the distance, and his hands were too numb to search for it. Emeka didn't seem bothered by the cold at all. His sneakers were still full of snow. Without his hat, now forgotten in the snow, the top of his balding head was revealed. How must Job appear now, shivering, his clothes scattered before him? He checked the houses up and down the street, so silent, so private. He was glad to be invisible.

Still, he couldn't let it go. He mustn't leave Emeka's home without a single understanding between the two. "I am not crazy. I am no fool. This is simple," Job said, leveling his eyes. "I am asking you to never enter my home again."

Emeka stared back at Job. "I never entered your home."

"You arranged the crib. In my own room."

"My only hand was in giving it to your wife."

When Emeka's gaze didn't waver, Job suggested, "Well, then your wife."

"Gladys was here. With me." With a wink, he added, "I should know." After a moment, Emeka furrowed his brow and eyed Job. "Perhaps it is *your* wife who should worry you."

Emeka's words haunted Job throughout his shift at the hospital. *What can I say to Ifi?* he thought. *How can I dignify such a claim?* Yet at the same time, he was convinced that Emeka's accusation was true. Even after many months together, Ifi still had strange ways that Job couldn't comprehend. For the first time, he began to wonder what she did with her hours alone throughout the day. When he arrived home in the afternoons, the television was usually off, but he always noticed that the radio would be on. Usually he was the one to turn on the television. It helped him sleep. Now, he wondered, *Which American stations does she listen to?* Were the rhythms strange on her hips as she moved to the music?

Patients tousled awake as he made his rounds, emptying bedpans and rearranging sheets. During first rounds, Job found Captain sprawled across his sheets, staring at the mottled ceiling with unmoved eyes. Ishmael, a lanky Russian nurse with a thick accent, accompanied him. The two flipped and turned Captain over to change his soiled sheets. Over the past few weeks, the accidents had become more frequent. Each time, Captain shrank in humiliation as the folds of his skin were spread so he could be cleaned. When alone, Job cleaned as quickly as he could, knowing that Captain's dignity was more precious than his cleanliness. But today Captain was perfectly still, staring up at the ceiling. Job followed his eyes and tried to think up a story to share with the old man, but Ishmael moved impatiently.

Just then, the old man's eyes rolled to meet Job's. His eyes were so vacant, so shameless, that it hurt to look into them. *What is a man if he can have no dignity?* Job thought in fury. Nothing more than a shrunken corpse, he allowed his flesh to slide one way and then the other without a care for how Job and Ishmael took him apart as they changed him. No longer did Captain walk with pride. All at once, Job was angry with Captain, Ifi, and the crib.

At break time, Job sat hunched over a bowl of dry cereal, his lids growing heavy. These days, between the hospital and the meatpacking plant, he was lucky to get four hours of sleep. Head resting lightly on his hands, he began to nod. Eventually, the humming refrigerator, buzzing fluorescent light, and creaking floors of the break room merged into one sound. Off in the distance, the intercom buzzed. An unanswered telephone rang. He drifted.

In his dreams, he was assaulted by a pack of faceless black American boys. They ran him down in his own car. They folded him against a wall. Headlights blinded his eyes. He woke just as the car was on him, finding, in its place, the bespectacled eyes of one of the nurses on his station. Mitzie was an older woman with a furrowed expression and dry, flaky skin. Her blue eyes were magnified behind the lenses, and her furious glare reared Job out of his seat.

He was up and out the back door, leaning against the brick back wall, breathing in the cold air, listening for the sounds of the night. Cars softly whirred on drying pavement. An owl hooted. All were so far away, yet everything was magnified in the dark, starless night. Four streetlights flooded the parking lot, and Job felt, even out here behind the large brick building, observed and scrutinized like he was on the line at the meatpacking plant. He had never forgotten the strange feeling of staring out over the floor from the large glass window, observing the bodies lined up like albino cockroaches in rows. How small that moment had made him feel, like he was merely a stain on glass.

Again, he reflected on Emeka's face as he delivered his accusation about Ifi. Job's cheeks burned in anguish. *Overconfident,* he thought of Emeka. *Like Samuel.* And Emeka's crib—a rickety thing that could be broken in two with minimal might. That's all it would take, and the nonsense would end. Perhaps Job would not even need to say a word to Ifi.

When the cold caught up with him, he breathed into his hands and tried to open the door. He was locked out. Job patted his hands together, blew in and out. He knocked wildly at the steel door. No one answered. He weaved in and out of the shrubbery guarding the door until he made it to the front entrance. A stern-faced security guard allowed him into the building. When he made it back to his station, everyone treated his absence as if it happened every night. No one wondered if he had locked himself out during a casual cigarette break, as had been the case with other employees in the past. No one worried if he went outside to vomit. Job breathed a sigh of relief.

Just as the early morning rays began their descent, his shift nearing its end, Job was asked to report to the main office. There, he was soundly reprimanded for his *frequent* negligent naps and undocumented absences. Further, the charge nurse reminded him that his constant appearances in inappropriate attire had not gone unnoticed. To Job's consternation, she produced a document with a series of dates listed. Each offense was outlined in boldface letters. At the top of the list was a familiar date. He stared at the numbers on the page, remembering the night that he had been beaten, kicked, and spat on by boys young enough to be his sons. Boys he could have handled with a belt, had they been his own children.

Drawing her finger to the bottom of the page, she said, "Sign here."

"Sign for what?" he asked. Why all of this fuss? He had been locked out; it happened to his coworkers all the time. In fact, he was usually the person to allow them in.

"Sign here, Job," she said again. "It's a formality."

"But I have done nothing," he said. "I was locked out."

"Job, please," she said, pursing her lips, smiling thinly. "Must you be difficult?"

"What am I signing for?"

"You are signing to acknowledge your compliance with the regulations of your workplace. That is what you are signing for."

"Well, I don't agree," Job said.

"It's not for you to agree. Just your acknowledgment. Any disagreement you have can be made through a formal petition."

Job frowned.

She frowned back.

He stared through the woman's white neck. The cords along her throat wiggled as she ground her teeth and swallowed. Slender ribbons of red mixed in with the muscles and tendons. His hands moved up. His hands gripped the cords of her neck. They squeezed. This is what he imagined of that neck.

"This is your second warning," she said, finally, after he had signed. "Your next offense will warrant immediate suspension without pay and possible termination."

By the time Job arrived at home that morning, his anger was a tight kernel in the pit of his stomach. His mind tumbled through a list of reasons for the assembled crib. *If not Emeka, then Gladys. If not Gladys, then who?* A curl of steam rose from a pot on the stove, an onion-smelling yam pottage. Instead of the scent calming him, it only infuriated him. Emeka and his haughtiness, the nurses on his station, and Captain, an old, imbecile man with nothing left.

Job flung the bedroom door open, finding Ifi curled on her side with a blanket wrapped around her swollen ankles. Dark lumps encircled her eyes. Her braids were clumped against the pillow in a frizzy halo. A ball at her side, the boy's hands gripped the loose tails of her wrapper. Job turned away from the two, finding the domesticity of the scene a distraction from the immediacy of his anger. His eyes met the crib. An ugly, imposing wooden thing, balanced against his back wall, squeezed in the only bit of space available to them. *Does the child even need a crib?* he thought. *I can purchase a bassinet, just as useful, a quarter of the size, at Wal-Mart.* He could purchase a better contraption with his MasterCard.

Rigid lines scored into his forehead, Job nodded silently and stood squarely in front of the crib. *An ugly thing!* Examining the length of the wood, he ran his fingers over each smooth, shiny piece of the frame where the railing met two sturdy pillars along the side. *An ugly thing,* he thought once more. He scoffed at the word Emeka had used to describe it, *antique.* What a silly way of appraising a piece of junk they needed to rid themselves of. He jiggled the handles, pulled the lever, and the rail promptly lowered. A fit of rage overtook him. Then he kicked it in the middle, hard.

Ifi jolted from sleep, indentations from the braids along the sides of her face. She clutched their son to her body, wildness in her eyes. The boy threw his head back and let out a wail, the beginning sound of his furor. But Job wouldn't be deterred. He kicked the crib again, as hard as he could. Ifi shrieked. The boy vomited. Job's foot caught in the bars, but the shiny, dark wood remained unscathed. For a moment, Job dangled precariously at an angle before he untangled his leg and crashed to the floor, howling in rage and pain. At first Ifi gasped, watching Job bellow in rage. Then she laughed.

"Fucky, fuck that, fucker, motherfucker," Job sputtered.

And she laughed harder. His features were a mixture of confusion, surprise, and pain. It seemed, for a second, that he might join in with her laughter. But once more rage surged through him. "Help me up! What are you laughing at? Stupid woman!"

Ifi tried, unsuccessfully, to bite back her laughter. She set the boy down on the bed and helped Job up. "Job, darling, what is the meaning of this?"

"You laugh, but I am the breadman in this household. Other men force their wives to work. Emeka forces his wife to work and kills their child, but me, I leave you here like a queen, and you treat me like a joke."

Regret showed on her face.

"Any man would see what they had done to me and make it an excuse to stay home," he said, pointing to the scars on his face, to the scar on his hand. "But night and day, I work. For you." He turned away. "And him."

"Ndo, I am sorry," she said softly. "What happened? You are not at hospital." Ifi rushed from the room and returned with a plastic bag of ice cubes and set it on Job's thigh.

Avoiding her gaze, he looked out the window before grasping the bag and setting it against his throbbing kneecap. Finally, he turned back to her, speaking quietly and seriously. "Ifi, tell me now, who assembled this crib? It was not Emeka or Gladys as I thought. Who then? Tell me."

At first, Ifi gazed at him strangely. Then relief spread across her face. "The boy," she said, simply.

Anger clouded Job's face. "You think I am an idiot."

"Not our son. The criminal, Jamal. It was him."

"That thief broke into our home? That gangster."

"Job, what is this? The baby. You are waking the boy."

The boy sputtered, spat, and flung his arms every which way. Ifi claimed him in her arms, but he wouldn't relent, struggling to free himself from her grasp. She swung him this way and that until finally she angled her breast into his mouth.

"Under my dead body will that thief ever enter my house again. Do you understand?"

"What is wrong with you?"

"What is wrong with *me*? That boy and his gangster friends nearly killed me and you are asking what is . . . What has happened in your head? Tufia!"

"How can you hate him, eh?" Ifi asked. "He is just a child. You must forgive him." After a moment, she continued in a whisper, "He came with his aunty and begged your forgiveness. He arranged our crib. Is that not enough?"

"You think I am silly? You are the fool. They've done nothing to you, but they will one day. You wait and see."

"Job," she said quietly, patting the boy's back, pushing a cloth across his dripping mouth. "Who took me to hospital? Eh? You don't know?" she implored. "It was that criminal boy. I say, he has begged for your forgiveness, arranged our crib, and taken me to deliver our first son. You must forgive him!"

As the truth of her words sank in, he struggled to cling to what he had previously held as the facts. "You took the taxicab."

"Do you know, if that boy had not come when he did, only to arrange the boy's crib after all, I would not have been able to deliver this boy? Who knows what might have happened? I am, after all, alone in this country."

"I'm here," he started to say, but the words ran from him. "Well, what of Gladys and Emeka?"

Silence. Even the boy, in a strange stupor, vibrated against Ifi's heaving chest. Strange how the stars that had hidden away from Job earlier that night seemed to appear just then. Jagged rooftops cut sharply into the lightening sky, and Job realized that the old houses along his street, each filled with various apartments, were taller than Emeka's house. But none of the houses belonged to Job.

"This thing will go back to Emeka and Gladys tomorrow. I will buy you a new one," he said with finality. "And that boy will never enter my house again, you hear?" Still, even as he said the words, he knew the crib would remain. It would be there, blocking the last ounce of free space in the small room, like a stubborn in-law.

CHAPTER 10

LATER THAT AFTERNOON, WHILE JOB WORKED, WHILE THE BOY SLEPT IN HIS crib, Jamal returned. Except for the hum of the fluorescent lightbulb over the stove, the apartment was still. Grainy particles, split by the permanent crack, floated across the mute television screen. Between rushing back and forth to feed the boy, cleaning the living room, and fixing Job's dinner, Ifi was run ragged.

Her first thought in response to the knocking was that it belonged to Mrs. Janik again. Mrs. Janik had come, twice, to see their son while Job had slept. But each time Ifi had announced herself at the door instead of Job, Mrs. Janik had settled on peering through the crack in the doorway at the boy, who was tied to Ifi's back, where he bobbed with her heaving shoulders, deep in slumber. Mrs. Janik had never recovered from witnessing Ifi speak to Mary and Jamal. Each time, she refused to come in. Ifi refused to come out. So the two merely traded wary glances at one another through the doorway until Mrs. Janik found some excuse to slink away.

This time, Ifi flung the door open in impatience, intending to shout harsh words at the woman—*Do you mean to wake the boy?*—but in Mrs. Janik's place was Jamal. Hands squashed into the pockets of a pair of jeans too large for him, he hunched forward so that his skinny shoulders pushed through a lean sweatshirt that was too small.

Ifi regarded him carefully. "Why bother yourself with knocking when you can simply come and go as you please?" The words that tumbled from her throat surprised her, but Ifi felt, in spite of herself, like she could say anything to this boy, who, after all, was nothing more than a mere child, a tall thirteen or a short fifteen.

"Sorry," Jamal said shyly. "I won't do it again."

"How many times have you broken into this place?"

"Only once," he said. Then he added, "When he first moved in." He nodded toward the back room. "But not since then. And anyway, I didn't take nothing."

"I see," Ifi said. She shouldered the door, and for an apprehensive moment, Jamal remained in the hallway. She glared fiercely until he dropped his eyes.

"Can I see the baby?"

"No."

Jamal nodded. "He don't want me in there, huh? He still don't like me."

"No," Ifi said again, slowly. "*I* don't like you."

His lean shoulders pinched at his ears in a forced shrug.

"He has every right not to like you. You're a troublemaker." And then Ifi launched into a furious lecture, shouting at Jamal, jabbing her fingers into his face. Aunty's intonations and movements swayed her body. Just once, exactly one week before the day Ifi was to be married to Job, she remembered Aunty speaking to her in such a way. Before that, Aunty had assumed that Ifi cherished the opportunity to marry and move to America. It had all been settled by then, that she would be married to the face marred by the flickering kerosene lamp; that she would be married to the Wal-Mart handbag with the gold chain and the jeans and the sweaters; that she would be Mrs. Doctor. That day, Ifi had been turned away from Aunty, beating dough flat with a large wooden rolling pin. Aunty had stood behind her, slicing raw onions, and the juices from the onions left Ifi's eyes watery. Aunty must've thought Ifi was crying, so she furiously spun her around to face her, yelling about everything and nothing at all.

"A boy such as yourself," Ifi said, following the sway of Aunty's large hips, "with many opportunities here in America, and you would rather follow riffraff."

Just then, the baby's furious wail climbed over her voice, but Ifi couldn't stop. "One day you will grow old, and nothing but missed opportunities will await you. You will wish that you had taken every opportunity. If nothing is as you had hoped, at least you will have tried. There is nothing wrong with that now, is there?"

Siren shrieks punctuated Jamal's nods. "You should get that," he said.

Ifi began to speak again but changed her mind and raced to the room. From inside his crib, the boy groaned and screeched, flailing blindly in every direction. Ifi grasped him, hoping her warm body would calm him. But it didn't. Instead, he thrust and kicked in all directions. As she attempted to calm him, she fumed. Jamal joined them. "You see? You woke him, and I spent the whole morning making him sleep. Take him."

Clumsily, Jamal's arms rocked back and forth in attempts to contain the boy's flailing and twisting body. Jamal glared into the boy's face, and the boy snarled and crowed back.

"You think it's so easy?" Ifi asked in satisfaction before reclaiming him. "Go in the other room."

Jamal went. Ifi shut herself in the bathroom, propping a foot against the closed door, just in case. She squatted onto the toilet seat, opened her shirt, undid her wrapper, and nursed the boy until he fell into a fitful sleep punctuated by sudden angry jerks and bends. Ifi placed him back in his crib.

"You shouldn't lay him like that. It'll cause SIDS. I read that." Him again. Jamal arced his lean body just over the crib gate for a good look at the boy. Suddenly, Ifi was reminded of how similar the boy's movements were to her own son's, his back coiling. *One day,* it dawned on her, *my son will grow to the size of this boy.* She couldn't imagine such a time. Remembering the pamphlets she had received at the two Lamaze classes Job had skipped sleep to attend, she warily dismissed the fear that growled in the pit of her chest. "Let him sleep."

After a moment, Jamal pointed to a corner of the room, where a small metal toolbox rested. "That's mine, forgot it." He knelt, picked it up, carefully opened it, and showed Ifi its contents before leading the way into the living room.

From the splintered window, they gazed out at the cold, barren street. How empty it seemed. Outside the sky was gray, and the mashed-up snow was tinged brown from the wet earth. A light freezing rain drizzled.

"What's his name?"

"Victorious . . . Victor."

"Victorious Victor. I like it."

"Only Victor."

The boy stirred again, and Ifi ushered Jamal to the door, suddenly remembering the crib and the split on the television screen, and Job's ineffectual rage. When they made it to the door, Ifi paused. "Who taught you to open doors that way?"

"No one." He paused. "My dad. But he's different now. Found religion. But I won't do it again. I promise. Anyway, I just come with these." He thrust some envelopes to her.

Ifi received the mail, but he didn't leave. "And?"

He handed another letter to Ifi, a letter in her own shaky handwriting. "I found it, when you had the baby." The envelope was open. "I didn't know where it was going."

She remembered her tears that night, the frustration, the anger and loneliness, and her desire to leave right then. She glanced back at the silent bedroom. Looking at the letter, she was alarmed to find that her feelings had changed once she bore her son. He would do everything he could in America. He would go to the best schools. He would make his family proud. He would do all that she could not do. Ifi crumpled the envelope into her pocket.

"Didn't think you'd want to send it," Jamal said.

He was right. After he left, she would tear it into pieces and force it down the garbage disposal. But she did not say this to him. For now, she simply said, "You open letters too."

"It was an accident." His words were snuffed into silence. After a moment: "I won't come back again. Just wanted to see what the baby look like."

"And what do you think? Does he look like his mother or father?" For this was a thought that had puzzled Ifi since the moment the doctor had produced the baby, wiped clear of her fluids. His puckered lips, slanted eyes, large nose, and misshapen head had gazed back into her face in a type of terror.

"No, he don't look like anyone at all," Jamal said.

Honest, Ifi decided. *After all, the boy is honest.*

"He look like a baby," he continued. It was decided. The boy belonged to no one.

Most of the letters were addressed to Job, bills no doubt. But there was one letter in an unmistakable long, pale-blue carrier envelope with a multitude of colorful stamps covering its face. Aunty's tall, looped penmanship filled Ifi's chest with a strangled cry. She tore the letter open and turned away from Jamal, leaving him standing there until he slipped away unnoticed. The letter was dated from almost two months before:

Dear Ifi,

Soon you will be a proud mother. I will come to bless you and the boy in America. Jesus has blessed you in this life. Who would have thought? An orphan with no one, and now you are a doctor's wife.

Tears started down Ifi's face. She looked away. Then she read on.

All my years of sacrifice have paid. You see, Jesus is listening to my prayers. I know that my ways were harsh, but I trained you well to make an obedient wife, an intelligent woman, a suitable doctor's wife.

Please, do not forget us now that you are in America. Your Aunty is not well, and hospital fees are mounting. Uncle is working hard, but you know that there is no money in Nigeria these days. It shames me to ask Mr. and Mrs. Doctor for money, so I will not, but please do not forget your people, who starved to pay for your school fees and train you to be an excellent wife.

The boy began to cry.

Ifi placed the letter on the table and went back to the bedroom. Only after she returned did Ifi notice Jamal's forgotten metal box. Shiny metal hammers, pliers, and screwdrivers with hard plastic handles were neatly fitted into the grooves of the container. Carefully, Ifi ran her fingers over each instrument. Her fingers traced the scarred body of a hammer until they reached the mallet that helped Jamal piece together the crib just days before. Hammer in her hand, she stood before the crib. Job had been so furious. *It would please him,* she realized, *if I were to take this hammer to the crib and finish the task that he started and failed.* But as she stood there, she couldn't bring herself to do it.

Before Job returned from work, Ifi searched for somewhere to hide the metal box. Ultimately, she settled on the location where it had gone unnoticed for so long, behind the crib's back legs. During dinner, she still sighed and fretted, worried that he would find the toolbox, and then he would shout and spit and kick at the crib once more.

Job asked Ifi if something was wrong. She seemed strange. She wasn't humming or singing. The house was silent. She turned on the radio. Carefully, he asked her what she had done all day. She told him she had received a letter from Aunty. Then his words were swallowed into a pit of silence.

After dinner, with the trickling sound of freezing rain outside, they lay on the bed, the sleeping baby between them. Ifi gazed at the boy's face, looking from Job's to the baby's, inspecting for signs of his mother or father, until Job fell asleep. Three hours later, Job woke again for his night shift.

In the morning, Ifi waited for Jamal to return for his toolbox, but he never came. After three days, Ifi surmised that her words might have had an impact on the boy after all. Perhaps he would stop his troublesome ways and go to school. Still, she wondered what to do with the box. Eventually, Job would find it. Eventually, he would ask questions.

That evening, she placed the box outside on the porch, away from their flat, so Jamal could retrieve it on his own. But the next morning, Job returned home from work, lugging the toolbox in with him and wondering where it had come from. Ifi said never mind it. Perhaps it belonged to a neighbor. She told him to put the box back where he found it.

Once he left for work, however, Ifi dragged the box back into the flat, behind the crib. *It could have been stolen,* she thought in alarm, *and then that will be on my head too*—like the limp Job left with each day and night as he headed to work. She should never have allowed the boy in the house, but Ifi couldn't help but gaze at the crib in satisfaction. In spite of Job's attempts to dismantle it, the crib remained sturdy and unharmed.

After so many months together, it was strange how Job's injuries could send them sprawling apart and then bring them closer than they had ever been. Just that morning, Ifi had stopped him in the doorway. Darkness still held daylight at bay, and so it was the glisten of his dark eyes on the light that she had held with her gaze as she pressed a pack of ice to his knee. Under her kneading hands, the lumps stubbornly resisted like the scowl on his face. Still, a small wave of delight had roused through her body. Perhaps their time was finally here.

By midday, the freezing drizzle of the last few days had cleared, and sunshine glared through the parting clouds, reflecting brilliantly against the white snow. This tiny break surely must be a sign. Brightness nearly blinded Ifi, and it occurred to her that in a given day, she spent nearly all of her hours indoors—bent over the sink sponging the boy, before the oven slicing okra, in the bathtub, and peering out the window at the empty streets below. Even as a child, during the rainy season, her chores had allowed her opportunities to go outside—to dodge the blood-red crags between the pebbled streets and, in the dry season, to dust the grains of sand against her feet. *Ah-ah, will winter last forever in America?*

Before setting out for Mary's house, Ifi bundled herself and placed the sleeping boy in his stroller, talking to herself the whole way, telling herself that she was doing the right thing. After all, Jamal had rushed her to the hospital and put the boy's crib together, two things that Job couldn't or wouldn't do. Once outside, Ifi was overcome by the strong scent of cooking meat and pulsing music. Along both sides of the street, secondhand cars were parked nearly on top of one another. Music blasted from a doublewide stereo tailed by a handful of colorful wires dragging up the stairs and in through the bottom of the door. Ifi jerked the stroller up the three steps. She took a deep breath. Before she had a chance to knock, the door swung open and two giggling teenagers charged out, tripping over a cord. A shout rang through the air as someone called to a voice in another room to reconnect the cables. An explosion of rap music that Ifi couldn't follow blared through the halls.

In spite of the wide-open door and the blaring music, Ifi pressed the doorbell. When no one answered, she tried again and again. It would surely be wrong to simply walk in. After a moment, she decided to set the toolbox by the door. Jamal would find it and know she had returned it to him. Just as Ifi turned, she faced the young couple again, lugging a large cooler up the stairs.

The girl: "What you got?"

"This is for Jamal," Ifi said, and immediately the boy and girl reached for the toolbox. Ifi stepped in front of it. "This is for Jamal."

The boy: "He inside."

The girl: "Yeah." And just like that, they tumbled through the doors, scraping the cooler along the melting snow on the porch.

Inside, a rush of scents and sounds, pulsating electricity, charged the air. Where to begin? A crowd of elevated bodies—some leaning, some dancing—swallowed the teenagers whole. Harsh chandelier lights were broken apart by colorful streamers and balloons, and the music raged on. A beet-faced man in a tall chef's hat and apron stalked across the room from the arched kitchen doorway. He made his way to the staircase and disappeared. When he reappeared, the music had changed, a mixture of Teddy Pendergrass, Al Green, and the Supremes. Now the bodies on the scuffed hardwood floor split apart. Scowling teenagers fell to the sides. Older couples replaced the teens' hard, jerkish moves with soft, stirring hips. Ifi couldn't help but smile—until a group of grade-school girls rushed past, nearly knocking her over.

"You get back here." The chef had three of the girls by the backs of their shirts. One escaped. He thrust the two remaining girls at Ifi, and the girls echoed noncommittal apologies before breaking away and sprinting out through the back door. Now the chef scrutinized Ifi. "You one of Mary's people?" he asked.

"Yes." Without thinking, she thrust the toolbox at him. "This is for Jamal," she said. "I've come to return it."

As if he hadn't heard her, he continued, "Mary's around here somewhere, celebrating, dancing it up. You only turn thirty once. Where you from?"

"Nigeria."

"I could tell you wasn't from here. You sure is pretty. That your baby? He'll sleep through anything, huh? Like my nephew, Jamal."

"Jamal?"

"Slept through anything. You should try my barbecue. It's that good, and I don't mean to brag." He talked nonstop, and Ifi was forced to sway one way and the other, avoiding the bodies that soon filled in around them.

Suddenly, a door swung open, and in walked Mary. She had indulged in her celebration a little too much. Her watering eyes slanted under the firm hold of her slicked-back bun. Wandering children, mouths pink with Popsicle juice, were snatched into her clumsy embrace. "You're gonna be bigger than your aunt tomorrow," she said. This was not true. At nearly six feet in height, Mary was the tallest woman in the room, perhaps the tallest person Ifi had ever known. *Why have I never noticed this?* Ifi thought. All those times she had gazed out the window with Mrs. Janik, following Mary's movements, reaching unfounded conclusions about her.

Mary fumbled her way to Ifi, gushing and throwing her into an awkward hug. "Jamal's been out of trouble just like I said, didn't I? He was just messing with the wrong boys. Stupid boys he's too young to hang with anyway."

Ifi nodded. Then she handed the toolbox to Mary. Mary grasped the box, then clumsily dropped it at her side and leaned over the stroller, cooing and ahhing over the boy. "Can sleep through a hailstorm, huh?"

Ifi bobbed her head delicately, gazing at the boy's closed eyes and his vibrating chest. "We must go."

"Come on, you don't want to go yet."

Ifi looked about the room at the swinging bodies. With a heavy heart, she thought, *This is what it is like to be surrounded by your own people.* She imagined her cousins all gathered on the front stoop, swatting away mosquitoes, listening to the sounds of the cracking church megaphones, the clucking chickens and roosters, the vendors in the streets, a sound that swelled with life. She missed them terribly.

"It's my birthday party," Mary said, following her eyes. "Stay awhile longer. Be my guest."

"Happy birthday," Ifi said.

Someone produced a Dixie cup with warm, tasteless beer, and Ifi was so thirsty and self-conscious that she forgot that she was nursing and sipped from the cup until it was gone, then someone placed another cup in her hand. Most of the afternoon was spent tramping from group to group at Mary's side as they laughed loudly at jokes, as they mused about years past, the relatives who were too far away to make it, and the plans for the rest of the week. Each time, the crowds clustered around the stroller, smiling at her son. Ifi pretended that the brown faces surrounding her belonged to her relatives and neighbors in Nigeria.

Strangely, it was as if the boy felt the same. Anytime Ifi peered into the carriage, she expected to see his red, bawling face, but the energy and life of the room filled him with peace. *He must believe he is among family,* Ifi thought.

Eventually, Ifi began to feel the effects of the beer. Before she knew it, she had lost Mary and all sense of time. Although it was too loud with the music playing, a television was on in a back room, surrounded by a collection of balding men and older women shrunken under teased wigs. Ifi felt warm with the life of the room, the generous smiles, the compliments, so much so that when she found an empty place on the couch and said "Good afternoon" to the elders, she was astonished to feel the harshness of their scrutiny—bold, direct glares.

Now is the time to go, Ifi thought. She had officially worn out her welcome. Ifi wheeled the stroller out of the room. But the house was a maze of leaning bodies clutching paper plates and plastic cups. Blurred oversized lips, hips, and feet flung into the darkened hallways. The stroller slipped away from Ifi, clipping toes, jarring the angleless hips. Apologies escaped her lips and drowned into the cacophonous swirl of sounds. Hot and out of breath, Ifi groaned as the boy began to cry, a wild, feverish pitch that was lost in the harshness of the new music. Counter to the music's melody, he jerked and twisted. Sick with the heat and the beer, Ifi limped through airless rooms until she was boldly thrust into the light of a kitchen.

Women in oversized tops, spandex leggings, and wedge heels cluttered the room. One or two babies peered through the fans of their mothers' glossy weaves. Each of the women drank warm red Kool-Aid from Styrofoam cups. Opening the spigot on the cooler, Ifi filled a cup and drained it. Panting, she asked for the toilet. The boy was hungry, and he needed to be fed.

The women sent an assembly of frozen stares her way. Ifi mopped the sweat collecting around her brow and glanced into the stroller in confusion. He was sound asleep.

"You Mary's friend," one of the women said.

"Yes."

"You from Africa?" She flung a baby from one hip to the other. He clutched a strand of her hair in his little fist, and she swatted it free without losing eye contact.

"Yes," Ifi said, "from Nigeria."

"I know someone from Africa." Another, softer in the face, slightly younger. She threw out a strange-sounding name, asked did Ifi know her.

"No, dummy," the first woman said, "Candis is from Jamaica. That's another continent altogether. Read a book."

Thoroughly chastised, the younger girl hung her head. "Sound just like her."

"So how long you been in America?" the first woman asked.

"Five months' time."

"Dang." The younger girl. "So why you come here?"

How to answer such a question? Should she tell her about her plans to be a nurse, to work in her husband's hospital, to raise her boy, to send him to the best schools? Knowing the facts of their present life, it all sounded foolish, like some fairy tale. Ifi searched for a face that would understand. These women would never grasp her world. With the simplest and most complicated response of all, she said, "To join my husband."

"What he do?"

Again, Ifi struggled to answer. His late nights, the evening homecomings strong with the scent of animal on his body. She lied. "He is a doctor."

They've heard enough of me, haven't they? Ifi thought. Now it was her turn to ask a question. But their questions continued, and Ifi realized that they had never meant to converse with her at all. They had only meant to cross-examine her. And if her answers didn't meet their expectations, they would simply prod and force more questions on her. *Why must Americans, even the black Americans, ask after the most intimate details of one's life without shame?* Ifi thought. *Perhaps we are not so alike after all.*

"How you join him here? You met in Africa, right?"

"No, well, yes. We met immediately before we married."

"So wait, you mean like an arranged marriage?" the first woman asked.

"Yes," Ifi said in relief. "We met in Nigeria, married, then I joined him here."

"I don't know how you could do it. I wouldn't let nobody sell me like that."

"Sell? What do you mean sell?" Ifi frowned. They had misunderstood.

"I'm just saying. I'm glad that don't happen here. How can you stand it? Being treated like a man's property? If my man even looks at me the wrong way, I have no problem telling him where to go."

A chorus of agreement followed, women tripping over one another's voices to add their horror and disgust at such an arrangement.

A boy entered the kitchen, headed straight to the fridge, and rifled through it until he found a bottle of mustard.

"I just couldn't. In America, people are free. American women wouldn't stand for that mess."

"I am no man's property," Ifi said in anger. "I have come from my own free will."

"I mean, I guess I don't blame you. It's a better life here, right?"

Again, Ifi was stunned. "What do you mean 'better life'?"

"You get to live in a house and everything. You get to wear clothes."

"We live in houses in *Africa*," Ifi said, imitating the woman's voice. She slammed the half-drunk cup of Kool-Aid on the countertop. It rose to the top and left a pink ring on the counter.

Ifi pushed the stroller past the group into an empty hallway, fuming. Job had warned her not to trust them. He was right. It was time to go home.

"They don't mean nothing." The voice belonged to Jamal. He met her eyes, grinning. His eyes pulled and flattened in the same slant as Mary's. "You probably the first African they ever talk to."

"Where is Mary?" Ifi asked.

"Somewhere," he said with a roll of his eyes, "probably bossing someone around." He smiled. "She my aunty, but she think she my mama."

"Oh?"

"Since my dad went away, feels like she has to make up for everything."

For the first time in a long time, Ifi spoke of her own mother. "My aunty raised me too," she said. "My mother died. My father died. I was too young." Ifi paused. Except for a faded wedding photo, she did not know her mother's looks. In her mind, her mother had taken Aunty's shape and Aunty's voice. Thinking of the two women, she felt pain and quickly diverted the conversation. "Your aunty sounds like my aunty."

"That letter, was that your aunty in Africa?"

"Yes."

Ifi remembered the letter with her shaky penmanship, the tears. She spoke sharply. "You want to know what made me cry that day?"

"None of my business," Jamal said with a shrug. "Just wanted to know where the letter with all them stamps come from."

"But you can see where it comes from right on the envelope."

"Yeah."

"So then you are asking me a question you already know the answer to."

"I guess."

"Is that not silly of you?"

"I guess."

"So, tell me, boy, what is it that you want to know?" When he didn't answer, she continued. "You want to know what was in the letter that made me cry that day. Well, I will tell you. Nothing at all. Nothing."

Jamal was silent. He wiggled his toes in shoes that were too large for his feet.

"I brought your box to Mary."

"Okay."

"So you have no reason to come back to my home."

"I didn't mean no trouble."

"You will not break in anymore or knock on my door to impress your friends."

"No," he said, "it wasn't them. They don't know nothing about it."

"Then to steal from me?"

"No, you don't have nothing I need." His voice was sharp. "Just forget it." Jamal turned to walk away.

"Wait, wait," Ifi said. Perhaps she had been too harsh. Anyway, she was alone, and suddenly the walls in the house felt too large, the music too loud, the voices too jeering. Simply put, she needed a friend. "Please. Don't leave. I don't know what I'm saying. I'm just angry with these women. And tired." *And drunk,* she admitted to herself. "No one can make me do anything I don't want to do," she said indignantly, thinking again of the women in the kitchen. "I am here, after all. Even *he* could not stop me," she said of Job. She peered down at the stroller, at the sleeping baby.

"So why you come to America, then, if nobody made you come, like they say?"

Ifi knew he was referring to the letter in her own shaky hand. "First, you tell me why *you* came in my home and fixed the crib."

Jamal paused, looked around. He smiled his soft smile. "My daddy. He told me to. My aunty told him about the trouble with your husband—always in somebody's business—so he said, 'Make it right.' So I come to your house to say sorry with my aunty. She thinks it was cause of her, but it wasn't. I did it 'cause I know my daddy wanted me to. Then I come to fix your crib. Then I come to see what the baby look like. And that's all. That's the whole story. Now, you tell me why you come to America if nobody made you. I never been anywhere but here my whole life."

"How old are you?"

"Almost fourteen."

"Then you're only a boy," Ifi said. "You have time."

"You think so? Hope so. I hate it here. I hate the way it smells. I hate the busted cars. I hate the trains at night. I hate the white people staring at me all the time. Don't know why anyone would want to come here."

Ifi was amused. She grinned. "Have you not heard of the American Dream?"

A loud crack, perhaps lightning, like a revolver's report. The music halted, and Ifi heard the sounds of confused voices shouting at one another. Jamal ducked around the hallway and turned back to her, groaning. "It's the police."

Two stalwart officers in snug-fitting uniforms balanced in the doorway, their hands clutched at their waists. They were speaking to the chef, who made animated gestures with his hands. His words climbed atop one another. His gesturing arms grew bigger and bigger. He was drunk, and Ifi knew immediately that it would go badly. *Someone will die tonight,* she thought in fear. Mary came up behind the chef. She accused the officers of looking for trouble, and the officers accused her of being drunk. Neither side was willing to admit guilt. And the whole time they were yelling at one another, and the sounds were getting louder, and they were moving farther away from the opening of the doorway and into the interior of the room.

Another crack, and the officer's baton crunched over the chef's head a second time.

The chef crumpled to his knees in front of them. "Now why'd you have to do that?" he asked. Then he was out.

Seconds passed in silence as the blackened beads of each eye shined on the officers in horror. An elder dragged her cane into the room, scratching the scuffed hardwood floor, one of the severe-looking old women from the TV room. When she was just inches from the officer's face, she lifted the cane and dropped it on his head. It thudded loudly against the carton thing that was his hat. Everyone laughed at the officer, an eruption of cheers and jeers. He bent to retrieve his cap. The music began again, pulsing, indignant. And the baby joined in with the crowd, wailing, shouting, hollering his protest.

"Turn that off!" one of the officers shouted. If they hadn't heard him, he made sure, clapping a pair of handcuffs on the old woman first, then the chef.

Everyone howled and shouted at the officers as they backed out of the room with the two captives. The officers shouted for no one to leave. They wanted to know the owners of the disorderly house. They said everyone would be cited. They were calling backup. By then the crowd had begun to thin, forgetting their protests. And the baby was spitting and shrieking, clawing the air.

"There's a back door." Jamal took Ifi's shaking hand and led her through a series of hallways and down a bank of stairs until she was facing a short door at the top of a steep set of stairs. Ifi pressed the boy to her chest and climbed the stairs. Jamal carried the stroller up after them. At the top, he dropped the stroller at her feet. Then he took off at a full sprint in the other direction. So red and angry, the baby's breath came in furious gulps.

Dusk was just beginning to settle. Ifi pushed the stroller up the backside of the street; she was surprised by how it appeared from a different angle. A graveled alleyway, barking dogs, and giant rusted dumpsters lined the street. Lights were on in each of the old apartment buildings. Screened doors swung open. Faces pressed into windows, taking in the shouts of the old woman as the officer dragged her to his cruiser.

"Arrest me, officer," she shouted. "I did it in the fifties. I did it in the sixties. I got a record. I'm trouble. Arrest me, officer."

Ifi knelt to the baby. "Biko," please, she said. "Stop this crying." She lifted him out of the carriage, but he only raged on. Ifi placed him back in the stroller. A shake rose through her, and she vomited in the snow. Spit foamed at her mouth.

As she pushed the stroller in a jagged line, Ifi's hands trembled uncontrollably—until someone came from behind and pushed the stroller away from her. An officer or criminal were one and the same to her in the encroaching night. Ifi spun and punched with all her might at the darkened figure, until she heard Job's quivering voice speaking to her in Igbo. Never in her life had she felt so much relief to see her dear husband. Never in her life had she felt so protected. As he pushed the stroller toward their apartment, she followed, and the words finally began to come.

"They took her," Ifi said. "They took the old lady. An old lady. A lady old enough to be your grandmother, sef. What kind of man arrests an old lady? Take the young boy instead. Not the old lady." *In America, what happens to people who are jailed?* she wondered. "Why did they speak to police like that? Why did they not listen? What is wrong?" She struggled for a way to justify what she had just witnessed, but the questions choked her. *Jamal, where is he now? Where has the boy gone?* All the good things he'd done would mean nothing if he was arrested. He would find himself in prison with his father when the police caught up with him.

As they crossed from the back of the street to the front face of their building, a pool of cruiser lights swirled in the street. A siren wailed. In the darkness, shadows flickered in and out of the headlights as figures dashed through the street. A light shined on Ifi and Job's faces, an officer.

Job smiled and bowed up and down, deeply, so low that his shirttail untucked and his naked backside bore witness to the cold. In choppy, broken English, he spoke like a man whose mouth was unfamiliar with English sounds, though he had been speaking English his entire life. "Me so-rry, Off-ee-sar."

What is he doing? Ifi thought. *Why doesn't he claim to be a doctor?*

To her astonishment, the officer nodded them away and stopped another black couple who had been watching the commotion. He yelled at them to go into their house with such ferocity that Ifi stumbled back in alarm. He even threatened to arrest the couple. And then it made sense to Ifi. She suddenly felt stunned at how well Job's performance had worked. In a matter of seconds, they had gone from being two menacing black faces to helpless, and moreover invisible, foreigners.

When they arrived at the apartment, Job carried the stroller, with the boy in it, up the stairs to their flat. Lights filled the room. Mrs. Janik peered at Ifi from her position on their living room couch. When she saw Ifi, her expectant eyes hardened. She started to speak, saying, "I warned her. I tried to warn her," but Job cut her off. "Thank you, thank you, Mrs. Janik. Thank you so much for your help. What would we do without good people like you?"

"Was nothing at all," she said. "Just being good people. That's all. I come from good stock. Like you." She nodded furiously at Job. All the while, he ushered her out the door.

Suddenly, one hand on either side of her body, Job shoved Ifi onto the couch into a sitting position, pinning her there. Only after he realized that it was not her body that was struggling and thrashing to free itself but his own trembling body pushing her one way and the other with force did he finally free her. He took the crying baby. He held his son to his chest, hoping that his own rapid heartbeat would calm the boy. It didn't.

His eyes rested on the frizzing plaits on Ifi's head, the unrepentant eyes, the shadows that whispered just about her eyes. This was not the shy girl he had met one evening in a darkened living room, the girl who was praised for her cooking, her quiet ways, her obedience. Again, it occurred to Job that he knew little about his own wife, little more than he knew about her those months ago when she arrived with her belongings, little more than he knew of her when he met her on the day of their arranged honeymoon. "Who are you?" he asked.

She was no mother. *What kind of mother?* he thought, could drag her only son into harm's way, could drink alcohol with strangers while her exhausted son fought for sleep. *I cannot leave my first son with such a mother,* Job decided. *I will take this boy somewhere else. No,* he thought. "I will send you back," he said aloud. Since he did not know anyone in America, he would take his son to Nigeria, to his mother, to his sisters. They would gladly raise his child properly. After all, in Nigeria it was customary for the child to follow the father during a divorce.

Ifi wept. *What of it?* he thought. *Your crocodile tears mean nothing to me. You have made your bed!*

Now the baby was howling and hiccupping with such vigor that his whole body erupted. Job rocked him slowly, shushing him. As the cries intensified, he rocked him harder. Ifi gripped his wrists. She was so close again that he could smell the alcohol on her breath. He did not know how to make the boy's wailing stop. She pried the boy from his hands. As she wept, she released her bra from her shirt and pushed her throbbing breast into his mouth. There was nothing Job could do but watch and wait. Both knew the boy would fall into a fitful stupor, drunk from the taste of her milk.

CHAPTER 11

THAT NIGHT, CAPTAIN PASSED AWAY. ONE MOMENT, JOB STOOD OVER Captain's slack limbs, wiping as his words came out in a rush of trembling accusations—"How can she be so careless? What kind of mother is she? Does she not see the danger of America? Does she not understand the trouble of akatta? Already, America has spoiled her!"—and the next moment, Job had his back turned to Captain as he emptied his bedpan. When he faced the old man again, the fragile light was gone from his eyes. Thirty minutes later the coroner arrived, and Captain's stiffened body was carried away on a stretcher.

Forms on state-issued letterhead acknowledged the time of death and the actions just before and after. For the rest of the night, Job briskly moved from room to room answering lights, rationalizing the events that had just passed: *Patients come and go,* he told himself. *Nothing has changed.* This was just his work, a temporary situation. Of course it was time for the old man to cross to the other place. After all, months ago his mind had already gone. Not only that, but the old man had nothing left inside him. Nothing at all. He was nothing more than a mere shell emptied of its contents.

Later that night, Captain's belongings—his letters all addressed to his imaginary son, his photographs, his clothes—were neatly fitted into four cardboard boxes and placed in storage for his family to collect. His bed was stripped of its sheets, his room sterilized, his chart removed.

By the next night, another patient occupied Captain's bed, a wide-eyed, elderly lady with a constant look of having been startled awake after a long night of dreaming. Job avoided the room. Each time her light came on, he found one task or another to divert his attention. At the end of his shift, he stepped outside into a retreating night, stippled by attacking strips of light.

Days later, Job, on the way to his car at the end of a shift, bumped into a middle-aged woman struggling at the door with a collection of cardboard boxes. She gladly accepted his offer of assistance. As he lifted one of the boxes from her hands, he identified it immediately as one of Captain's. Only then did he recognize the sandy-haired woman as one of the faces in the photographs dotting his nightstand and window ledge. *What was he like as a young man?* Job wanted to ask. Instead, he said, "I knew your father. He was one of my patients."

"Oh yeah?" she asked.

"I was his doctor."

"Oh." She looked grateful, so Job continued.

"He spoke of you often."

"Did he?"

"Every day."

"Really? I thought it took his mind," she said, twirling her finger at her head. "He never seemed to remember me when I called."

Finding a towheaded little boy waiting in the car, Job stumbled in awe. This was Captain's imaginary son. "No, no, he spoke of you often. Dementia," Job said, remembering Captain's chart, "it never completely melts the brain. If you have made a strong impression, the marks will leave a space in his brain, and his memory response will find a place for it, like a repository." Again, Job said, "He talked about you. He wrote you letters."

"Really?" She glanced at the box of letters she would soon find addressed to her son instead of her. She gazed out over the tops of the cars at the receding night. "Then I should've come more. I thought, well, it didn't seem to matter if he wasn't going to remember me anyway."

No, Job wanted to say. *He didn't remember you, but he could feel your absence in his aloneness. You are a bad child. You pushed him to his grave. In Nigeria,* he said to himself, *the old never forget the young, and the young never forget the old. Family is the most important bond.* Job placed each box in the trunk of the car. Then he waited and watched as the car pulled away.

A few days later, as Ifi, with a wooden spoon, pounded fufu on the heated stovetop, Job glanced at her, turning away from the blurry news on the television. "I've sent money to Aunty so that she can come look at the boy."

Nothing unusual about that. After all, it was custom for a female representative of the family, preferably an elder, to visit the family after the birth of the first child, to teach the new mother and to ease her into motherhood. Still, the real purpose was undeniable, a purpose they both refused to openly acknowledge. Since the night Job had pinned Ifi to the couch, the smell of beer on her breath, they had not spoken. Instead, they resumed their daily tasks. Ifi turned the pot, changed the boy's soiled diapers, and listened to the radio. Job rushed from one workplace to the next, rinsing his grimy body after each arrival before falling into the deep well of sleep.

Because Ifi did not work, and because of the sudden expenses the little boy had incurred, they really couldn't afford to invite Aunty for a visit. Nonetheless, she would come. She would be with Ifi throughout the day so that she would never have the opportunity to mingle with troublemakers. Between the meatpacking plant and the hospital, Job was already working the first and third shifts. Still, he refused to touch his father's tuition money. *If I cannot go to medical school, my son will,* he told himself. To make up the money for the travel expenses, Job picked up extra weekend shifts at the hospital on his days off and applied for three credit cards before one was finally approved.

At first it was exciting, the thought of someone familiar entering Ifi's new life in America. After Job left for work one afternoon, with the boy resting on one arm, Ifi sat down to compose a letter to Aunty. In excitement, she began by describing the boy's ways. He constantly cried. Always hungry and furious, he balled his small fingers into fists and blindly scratched and clawed at her until she fed him. Nevertheless, in the letter Ifi wrote, *Your boy is strong, Aunty. His name, Victor Ezeaku Ogbonnaya, the victorious king, is fitting.*

Then she remembered her first letters to Aunty on her arrival to the States—the wide, expansive rooms she had described, the brand-new furnishings, the curtained windows. A look around, and Ifi was suddenly reminded of the peeling walls, the holes, the taped-over windows, the old suitcases and boxes lined against walls instead of dressers filled with clothes. Shuddering in shame, it suddenly dawned on her that she couldn't possibly bring Aunty to this place. *What will she say?* Ifi thought with a tremble.

As she washed the dishes one night, Ifi called to Job, "Where will Aunty sleep?" Since the night of Mary's party, it was the first time they had exchanged more than a few cursory words to one another. With only one bedroom between the two of them, crowded by the boy's crib, the question had merit. Without saying so, the meaning was immediately clear to both of them: they needed to find another place.

Job said nothing.

Some husbands struck their wives with regularity, but Job had never been such a man. In fact, the day of Mary's party had been the first time he had ever laid a hand on Ifi, and even then, he had only pushed her to the couch and held her there. When she spoke of topics that displeased him, Job simply reacted as if the words had never been said. Ifi found herself believing that her husband's silence was a worse offense than receiving a blow from him. At least a blow would signify that he even acknowledged her. Today his silence would not be enough. With the sink running, she strode into the living room and stood before him, a plea in her voice. Her wet hands left a print at the waist of her wrapper as she demanded once more, "Where will Aunty put her head?"

Job didn't look up to meet her eyes. Instead, he thought of the time he had spent painting walls, taping over cracked windows, and patching holes before Ifi's arrival. He had even purchased a bed with a frame and a headboard. Before that, he had been comfortable enough on a simple mattress pressed into the floor. All in the hopes that his humble home would meet her needs. Nevertheless, he unwillingly admitted to himself that she was right. *What will the woman think?* he thought. His in-law had not been an easy woman. During the marriage negotiations, the first item on Ifi's bride price had been indoor plumbing for her aunty's home. That had been six months' worth of double-shifts. More importantly, he knew of his in-law's mouth. *What will she say to her neighbors and friends when she returns to Nigeria?* Job thought to himself. *After all, I am still Mr. Doctor.*

In the time that passed before Aunty's papers were in order, Ifi and Job spent countless hours patrolling the streets of neighboring towns in search of a new dwelling. The neighborhoods were inevitably the same: peeling siding, scratched paint, cracked walkways. Many canines howled on street corners, and women with chipped toenails in flip-flops answered the doors of the duplexes, townhouses, and multiplexes, their faces turned away in mock confusion.

"You must have the wrong house," one would say.

Another might explain, "Well now it's occupied."

And yet another, "Someone's looking at it today, but if you give me your number, I'll call you later."

One landlord even inquired up front if they were employed, if they were illegal. In defeat, they returned to their apartment, its stained walls, browning carpet, faded linoleum, and creaking floors.

With only a week remaining until Aunty's arrival, on the way home from work, Job noticed an apartment on the neighboring street. For months it had been unoccupied, with a faded red *For Rent* sign plastered in its window. It was a tall, sturdy brick building backed against a chain-link fence that wound down the street. There was no yard. Instead, like in Nigeria, a concrete walkway surrounded the building. From the outside, the building was taller and wider than the one Job and Ifi lived in, and he imagined that the rooms were larger, more expansive. Tentatively, he telephoned the landlord.

In spite of his accented English, the landlord arranged to meet with them immediately. The next afternoon, Job, Ifi, and the boy arrived. A balding white man, wiry, with the look of a spider, answered the door. His bent legs moved through the apartment, pointing out the two graying bedrooms and the single bathroom while avoiding the holes in the walls and the rusted piping. Job and Ifi shared an eager glance. While the apartment was not ideal, it was an improvement. Without a word exchanged between the two, it was decided: they would rent the apartment.

The landlord was indifferent but not unpleasant. He curtly discussed tenant and landlord responsibilities. He explained the cost for rent, the preferred payment method, and the length of the lease. Job filled out the form. As a formality, he also filled out a release to review his credit history. Before they left, the landlord shook hands with Job and said, "Welcome to your new abode."

At the landlord's call the next morning, Ifi shrugged Job awake and eagerly handed him the phone. Minutes later, the phone call ended with Job slamming the phone into its cradle.

"What is wrong?" Ifi asked.

Job smiled, nodded, and told her, "Everything is okie," though the deep recesses in his forehead told her that something had gone terribly wrong.

❖

The Somalis were praying. Job slipped out among them, finding his way to a payphone just outside their prayer room in the meatpacking plant. No longer could he wait. A blinking fluorescent light was the only sign of movement left in the hallway. The phone was beat up and smelled foul. He put his change in twice before he heard a dial tone. His hands shaking, he placed the call. Listening to the ring, he anxiously coiled and uncoiled the telephone cord around his palm.

In a low, raspy whisper, Cheryl answered on the fifth ring. "Hello?"

Anger rose like bile in his throat. "What have you done to me?"

"What?"

"You have ruined me. They will not allow me to rent in this city."

"Job?"

"Yes," he said.

A pause. Then, "Job, I'm sorry. It just happened. I fell behind. I tried. Just couldn't make it. I sold everything I own. Now it's just me and that empty house, and they're going to take it away."

"You are lying to me. As God is my witness, you are lying to me. What of the money I sent you last?"

"It wasn't enough. You fall behind once and the late fees. They get you."

"What about me? I did nothing. What about me? Now they will not rent to me in this town. You have crooked me again."

"No, that's not fair. I've been good on our deal. Besides, we were still married when this started. I was within my rights. Married couples share everything."

"You were never my wife. That was," he looked for the right word, "an arrangement."

Another pause. "Look, I'm sorry. I can't ask you for more money now, so I won't, but if this house forecloses, it'll be a stain on both our records. We won't be able to rent or buy another property for the rest of our lives."

"You use me and lie to me again!"

"Job, my daddy built that house for my mother." Her voice trailed off.

"You lied and used me."

"You used me too. And you lied too," she said. "You're a citizen because of me. You brought your pretty wife to this country because of me. You can practice medicine legally in this country because of me. I think that makes us even."

He pushed the phone so close to his mouth that his lips wet the mouthpiece with each word. A muscle on his jaw was so tight that it twitched with the effort. "I did nothing wrong. You stole my identity. I cannot even rent an apartment in this America because of you." Job had been in America long enough to know the single threat that Americans issued with the most vigor. "I will take you to court!"

She only sighed. "You and everyone else."

The Somalis were pouring out of the prayer room in a single-file line. "That is it?" Job asked.

"Look, I'm sorry, Job. I mean it."

"That is all you have for me?"

"I feel bad," she said. "Just let me see what I can do, and I'll get back to you."

Before Job could say another word, she hung up. The dial tone followed. Job shuddered and pulled the phone to his chest. His body quaked. *I will call police,* he thought. *I will tell them about this crook!* He would tell them all about Cheryl's scheme, how she had used his name for money and then refused to pay it, how she did this all without his consent. Married or not, surely this was illegal.

A voice answered immediately when he dialed the police, a thin American voice, dull and bored. *How will I explain the marriage and the divorce?* Job wondered. *What will these people say?* Again, he was reminded of the horror at the police station on the night of the attack. They would fingerprint him again and photograph his face. They would order him to strip this time and search his body before finally deporting him. Their excuse would be that he sold drugs, and that he stole from law-abiding Americans.

Job let the phone fall from his hand, the voice asking, "Yello?"

Blending in among them, he joined the march of Somalis, his shoulders tucked, his eyes low, as they returned from their prayer break. Listening to their joyful, energized voices as they reentered the main breezeway, Job stopped to scrub his hands and snap his hat and gloves into place before resuming his position on the line.

Throughout the remainder of his shift, he struggled to stay focused, but his mind wandered. Regardless of what happened, there still remained the apartment. Perhaps if he called and explained the situation, explained that he had been crooked by a way-o American, the man would understand. But Job recalled the indifference in the man's tone. Deep inside, Job knew that whatever he said would not matter. *What will I say to Ifi?* he thought to himself. *How can I tell her that we have lost it? What will my in-law say when she visits? What will she say to my family when she has returned to Nigeria?* Again, his mind returned to Cheryl. Everything bristled inside. She needed to make things right. He would have to find a way for her to do so, even if it meant that he must plead with her.

Once his shift ended, Job dialed Cheryl again. Two other men stood in line behind him, so he huddled with his back to them, covering the mouthpiece. Before she had an opportunity to speak, he said the first words. "You are an American. Talk to him."

"Job?"

"Talk to him," he said again. "Explain to him."

"Who?"

"Talk to the landlord. My in-law will be here in one week's time. Explain the misunderstanding. I work hard to pay my bills. Tell the man that it is your debt so he can rent me the apartment."

"Right, Job, I'll walk right in the door and say, 'Hello, excuse me, sir. My ex-husband that I married illegally for papers twenty years ago wants you to forgive our debt so he can rent your apartment.'"

"I work hard," he said.

"Say what, Job? Say what?"

"Talk to him like an American, I beg of you."

"Like an American. What does that mean? *You* talk to him like an American. You're an American too. Because of me. I made you an American."

"Hurry up, man," one of the men behind him growled.

All Job could think of was standing in the examining room at the police station as they peeled off his clothes. All he could see was the police officer's flashlight the night of the party. All he could remember was forcing a crooked smile and speaking broken English. All of this in spite of his education, his family name, and his success. A man from Job's background stood stinking of pig in line with an illiterate Mexican and a famished Somali. "I am *not* an American," Job said with ferocity. "I was born an Igbo and I will die an Igbo, no matter where I am, you hear me?"

"Fine. You're an Igbo."

"You can take your stinking papers back. Just call the man. Tell him what you must."

"Don't talk to me like that," Cheryl said. "I'm not your slave."

"Slave? What slave?"

"Wasn't for me, you'da been deported twenty years ago, so don't you talk to me like that." All that was left of Cheryl was the dial tone.

Still, later that night, as Job readied for his shift at the hospital, the phone rang. With the shrieking baby slung on her back, Ifi brought the phone to him. Surprise filled her face. It was the landlord. Again. Job dragged the phone into the bathroom.

"Hello?"

"Is this Job Og-ban-ooya?" the landlord's voice croaked.

Job stopped himself from correcting the man. "Yes," he said, feeling a twinge of excitement. "Yes, I am him."

"Well, Job, got a call from a lady says she's your current landlord. Says you're honest and good and dependable, and there's a mistake with your credit report."

"I work hard," Job said.

"As it were, the place is rented. I got one more property left in that building, though. It's a one bedroom, and I'd be willing to rent that to you."

"No, no," Job said. "I need two bedrooms."

The man's voice shrugged in nonchalance as he said good-bye.

This is what he told Cheryl the next morning after his shift at the hospital, to which Cheryl replied that she had a plan. "Job, I've been thinking," she said. "I'm going to lose my daddy's house, and you need one. Both of our names are on the title. Isn't there something we can do to help each other?"

"Yes?"

"I can't talk now, but let's meet somewhere."

"No, now. Talk now. I am here. You want money? I am Mr. Moneybags, eh? Say what you have to say."

"Job, this isn't a matter that can be discussed over the phone. But I will say this: I will do anything to save this house, and you need one. It only makes sense for us to talk."

Job suddenly understood. "When?"

"Tonight."

"No, I am going to work."

"Well, we have to talk soon. There isn't much time. There's a diner around the corner from where I live. Let's meet there." She gave him the address.

"Fine," he said tiredly.

"Sunday."

"My in-law will come."

"Well, Job, it's the best I can do."

Again, Job marveled at this American woman. He was brought back to the day twenty years earlier when he had arrived with the money and the papers. He had entered into an agreement with her. She took his money and his name. He became an American citizen. *Can I trust her?* he wondered. She did speak to the landlord on his behalf, even if it was too late. *Should I consort with riffraff once more?* Emeka would know what to do. Perhaps Job should speak to him. Job paused at the phone only to be reminded of Emeka, back pressed to the snow outside of his house with Job's money raining around him. Job couldn't swallow any more of his boasts. Still, in spite of his doubts, Job determined that Emeka would have the proper response. After all, he had been in America far longer than Job, and he had known many more Americans than him. Sullenly, Job agreed. "Sunday."

CHAPTER 12

O N THE DAY OF AUNTY'S ARRIVAL, IFI BURNED A CLUMP OF HER HAIR OFF while relaxing it over the kitchen sink. The boy was to blame—howling, crying, frothing at the mouth until she placed the plastic container of pinkish paste and the wooden stick aside to hold him. She rubbed Vaseline on the burn. Stinking of sulfur, Ifi made her way to the thrift store and reluctantly purchased a wig. The boy, in his stroller, cried the whole way there. Her scalp and neck itched where the wig touched them. The store clerk, an older white woman whose hair was a little too dark to be her own, stood behind Ifi, the woman's large spectacled eyes peering at the mirrored reflection. Ifi gave the wig a jerk in one direction, adjusting it so the dark curls fell around her face giving her just a hint of bangs, resting the part to the side. "No, dear, like this," the store clerk said, tugging the wig in the other direction.

Aunty arrived later that afternoon, fitted like a sausage into a colorful dress of bright prints, her lips thickly coated in red lipstick. Her hair was draped in layers of cloth matching her dress's print. Suitcases surrounded Aunty. Somewhere among the suitcases, Job clutched a stinking paper sack with the foodstuffs she had managed to finesse through customs.

Before they embraced, Aunty took a long look at Ifi. One plump finger darted out and tugged Ifi's wig hard in the other direction, the direction Ifi had her wig in to begin with.

Aunty ambled through the narrow entryway, her neck craned, her eyes upturned. Ifi waited expectantly, but Aunty said nothing of the creaking floors, the holes in the walls. A cockroach boldly marched into the entryway and nodded his greeting to her, but Aunty only widened her step. When Ifi had the chance, she squished the roach under the heel of her foot.

In shame, she could only think of the hours she had spent at Aunty's home in Port Harcourt, sweeping the sand and scrubbing the rust buildup along the walkway where the water discharged during the rainy season. Many times, Aunty would purse her lips and send Ifi back a second, sometimes a third time because she had tracked the grainy pebbles in on the bottoms of her feet. "You have not finished," she would say, pointing a red, lacquered fingernail at Ifi's small, red footprints on the tile floors. Yet here, now, Aunty said nothing at all.

It was a given that Aunty would visit for several months, but because Job worked the night shift at the hospital, they decided to give Aunty the bedroom and sleep on the living room couch in shifts; nonetheless, when Aunty heard of this, she was insulted. "American girl, Mrs. Doctor, are you so big that you cannot share a bed with your da?" she asked. "Your da that wiped nshi from your ass?" This was untrue. In fact it was Ifi, at eleven, wiping the bottoms of Aunty's new babies when each was born.

Eventually, they must attend to the real business. Ifi cringed and braced. Job leaned heavily against the kitchen wall. They were waiting, waiting for the eyes to burst, waiting for the mouth to rip, for the saliva, mucous, and breast milk to spray, waiting for invisible fingernails to scratch furiously. Ifi's breasts and arms were lined with scars from the boy's outrages. Although she attempted, frequently, to clip his fingernails when he was asleep, he had won nearly every fight. For now, Ifi prayed as fervently as she ever had for the boy not to disgrace her.

Forcefully, Aunty unraveled the boy from Ifi's back, where he was secured by her wrapper. For once, the boy's eyes were creased shut. At a plump four months, his cheeks were puffed out in sleep. She scraped her fingernails over the rectangular bald patch on the back of his head.

"He is sleeping, Aunty," Ifi said.

Aunty swatted Ifi's hands away and roughly bounced him back and forth. His eyes were still closed. "What is wrong with this boy?" Aunty asked. She turned him around and smacked his back hard, as if freeing food from his chest.

"Aunty," Job said, "let me help you."

"He has taken your hair, oh." Aunty jerked at a tuft of the boy's hair. "Don't worry. In America, his hair will improve."

Ifi's fingers slid up to the smarting bald spot under her wig.

Aunty jerked his toes. Still the boy slept. Ifi and Job exchanged a glance and finally began to step back. Suddenly, the volcano erupted. Fluids spewed from his crimson face directly onto Aunty's dress. He flung his head, arched his back, scratched furiously. Aunty nearly dropped him. "Chineke!" she hollered.

Ifi and Job simultaneously stepped forward, arms out. Still holding the boy, Aunty turned away. He twisted from her. The button holding his onesie together unsnapped, and his diaper fell away, swollen with urine. His flabby brown thighs were prickled. In all the chaos, Aunty couldn't help but to pull him back a few inches to inspect his naked lower half. "Ehe!" she said in triumph.

Just like that, the boy let a full-bodied arc of urine spray her.

"*A-ah!* What is this?" Aunty said, but she continued to shield the boy from Ifi and Job. "Bring me a bottle," she said. "Have you not fed this boy today?"

"Aunty, he is tired," Ifi explained.

"Bring me a bottle," Aunty said again.

"He will be like this until he sleeps," Ifi said.

Job was caught between wife and in-law.

He reluctantly heated a bottle of milk for the boy under the running tap. Aunty complained that the bottle wasn't warm enough, but took it anyway. "You see?" she said. "You see why the boy cries."

For his act of betrayal, Ifi refused to look at Job the remainder of the day. She wanted nothing more than to announce to Aunty that Job was not really a doctor. Because of this, he was onye ohi, a thief, a crook. He had lied to her, to everyone, and he continued to lie to his own family. Their very marriage, arranged so meticulously by Aunty, was a sham. But to share this with Aunty would ruin the visit and infuriate her. In her anger, Aunty would shout Job's failures through the streets.

To the boy, who relaxed into calm when the bottle was in his mouth, Ifi was cold. Later that day, he clawed for her breasts, but she refused, still smarting with rage at the alliance the small boy had already formed with his great aunt. Ifi only relented when Aunty suggested that if she placed her own ample, yet milkless breast in the boy's mouth, he would be calmed.

The next day, Aunty and Ifi stood barefoot on the cold kitchen tiles, leaning over the sink, the wig flung on the counter, as Aunty clipped away at Ifi's hair. "American women do not know anything of hair," Aunty said. "Mrs. Doctor marries a big man and forgets her Igbo ways."

Ifi bit back tears. *Why am I crying?* She thought of the difficulty of relaxing her hair once every two months on her own, the hassle of sleeping on curlers each night, her achy muscles after attempting to part straight braids on the back of her head with only the aid of a broken hand mirror.

When the task was finished, Ifi's hair was cropped so close that in some places she could feel her scalp. The site of the offending burn was an accusatory scaly patch of pink that flaked until Aunty spread a dollop of petroleum jelly over it. Ifi's eyes were full moons. Her ears stuck out from the sides of her head like they had when she was just a girl. Aunty folded one of Ifi's ears in her fingers. The two laughed. This was how Ifi wanted to remember herself, before the baby, before Job, before America.

When she washed off the bits of hair from her neck and shoulders, she felt, in spite of herself, as if a weight had been lifted. She enjoyed the pleasure of the warm water running over her scalp in the shower. It reminded her of the kerosene-heated baths of her childhood. Since the night before her honeymoon, when Aunty had relaxed Ifi's hair for the first time, Ifi had never washed without a shower cap. She had been relegated to the kitchen sink, pushing her relaxed hair as far under the tap as she could manage. After the rinse, Ifi sat, chin between her knees, as Aunty scratched and moisturized her scalp. Aunty updated Ifi on matters at home that had happened since her last letter.

"Uncle is sick again," Aunty said with a sigh. "Medicine is so expensive. Life is hard in Nigeria, Mrs. Doctor."

As Aunty attempted to gesture and massage at the same time, Ifi nodded her agreement, her head tugged one way then the other.

"Your brothers," Aunty said of Ifi's cousins. "Such intelligent boys. I am not lying, Mrs. Doctor. The instructors would not allow the boys to sit for their exams last term. Simply because your uncle paid the school fee late."

As Aunty moved on to discuss the pains in her ankles and wrists from early-onset arthritis and the mounting costs for her analgesic rubs, Ifi remembered standing, as a little girl, in front of her uncle's favorite sagging living room couch. Uncle sat back in the chair, his face furious.

"You say the girl did not wash the rice at all?" he asked Aunty. "On purpose?"

Aunty stood over Ifi with the offending bowl of rice in her hands, her chest and backside pushed to opposite extremes. With one hand knotting her wrapper together at her chest, she exclaimed, "This child, my brother's child I am raising, who is ungrateful."

"Ungrateful," Uncle added—with a wink.

"Spoiled," Aunty said.

"Spoiled," Uncle agreed. "What is this slipper? Bring me a belt."

When Aunty returned with a belt, he sent her to bring him a bottle of Heineken to calm his blood pressure. In the time that she made her way to the refrigerator and opened the bottle with the opener—a task she completed with difficulty—he raised his hand to an exaggerated height and slapped the tiled floor in fury. With each jerk, he nodded to Ifi and she let out a tremendous wail. By the time Aunty returned from the kitchen, the deed was done. Ifi scrunched herself into a ball on the floor and continued to wail and beg for mercy on her life.

"Darling," Aunty said, gentleness returning to her voice as she looked over Ifi's writhing figure, "you don't think you have been too harsh with the girl?"

"*A-ah!* I am trying to train her. It is you who will spoil the child," he said. "Women are too weak."

Aunty agreed. "Yes, we are too weak." And as evidence of the weakness of her sex, Aunty reluctantly apologized. "Ndo. Your uncle is only trying to teach you." Ifi continued the charade, balking each time Aunty tried to touch her until Aunty returned with a warm bottle of Fanta and presented it to her.

When Uncle protested, Aunty said, "Darling, you do not want our neighbor to think we are killing my brother's only child." It worked every time.

Now, as Aunty's coarse fingertips raked over Ifi's scalp, Ifi laughed to herself, thinking of the way her scalp burned with each touch only to subside into calm, like Aunty, whose harsh ways came from a tender place. Ifi realized that Aunty had known of their charade all along. *Perhaps,* she thought to herself, *my husband is the same.* In his own way, he was a soft man.

Patches of snow clumped the brown earth, but in spite of this and the cold, the sun shone brightly overhead. Mrs. Janik arrived with a basket of stale rye bread, and, in her choppy, suspicious manner, inquired after Aunty's trip, fondled the baby, and spent the greater part of the morning ignoring Ifi. By afternoon, Mrs. Janik had gone. After a bite of rye bread nearly chipped Aunty's tooth, she hissed over the inferiority of American food before launching it across the kitchen at the trash can. With a metallic clunk it landed in two pieces. As Aunty started a large boiling pot of stew, Ifi retrieved the two pieces, haughtily carried them outside to the large, metal, rubbish bin, and neatly placed the pieces atop the lid, where Mrs. Janik would surely see the bread.

Across the street, Jamal was sitting on the porch alongside two similarly sized boys, wringing his hands at his waist. When he saw Ifi, he leapt down the stairs and crossed the street. Before she could turn away, he was at her side, stopping only to collect the mail from the box. He thrust the letters into her hands.

"Is that her?" he asked breathlessly. "All the way from Africa?"

"Yes," Ifi said carefully. Job would be home soon, and she'd had enough of their fights. Now that Aunty was here, she felt a bit more whole, like the fragments of her new life in America were finally coming together into one. How strange that the past and the present came together in such a place, a cold, snowy America. Yet with all the pieces coming together, Ifi still yearned, more than ever, to return to her real home.

"I saw her yesterday," he said. "She was wearing a big, colorful hair tie, like my people in the south." In response to Ifi's bewildered frown, he continued. "They from the Gullah. They talk and dress so different from anybody up here. That's what Mary says. She says they look African or Caribbean. They even dance the same. It all looks the same."

"Oh." Ifi was reminded of the women in the kitchen at Mary's party, the snideness of their interrogations and accusations about Africa. "You should tell the women in your family about this."

He smiled knowingly. Then asked, "How long she staying?"

"A few months."

"Long time. You showing her around?"

"I don't know," Ifi said.

For a long time he thought. "Yeah, I guess there ain't a lot to do here." After a moment, his eyes flashed eagerly. "Last year we went on a field trip to see the cranes." He twitched eagerly. "The sandhill cranes. They come from all over the world. All over. And they stop just to rest and get fat before they go the rest of the way. Take her there. People come from all over the world to see."

"Why?"

"I don't know. They dance, they sing, they eat. Sounds corny, but it was cool. I mean, why they want to come here? And yeah, they come here, but at the same time they know this ain't the place for them. It's temporary."

"Then this can never be home for them," she said softly, sadly.

"No," he said, "and it was never meant to be like that."

"I see."

"They're like people, ain't they?" he asked.

"Yes," Ifi said, thinking of Job and her small boy. "Like some."

Reflecting again about the night of the party, she fixed a hard gaze on the withered exterior of the wooden house across the street, remembering the way Jamal's family had been driven every which way by the police. Yet today, a collection of boys lounged on the porch as if nothing had happened. Jamal's family was not calamitous. They were resilient. "What happened to the old lady and the chef?" she asked.

Jamal shrugged. "She fine. Gave her a ticket for disturbing the peace, then dismissed it and sent her home the same night. She so proud of herself though, been talking about it to everybody, trying to get petitions for police brutality." After a moment, he nodded. "She a tough old lady."

"And the chef?"

"Not so good. Nobody had the money to bail him, so he sat it out. Came out of there angry and mean."

"That's sad," Ifi said, thinking of the chef's special barbecue recipe.

"Yeah, well." Jamal shrugged.

Just then, a Buick pulled up the block, humming and shaking from the weight of blaring speakers. A honk sounded. Through the car's windows, Ifi could see that some of the boys looked to be in their late teens, but at least two were old enough to be in their twenties. One of them rolled the window down and peered at Ifi and Jamal. A boy in the car catcalled and licked his lips at her. Heat burned her cheeks. When she turned away, she found Jamal examining his shoelaces.

"Are these your friends?"

He looked as embarrassed as she felt.

"Are these the boys you helped that night?" *How can he speak to them once more?* she wondered.

"They won't bother him again. I promise."

Ifi glanced up and down the street, but there was no sign of Job's car. Finally, her eyes returned to Jamal, a skinny boy with ashy knuckles and uncombed hair, a mere child. "Jamal, why do you roam with such boys? They are too old for you. Too much trouble."

"You ain't my mama," he said stubbornly.

Another honk blared, and he cut across the grass into the street, hollering and hooting. Before jumping in, he pounded the hood of the car with his fists, and the guys inside roared and set off a series of honks.

Ifi sighed. *Only trouble can follow.*

Binoculars were on the short list of items to bring. Unfortunately, they forgot the cold. As a result, Job's nose dripped. Shocks of cool air rippled, and Ifi clutched her skirt to her knees, heels digging into the damp earth. Purple ash split the sky, and the sun was just beginning to rise, casting a brilliant orange pool on the water. It was the time of day that Job only witnessed from a patient's open window; today, he would share it with Ifi, Aunty, Emeka, Gladys, and their children. And then tomorrow and the day after, he would work double shifts to make up the lost money.

A shallow, braided stream no more than six inches deep rippled. At its surface, the Platte River was a dark blue with sharp folds, like seams. Cars were staked along the edge of the dirt road. Already a crowd had gathered, spread out on blankets and lawn chairs. Others stood in a line along an old wooden bridge, a child or two dangling sneakered feet between the gaps in its struts. A few pickup trucks had lowered their gates, and inside, couples were cocooned in one another's arms with flasks of hot coffee drawn to their lips, their eyes eerily large behind binoculars.

Aunty rocked the baby in her lap in sudden muscle spasms that could only be a result of the cold. At least she didn't complain, not exactly, not about the cold or the smell of the river or even the noise of the honking birds.

Instead, with a shudder, she loudly compared the sunrise to urine that had missed the commode. Emeka laughed, hard and loud, in a crackle that burst the air. Other couples glared at them, as if the birds could hear him over their own noise. Emeka's youngest, cradled in his lap and kneaded together by his arms and legs, whispered for him to quiet. Gladys told the girl not to disrespect her father. Then she sent Emeka the same withering glare she had on her face when they had all arrived in a caravan, one car containing the Ogbonnaya family and the other Emeka, Gladys, and their two youngest daughters.

Coming to this place had been Ifi's idea, an idea that Job still had yet to understand. There was nothing spectacular about this event. Nothing at all. Days earlier, as he had pulled the car up to the curb, she stood out on the steps, the mail in her hands, waiting for Job to come home. Seeing her waiting expectantly, like a good wife, had pleased him. Then his pleasure quickly dissipated. She offered him the mail and told him about the sandhill *cranks*—that's what Ifi had called them—and Mrs. Janik's visit that morning with the bread that Ifi had foolishly thrown away.

Before he could hear another word from her, Job stalked right past Ifi and retrieved the bread from the rubbish bin, where it was split into two halves. There was nothing wrong with the bread. For nearly two decades, because of his frugality, he had survived on his own in America while others could not keep their lights on. Ifi would have to learn the same. He dusted the bread off, warmed it in the oven, then sliced it and ate it with his coffee, dipping it in long enough to soften its edges before swallowing the moist chunks whole.

Aunty agreed that things went to waste in America, that it was the American way, though she refused to sample the bread. To prove his point, Job had been forced to eat the entire loaf on his own. Afterwards, he visited Mrs. Janik to offer his thanks. While there, he asked her about the *sandhill cranks,* and Mrs. Janik told him about romantic trips out into the prairie to see the *sandhill cranes* twice a year, and how it was world renowned, something every American needed to do once. Just the perfect occasion to show Aunty the America the Americans knew.

When Gladys and Emeka agreed to come along, it was settled. The whole idea had pleased Job. It would be an opportunity to talk to Emeka about meeting Cheryl the following morning, Sunday. For Ifi, it would give her a chance to develop her friendship with Gladys so Ifi would find no reason to consort with troublemakers any longer. Gladys could teach Ifi about proper clothes and the proper way to wear her makeup and which Americans to speak to and which to avoid. *Perhaps if this information comes from a fellow woman,* Job thought, *my wife will not be so stubborn.*

All morning, Job had debated how to corner Emeka and ask him about Cheryl. This was their first time out since the big fight, and Job still burned with fury at the way Emeka had laughed off his rage. In spite of this, when he had called, Emeka acted as if nothing had happened. When they had first arrived on-site, Emeka made some silly joke about Job's twenty dollars buying his daughter candy. To illustrate his point, he called the girl over to him. A wet, sticky string of licorice dangled from her mouth, and she gazed suspiciously at Job. To rub salt in the wound, Emeka ordered the girl to share some of her candy with her uncle. Job almost spat in his face, but he kept his composure and corrected Emeka, saying that it was, in fact, two hundred dollars, and that Emeka could spend it however he pleased. Gladys, who up until then hadn't paid attention to the two, fractured their heated exchange with her own severe expression.

Since that time, Emeka had been avoiding Gladys's furious glares. Her anger was so satisfying that now as he sat thinking, Job wound his fingers around Ifi's and pulled her closer, feeling the heat of his breath moisten the skin of her forehead. It did not occur to him to wonder what the source of Gladys's anger was. He had not felt so warmed and calm in such a long time, and thinking this, Job pushed away his worries of the last few weeks: Emeka, Ifi and the criminal boy, Aunty, Captain's death, and even his meeting with Cheryl. He would hear what she had to say later. *This problem,* he decided, *I will worry tomorrow.*

Hundreds, maybe thousands of cranes, gray like dust, roosted along the river and clumsily made their way out past a fan of trees, their deafening cries like rusty horns. One at a time, their stick legs lifted, shaking the water free before bursting into the air. From a distance, patches of tremendous lush greenery weaved through the brown fields. Up close, the ground was damp and dark from melting snow. Mostly the fields were flat, but occasionally a crest or a rise gave the appearance of valleys that went forever into the distance.

Someone whispered, "They're dancing," and a collective gasp escaped. Both feet touched down in a leap, wings outstretched. In turn, one after another, the cranes shot forward with their wings thrown like flipped umbrellas.

Job thought it was Gladys's voice that whispered, "They're dancing," so he glanced her way, but she was only watching the sleeping boy in Aunty's lap. For the first time, it occurred to Job that Gladys had yet to visit with the boy, even to touch him. And even then, he couldn't remember a single time that he'd witnessed her with the baby in her hands. A tear moistened her face in a shimmering path. His eyes fixated there. A memory came to him. Many months earlier in the hospital room, overlooking Emeka and Gladys's newborn son's lifeless body in the incubator, Gladys had looked nearly defeated. *She still yearns for her dead son,* Job thought. Why hadn't he ever put it together before? But she had seemed so strong. It was Emeka whose face had contorted into various poses. It was Emeka who had seemed so weak. Their eyes met, Gladys's and Job's, but she did not wipe away her tear. He was suddenly overcome.

Exactly how he did not know, but on the way back to the cars, Job found his strides matching the rhythm of Gladys's instead of Emeka's. He forgot everything. He forgot about his decision to discuss Cheryl and to figure out a plan of action. He forgot his decision to stomach his pride in favor of counsel. Together, in silence, Job and Gladys watched the backs of the others grow smaller and smaller as the distance grew between them. When they were far enough behind the others to not be heard, Gladys spoke. "You talk to him," she said. "What does he say?"

In the distance, Emeka suddenly flipped his youngest daughter up onto his shoulders, and she squealed. Licorice slipped from her fingers onto the damp, muddy earth, and she howled in horror. As she twisted in an effort to reach her candy, he flung wild promises at her until the cries finally subsided. He told her he would buy her the whole store. He would ask the candy maker for the ingredients, and her mother would bake it in the oven for her and fill the shelves in her bedroom with ropes and ropes of licorice.

At this, Job couldn't help but laugh. But when he glanced back at Gladys, the same pained expression was on her face. He wondered how to answer her. *What can she mean?* he thought. *Does she know of Emeka's women?* Well, she would be angry. Job would have to promise to chastise Emeka. And then things would move on. It was the best counsel he could offer. Some men simply must stray. Still, he couldn't help but believe in his heart that Gladys could do better. If Gladys were Job's wife, he would never stray. A man with Emeka's stupidity simply didn't deserve a classical woman like Gladys.

"Job, my brother," she said, "we have known you for many years, since you first arrived in this country, no?"

"Yes," he said quietly.

"Is it not us who taught you how to walk when you first came to America?"

Job cringed. Even after all these years, this was the foolish thought that Emeka had taught his wife. Job fought the urge to retaliate against Emeka, to tell Gladys that he came to this country walking, that he came walking because he would never make the mistakes that his brother had made. *Emeka, so much like my own senior brother, the fool.* Emeka was the joke, and one day everything would collapse around him. Gazing at Ifi, Job wondered if that was happening right now. Deep in his gut, he felt a pleasure that he refused to shrug off. *Gladys,* he admitted to himself, *is a woman!*—in fact, the same age as himself. *Ifi is a mere child.*

Instead of telling Gladys that her husband knew nothing, that he was the fool, Job reminded himself that Gladys was only repeating what Emeka had said to her. Surely she couldn't believe it. After all, when he first came to America, Gladys and Emeka were the only two people he knew. For many years. Indeed, Gladys had always treated Job like her own brother, cooking meals for him, bringing him beer, sharing in the surprise and pleasure when he announced his plans to marry and when he announced that his first son was born.

In the Nigerian way, she did not come right out and ask for her favor immediately, but as the conversation developed, it became obvious that she was in need of Job's aid in some way. "You know, my brother, things are hard here in America," Gladys said. She leaned into him just a bit and ran a finger past her tired eyes.

Job agreed with her. As he watched her, he was again humbled by her beauty, her grace. She was a tall woman with smooth chestnut skin, shapely thighs, hair plaited into a neat bun—the kind of woman Ifi would surely become with a little more time and patience.

"My husband has sent every relative to school. He has paid for every business, repaired every home in Nigeria. Because of our success. My entire town remembers my husband when there is sickness. But, you know, we need to grow our family here in America. Isn't that so?"

Job agreed. He told her about the money he'd sent to his relatives and in-laws. He told her about his father's construction business, his mother's hair salon, his junior brother and sisters' expenses for school, and the family of his wife. As he spoke to her, he turned up his palms and gazed at his hands, finding the shine of gnarled, hardening flesh.

"Some people are not grateful for the sacrifices we make in America," Gladys said. "They don't know because we are too humble to announce them to the world."

Job agreed, his eyes settling on Ifi up ahead.

"Money for everything. For clothes, for car, for school, for light." She sighed.

Isn't it plain? he thought. *She is asking for the money her husband is too proud to ask for.* Job would give her whatever she needed. Whatever she asked for. Delight filled him. After all these years and all of Emeka's boasts, his beautiful wife was here begging Job for money. Hadn't Emeka admitted that Gladys was spending their money on juju so that she could finally have her son? How much had they spent? What was left of their fortune? Emeka had needed the two hundred dollars Job gave him, but he was too proud to accept it on his own, so he had tossed it to his daughter. In his excitement, Job threw out the first words that came to mind. "Stop sending money to native doctors," he said. "What good has it accomplished?"

Gladys said nothing at first. Instead, her pained expression hardened. "My sister has three sons. Me, I only have girls, six daughters. Not even one boy. My girls are intelligent and beautiful. Still, all the money in the world cannot make his family respect me."

Up ahead, Emeka lifted his child off his shoulders and tickled her. Midswing he turned back, his eyes settling on Gladys and Job. For a second, Job was sure he saw an anxious frown flicker across Emeka's face before he returned to his daughter.

"Stop wasting your money on juju," Job said again, thinking of the two hundred dollars he'd lost. Throwing such money away wasn't easy. He would suffer for it. Just the same, he would give her whatever she asked. *How can I say no to Gladys?* he thought. *No one can say no to Gladys.* "Times are hard in America, but we must help one another," he said.

"Yes," she said. Her face suddenly filled with anxiety. She stared deep into Job's eyes and then turned away.

How much? Job wondered. *Three hundred? One thousand?* Again, he felt startled by her beauty—her eyes, her lips, the fullness of her cheeks.

"My brother, are you hearing me?" It was the second time that she had asked her question, and Job realized he had been caught up in her beauty.

"Yes," he said with finality. He waited for her to announce the number.

"Your wife will not understand," she said. "This business happens in Nigeria, but it is not understood in America."

Job frowned. *What can she mean?* he thought. *A-ah! This woman's pride.* "No problem," he said. "I'll dash you."

Now Gladys frowned. Again, she stared hard at him. "Dash me?" Her gaze softened. "Yes, that is exactly what this is," she said. "Just one," she answered, "before my time has passed."

A balloon of pleasure rose in his chest. He still didn't quite understand, but he nodded in agreement anyway.

"Job, I have always known that *you* would do anything for me." Her glance hardened as it settled on her husband, but when her face returned to Job's, her lips turned up in a smile. She moved girlishly, swinging her round-ish hips.

His stomach flipped. "Yes, of course," Job said. "Anything."

By the time they'd made it to the car, Gladys and Job had agreed to meet at a restaurant after his shift at the hospital the next morning. In his elation, he forgot about his meeting with Cheryl at exactly the same time across town.

CHAPTER 13

EXTRACTING ONE THOUSAND DOLLARS FROM HIS SAVINGS ACCOUNT IN the early hours of Sunday morning had been a challenge. In his haste, Job forgot that the bank was closed, arriving only to press his face against the dark window before being forced to stop at four separate ATMs to collect the entire amount. At the time, he had ignored the shame in the pit of his stomach. Now that Aunty was visiting, there was not a cent of extra money. This was his father's money, money now meant for his son's future. Still, as long as it would take, he would work harder and pay every cent back. Now, he nervously clasped the damp stack of bills in the pocket of his lab coat.

Gladys arrived on time at the Union, a sports bar restaurant on the lower level of the Airport Holiday Inn. Even from a distance, Job was overcome by the tall plaits gathered in a single ponytail, the shapely body, and the soft eyes. Clutching a heavy tote bag, she frantically peered around the empty restaurant until Job stood and waved her over to his corner booth. Gladys was drenched from the rain and shivered as she set down her things. He waited for her to peel off her coat, but she didn't. After hurriedly greeting him, she remained standing. Only after several moments did she finally take her place at the table.

Once she was seated, Job asked after Emeka and her daughters.

"They're fine," she said.

"And what of your eldest?"

"Fine."

"Are they faring well in their studies?"

"Yes."

When she didn't ask after his own family, he began immediately, telling her his son was holding his head upright. Gladys stiffened at his words, and he quickly shifted the discussion to work. "I am considering developing a practice of my own," he said calmly. "Many have advised against it, but I think it's wise at this juncture in my career." After a moment, he added, "Don't you agree?"

"Yes."

Again, he waited a moment before continuing. "It is out of the question while my in-law is visiting."

"Yes, of course." Her words were blind.

Job's ramble was snuffed into silence.

A chomping Tchaikovsky erupted in the background, out of place among the large television screens and the shining wraparound bar. Job anxiously looked about the room at the round tables, the harsh lights, the dusty plastic trees bunched together at the center of the room, obscuring the only other couple in the restaurant, two men in dark suits. Both of the men ordered coffee, grits, and eggs. When the waiter stopped at their table, Job began to order the same, but Gladys stopped him. Instead, she waved away Job's order and asked for two coffees.

Golden baubles at her wrists clinked with her every motion, and it was the flurry of her movements more than her anxious eyes or her dismissal of his breakfast order that immediately set him on edge. In his anxiety, he told himself that he should place the money on the table and go home. He would arrive only a little later than he usually did, and he would not need to make any excuses about emergencies at the hospital. He would not need to bounce the wailing boy against his knee as Ifi and Aunty quarreled over the best way to reheat the soup that would already be cold.

Even as the thoughts ran through Job's mind, he knew that he would not leave. *How can I?* he thought. He was here with Gladys, giving her the money Emeka had been too proud to ask for on his own. Emeka's fancy education and expensive salary couldn't disguise the fact that he was nothing more than a bushman. After all, it was Job's family that had the good name. *What of the fact that Americans don't understand family name and heritage?* Job thought. For the rest of their days, Job would regard Emeka with a scolding look of pity.

Two piping-hot black coffees arrived, but Gladys did not drink from hers. Job sipped from the coffee and grimaced at the taste of stale coffee grounds. He waved and hollered to the waiter. A tall man in head-to-toe black arrived, and Job chastised him for the coffees and ordered two fresh cups. When the cups came, Job sipped, but the coffee was lukewarm, and it had the same stale, earthy taste. Just the same he grunted, split open a packet of sugar, and dumped some crème into the coffee. He grabbed a handful of packets and offered Gladys some, but she refused.

"I can order again," he finally said.

"It's fine," she said. Still, she refused to touch her lips to the mug in front of her.

He hastily ripped a packet of sugar open and dumped it into the cup for her before returning his hand to the money in his pocket.

"It's fine," she said sharply.

Job jerked in nervousness, and the bills came up with his hand. It was too late to put them away, to offer his deliverance with finesse. Clumsily, he placed the bills on the table between them.

Her eyes widened in shock, then doubt, and then suddenly something that crystallized into horror. Gladys thrust the money at Job, and the bills rained around him. "What is this, huh? What is this?"

One of the businessmen at the other table stopped to watch the two. Leaning into the bar, the waiter crossed his arms and stared. Smiling and nodding, Job scrambled to collect the money. Perhaps she was ashamed to receive the money in public. Still, hadn't she suggested this place?

He was reminded of that afternoon all those years ago, waiting for Cheryl outside of the county clerk's office. A weight dropped to the pit of his stomach. In his haste and excitement, he had forgotten about the meeting he had scheduled with Cheryl about the house. *If she takes the money now,* he decided, *I can drive across town and meet Cheryl in time.*

Gladys's eyes thinned into slits. "You think I am doing this for money?"

Thinking of Cheryl, Job stiffened, and his own shock curdled to anger. "You should be so proud. For what? For nothing. You are just like Emeka. Take the money. Take it and I will go. Give him the money."

"Take your money." Gladys collected the straps of her tote bag and began to rise. "What do you think I am, eh?"

"If you don't need the money, then why have you asked me here? Why are you wasting my time?"

"This is just time to you," she said near tears. "Yes, this is all about time." Even as she stood before him, shaking with her anger and tears, she backed into her seat and remained there, her gaze cast out past Job to the large, dark windows overlooking the hotel's near-empty parking lot.

Job collected the bills, stacked them together, and once more placed them on the middle of the table.

"Take your money," she said softly. "My son. That is all I want."

"Your son?" Job asked.

"My son." With an even voice, her eyes rested on him.

Suddenly, it began to make sense. All the money in the world and all of Emeka's boasts. All the native doctors in the world could not give Gladys the boy she wanted. Emeka had failed at the largest charge for any man. *She wants me to give her a son,* it dawned on him. Numbness spread through his limbs. It settled at his lips so that when the first words issued from his tongue, he was forced to repeat himself for Gladys to understand. "Okie," he said. "Let us go."

By the time they made it up the three flights of carpeted stairs, smudging the red floral print with their damp shoes, the weight in Job's stomach had ballooned up to his chest. As he slipped the plastic key card into the lock, his hands trembled in anticipation. Even before the door snapped open, images of Gladys sprawled on the bed, breasts bobbing, gasping in elation, passed before his eyes.

Inside the hotel room, the air was still and musty. He flung open the curtains, but it only swathed the room in a rectangle of bleached sunlight. Patches of brightness flickered across the bed and the desk just as the sun began to break through the clouds. Particles of dust rained on Job, and suddenly he felt dirty.

Standing in the room, staring at the pillows propped on the bed and the still-life paintings on the wall, Job thought of his honeymoon with Ifi. Strange how no matter where he was in the world, a hotel could have the same haunting familiarity. At once he pushed the image of Ifi in her yellow dress on their honeymoon night to the corners of his mind. It took little effort, and this, more than the business at hand, gave him pause.

"Will you hurry?" Gladys was standing in her undergarments, plain beige cotton panties and a bra that looked dirty under the slanting flurry of sunlit dust. Her clothes were in a heap by the door. He had imagined Gladys to be the kind of woman who would take her clothes off slowly and fold them into neat squares before laying them on a chair. The woman before him, with her clothes tossed about, would surely climb up after they had finished and slip into wrinkled clothes. Not his Gladys.

Her eyebrows were furrowed. Impatiently, she crossed the room in three strides and hastily removed his lab coat for him. By the time he was down to his underwear, Fruit of the Loom briefs, he was overcome with shame. The underwear was tighter than he remembered, and he compensated by sucking in his hairy gut.

When she began to advance toward him, a determined look on her face, he realized that she had finished undressing him.

Thrusting his hand out, Job said, "Wait, Ifi—"

By the time he caught his slip, Gladys's scowl had deepened into a sneer, sending her penciled eyebrows up in stark arcs.

"Sorry," he said respectfully, "you are just too beautiful."

No reply. Feeling hot, suddenly exposed in the shaft of light, Job glanced about the room in search of a remedy.

Without her smile, Gladys was nothing more than a scolding schoolteacher. After a moment, the scowl softened into a tight smirk. "Well?" she asked. "Come now."

A tan skirt and plum-colored blouse littered the floral-print carpet. Hose, the shed skin of a snake, was bunched up and tossed to a corner. *I can't,* he thought to himself. Not with her clothes piled in a corner on the floor. *Not like this. What kind of woman comports herself in such a way?* He couldn't cast away the image that would follow, of Gladys picking up the wrinkled clothes like a used carton of cigarettes.

Job stepped out of the light, and as he folded the clothes, he remembered the night of his honeymoon. He reflected on Ifi's face, the warmth that suddenly radiated as she had laughed at his body bulging through her yellow dress. Hadn't it eased her anxiety? At just that moment, Ifi's fierce expression had fallen away, and she was the easy-to-laugh girl that his in-laws had assured him of during the arrangements.

At first, the look of interest on Gladys's face inspired Job as he pulled on each article—the blouse, then the skirt, then finally, seductively, the stockings. Stockings were a mystery to him. Once on, they itched and were too snug in the crotch. His sweat and leg hair were trapped in the tiny punctures of the porous fibers. Tiny glittering buckles, like frog eyes, stared at him from the floor. Job slipped into the shoes. His feet dangled over the backs, and his large toes struggled to peep through the opening at the front. There was no makeup bag, no articles of jewelry, just Gladys standing before him in her faded panties.

Like Ifi's had, Gladys's furrowed expression divided into a smile. Staggering for a moment, laughter bellowed from her chest, a deep, cavernous laugh that Job had never heard from Gladys. Strange how the wrong man could do that to a woman, keep the real laughter bottled up inside until the right man came along with the proper key. His mother had always said so. Now, Job was certain that he had unlocked such a place in Gladys. A twist there, a bend there; he smiled and did his dance.

How marvelous! he thought, the way her eyes opened up, the way the laughter spilled from her body, rippling up through her ribs and her large breasts to her beautiful, full lips until the laughter was magnified—but Job began to realize that the look on her face was not one of pleasure, but derision. Now her lips were giant, her teeth too large, her eyes too open.

Once he discovered his mistake, Job stopped immediately. But it was too late.

"No, no, don't stop!" she said through her laughter.

But he couldn't continue. Hastily, he struggled to peel off each article.

"Is this what makes it work?" Gladys asked. "I have seen everything in America."

How could he explain himself? Suddenly, and with ferocity, he hated her. More than Emeka. More than Samuel. With his eyes turned away from her face, what he saw was the loose, dented skin of her thighs. Discolored scars stretched across her stomach. Pimples beaded her back. Clouds of acne peppered her shoulders.

"Well?" she asked. "Come now."

When it was all over, Job apologized as he caught his breath. "We can do it again," he said. "I need just five minutes." But by the time he had flipped over onto his back, Gladys was already half dressed and heading for the door.

"That was good enough."

Alone. A chill found him. The sheets were damp with his sweat and fluids. Wisps of smoke clouded the sun outside, but as the clouds split, he saw them for what they were: the skyward sandhill cranes.

What would I say differently if I could do the morning all over again? he wondered. Standing naked in the hotel shower, his stomach suddenly and insistently growled. *Well, for one, I would not have allowed her to cancel my breakfast order,* he decided. That was the beginning of a bad ending. He would have forced Gladys to eat breakfast like a civilized person. He would have scolded the waiter for serving them that rubbish that he called coffee. *I would have.*

As the water washed over him, rinsing the crusting semen and dust from his legs, Job remembered his meeting with Cheryl. By now she was surely heading home. By now she was shredding her housing documents.

It is just the same, he decided. Emeka. He could hear his voice: *"Ah-ah,* A-mer-eeka. Job, my friend, me, I would not enter into any other agreement with a quack-quack. The woman has already made you a fool."

Fool. Meeting Gladys instead of Cheryl had been foolish. Gladys, like Emeka, had planned from the beginning to compete with Job. Hadn't she said that it was they who had taught him to walk when he came to America? Job shuddered at the thought. Well, he would do exactly the opposite of what Emeka would advise. Job would be strong and forceful with Cheryl. Things would be done his way. In time, he would own a home, raise his son, and send him to the best schools, better than anything that Gladys and Emeka could offer their own children. Job remembered that day, sitting in the police station. Even then, the realization had begun to form: His own dreams no longer mattered to him. Nor did the money he had been saving all these years to return to school. *I have been foolish,* he thought. *For too long.* Now, he silently insisted: *My son will be the doctor instead of me. My daughter will be the nurse instead of Ifi.*

Outside, the house was tall and willowy. Inside, it smelled of used cigarettes. A faint blue glow leaked from behind a closed door. A large, ragged hole stained the wall. Every space was filled with furniture, large plush couches and old wooden tables. The dining room table was piled with fashion magazines and books. On the chairs around the table lay broken computer parts and clothes. He sat stiffly on one of the plush couches and fingered the magazines on the table, careful to set each *Cosmopolitan* and *Glamour* magazine back exactly the way it was. He did not want to be labeled a thief in a white man's house. Then he corrected himself: *This is my house.*

All the arrangements had been made under the table. He'd handed over the one thousand dollars he had meant for Gladys to secure the late payment. Only a few final steps remained. It was quite simple. Job's name already appeared on the title alongside Cheryl's, so there would be no legal trappings to deal with. As soon as he withdrew the money from the savings account and made the payments, the danger of foreclosure would no longer be imminent. Cheryl wouldn't even be in the picture anymore, renting from a friend in a nearby neighborhood. It had already been handled. Her only request was for her name to remain on the title. *It's only fair,* she had said. *I put so much into the place. It's my daddy's house and all.* Together, when Job and Cheryl sold the house sometime in the distant future, when Job was ready to send his son to medical school or return to Nigeria and retire, she would have had enough time to raise the money. Then she would simply buy back his portion of the mortgage. *Like an amicable divorce,* she had said. *People do it this way all the time.* There was just one final step. Monday morning, Job would withdraw every cent from the savings account and make the mortgage payment. Once that was done, all foreclosure proceedings could come to an end.

Of course Job felt some uncertainty. *Will this woman crook me again?* he asked himself. But something told Job to believe her this time. He knew how desperately Cheryl wanted to hold on to this house, this legacy of her father's. After all, it was her desperation that had forced her hand in their arranged marriage. In a strange way, Job understood the feeling. It was the same pang that forced him to collect his father's tuition money and keep it stored in his saving's bond, despite his meager life.

Not to mention that he would finally be a homeowner. All through the discussion with Cheryl, Job had flushed with scorn, picturing Gladys's derisive laughter. Sitting in his new house, he pushed the hurt out of himself. Everything Gladys and Emeka owned and more would be his. His son would go to the best schools and befriend wealthy, successful, apple-cheeked Americans who lived in cul-de-sacs. It all began with this house.

Underneath the piles of magazines, he noticed a book: *Lonely Planet: Nigeria.* He thumbed through the pages, recognizing the names of towns and monuments. There was a brief explanation of the Igbo, the Yoruba, the Hausa, and the Fulani. Someone had underlined passages and made notes. He pulled the book close to his nose. In astonishment, he read a question that someone had penned: *Is he Yoruba or Igbo?*

Just then, Cheryl returned to the room, her hands full with two mugs of coffee. At the sight of him thumbing through her book, her pale complexion colored. He couldn't help but smile. *She wants to know about me,* he thought. There *were* things that no one knew about him. All of his years of being acquainted with Gladys, and she knew so little about him. Sharing a bed and a home with Ifi had at first convinced him that she knew him inside and out. Now, he realized that it just wasn't true. Cheryl, on the other hand, had the wherewithal to wonder about him. He felt the pride a man should.

One of the cups flipped sideways and spilled on the book. In a wild panic, she rushed to blot out the coffee with her faded blue shirttail. "It's not even mine," she moaned. "How am I going to take it back to the library?"

He took the book from her fumbling hands. "It's okie. It's just a book," he said. "You can ask me whatever you like. I have all the answers here." He tapped his head. It was the simplest gesture, but she relaxed into girlish laughter that smoothed the lines in her face. He saw himself in her eyes— tall, dark, and elegant in his suits, with his crisp, cultivated English, a mystery. "For example," he said gently, "I am Igbo."

"You read my notes." The flush returned to her face. "I just wanted to know some things."

"I come from a great family. My father is a chief," he said with pride. "He sent me to America to become a doctor."

"A chief," Cheryl echoed. "A chief, that's like the president or a king?"

After a moment of consideration, Job agreed.

"It's funny," she said softly. "My daddy always said I'd marry a doctor. Well, here it is. I married a doctor." She grinned at Job.

"And I married my nurse," he said of Cheryl's current occupation, which as a veterinarian's assistant was roughly equivalent.

He assumed she'd ask about lions and tigers and jungles. Surprisingly, she didn't. "Been in Nebraska my whole life," she said solemnly. "What's your favorite memory of home?"

Could it be so difficult to answer her question? What was so special about the place he now considered home more than ever? "My family, my friends . . ." he started. But that wasn't it, not completely. An image began to form in his mind, of him and Samuel, Samuel with his arms extended before him, gripping Job around his waist, hoisting him high enough to peek over the concrete wall surrounding their estate. Glass and shoots of wire, meant to keep out intruders, jutted from the top of the wall. From above, Job saw the world, or what he imagined of the world at age five. Cars whizzed up and down the busy street. Hawkers weaved in and out of traffic with baskets of corn and fresh fish. Guards, dark and shiny from the sun, with semi-automatic rifles at their hips, lazily gazed out over the distance. One of them glanced up, catching Job's eyes. Surprised, the guard let out a sharp exhale as he clapped and thudded on his partner's side. Job angled his hips and waved his arms, pretending to be the evil spirit the man believed him to be. Job saw himself the way he imagined the guard saw him, a small boy suddenly a giant. *This she cannot understand,* he thought, so he said simply, "My brother, Samuel. Before the war."

He continued thumbing through the pages, not quite paying attention to the words on them. The pool of dark coffee quickly dried. As he handed the book to her, Cheryl's hands stretched to meet his, palms up.

It was then, as he was placing the book in her hands, that their fingers touched. Her hands were wet. By the time the coffee had splashed her skin, it had cooled to lukewarm. Just the same, he couldn't help himself. "Be careful," he said. He ripped a page out of the ruined book. Cheryl jerked at the sound of the page tearing, but she didn't try to stop him. Where Job dabbed her wrist with the torn paper, Cheryl's skin was a warm, pinkish hue. She allowed him to sop up the moist beads of coffee from her arm. She pretended, just as he had, that the coffee was too hot.

"I think it's okay," she finally said.

"Run it under cool water," Job instructed her. "That will soothe the burn. Apply hydrocortisone treatment to it. This will prevent infection from developing."

Her eyes widened into full moons. "Really?"

"Like this," he added, making circular motions on her skin with his thumb and forefinger.

She nodded, hanging on his every word. Still, she didn't stand up. Instead, her freckled hands grasped at the scar on his hand, trembling. In silence, their eyes met more than once. Reluctantly, he admitted to himself that she was not such a terrible-looking woman. Frankly, she didn't look older than him, though she was two years his senior. Had they grown up in Nigeria, they would have been agemates. Red hair, at the right angle, glowed. Freckles and small teeth on the right face evoked character and youthfulness.

Bristling under his gaze, she asked, "Job, what do you do for fun?"

"Fun?" Job furrowed his brow.

"Yeah, I mean, like when you don't work, where do you go? What do you do?"

"I go home," he said.

"But come on, what do you do?" When he didn't answer, she pressed on. "I make things. Scarves, sweaters, stuff like that. I have an elliptical machine in the basement that I run on sometimes. When he's not shitting on the world, my asshole brother tinkers with computers." She gestured broadly at the remains of scattered computer parts. "And I read," she said, indicating the magazines cluttered on the table.

"Ah, yes," Job agreed. "I read too."

"Really? Job, I thought *I* had no life," she said sadly. "You have no life."

"You say, 'Have no life.' What does this mean?"

"Nothing. Just, I'm running out of things to say, but I don't want you to go yet." Her hair was red like a fresh wound, and she picked her fingers through it. "I don't know. I'm alone here. I'm scared. But I want to do what's right. Job, I can't lose this place. It's all I have. You know, Job," she said softly, "it's strange, but you've come to save the day again. You're like Superman."

"I won't let anything happen," he said.

As midday approached, they remained sitting together in silence, Cheryl's dry wrist still upturned in Job's palm. By her side, he forgot completely about the horrors of that morning—Gladys's derision, Ifi's looks of disappointment, Aunty's complaints, more of which surely awaited him.

On the way home, the darkened sky divided into a V formation. From his windshield, Job was astonished to see a flock of ascending sandhill cranes alight the sky, a roiling, honking gray mist. What was left of the morning sun staggered through its gaps. In awe, Job's eyes left the yellow lines splitting the highway ahead of him and took in the moving sky. Just then, a splatter of bird excrement painted his windshield. For the rest of the way home, his vision of the sandhill cranes' grand flight was obscured by four white streaks of shit.

CHAPTER 14

THEY WENT TO THE BUSH, IN BELATED HONOR OF THE BOY'S BIRTH, TO butcher a goat. It had mostly been arranged by phone. There was a farm on the edge of the county in a town called Hickman. An aged man and his wife ran it. Their ad boasted of the biggest, meatiest Boers in the entire state. They would even prepare the goat the Nigerian way—roasted, skin on—free of charge. To Job, this was the biggest relief of all. After hosting Aunty for nearly four months—enduring the cold, sexless nights on the scratchy living room couch, enduring Aunty's optimistic complaints—Job fervently hoped that everything would go well.

Still new enough to America, Ifi believed that because the farmers were American, and because English was their native tongue, they must be educated, as the upper classes were in Nigeria. And because they were educated and lived princely lives, they must not tell lies; it was surely beneath them. In his own way, Job believed this as well, presenting the ad to Ifi only after all the arrangements had been made. He was, after all, head of the family.

The original plan was for Aunty and Ifi to stay behind with the boy, to wait for Job to return with the goat. Then the women would stand over the sink cleaning, cutting, and curing the meat for pepper soup, jollof rice, garri, and egusi. However, Aunty insisted on coming along—to see America. She had only a short week left before her return to Nigeria, and for the four months she had spent with them, she had seen, at most, the local theater, grocery store, and a couple of restaurants. Her memory of the sandhill cranes was still clouded by her vision of a ruined commode. Because she was determined to spend as much of her remaining time as possible with her "son," she refused to attend without the boy. As a result, Aunty rode in front alongside

Job, holding the boy to her chest throughout the ride—despite Ifi's attempts to convince her that in America it was illegal for a child not to be buckled into a car seat. Ifi, who sprouted budding tufts of thread-tied hair underneath her wig, sat in the backseat.

On the ride out to Hickman, Aunty saw nothing of the skyscrapers from the tabloid magazines she purchased during their weekly outings to the grocery. Unlike Ifi, who bit back her disappointment in silence when she first arrived, Aunty did her best to encourage the young couple, remarking, as they passed the lone steer dotted along the Nebraska skyline, "Don't count your chickens; they might hatch," a phrase she had picked up from television during her short time in America.

The first sign that something was wrong happened when they arrived at the old man's farm. They saw the mailbox, the wire fences, and drove up the dirt road until they found the faded two-story house sitting on a slight rise. At first no one answered the door. Job knocked again and again. He rang the doorbell. A very old woman wrapped in a shawl and smelling of urine finally answered. She was wrinkled but ruddy faced. Her hands were strong. Her forearms were tight and corded with veins. She had the sturdy look of a farm wife.

"He's ill. Didn't you get the message?" she asked.

"There is no message," Job said. But he recalled the phone ringing on his way out the door. He remembered Aunty wondering aloud if it was Uncle. And he remembered, that for exactly that reason, he had rushed them out the door in the interest of putting the money toward the goat instead of another international call.

"You'll have to come another day," the farm wife said.

Job could see Ifi's face in the car window, strained with annoyance. He was responsible for making the arrangements, yet she must always look as if she was begging him to fail. The last few months, he had seen that face again and again: each time he groped Ifi from behind while Aunty washed in the bathroom, each time he attempted to handle the boy, and each morning on his return from work. For this reason, he had chosen not to share the news of their new home with Ifi until Aunty returned to Nigeria. "Please, Aunty," he said to the old lady in such desperation that he forgot: this is America.

Her face softened. "I'll ask my son if he can help." She hesitated for a moment, but went inside, made the call, and returned. "He'll be along in

JULIE IROMUANYA

fifteen minutes or so. He's up the road." She beckoned to Ifi and Aunty until they met the two on the porch steps.

Inside, they sipped iced tea that was thick with sugar and lemon seeds, and the old lady asked them question after question about Africa: "How long you been here?" she asked. "Do you live in houses in Africa?" And, "What's the goat for?"

From a distance, the farmer's son appeared as a teenage boy, shrunken, with blue overalls free on one shoulder and a T-shirt a little too big for him. He wore a backwards baseball cap. Job wondered if a boy should be left in charge of such a task, butchering a goat, but he reminded himself that the celebration must take place the next day. His own father had butchered a goat in honor of his birth forty years earlier. And his father before him. Reluctantly, Job had even gone to the trouble of inviting Emeka and Gladys to the festivities.

When the farmer's son was closer, his stained, leathery face revealed his age. The two men shook hands, exchanged money, and headed out the back door, leaving the women in the parlor. They tramped across flat, damp earth, and he led Job out past the goats that were scattered behind a wire fence with sturdy wooden posts. He retrieved a .22 from the shed while Job waited outside, heating the insides of his hands with his breath. It was late March. Winter was just beginning to thaw. The sun was without warmth.

He told Job to pick the one he wanted, and Job puffed out his shoulders and marched toward the goats as if he had done this before. To be honest, they all appeared the same to him: skinny and meatless with long, flattened ears, nothing like what the ad had described. Evidently, the man had been ill longer than his wife had implied. Job thumbed one. But he made the wrong choice.

"Are you sure?" the farmer's son asked.

But Job would not look like a fool and refused to relent, even after the man explained to him that wethers were best. Instead, Job replied, "Remember, it must have skin."

The farmer's son wrangled the goat and hauled it to a slaughtering pen near the shed. The goat bleated and whipped its tongue in protest. The slaughter was supposed to be included in the price, but only after Job paid an additional fifty dollars did the son proceed. The farmer's son slapped the goat on the rear, and it trotted around the pen. He spread some feed on the ground, stepped away, and watched the goat circle and bend to taste. Before Job could turn, the .22 cracked off; the goat dropped. Job was so near the goat he could feel its warmth. A flock of birds perched along the roof of the shed scattered.

Inside, Ifi, Aunty, and the old lady paused when they heard the sound. The boy began to cry. But then they heard it again. Another crack.

And then another crack before the old lady came charging out the back door. Job was turned over, gasping into the dirt. For a second, it looked as if he was the one who was wounded, and Ifi's throat closed up. But the old lady put a finger in her son's face. The goat was limp and bleeding from three places. Vomit ran down the sides of Job's mouth.

The farmer's son refused to meet his mother's eyes.

"One shot, Scotty!" she said.

"It's not my fault," he said. "It misfired."

Job could smell it now, the alcohol on the man's breath.

Ifi and Aunty were still on the back porch, peering out at the commotion. When the farmer's son wrung the goat's neck until it cracked, Aunty turned away. The boy, held over her shoulders, inadvertently had a direct view. His tongue out, he watched as the farmer's son slit the goat's throat and tied off the gullet. The farmer's son nicked the goat at each Achilles tendon and hoisted it onto a hand-cranked pulley. Blood ran down its sides. Automatically, he began to fist off the hide, but halted and torched the bleeding goat instead. He rinsed off the ash with a hose. He emptied its insides. Then he hacked the limbs off in pieces with a saw, muttering to himself each time metal collided with bone. Panting, he mopped his damp forehead with the crook of an elbow, spreading small streaks of burnt blood across his face.

Instead of envisioning himself in place of this small man dressed like an American teenager, Job imagined his father sturdily holding the goat's kicking legs together, tying it upside down, slitting its throat, and watching the life tremble out before setting it ablaze. Job stepped outside of himself, but all he could see was the back of his body as his hands worked vigorously on the line in the meatpacking plant. He hated what he saw.

The farmer's son bagged the broken goat so that it could be packed on ice, so that the "cleanup" money could be exchanged, and so he could go back to his whiskey. On their way back to the farmhouse, without noticing, they passed the goat that had been meant to be slaughtered, left hungry overnight by the old farmer, collapsed on the floor of an isolated pen in exhaustion.

On the way home, Job pulled over twice before the contents of his stomach were finally emptied. Each time the car stopped, Ifi's eyes remained fixed out the window, staring at the grainy landscape. She ruminated again and again on the feeling in her throat when she thought, for just a second, that Job had taken a bullet. Aunty said little and pushed the baby more firmly into her breast, willing, with all her might, her body to protect the small boy, but knowing that soon she would be gone. The heat of the boy's flesh and the warmth of his breath dampened her neck. She was reminded of a saying she had heard nearly her entire life. In a whisper, she said, "A goat that dies scared will taste of fear."

When they returned home, they pushed the goat meat into the freezer. It was so large they were forced to move everything else into the refrigerator. They would be eating the goat's remains for many months.

That night, Job lay flat on his back, staring at the streamers and balloons hanging from each corner of the living room ceiling. His belly ached with failure. He wished he could do it all over again. But he could not. He wished he could go somewhere, get away from his life, just for a little while. *Where is Cheryl right now?* he wondered. Walking dogs, sipping a milkshake, reading one of her magazines? Already, he knew the answer. Sitting at her dining room table, her neck craned, her eyes pinched by the dull blue glow from a nearby room, she flicked through a book with pages well worn by her fingertips, a book about Nigeria, about him, about the exotic life she imagined he lived. The corners of Job's mouth drew into a smile.

Soon he would tell Ifi about their new home. Everything had been finalized. The whole time he had stood before the bank teller withdrawing the money, executing the close of the account, it felt right.

Tomorrow, they would cook the goat, drink Sapporo and Heineken, chat about politics, tease the boy with the taste of food from his native land, and pray for his future. In the safety of the time-honored preparations, preparations that had been made before him and would continue to be made after him, Job found sleep despite the boy's wails.

The boy cried as the pitch-black darkness escalated into a purple, then a steel gray. In the bedroom, Aunty and Ifi were spread out on the bed. Whispering, Aunty explained that the boy was crying because he could sense that she was going away soon. Although it was clear that he had a fever, Ifi couldn't help but feel that in part, Aunty was right. Rather reluctantly, she had grown so used to Aunty's place in her home that she couldn't imagine herself returning to the kitchen to cook a meal alone or sleep with her husband so close. Throughout the night, Aunty bathed the boy's face with a damp cloth and shined his chest with a mentholated rub. Each time she spread the salve across his body, she leaned in, eyes closed, and puffed her breath on his skin so that the heat could warm him on the inside. Of course, Ifi was not allowed to touch him.

When morning arrived, the boy had cried so long and with such gusto that his throat was strained, and he fell into an exhausted, fitful sleep at Aunty's breast. Each time the boy tossed in his sleep, she scraped her lacquered fingernails across the back of his head. As Ifi watched her, she imagined the tenderness that her mother must have had for her as a baby girl. Not like her aunty's forceful ways. She wondered if girls raised by surrogate mothers could ever replicate such a feeling with no memory of their birth mothers.

A sentiment so sudden and hard filled her chest and closed her throat. It was the same pang she had when she saw Job upended at the slaughter. She wanted, now more than ever, to be home. Not in this America. "Aunty," Ifi said.

Aunty's eyes opened slowly.

"I would like to see Uncle and my cousins."

Aunty sat up slowly, cupping the boy's head in her palm. Her voice was cheery, yet hesitant. "You are such a lucky girl—no mother, no father, sef. And you are in America driving a big car, living in a big man's house, eating goat meat and stockfish every day of the week while we are eating overripe yam."

Aunty placed the boy down on the bed between them and turned her back on Ifi. Even in sleep, he turned away from his mother to join Aunty.

Ifi tried again. "I am not happy."

"What is this talk of happy?" Aunty asked without turning. Then, gently, she added, "You have been in America too long, Mrs. Doctor."

Angrily, Ifi said, "He is not a doctor."

Now Aunty faced Ifi. "Do you think you are shaming your husband with this nonsense talk? You are his wife. Do you understand?" Ifi did. Aunty had known all along. "You are everything he is. Do not expose yourself. I will never hear you say that again. Do you understand?" Her words were low, yet sharp. "You *are* Mrs. Doctor."

3.

CHAPTER 15

O N THE WHOLE, VICTOR WAS CHEERFUL. HOWEVER, HE CAME TO appreciate the fact that his mother's sole purpose in life was to deny him the delights of the world. His father agreed. When he burst into a mirthless room, roaring at the top of his lungs in imitation of the famed X-Men hero, Wolverine, forks and butter knives attached to each hand, his mother lifted him by his shoulders, held him up to her eye level, and threatened to beat him. His father intervened. "Let the boy play." Everyone approved.

For Victor's fifth birthday, the house was filled entirely with strangers, mostly Nigerian. When he somersaulted into laps, marched through the room tasting the food on their plates, and banged pots and pans during *World News,* the guests joined in and agreed with his mother:

"*The boy* is wild."

"*The boy* is uncontrollable."

"*The boy* must be spanked."

"America is spoiling *the boy.*"

Still, there was an air of secret pleasure in their tone.

Victor's father swept his son's gifts aside and presented him with a Big Wheel tricycle wrapped in a shiny red bow. At first, Victor wasn't particularly drawn to the contraption. He didn't even bother to mount it, suspicious of its look. It didn't have arms and legs, monster eyes, or claws like his other gifts. It didn't have bright lights that swirled around or a horn that blared like his fire truck. His father heaved the tricycle in his direction, and it spun and spiraled as if unraveling. Victor heaved it back. This excited him; they shoved the Big Wheel back and forth until he grew restless. He did not grow to love it until months later.

An ugly old man with trembling lips presided over the celebration. His voice warbled as he made one pronouncement after another during the passing of the kola nut. Victor was supposed to call the man Uncle. Adults filled the room in long gowns of bright prints, swallowing balls of fufu, akra, and garri and drinking palm wine. They boasted of their newly purchased homes, computers, SUVs, and their second and third degrees. They disagreed about politics.

Most of the women were in the kitchen. Victor's mother was among them. She had banished Victor from the kitchen. Days before his birthday party, she found Victor in the kitchen, peering into the frozen, lifeless face of the goat that had been butchered for the celebration. Victor's cheek lay flat against the counter, his tongue waggled out like a goat's.

He was well aware that his mother wanted no part in the festivities, yet there she was bent over a pot of soup, flipping through ingredients in the cabinet like fabric swatches. She had wanted to feed Victor ice cream and cake and hot dogs. She'd wanted balloons and streamers and to invite one or two boys from Victor's school to join in. She had intended to take them to the children's museum or a movie afterwards. His parents had fought over this as they fought over everything.

To Victor, adulthood was equated with displeasure and disagreeableness. Instead of feeling frightened during the fights, Victor was merely annoyed that the attention was drawn away from him. Although nearly every one of his parents' fights began with *the boy,* he suspected they were fighting about something that had nothing to do with him. He thought this unfair and rivaled for the attention that was due to him. He banged louder on pots and pans. He cut holes into the living room couches and didn't bother to flip them over to disguise his artistry. He marked up the walls with his crayons. He pushed food around on his plate, chewed it up, and spat it out.

Each time, without fail, his mother raced around the table, grasping him in her fingers, holding him to her eye level. She threatened, "I will break your head!" Or, "I will send you to Nigeria!"

When the threats were issued, he was freshly wounded. He wailed as loudly as he could.

His father always emerged from the wings. "Are you raising a girl?" he would ask his mother.

With this, his mother couldn't argue. After more threats, she set him down and turned her fury on his father.

Of all the threats his mother had issued, the most perplexing of all was the threat to send Victor to Nigeria. He had mixed feelings. On the one hand, his father spoke so joyously of his days there as a child, running as freely as he wanted, climbing trees, playing with goats and chickens, swimming in rivers, surrounded by adoring adults and children. His father shared these delights with him as they nibbled moi moi, or when his father secretly allowed him a sip of palm wine, which he sucked down so quickly he came up choking and gasping for air. No one in Nigeria would make him put away his toys. After all, there were houseboys and housegirls for that.

On the other hand, his mother told him that in Nigeria, there would be no pizza or chicken nuggets. There would be fufu and jollof rice, which he liked well enough, but nothing could take the place of pizza. The children would make fun of the way he spoke. He would have to leave his Big Wheel behind. Worst of all, he would be beaten if he misbehaved. Of one thing Victor was certain: anything that evoked any pleasure in the world was considered naughty. Because of this, he would be beaten by neighbors, family friends, schoolteachers. In his mind, Victor imagined a long line of men and women with his mother's arms and fingers grasping him by the shoulders, flipping him upside down, beating him with the soles of their slippers, beating him with switches from trees, beating him with belts, beating him with whatever they could grasp.

When he was six, Victor's mother ran away with him. It was night, and he woke with her face so close to his that he could smell the stockfish on her breath. Victor was too groggy to put up any fight. She must have known this, because she wrapped him in her arms and hugged him to her chest. She pushed her lips to his forehead in a dry kiss. He was completely defenseless.

They were in the cab before he realized that he was in his shoes. Over his pajamas, he was wearing his winter coat, mittens, and hat. The pajamas were cotton and too thick to comfortably wear underneath the coat. Sweat dampened his arms, legs, and throat. He began to itch. In a futile attempt to free himself, Victor kicked and beat his arms. His mother, anticipating this, had buttoned and zipped him in so securely that his efforts were in vain. Victor cried and wailed. In his despair, he wanted his favorite item in the universe. "Big Wheel!" he shrieked.

She hadn't thought of that.

At first, the cabdriver just glanced at him in the rearview mirror. When the crying became a choking, spitting fury, the driver said, "Make him stop."

"I am paying," his mother said in return. But something about her tone told Victor that the driver was winning. "I will buy you candy if you are good," she said to Victor.

When the car finally stopped, they were in front of a brick two-story building. A pink light flickered outside. The cabdriver dropped them off in front without bothering to bring their luggage to the door. His mother grudgingly paid the tip anyway. Victor flung himself on the sidewalk, screaming, kicking, and punching.

"There is a swimming pool," she said to him. "You will eat pizza and ice cream for breakfast."

Eventually, a crowd surrounded them. His mother shielded her eyes. She attempted to collect their luggage, to collect him, to smile, to speak to him in hushed Igbo, which she rarely spoke. They looked at his mother as if she was stealing him. He felt taken.

"Your Big Wheel is inside," she said to him. Victor gazed at his mother suspiciously through the tears. If she had his Big Wheel, she would not allow him to play with it while he cried. *Is it hidden somewhere as a surprise?* he wondered. He decided to believe her and sucked back his tears; his cries diminished to a whimper.

By morning, Victor's father had arrived. Striped under the slanted rays of light that spread through the window blinds, he hugged Victor to his chest. Victor felt each inhale of his father's staggered breaths. He tasted his father's sweat through the suit and tie he wore to work. His fingers clasped around the tubes of the stethoscope that dangled from his father's pocket. His father headed to the car, leaving his mother to collect the unopened suitcases and store them in the car's trunk. Victor sat alongside his father in the front seat. The whole way home, his mother wept. Her cries were a steady, uninterrupted moan, wet with her tears.

❖

The boy had inadvertently become Job and Ifi's battlefield. Nearly a year earlier, when Victor first enrolled in kindergarten, his parents had battled over whether to place him in the local public school or to send him to private school. Although they were not Catholic, his father had insisted that Victor should attend the Catholic school, where the fitted and ironed uniforms reminded him of the refined boys' academies in Nigeria. Most importantly, the boy would be away from the influences of hoodlums, namely the black Americans and Mexican Americans at whom he still shuddered.

Ifi had insisted that Victor should attend the neighborhood public school. After all, it was free and just a few short blocks from their newly purchased home. She wouldn't have to worry over washing and mending uniforms. This freedom from restriction that she had observed over her few years in the country was what she considered quintessentially American.

Job had nearly won the battle when a local Nigerian teenager was on the news for attempted murder. He blamed it on the influence of black Americans. Ifi's arguments were entirely useless. In defeat, she starched and ironed Victor's clothes, lotioned his face, and wiped his nose so that the three could visit Sacred Heart Catholic Academy. They sat along a long, noisy corridor and watched as boys and girls of various sizes tramped up and down the stairs to their classrooms.

The first surprise was that the school was coed; however, Job dismissed the disappointment. Eventually, they would have a daughter. It would be easier to have them take the same bus to school each morning. The second surprise was that the children were loud and rambunctious, not at all disciplined and scholastic like the boys on the glossy pages of the school catalogue. But the final and most damning surprise was the cost. Even Ifi had counted on an installment or good faith plan. Surely good Christians couldn't turn potential parishioners away. They had already agreed to join the Catholic Church for the promised discount.

At the end of the afternoon they drove home, accompanied by the sound of the car's engine knocking. The next morning, Victor was enrolled in the neighborhood public school. As a compromise, whenever Victor went out to play, Job stood out on the porch, eyeing the neighborhood boys if they approached until they knew to leave Victor unharmed.

❖

The house was the first purchase Ifi and Job made together—well, not exactly. Just the same, like the boy, the action further solidified them as a unit, not the two strangers who met alone for the first time on the day of their arranged honeymoon. On the day they were to move in, as they drove up to the house, Ifi burst into tears. It was nothing like what she had expected of her first home. She had expected a garage, a picket fence, and a porch overlooking the neighborhood. She had expected, by then, to be a nurse. Instead, what she saw was a haunted aberration with peeling siding and cracked walkways; the windows were agape, like cavernous mouths.

Haven't I been in America long enough to realize that anything is possible, but things take time? she asked herself later that day. *Isn't it so that real estate is a financial investment that will make us millionaires, like Ed McMahon?* Then and only then would her dreams finally come true.

In her own way, Ifi grew to love the house. Like the boy, the house gave her a sense of use. Although she continued to send money home to her uncle and cousins, now that Aunty was gone and a new woman had replaced her, it wasn't the same. Although Job had begun to build their retirement home in Nigeria almost as soon as they married, the house in America became the focus of her dreams. It was her claim to America and all that was American. She could fill her kitchen with shiny appliances, watch American talk shows, and order hamburgers and french fries.

Like any new homeowner, Ifi threw herself into improvement projects. Some of the first repairs in order were a result of Victor's roughness. He shoved objects into open drains, pried at loose tiling in the kitchen, burrowed his little fingers into the gaping holes in the walls. At first, Ifi attempted the repairs on her own, plastering open holes, resealing lifting tiles, plunging drains. She looked on in satisfaction after the tasks were completed and looked on in dissatisfaction when sealed holes sank, when tiles began to curl once again, when ankle-length water rose in the shower. Of all the damaged areas of the home, the one that irked her the most was the giant, cavernous hole in the living room. It stared at them like a gaping mouth, with ragged bits of plaster for protruding teeth. Of late, Victor had taken to slipping his little hands and even his face into the hole. Each week it seemed to grow larger and larger, a hungry maw observing the family in mockery.

Ifi flipped through the pages of classified ads looking for plumbers, electricians, and carpenters to hire, anyone who knew a thing about a house. But when she called, the men who answered the phone were confused by her accent. They asked, "Excuse me?" "Come again?" They convinced themselves, as well as Ifi, that she surely couldn't afford their services. She nearly gave up on her search, but standing in the checkout lane at the grocery one day, Ifi found a handmade flyer for a handyman: FIX ANYTHING. GOOD PRICE. On a lark, Ifi called the number, and a woman's buttery voice answered. She took Ifi's particulars and said she would dispatch the handyman.

A week later, a tall young man with slanted eyes and a taut jaw arrived. He carried a steel box with his tools. His jeans were baggy at the waist. His hair was neatly braided in rows. He looked to be about eighteen.

Job answered the door. In the background, Victor hollered and slammed his toys like the wrestlers on TV. Ifi sliced fresh okra into her palm.

With still eyes, he stared Job down. "Hey," the man said carefully. "I got another job at three, so we have to see what I can do till then."

Job frowned. "You have the wrong house."

The man had a slip of paper in his pocket. He retrieved it and matched it with the numbers over the porch.

"You have made a mistake," Job said. Heat rose. He began to perspire. "Sorry," he said to the man. "I will help you find your friends."

When Ifi saw Job standing stock still in the doorway, she crowded into the door next to him. "Hello?" she asked.

Again that strange look on his face. "Listen, I'm supposed to be here until three, but then I have to get going," he said again.

Ifi smiled at him. Still, she said the words that Job had been searching for during the entire exchange. "We don't want any trouble."

He peered into Ifi's face thoughtfully. "Mary said," he began, but then stopped himself.

Immediately, the stern expression on Ifi's face relaxed. "Jamal!" she exclaimed.

Slowly, he nodded.

"The boy, Jamal? You have grown, oh. You are a man."

His face broke into a crooked smile, and his eyes slanted on his face.

Ifi turned to Job. "Jamal is here to fix our house."

Job's face deepened into a smile. "Oh, I see," he said. "Thank you for coming, but we have found someone else." Not an ounce of recognition was on his face. He reached into his pocket and produced a twenty-dollar bill. "Here, for your trouble."

Jamal shrugged, took the twenty, and drove away. Ifi did not stop him. Ifi did not remind Job of the teenage boy with the slanted eyes, of the night the boy had lifted her down the stairs as she went into labor. She did not remind him of the crib the boy pieced together for them the night she gave birth to their first son. Still, Jamal did not leave her mind.

Instead, as Job asked, "What were you thinking, bringing akatta into our home? Have you not learned anything?" Ifi only listened.

"Do you know," Job said to her, "if I had not paid him for no work at all, that man would come with his friends at night to rob and beat us?"

Ifi called him a racist. She told him she did not see color. *In America, everyone is equal,* she thought. She said all the things she had heard on television and read in newspapers. She added, "How can you discriminate a man who is your color?"

But then, inevitably, the fight turned to *the boy.* In the first place, *the boy* was responsible for all the repairs the house needed. He rode that clunky red *thing* his father had insisted on buying him in the house. Because his mother was not watchful, he banged into walls. He overturned trashcans. He circled the kitchen, leaving skid marks and curling tiles underfoot.

As if to prove her point, Victor came pedaling into the entryway, his voice loud like a fire siren, and struck the wooden front door with such force that from the outside, passersby witnessed a great tremble.

CHAPTER 16

JUST AFTER TWO ON SATURDAYS, WHILE HIS MOTHER BOUGHT GROCERIES, Victor and his father drove through town, stopping at one garage sale after another. They began their afternoons with a stop at a gas station. His father gave him money to purchase the candy of his choice. Then his father leaned back and scanned the classifieds, circling each destination with a felt-tip marker. Victor took the Laffy Taffy, Jujubes, or Skittles and the bill to the cashier; he grinned wickedly when the cashier not only gave him his candy, but also some money in return. Each time, he presented the change to his father in astonishment. His father chuckled and told him he was a clever boy.

The neighborhoods they visited were unlike their own. While the houses in Victor's neighborhood were tall and thin, with missing siding and cracked walkways, the houses in the garage sale neighborhoods were larger, pristine, with undisturbed yards, garages, wooden fences, and flowery gardens. These neighborhoods were a bore to Victor. At the end of every trip, he gladly returned to the broken holes under porches that led to crawl spaces, to poking sticks at beasts behind chain-link fences, to the misshapen shrubbery that shielded him in hide-and-seek, to tearing through the streets on his red Big Wheel.

In the summer, the yards of each garage sale were identical. Hand-painted signs hung on trees, sometimes with airless balloons collected in a wilted bouquet. Rows of tables were positioned with tennis rackets, dog-eared dime novels, scratched records, and worn shoes. They stopped at garage sale after garage sale, overturning different objects in their hands, flipping switches, poking and prodding. It was on one such journey, Victor suspected, that his father had purchased his Big Wheel.

Victor enjoyed these outings. No one told him to put his hands in his pockets. No one told him he couldn't try on the roller skates if they were three sizes too big. No one told him he was too small to fling the beads of an abacus, or too big to taste the cool, smooth surface of a snow globe. In fact, the sellers encouraged it, following them with oversolicitous smiles, instructing him to step this way, push that way, to get the full effect. His father seemed to enjoy these trips as much as Victor did, standing importantly in his suit and tie in spite of the heat, in spite of the sweat that dampened his arms. His father picked up one object after another and inquired, in crisp, overpronounced English, "Tell me about this."

On one such trip, Victor's suspicions about the Big Wheel were confirmed. A red-haired woman with high-waisted jeans and a baseball cap met them. Victor didn't notice her at first. Nor did his father, it seemed. But suddenly, abruptly, she was standing at his side. She patted the top of his head. "Victor, do you like your Big Wheel?" she asked.

Although it didn't occur to Victor to wonder how she knew his name— surely everyone knew Victor Ogbonnaya—he was struck dumb. He didn't like the way she looked at him. He didn't like the way his father stood stiffly at his side.

"Victor, answer," his father said.

Only then did he reply. "Yeah," he said, "I like it."

"Victor," she said, "you're a big boy now. You look just like your father."

His father and the lady exchanged a glance that he didn't understand. She picked up a stuffed bear from a table and handed it to him. "You like this?" she asked. "I'll buy you this."

Just then, Victor had had enough of the woman. He wheeled around and knocked the bear free from her hand. The bear was insulting. "I'm a big boy!" he said to her. He thought of his mother, who just that morning had scolded him for wetting his bed, asking him if he was still a baby or if he had decided to be a big boy.

The lady's face was crimson.

"Victor, behave yourself!" his father said. He jerked Victor with such force that he expected his arm to fall off. He had never been spoken to so sharply by anyone, not even his mother. His eyes screwed up and he howled. But his father didn't relent. "Take the toy," his father said.

Victor refused.

"Victor, behave or I will beat you," his father said in Igbo. And then, "Do not disgrace me."

Still, Victor refused to submit. When the lady bent to pick up the bear, he kicked it beyond her reach. Tears streamed down his face. He wanted his mother, so he said so. "Mommy!" he wailed.

"Hey, Job." The lady let out a dry laugh. "It's okay. We'll pick something else out that's just right for a big boy." When she winked at Victor, he regarded her with distrust. Finally, she began to back away and replaced the teddy bear on the table.

It seemed like it was over. She said good-bye to his father. They hesitantly hugged, bumping shoulders as they leaned into one another. She turned to Victor. Victor whipped away from her.

"Victor." His father's voice was low.

"No," Victor said. His father pulled Victor's arms apart and forced them around the lady, who was stock still in the captive embrace. She smelled of cigarettes and strawberry shampoo.

Victor was utterly humiliated. He shrank into himself. Nothing, not even the woman's plaintive glance, not even the candy she offered, could make him smile again for the rest of the outing. When they returned home, his mother asked what was wrong. Victor's father told her that Victor had fallen and bumped his head.

After the garage sale fiasco the outings stopped, and Victor endured long, tedious summer afternoons watching Bugs Bunny and the Road Runner while his father snored on the couch. Inevitably, Victor stopped the sound through his father's nose with his fingertips until his father woke up, sputtering and choking, looking every which way for his assailant before pulling Victor into a bear hug. It was the only thing that seemed to make his mother laugh before heading to her job at the motel in the afternoons.

In late summer, the grasses of the various parks throughout town were beaten flat and browned from the scalding Nebraska summer heat. Nonetheless, knobby-kneed men in mesh shorts and worn polos frequented the parks. Caravans arrived in the early evenings during the time between an early shift's end and a late shift's beginning. The men ran themselves ragged after soccer balls while dodging holes in the ground. Along the side of the fields, their wives were spread out on blankets, feeding their children curried rice, burritos, or greasy plantains from plastic Tupperware containers covered in foil.

In his earliest days in America, when Job was still a university student and he and Emeka were still friendly, they would shout and holler along the sidelines, teasing the losing team until one scrunch-faced defender would charge the sideline and demand that they join the game. Emeka always announced that he was too old. *How could young men shame themselves by demanding that an old man with four daughters—one already grown—should run among them?* Because he was just that, they always relented, focusing their attention instead on Job. From then on, he had tried his best to avoid the humiliation of running the field by not coming altogether. At his ripe age, as a father, Job could finally join the older men resting along the benches, sharing cigarettes, sipping from sacks of beer, and placing bets they would never be forced to pay.

One evening, Victor announced that he would play for the Super Eagles when he grew up. The ripple of pleasure that spread through the crowd of Nigerians filled Job with such pride that he made a point to purchase cleats, shin guards, and a small jersey. From then on, to the nods of onlookers, Victor stylishly paraded the fields, kicking and elbowing past the little boys in their miniature soccer game. Victor wasn't exactly good, but the key, he had discovered, was to elbow, push, and pull the other players around, preventing them from scoring.

Only the mothers complained, confirming Victor's certainty about the purpose of all mothers. He was neither resentful of nor charmed by this affirmation. He unquestioningly acknowledged this fact, as he accepted the fact that the sky was blue. At once he became the most hated child on the field by mothers and fathers alike. Mothers were straightforward in their contempt, attempting to revive their whimpering boys. To save face, fathers declined to intervene, sometimes siding with Victor, insisting that a scraped knee or a bloodied nose was the cost of a hard-fought game before reluctantly shoving their trembling sons back into battle.

Job felt the need to apologize to Cheryl for Victor's behavior at the garage sale. His chance came one evening when Cheryl agreed to meet them at the soccer field. As Cheryl looked on, Victor huffed up and down the field, elbowing and knocking little boys out of his way. Although the crowd was primarily international, with representatives of India, Malaysia, Kenya, Brazil, and Nigeria, there were a few pink-faced, jeans-wearing American wives and girlfriends sprinkled throughout the crowd. Among them, Cheryl sat on a blanket with potato chips, slices of fruit, cold cuts, and juice boxes.

As is eventually destined to happen to all Goliaths, the Davids of the world—boys who nightly limped home swollen, bruised, and teary—launched an attack on Victor. In a wall they united, breaking one way, cutting that way, forcing their bodies into steely alignment each time Victor neared, knocking him to the ground, tripping him, elbowing. The onslaught happened from all sides and was thoroughly unexpected. In stubborn denial, Victor refused to acknowledge their blows, offering them a dull smile. Until then, he had assumed that the object of the game was for the other boys to fall. Not him. At one point, the great giant was knocked to the ground so viciously that groans issued from the crowd. Even the adult soccer game paused.

Job didn't interfere. *How can I?* he thought. *This is the duty of a mother.* But Ifi was at work, at the motel. She had never even seen the soccer field. And the mothers along the sideline, ever vigilant, were suddenly distracted by the babies in their laps, the runny noses of younger children, the articles of trash.

Cheryl charged onto the field. Victor was limp with cries. She smothered him in the embrace he earlier denied her and carried him back to her blanket, where she fed him browning apple slices coated in peanut butter and raisins, where she burst open a juice box and encouraged him to sip.

He felt tricked. But there were no friendly faces in the crowd, not even his father's, and so he allowed Cheryl to hold him, to speak to him.

"Is it true that you're a smart boy?" she asked. "Have you been playing with your Big Wheel?"

Although Job had seen Cheryl's subtle tenderness the nights and early mornings they had spent together—tucking extra pillows behind his back, running her fingers through the knots in his hair—her reaction to Victor was unexpected. For days afterwards, he lay awake in bed, thinking the moment over. It seemed strange seeing her there, his little boy paralyzed in her arms. The picture should have been a great comfort to him; frankly, it was not. He hadn't even wanted Cheryl to take part in these outings in the first place, but after the garage sales, she began to insist on the soccer field too. She wanted to see the boy. *Just get to know another part of you.* For the most part, it had never bothered Job. After all, Victor was too young to understand such "friendships." But to see his Victor in her arms like this was suddenly disturbing.

From that day forward, he didn't call things off exactly, but he answered the look in Cheryl's eyes less and less each time they were together. Now, something was different. What, he did not know.

For the first time, as they lay awake in bed together one morning after his shift, Cheryl lighting a cigarette, Job asked her why she had not made good on her efforts to stop smoking. "In Nigeria," he said, "smoking is for men."

Cheryl didn't even bother to put the cigarette away. He expected her to argue with him, to tell him that in America women were equal to men or something to that effect, to say she was not his slave. But she stared numbly at him. He never saw her smoke another cigarette again, yet he could smell the scent on her now, pungent as ever. That she had taken to smoking in secret, just before and after his arrivals, he was certain.

Scalding afternoons made up the days leading into August. The living room fan, draped in a misted towel, circulated stagnant air about the room day and night. Job worked the night shift at the hospital and slept through the mornings and afternoons, rising just as Ifi left for alternating late afternoon and evening shifts at the motel, where she vacuumed rooms, emptied trash bins of condoms and beer bottles, and replaced semen-stained sheets. Few nights were shared by the two. In the event that they did share a night together, the sex was in the dark. Neither bothered to shower before or after, so their musky bodies joined together in a mingling of scents: onions from dinner, vomit from the boy, urine from a patient at the hospital, stale cigarettes from the motel. It was over just as quickly as it began, and the two retreated to their sides of the bed before falling into heavy slumber.

One night, after the boy had gone to bed, Ifi and Job were lumped on the couches in the living room watching television when they heard a scraping outside.

Ifi's eyes opened in alarm. Job raised his finger to his lips and went out the back door. Ifi followed. At night, the backyard was a frayed forest. Bushes were tangled and unkempt. Half-grown grass caught at the backs of their ankles. In the distance, they could see the outline of the full-bodied moon. Ifi clung to Job. He told her to go inside but leaned into her anyway. Then they saw its eyes, large and shining. The raccoon flipped into the air, letting out a squeal, which incidentally was identical to the one that Job issued as well. The suddenness of the two sounds, and their similarity, made Ifi laugh. Then Job laughed. And when they saw that the overturned trash cans and scattered refuse were not *the boy's* handiwork after all, in a small way, they rejoiced.

Such was the sentiment that compelled Ifi to suggest a family outing the next day as they ate toast with runny eggs for breakfast. Job acquiesced. By Sunday of the following week, Ifi, Job, and Victor were sweating in a hot open-air tent, divided by pens of stinking hogs and sheep at the 4-H exhibit of the Lancaster County Fair. A week before the commencement of every school year, a parade of tents was positioned alongside the abandoned fields and hollowed-out buildings of Zonta. A beer garden, concerts of howling country singers, a dubiously erected Ferris wheel, and the usual pageantry of horses and apple-cheeked schoolgirls in drooping sashes rounded out the stale days of the retreating summer.

Ifi had the day off. Though she had lived in America for nearly six years, this would be her first time attending. Shaking off the disappointment of the sandhill cranes all those years before, she took in the sights with forced vigor and appreciation, finding herself slipping in and out of Aunty's platitudes. "Never count the eggs that might hatch," she warned Victor as they overlooked a small-game exhibition.

At the 4-H exhibit, a small African boy about Victor's age trotted out a limping calf and carefully mounted wooden stairs to a stage. Three other children, small, bowlegged, and uncertain, marched along with a scowling sheep, hog, and chicken. They stuttered and spat prepared speeches into the microphone. An announcer followed, haltingly shouting and proclaiming them all winners before pinning each child with identical blue ribbons. In the tight, packed crowd, parents beamed from the sidelines. An array of camera flashes lit up the crowded tent.

"What kind of competition is it that everyone is the winner?" Ifi asked Job.

"Nonsense," he replied.

Still eyeing the blue ribbons, Ifi turned to Victor. "You see, that boy is smaller than you." Victor's mouth was full of cotton candy. To no one in particular, Ifi said, "My son can do better." And she could see it: just like the other American children, her Victor would stand in a cowboy hat and boots, proudly looming over a bleating sheep as he was presented with a ribbon. Ifi and Job would beam from the sidelines like the other parents, lighting the sky with their cameras. By then, she decided, the holes in their house would be repaired. There would even be a white picket fence. She turned to Victor. "Next year will be you." She took Job's hand. "Anything is possible."

Under the sun's glare, Job frowned. He had the bloated look of flayed dough. It was the heat.

"You were right, you know," she explained. "I didn't believe you then. When I first came to this country, I saw the cold and snow and empty fields. But there is more." *What vanity!* she thought of herself. *Coming to America with the glitter of golden streets and diamonds like apples in trees.* How wrong she had been. All it took was hard work and pluck. Hadn't Job known all along? Hadn't he tried to make her understand? They did not own their clinic, but they did have a home of their own and a son. *Amazing!* she thought.

A little girl in a yellow dress skipped past them. At the same instant, Ifi and Job both recalled that silly night, bucking and sweating under the Port Harcourt heat. They remembered the darkness and then the sudden light. Ifi remembered Job, swollen and pitiful in her yellow dress, with crooked lipstick on his teeth.

"Mr. Doctor," she said, a tease to her voice.

"Mrs. Doctor," he said back. "Do you still have that yellow dress?"

Ifi's head said no, but her eyes said yes. "I have had to repair that dress because it cannot fit properly." A deliberate pause. "A big, fat woman with large buttocks damaged it."

Job quipped an American saying he had heard many times before. "No, no, not fat, big boned."

Another pause. "Big bones? I don't understand," she said.

"Nothing," he said, shaking off his failed attempt at humor. "Nothing."

"Tell me now," Ifi said, her tone taking on irritation. "What is this talk of big bones?"

"I am saying that I am not fat. It is only that my bones are big," he said.

Her eyes flicked dubiously to that thunderous belly of his, not so subtly disguised under his dampened shirt.

"Come now, it is an American joke."

"Oh, yes-yes," Ifi said back uncertainly. And then she laughed hard and suddenly, imagining bones thick enough to fill up her husband's round belly. Job, caught up in the sound of her perplexed laughter, joined in.

Just three hours remained until Job had to leave for his weekend shift at the hospital, so they moved along the various stalls and exhibits in haste, stopping only to pose for pictures in front of a clown, a cutout, and a glittery poster. Victor's fingers and mouth were sticky purple from cotton candy, and he made the usual menace of himself, stuffing his fingers through the gaps in the fencing to grasp at a swinging tail or ear. Twice they had been warned by one of the bulldog-faced attendants to contain him. On Victor's third move in the direction of a surly pig, Ifi grasped his sticky palms, only letting go after she had dragged him far from the tent. A row of portapotties was next to the tents, and Job disappeared into one while she and Victor waited outside.

Facing them was one of the winners of a blue ribbon, the African boy. In one hand, an ice cream cone dripped; in the other, the hand of a girl with her back to them. Tall, with gangly legs, she fanned herself from the heat while flirting with a merchant, a teenage boy. Before Ifi could stop him, Victor scrambled at the boy, swiftly exchanging his dissolving cotton candy for the boy's ice cream cone. At first, it looked as if the boy would cry or fight or yell.

Ifi moved to grab Victor's hand. "What is wrong with you, eh?"

Another merchant, a grown man dressed head to toe in a striped uniform, admonished, "Hey now, hey now. Brothers shouldn't fight. Gotta look out for each other." It was enough to stop the two small boys from getting into a fistfight. The other boy took an uncertain bite at the cotton candy, shrugged his shoulders, and continued to eat without another thought. Victor licked furiously at the dripping cone he had claimed as his.

Ifi made a move for the cone in his hand. "That is not yours."

"Boys," the man said to Ifi, putting his hands up to stop her. "Listen, don't sweat the small stuff, huh? They're only being boys. I fought with my brother too, every chance I could. For no reason at all. "

By then the girl had turned around. "That's not his brother," she said, screwing up her face. "He's *my* brother."

Only then did Ifi see it, the striking similarity of the two boys with their identical bulbous heads, their wide, flat noses, full lips, and chestnut-brown complexions. Really, the only difference was that the other boy was slightly smaller, perhaps no more than a year younger. Openmouthed for a few moments, she gazed at the boy. "They could be brothers," she finally said.

"Yeah, I guess so," the girl said. "Come on, let's find Mom and show her your ribbon." She took the boy's hand and trotted away with him.

Just then Job reemerged from the toilet. Halfway through telling Job about the small boy, Ifi abandoned the tale, remembering the confusion that big bones had caused earlier. Instead, they stood in line for a turn at the dunking booth.

As the new school year approached, Victor spent his afternoons furiously pedaling through the neighborhood streets on his red Big Wheel. Only after dusk began to settle did he traipse home, ragged and damp with sweat, his stomach hissing in hunger. By now, his parents had relented. No longer did his father stand on the porch steps eyeing the neighborhood boys— the Mexican Americans and black Americans who, frankly, didn't particularly like Victor. In fact, *he* was the neighborhood boy parents warily eyed as they watered their plants, plucked their weeds, and checked their mailboxes. Postal workers were in the habit of ducking and stepping aside or widening their legs so he could pass through. Trees retreated when he approached. Dogs that once barked without abandon withdrew just as they heard the grinding and swishing of his tires.

One night, Victor did not return home for dinner. Ifi and Job exchanged glances across the table, but continued slowly swallowing garri. After all, they both remembered the Sudanese boy who had disappeared just months earlier. His mother had called 9-1-1 to report him missing. When he turned up playing basketball on the other side of town, she'd wept openly. Not because she had found her boy, but because the authorities made the boy's single mother pay the expenses for the fire trucks, ambulance, and police cars; because they charged her for being an abusive mother—*after all, what kind of mother doesn't know where her boy is?*; because they raided her home and, seeing that her three small children shared one mattress at night, fined her for negligence. Job and Ifi had agreed then, as they did now, that in Nigeria, there was nothing wrong with a boy being a boy, sef.

After their slow swallows had digested, Victor still hadn't turned up. Their minds raced to all the things that could have happened to the boy. Most frightening was the thought of the men they had read about in the newspaper. Yes, they had heard of that sort of thing happening to girls, but a boy? Only in America. Ifi called in late to work, and she and Job staggered through neighborhood after neighborhood, mixing Victor's name with threats.

"Victor, boy, you come home at once!"

"This is your father, Victor! I am not playing games!"

"I will beat you, oh!"

When the houses along the streets were nothing more than outlines, their threats were whimpers. "Victor," his mother pleaded, "I will buy you candy."

On the way home, Job and Ifi turned on one another.

Job said, "You see? Let the boy play in the house in peace!"

Ifi said, "Why did you buy that foolish toy?"

Just as they made a final loop around the block, heading for home, a girl hurrying past jostled Job. It wasn't until they were halfway down the block, shaded by the tilt of trees, that Job looked back, suddenly putting the pieces together. Something about the girl's lean, something about the whimper in her breath.

"Hey!" he shouted at her back. "You come here!"

She stopped short and turned to face them. She was no more than a girl, a teenager, pale wispy bangs dripping around her glasses frames. Suddenly he was struck with the image of a gleaming metal smile, the girl on their porch steps, grinning as she demonstrated an arpeggio on her clarinet not even two weeks before. She had been selling boxes of candy for a trip to band camp. By the time she had left, Job had succumbed to her entreaties, purchasing three boxes of overpriced gummy bears, which Victor had gleefully dissolved in a matter of minutes while Ifi complained that Job should never have opened the door to begin with.

The girl was shaking, and Ifi was shrieking, "Where is he? What has happened?" But the girl quietly trembled as she gestured up the street.

Then he was in a full sprint, running as fast as he could. Two blocks from them, he could already make out the frame of the silver Camaro and the glow of headlights bracketing the street. A burning climbed up Job's sides as he sprinted past the lit windows, the faces of strangers gaping from their porches. He hadn't the time to think of what could be wrong. He hadn't the time to even catch his breath. The red Big Wheel, torn into pieces, was in one direction, and in the other, a small crowd had begun to form, leaning over what Job could only guess was his Victor. He pried apart the shoulders and thrust his way into the commotion.

He let out a sigh of relief. *No blood,* he thought. *The legs are even moving.* If Victor's legs were moving, then he was surely conscious. He was fine. There would be a broken bone that could easily be set and wrapped in a cast. He would hug his arms around his boy, scold him gently, and remind him of the danger in the world.

"Victor!" he shouted.

Just the bare whisper of movement in the boy's chest was the only reply. Perhaps he was in need of CPR.

"I'm the boy's father," he said to whomever would listen.

"Please, you have to stand back," someone said. "We called an ambulance. They're on their way."

"No, no," Job said. "There isn't enough time." *Five minutes? Ten minutes? Twenty minutes?* he wondered. Regardless, it would be too late.

He made a move for Victor, but the man restrained him. Then another and another came, each securing Job's arms behind his back, keeping him from his only child, his only son. "It'll be okay," a voice gently whispered. "An ambulance is on the way."

"Let me go, you idiots!" Job hurled in fury. "I am a doctor, damnit!"

They let go, eyebrows raised in surprise. One by one they stepped aside, parting the crowd. Job was close now, so close he could see the trickles of blood coming from Victor's eyes, nose, and mouth. *His legs will be broken,* he thought, *but those can be reset.* His arms too perhaps. *But it will be okay.* He looked up. He found Ifi among the crowd, shivering, her eyes wide in alarm and fear. He exchanged a glance with her, a glance that said, "It will be fine. Trust in me." For once, the hard look in her eyes softened, acknowledged, agreed. *It will be fine,* they said, together.

After all, his legs were moving. There was the slight murmur that echoed up to Victor's chest. Job crouched and lifted Victor's neck toward him. "I am here," he whispered. He parted Victor's lips, cleared his mouth so that he could swallow his father's breath. But there was blood, so much blood, and it would not stop. He turned him on his side. Victor's legs were trembling. *It will be okay.* Sirens were sounding in the distance. But they were so far away. Job lifted Victor's chest off the pavement. A ring of blood marked the concrete.

I am a doctor, he told himself. *I am a doctor.*

The longer Victor was without oxygen the worse it would be, and so he must elevate his head. He must proceed to breathe his life into his only son. He placed his mouth over Victor's, tasting the blood in his throat. He fixed his fist against his Victor's chest and pumped as hard as he could. Now, more than ever, he wished for his stethoscope. He wished for the whisper of Victor's heartbeat.

But the moving had stopped. There was no more tremble in the legs.

Job lifted Victor off the concrete, first his shoulders, then his head. He shouted air into his son's lungs. He beat harder at his chest. And then he felt it, a sudden hard ripple of breath, the starting of the boy's engine. *Soon, I will have my boy,* he thought—and the smile, the dull smile, and the pranks, and the unruliness.

"Let him go." Someone grabbed Job's arms.

Without looking, Job angrily batted at the arms. "I am a doctor," he said.

"Doctor, let him go."

"I am performing CPR."

A pair of arms knocked him back off his feet. A calm whisper in his ear: "Doctor, you did all you could." Two sets of arms paralyzed him, grinding his face to the concrete until the deafening peal of sirens, the swirl of lights, the glowing haze of headlights was cutting through the night air like a fog. Now the street was filled with neighbors, all whispering among themselves; and there was the girl, standing with her back to a police car, the arms of her mother wound around her as an officer questioned her. And Ifi, her eyes filled with that unmistakable frown of disappointment.

Above it all, Job could hear the man's voice: "Doctor, you did all you could."

Soon, the ambulance was taking his Victor away, and the men were leading Job to one of the police cars; and Ifi was standing with her back to him, talking to one of the officers; and Job was wailing and angry and hating himself, wishing for his stethoscope, flipping through the channels of his mind, trying to replay every minute, trying to find the moment between the last tremble and the sudden release, realizing that for just one moment, he had his boy's life in his hands, and he let it slip away.

CHAPTER 17

I F ONE APPLIES, THERE IS PAID TIME FOR GRIEVANCE. WHEN AUNTY DIED, IFI thought to apply then; she didn't. How to explain that her father's sister—her surrogate mother whom Ifi had hated all those years without even knowing it until her aunty's one visit to America—had died from a heart attack? Now in Aunty's place was another woman, half her uncle's age and half her aunty's size. From then on, Nigeria was no longer home.

When the baby girl died inside Ifi's body, how to explain that a child who had never been born needed proper bereavement, that somewhere inside her, she knew that she would never recover from the pain? She could never have another child.

The exchange never made sense to her then, as it didn't now: a penny for every second of pain. With the forms spread out in front of her, Ifi imagined the stacks and stacks of pennies filling the room, rising from the dusty, hardwood floors past the gaping hole in the wall to the ceiling. *What can I do with these pennies?* she asked herself. She could never spend them, because they would continue to replicate forever, like a cancer. Under the bold heading, REASON, Ifi left the space blank. Her application was denied.

A night before Job planned to fly to Nigeria alone, to bury their son, Ifi parked the car outside the junkyard where the damaged vehicle that had killed her boy rested. Bats screeched well into the night. It had just rained. Mist salted the air. A high chain-link fence wrapped around the junkyard. It was secured with a rusted padlock.

Ifi's mind was a revolving door of blame. Yesterday it was Job's fault. He bought that foolish Big Wheel. If Victor had never ridden it, he would never have wandered into the street. If they had never moved into that big, ugly house, they would never have lived in such a neighborhood where a boy couldn't play in the streets without fear. If she had never met Job . . .

Today it was Ifi. *Why didn't I allow the boy to play in the house?* She should have permitted him to be as rough as he pleased. Then he would never have had any reason to be out in the street. He was a boy, sef. Anything he broke in the house could be repaired or replaced. *Why was I so insistent on scolding the poor boy for a mere scratch on the wall?*

Why must Job look at her that way with his probing eyes? Why couldn't he go to work like a normal human being? After all, people lost children every day of the week in every part of the world. Immediately after it had all happened, Ifi returned to the motel. She went about cleaning each room as if nothing had happened. But Job stayed home. He hardly ate a thing these days.

Until today. That morning, he'd collected himself and acted as if everything was fine. And suddenly it didn't seem right for him to pick up and move on as Ifi had. Without her realizing it was the case, Job's pain had been a comfort to her. It was as if everything that had been holding Ifi together began to crumble once she saw Job go about his day. She'd left the house and kept driving, even after she crossed the path of the motel's flickering lights— until she was here, again, at the junkyard. And now, instead of remaining behind it as she had done for the past few weeks, Ifi found herself mounting the chain-link fence. Tonight she needed to be closer.

Feeling a rip in her uniform slacks, she scaled the fence. A red gash on her thigh screamed. Puddles rippled beneath her heels. Cars were lined in rows, their broken frames pushed into the mud. A light glowed. The fading outline of a row of buildings some ways out was illuminated. Off in the distance farther still was the highway. Wet tires hissed on the pavement.

In the newspaper, the article had been exactly one paragraph in length. Victor was unnamed. The first line, which Ifi remembered by heart, read "One boy dead in a vehicle-bicycle accident on the corner of Ash and Leighton." There was no mention of Victor's beloved Big Wheel. No mention of his antics. No mention of the light in his eyes. Silence hung between the words on the page. When reporters called the next morning, Ifi and Job refused to comment. In the place of words was a picture of a dented silver car. Missing from the picture were the pieces of Victor's broken body.

Dusk shaded the coup's silver color. Although the license plates had been pried free, Ifi found the car immediately. Among the rows, it was obedient and cowed. At first she stood, simply gazing at the car. Ifi and Job had joked since Victor was born that he had a big head. His thighs were lumpy. He had been a plump baby and chubby for a boy of nearly six. As he had lived his life full of noise, he refused to go out in a whisper: the windshield was shattered where he had been flung.

Ifi meant only to look at the car, to think about Victor's last few moments pedaling through the streets, probably hollering like a fire truck's siren. She meant only to run her fingers over the frame, to touch the parts of the vehicle that had felt her son last. Her fingers slid over the car's surface. Wet with rust and dirt, Ifi brought her palm to her face and touched. The smell of metal and iron was so strong in her nose and throat that she gagged and hacked saliva on the ground. Her heel pressed into the spit. Then, as if by reflex, Ifi's foot came forward and struck one headlight, then the other. Her fists closed over the hood. Ifi struck again and again until she was haggard and bloody with fury.

She stepped away to inspect the damage. But for a dent and a few cracks in the headlights, there was none.

Not more than five feet away, a metal rod was strewn among the debris. A surge of energy lifted Ifi, and she raced to the car, rod in hand. She shattered the windshield and pummeled the hood.

Then she heard it, a whinnying. The sound stopped and started again. And stopped again. The broken vehicle that had killed her son offered the most immediate shelter, an irony that, even in the moment, Ifi had the wherewithal to recognize. From behind the car, Ifi watched as a teenage boy stepped out into the night. He was stripped from the waist up. His pale skin was wet and luminescent.

"Listen, asshole," the boy said after a pause. "I got a gun, so don't fuck with me." The boy peered around, knocked on a few cars, then, satisfied with his show of manliness, returned to a busted-out sedan.

From where she was crouched, Ifi witnessed the rocking of the car. Throaty giggles. The whinnying resumed. He had acted the hero, and here was his reward.

Safe at last. Ifi stepped out from behind the car.

Suddenly, the boy returned. Sweat glistened on his shoulders. A large metal bar was raised over his head. It began to come down—on Ifi.

A girl. "Danny, no! It's a lady." Her slim pale shoulders were drowned by the tan shawl draped across them. "What are *you* doing here?"

Danny erupted into chuckles.

The girl's eyes met his. She laughed with him. Their lidded eyes rested on Ifi.

"Whoa, man," Danny said. "Whoa."

The girl reached into the car and offered Ifi a hit on their joint. Ifi, still frazzled, took the joint in her trembling fingers. Never before had she even held a cigarette. She started to say no, but the hungry look in their eyes. She put the joint to her lips, sucked on the smoke hard. Her lungs caught on fire. She coughed. The couple laughed.

"*You* did that your first time," the girl said to Danny.

"I didn't."

"You did."

"Because *I* inhaled. *You* didn't."

"So?"

"Forget it."

"Yeah, fuh-gedd-a-bout it." They laughed at their joke.

"What you doing here?" the girl asked again.

For the first time, Ifi spoke. "My boy," she said.

They looked around the junkyard at the shells of cars. "Won't find him here."

"No," Ifi said back.

"Maybe," the girl said, "hiding here somewhere."

"What's he look like?"

"He is a boy, a beautiful boy, my son."

"What's his name?"

"Victor."

"I don't know a single Victor."

"How old is he? We'll help you look."

"Five."

Danny crouched and called out in a low voice, "Victor, Victor, where are you?"

"What if we never find him? Oh, that would be terrible," the girl said.

"Then we'll break shit." Danny still had the bar in his hands. He smashed it over the top of the car they had camped in. They all listened as the splintering glass ruptured the night air.

"Nice move," she said sarcastically.

He smashed at another car.

Ifi collected her bar and attacked the silver coupe. They joined. In turn, the three demolished the vehicle, their silhouettes throbbing from their laughter.

Sirens wailed in the distance. By the time the police arrived, the car had stopped rocking. Only the scent of marijuana and alcohol lingered in the air. Into the blur of the highway the boy and girl had vanished, giddy and breathless with their raw defiance. Because of her bleeding thigh, Ifi made it only midway down the fence before a yellow light burned her eyes. A policewoman with a wide gait stepped into the light. But the glare was too intense for Ifi to make out her features. A staticky walkie-talkie merged into the sounds of the officer's voice. Her questions were a disconnected stream of guttural syllables that Ifi had trouble understanding. Her blood was hot. Her throat was thick. Her eyelids were heavy.

Ifi's bloodied hands were handcuffed. "Please," she said to the officer, "I will not come back. I am sorry."

"You have the right to remain silent," the policewoman said. "Anything you say can and will be used against you in a court of law."

A male officer ran her license on a computer.

Will they deport me? she wondered. *I cannot go back to Nigeria,* she decided. *Not without my son.*

At a hospital, Ifi's wrists were bandaged. Asked not to return to the junkyard, she was suddenly released. Job waited for her with a white woman. The woman's eyes were sleepy, her red hair in a tousled ponytail. Her high-waisted blue jeans tapered at the legs. She smelled of cigarettes and strawberries. There was an awkward introduction in which their eyes met and Ifi mumbled hello. She turned to go, but the woman spoke to her.

"Job and I, we're friends from the old days," the woman said in a rush.

"Anyway, I took care of everything. The cops, they understand. They won't press charges." Then she looked at Job. "But she can't ever come back, okay?"

Job nodded.

On the way home he said nothing, but the woman kept talking. She commented on everything: the still night, the full moon, the rattling of the car's dash, the feel of the breeze. Ifi spread out on the backseat of the car, spent, unable to sleep.

They arrived at a corner apartment not far from where Ifi and Job lived. Just before they drove off, the woman glanced in the direction of the driver's-side window. One soft look suddenly revealed to Ifi all that the years of late arrivals and early departures hadn't. But she was too numb to react. Her tongue was too thick in her mouth to speak.

Job let the door to the house close before he finally spoke. "What is wrong with you?" he asked Ifi. "Are you trying to disgrace us, acting like onye ara?" a crazy woman.

She said nothing.

"They will deport you like the Mexicans," he said. "I begged that woman to speak to them as an American."

Ifi's eyes sharpened at the woman's mention. "I don't care. They can take me. You can go back to your woman and tell her I said this."

Job shook his head. "You must stop this. At once. I beg of you. Please, biko." He took her bound hands in his. Tears were in his eyes. "Tomorrow, I am going to Nigeria alone to bury my only son, my only child. You have left me to do a father and a mother's job as one. And now you must do this?"

"You do not have to go alone," Ifi said. "Take your 'friend from the old days.'"

Job emptied cans of pork and beans into a pot and heated them. After dishing for Ifi, he scraped away the burnt bottoms of the pots. Hot mugs of Ovaltine, sweet with evaporated milk, would finish the meal. Ifi did not eat. She did not drink. *Is it because of Cheryl or Victor?* he wondered.

For a moment, sitting across from one another at the table, Job's mind returned to the image of Victor spread out on the concrete. When he had tried to explain that Victor had been moving when he first arrived, the

JULIE IROMUANYA

doctors reasoned that Victor was already going into shock as his systems were beginning to shut down. His lungs had collapsed, his heart could barely pump blood through his body, his bones were broken under the surface of his skin, and his brain had already expired. They had said there wasn't anything that Job could have done. But they hadn't hung on to Victor in the last moment like he had. They hadn't felt what it was to feel the last ripple of life escape through one's fingertips.

Job gave Victor life. *Why didn't I save my boy?* he thought. Sons were supposed to bury their fathers, not the other way around.

Ifi sat silently across from him, her face resting on her palm, her eyes vacantly gazing across the room. She had returned to work, but she hadn't cried, she hadn't wailed, not like him. He remembered the look on her face that night, how for just a moment, she had seen Job, the doctor, and known, believed with all her heart, that he could fix their son and fix their futures. Then how suddenly her face had gone from hope to dashed dreams as she watched Victor's life slip from his father's hands.

Job's breath caught. He set down the salt shaker. He pushed thoughts of his son from his mind. In silence, he ate both of their portions; later, he strained over the toilet to push out the hardened stool.

Before Ifi's arrival, the years before the arranged marriage, he had imagined that the indignity of these American meals would be no more. No more spaghetti from cans and frozen hot dogs. Now, his life had turned in on itself. Before flying to Nigeria to bury his boy the next morning, he promised himself that he would rise early and prepare a soup—despite what he already predicted: the soup would be runny, with okra sliced too thin, mushrooms too thick, blocks of beef too tough, and the fufu would be stiff and crumbling, overcooked on a too-high flame.

That night, Ifi's eyes closed, feigning sleep. Job pulled her close and wrapped his arms around her back. Without comment, she neither balked nor relented. He took it as a sign that she had forgiven him, that without his having said so, she knew he had finished with Cheryl. Things had been over for some time anyway. He had only called on her help in releasing Ifi from jail. He pressed his face into her back and ran his fingers down the side of her dry face. She had never cried, not even once. Job suspected—in all honesty, hoped—that she at least cried in his absence.

Daylight was just beginning, a fuzzy patch of clouds through the window screen. In an hour's time, Job would be leaving for the airport to fly to Nigeria to bury his only child. For three weeks, he would sleep under mosquito nets at night, eat his mother's stew, and listen to his brother rant about his latest ex-girlfriend. All of this would be pretense. *Forget about the boy,* they would say to him in their own silent ways. *Move forward. Begin again. There is still time.* Job dressed in his good pants, shirt, and tie. He had spent the morning ironing them. The phone rang.

"Who is calling at this time?" Ifi asked. She was hoarse; nonetheless, she looked more like herself.

"No one," Job said. But when the calls didn't stop, in exasperation, he finally answered.

Cheryl.

Before she could speak, he began. "Please, I beg you not to disturb my home." He glanced back at Ifi. "My *wife* is not well."

"Don't shut me out, okay?"

Once again, he glanced back at Ifi, hovering in the bathroom doorway. "You hear me?"

"Job, don't do this. Don't be unfair." Cheryl's voice was flat and still, with the same gravel undertow he'd grown used to over the years. A smoker's cadence. "I helped you."

Ifi silently regarded him for a moment. Job forced a reassuring smile. After a moment, she retreated to the bathroom. She would sit on the toilet seat staring blankly at the walls surrounding her. He waited a moment for the sound of the water faucet. "You were not supposed to be there," he said into the phone.

"You needed me. And I was there. Now I need you."

"This is how it is," he said softly. "My *wife* is not well. Not while she is like this."

"Don't be an asshole, Job. I get what we are. I never tried to make it anything else. I been married two times already, okay? I don't need another one under my belt. Only thing is, what you're doing, it ain't fair." Her voice was thick and churlish.

It softened him. He tried to understand where her ache came from. Hadn't he been thinking the very same thought since that night? "What is this *fair*?" he asked. Truly, he wanted to know, because he couldn't understand what the word meant anymore. What was fair about a boy losing his life just as it had begun? Was it fair the way things had turned out with Samuel, with his education in America, with Gladys, with Ifi?

"We can be there for each other, Job, like we've always been. I know things have cooled down lately. I could feel it. But it don't have to be that way. Let's go somewhere. A trip. Someplace brand new."

"No, no brand new."

"Why not? Why do we have to make ourselves miserable? We can help each other. Just for a weekend, okay? We go away and come back, and then everything'll be calm."

Water still ran at full blast. Job sighed. Ifi had left the water running again. "We can't do this anymore," he said. "I have tried . . ."

"We can."

"No," he said weakly.

In spite of his words, he felt the need to break away, escape from this empty house and Ifi's dead eyes. *What if I do it?* he thought. *What if I travel away and return with a renewed spirit?* It would help him clear his head. It would help him understand. Because he could not understand it. *What is all of this anyway?* he asked himself. *What is this marriage without the boy? What is this house without the boy?* All that was left were objects. Objects were hollow inside. Like Ifi. "Where will we go?" he whispered.

"A cabin up north. My folks used to take me and Luther up when we were kids. Haven't been back in years."

Cheryl standing along a beach, her red hair swooped back by a breeze, her eyes lovingly set on him. He imagined it. Not like Ifi; her eyes were missing something, like a piece was gone, a piece that would never be retrieved.

"Okie," he said. A weight lifted from his chest. He couldn't believe he'd actually said it, and once he had, the arrangements began to take shape. He would make a cash withdrawal from his credit card, enough for a few days. He would ask for some extra leave time from work. They would understand. He would tell Ifi that there had been a delay, that he would be in Nigeria longer than expected. He would leave, with Cheryl. They would go away to this lake cabin. "I am going to my son's funeral in Nigeria," he said to Cheryl. "After I return."

"Yes." Cheryl let out a hoot. "This is so right," she said. "Doesn't it feel good already?"

"Yes, it does," he admitted.

"This has been so hard for me, you know? I been fighting with everything inside." She began to whimper. "God, I miss him so much."

Job recoiled. He hated that sound, like snot trapped in her nose and wheezing its way through her lips.

"This trip will be so good for us, Job," she said. "I just need to be with you. Then, you know, we can make it through this. And if we make it, we can make it through anything."

"*We* are not miserable," he said, glancing at the bathroom. Water still poured from the bathroom faucet. "*We,* my wife and I, are fine."

"Job, I loved him too. You *know* that."

Her voice softened, and the whimper turned into the crunch of tears, an ugly sound, a low, deep cry, the sound that he hoped day and night to hear from Ifi, a mother's cry for her lost child. Not from Cheryl. *She wants to cry for my son? I won't have it. She is not the boy's mother.*

"No, you didn't know him," he said. He could handle her anger, her shouts, even her cigarettes, but not this. "You are nothing to him."

"*That's* not fair." Like a child, a whining, foolish child, the harder she tried to protest, the more guttural and pathetic her cries. "Job, Luther's gone. My folks are gone. You and Victor, you're my family."

Family? How had it all begun anyway? This thing with Cheryl. At first he couldn't recall, then suddenly he remembered that day all those years ago, the derision in Gladys's laughter. Right then. That's where it began. *Well, I was weak then,* he thought. Cheryl took advantage. He was suddenly overwhelmed by the sickening scent of her strawberry shampoo and the cigarettes. Her whiny voice. She never let him be anymore, always calling, always with that hungry sound in her voice, a voice so hungry that it had almost consumed him.

He wouldn't have even called her if it hadn't been for Ifi's accident. Only Cheryl could talk to the police and get Ifi out of trouble. *Because she is white,* he told himself. *Because she is an American.* And she knew this. He had been forced to call her. *She used it to her advantage,* he thought. *A conniver, she is. But I will not fall to her again. Never again.* "No," he said with ferocity.

At once, Ifi stood in the doorway, her eyes on him. Water still blasted behind her. He smiled, threw up his hands in feigned exasperation. "Telemarketers," he said to her. "I am hanging up," he said to the invisible merchant. "Stop disturbing my family with your calls. Never ever call this number again."

After he hung up, Job marched past Ifi into the bathroom and turned off the running water faucet. By the time he returned to the living room, he had collected himself.

With the morning news blaring, Job and Ifi ate runny soup together on the couch. He watched her slow swallows, the exhaustion in her eyes, and it occurred to him that she was quite beautiful. In a plain, unencumbered way, her imploring eyes had a way of reviewing the world with calm incredulity. It was magnificent. As he watched her, it was impossible not to make comparisons. Ifi and Cheryl. Ifi's caramel to Cheryl's crème. Ifi's fluffy, dark hair, thinning around the hairline from tight braids, to Cheryl and her flyaway red hair, with slants of gray straining around her pinkish ears. Ifi's hard, set look; the whiskers around Cheryl's eyes. Ifi's slim waist, her lumpy round rump in a towel or a wrapper, like now. Cheryl . . .

Ifi was beautiful and soft and hard all at once. Like his mother and his sisters and Gladys, and the first girl he fell for in secondary school, the girl with the gapped front teeth and crooked smile. She was a grown-up version of the Nigerian girls he and his friends taunted as they marched by, their massive backsides rhythmically drumming with each step. She was a Nigerian, like him.

Now she was the mother of his son, his wife. She was beautiful. This must have been what he saw that first time so long ago, the photograph that stood apart from the others. He must have seen it in her, the ability to become a part of him. All these years, he had imagined it as a random shuffling of a deck of cards in a hand, that his eyes should land on hers; that his parents should agree with his choice for her skin color, her shape, and her family name. But it was more. Perhaps his eyes were destined to stop on her picture, to return a second and then a third time, before the decision was made.

Before leaving for the airport, he pulled Ifi to him by the waist. A rush of feelings enveloped him. *Is this what it feels like to truly love someone,* he thought, *like in Hollywood?* He kissed her tenderly along the side of her face and told her he loved her. "When I return," he whispered, "we can start over. We will have other children. This will not be the end of it."

In ten minutes' time a cab would arrive.

All of a sudden she clawed at his thighs, his chest, his penis. It excited him. Her eyes were fierce and probing. She forced her tongue into his mouth. *This is not her way,* he thought. Normally, her kisses were dry, her movements soft. She hissed. He fought to keep up with her tongue's movements just as he struggled to keep up with the movements of her hips.

A car horn began to honk outside. The cab. *I will miss my flight,* he thought in panic.

"Biko," he said. "Not now." Still he dared not push the bound hands away. "Biko," he said again and again, suddenly realizing her plan. Holding her damaged hands gently, he pulled away. "You will cause me to miss my plane." When he pulled his shirt back on, he found the skin of his back and chest shredded from her fingernails.

At last Ifi said, "You will not take my son away."

"What are you talking about?" Job asked.

"We will bury him here. In America."

"No," Job said. "He is a Nigerian."

"He is an American."

He should say something about the silly way she filled the boy with hot dogs and pizza, about her insistence on only speaking English to him instead of Igbo, but he didn't. How could he dignify her claim with a response? None of it mattered anymore. *My boy, he will never be a man,* Job thought.

In a final stand, Ifi grabbed the squat center table and lunged forward with it. The table met the wall in a heavy thud that widened the hole that was already there. Surrounded by broken glass and papers, a huge, toothless mouth laughed at them.

CHAPTER 18

JOB THOUGHT IT FITTING FOR VICTOR'S REMAINS TO BE FLOWN BACK TO Nigeria and buried in his father's compound among the ancestors, so that the boy could rest in peace. In his mind, the small boy's mourning would be fit for a chief. They would mourn the old way. A caravan would follow the boy's small casket through the village. Ifi would shave her head. Among the female relations of his village and family compound, she would ululate her grief through the night. Under her rigid stiffness, Job would at last witness Ifi's beating heart.

But these plans existed only in his mind. His wishes had been put to rest when Job woke to find Ifi's date-stamped bereavement claim denied.

In his foolishness, he still hoped right up until the last minute that Ifi would arrive at the airport, that all would go as it should, but the funeral was nothing like his dreams. His old father and his youngest sister arrived at the Port Harcourt International Airport to pick him up. The rainy season had just ended. The air was dry. Soon, the dusty Harmattan winds would start. But he would be gone by then. Although his father leaned heavily against a cane, he looked well. His youngest sister Jenny's lips and fingernails were glossy with red paint. When she hugged him, he could feel the sharpness of her nails against the frayed skin of his back. She ordered around the driver, an ashy-faced boy of sixteen.

After collecting all of Job's suitcases, the driver motioned to the one remaining, the black leather briefcase containing Job's stethoscope. "Docta?" the boy asked. "Me, I de take?" Although it was not a question, his voice rose at the end. After all, he was nothing but a houseboy dressed in a driver's cap. He would also wash their linens and underpants, iron them too. The family had fallen that low. No more grand parties. No more visits from important diplomats. Just enough from Job's monthly remittance to furnish the house and pay for a catch-all houseboy.

As always, Job forgot to respond. It was the first time that Job felt the weight of his lie.

"Docta?" the boy asked again as he reached out.

Job recoiled, hugging the briefcase to his body, thinking of Victor's life slipping away from him, thinking of the voices of the men who called him doctor that night. "No, no need."

Before heading to Abba, they spent the day in Port Harcourt making the last preparations for the funeral. His mother, sisters, and the housegirls filled the kitchen, preparing food for the feast that would follow the service. In a sad way, it was a joyous occasion, a reminder of the bygone wealth that had furnished Job's trip to America to begin with.

In the parlor, his junior brother, Obi, and his father accepted guests who came to pay their respects. Clay walls and stiff leather furniture made up the room. Three knotted curtains of muted pastels blocked out the fierce sunlight. An air conditioner blasted cold, ragged air into the room. Each voice shouted to be heard over the sound of the air.

Among the visitors were a man and his boy, a relative of a relative, someone Job only knew vaguely, someone who had come to show his respects to the man who was celebrated up and down the street and in church once a year when they received his annual endowment. Clearly, the son was suffering from bowlegs. The father insisted that it was something more.

"Doctor, he walks like k-leg, k-leg," the man said, turning his legs out. "He sleeps with pain."

The boy's hair was all tough, tight curls. He was thin, with gangly limbs and a belly like a ripe melon. He had arrived in his best slacks, and now he held them bunched at his knees.

Job leaned heavily into his father's low leather couch and beckoned. The boy came forward, and Job ran his fingers along the length of the boy's legs. He looked nothing like Victor, half his size and nearly a foot taller, yet Job recognized in his shy smile the same pleasurable unruliness as his own Victor. He imagined the boy's skinny legs ducking in and out of the housegirls' thick calves as they prepared meals in the kitchen. He could see the boy dumping bowls of rice, upturning roots in the garden, yanking the braids of his sisters' fresh and tender scalps. It nearly broke his heart even to examine him. Job took a deep breath and began, casting aside the images from that night.

He asked the boy to spread his arms, and Job patted him down. He asked the boy to walk on his tiptoes, to jump, to kick. The boy did everything, his knees buckled from his bowed legs.

Job produced his stethoscope and listened for the boy's rabbit heartbeat. He told the father, "His heart is slow. It is not the boy's legs. You must feed him coconut milk."

"Yes, yes." The father nodded solemnly.

But Job didn't stop there. He sat back in the chair pensively, then tilted forward, arching his eyebrows in seriousness. "The coconut milk must be fresh. Not in a can. The enzymes will thicken his arteries so that they can pass more blood throughout his body. His body is thirsty for blood. Especially there." He indicated the misshapen legs.

The father agreed. "Yes, the enzymes."

"And," Job could not resist, "tell the boy's mother and his sisters that he must be left in peace if his legs are to grow properly."

"*Eh?*"

"Let the boy play," Job said softly.

By evening, the arrival of guests had temporarily waned. Job escaped the parlor and disappeared into the dark hallway dividing the main quarters from the boys' quarters at the back of the house. A tall portrait was positioned on the wall. With thick eyebrows and vicious eyes, his brother was no more than nineteen years of age in the photo. Standing before the portrait, Job trembled. Samuel's eyes probed his with distaste. He laughed at the briefcase in Job's hand. *Doctor,* the voice said mockingly, *it is not even real leather. What a grand pretender you are.*

On the drive to the village in Abba, Jenny sighed and shouted her praises of Ifi. She wrapped her sharpened fingertips around Job's hands. "Don't mind, my brother. She is mourning. Our Jesus will not leave us."

But later, as he washed his face over the bathroom sink of the chapel, he overheard her in the hallway. Her voice overtook those of other parishioners.

"Why my senior brother married such a woman, I do not know. He had many choices. A mother who will not bury her own son, oh. This is Satan. *A-ah!* This is abomination."

Jenny's accomplices were other thirty-something women, fully regaled in ichafu headscarves, long dresses, and wrappers of various prints. His sister stood out among them in a tailored western suit. Job clutched Jenny at the elbow and led her away from the women. Flashing a sympathetic smile to her friends, she followed him to the other end of the hallway. Low overhanging bulbs elongated their shadows. A pool of light poured in through the exit door.

"You are insulting my wife?" Job asked.

"What is this?"

Job turned his body to block the streams of parishioners making their way into the chapel. "She is not well. It's not her fault. Can't you see?"

"Not well, oh. That is speaking lightly," she said. "Do not deny it, brother. She is onye ara."

"Don't speak of my wife in that way."

"This woman, who was as poor as a church rat, you take her to America and make her a queen, and it spoils her brain. But don't worry, my brother," Jenny said. "We will find you a new wife."

"She is a good woman," Job said, suddenly reminded of his great joy in seeing Ifi smile. *We will have another child,* he told himself. *We will go to another city. We will begin all over again.*

"Your wife is a liar," Jenny said. "Imagine this rubbish woman calling the day the son of my senior brother will be buried. Imagine such a woman calling to disgrace her husband. Imagine such a woman calling the father of her husband to share such lies. I tell you, this is Satan. I am not surprised if it is not juju that made you marry this woman."

"What are you talking about?" Job asked.

"I do not need to repeat such nonsense," Jenny said.

His forehead swirled. Already he knew the answer.

"But if you must force me, I will tell you." Jenny looked around and bowed toward him. "She says that you are no doctor. She says you wipe the ass of diseased Americans. That you do not even have a first degree."

In silence, Job took it all in. He swallowed a deep breath through his nostrils. He could only listen.

"I never liked that woman," Jenny said, resuming her normal volume. "With her big nose and flat buttocks. It was juju. But don't worry, my brother. We will find you a new wife."

What could he say in defense of such a charge, of such a glaring fact? At once he hated Ifi for her truths and hated his sister for so completely believing his lies. At the same time, the ache in Job's chest swelled into a feeling caught between hate and love. *How could she expose me?* he thought. Suddenly remembering the look on her face that night as she watched Job's slippery fingers lose their grip on Victor's life, Job bristled at the accusation in her expression.

A hand clutched at Job's elbow. His heart thudded in his ears. He started to push the figure away, but he heard his father's voice. "Bia, come," his father said, "the service will begin."

With great difficulty, Job followed.

The service took place in a cooled chapel filled with those Job had known nearly his entire life and those he barely knew at all. Stunned into silence, Job felt the absence of the most important person of all, Ifi, and the shame began to crystallize into hate. As Victor was eulogized, the air conditioner rattled in the background between bursts of loud air. The pastor was a red-faced white man, no doubt commissioned by Job's family on behalf of *Doctor.* The pastor pronounced Victor's full name slowly, with difficulty. With the correct pronunciation, Job repeated his son's name in his head: *Victorious Ezeaku Ogbonnaya.* His first son, who was supposed to grow to be the victorious king Job could never be for his own father.

He thought of Samuel. Samuel had been careless. He was the first son. He was not supposed to try to be the hero. He should have left the heroism for Job, the second son, the one who could make mistakes and be forgiven. But now, forever, Samuel would be nothing more than a set of accusatory eyes in a portrait, aged no more than nineteen years. Samuel would live forever in all of Job's failures.

For the first time, Job wondered about his father. All those years ago, how had his father been able to cope? What had it meant to bury his dreams along with his first son?

Throughout the service, the pastor pressed a handkerchief to his temple. After the viewing, the casket was closed and dumped into the ground. Once covered, the plot swelled with dry earth. No one ululated for the boy. On Ifi's behalf, Job's mother quaked and sighed next to his rigid father, two sisters, and younger brother, mourning the boy whose growth they had only witnessed through photographs. They knew nothing of his Spider-Man, Wolverine, or his Big Wheel. They knew nothing of the clunky sound of Igbo in the small boy's mouth.

After the funeral, the mourners ate tureens of jollof rice and moi moi. One parishioner after another shared condolences. Women embraced Job thickly. Men clasped his hands in theirs. By now, everyone had witnessed Ifi's absence. In her place Job's mother stood, her face wet with tears. She grasped Job's hands in hers and held them through the day.

But Job could only imagine Ifi, with unmoving eyes, curled in front of the television. He willed the tears to spill from her eyes. But the harder he tried, the angrier he became at her resistance.

And then the anger turned into humiliation. *What kind of father allows such a thing to happen to his son?* he thought. *What kind of doctor is it who cannot save lives?*

One by one parishioners stood before Job, each nodding furiously. "Doctor, God is good, oh. We cannot understand his ways. The boy is in His kingdom." Always, they asked after his wife's health. Always, they began each statement with "Doctor."

Eventually, a tall old man stood before Job. His wife was a small woman. She supported the sagging man with her shoulder.

"Doctor, this cough will not allow my husband to sleep, oh."

A hard lump knotted in Job's throat. Thinking of his Victor, thinking of the sliver of life in his palm, he tried to swallow it away. "I am sorry."

"Doctor, please treat my husband."

"Leave me, oh," Job said. *I can't do this again. Not now,* he thought. He had never been meant to be the doctor. That was for Samuel. Job had been playing an expensive game for far too long. If Samuel had stood over his son that night, Victor would still be alive. Even as it pained him, he decided that he must own up to it. When he was finally alone, he would throw the stethoscope away. He would finish this game. Once and for all.

"I am not lying," the woman insisted.

"I do not have my tools," Job explained to the husband.

When the woman still wouldn't listen, his voice broke. "I am not a doctor."

As if she had not heard, she continued, her voice growing shrill. "I beg of you. My husband will pay." She lifted her purse and sifted through, finding ragged naira notes bound by rubber bands. She began to lower herself to her old, cracking knees to bow in supplication.

"Put your money away, Aunty," a voice boomed from behind Job. The voice belonged to his father. His father dipped and leaned into his cane until he was standing to the right of Job. "My son is humble. He will treat you." With that, he produced Job's briefcase and unclasped it. All that filled the briefcase was Job's accomplice, the stethoscope.

With wavering palms, Job touched the man's heaving chest. He pushed in and out and asked him to breathe in deeply. The man struggled through coughs. Job plugged his ears with the eartips. All he could hear was the suction of empty air. As his father watched him fumble with the stethoscope until he found the man's heartbeat, Job felt his own thorough disgrace. Thuds pounded in his brain. He fought for the words that would interpret the tall man's maladies. He struggled for the words that would make the man go home with hope. Wasn't this why his father stood alongside him, urging him to continue his charade?

"Your lungs," Job started.

He felt his father's breath over his shoulder as he looked on.

"You see?" the wife asked. "You see. As God is my witness, I am no liar."

The cough, Job had noticed, was wet and thick like a rag. "Your lungs are filled with fluid instead of air," he said, though his heart was not in it. "Your lungs are two balloons filled with water." He thrust out his chest and sucked in air to demonstrate. "You must take," Job paused for a word that would produce the proper sentiment, a clinical word that rang with finality, professionalism.

"Acid-o-mana-phin."

"Yes, doctor, yes," the man said through a cough.

CHAPTER 19

FOR THE PAST THREE DAYS, THE PHONE HAD RUNG. IFI DIDN'T ANSWER. IT must be Job. *Now we are even,* she said to herself. Was there such a thing? *Now that the world knows he is nothing in America, like me, a mother without a child, what will he become?* she thought. What was left of nothing? What had brought her here to begin with? His lies.

Seduction was an art Ifi knew little about. Yet, she must have understood its ways. She must have mastered it before she even met Job. Yes, in the photograph that Aunty had mailed to his family without her knowledge, she had seduced him. Perhaps it was an innocent glance that presented her. Perhaps without knowing it, Ifi had exercised the subtleties of grace and coyness during that awkward meeting with Job in Uncle and Aunty's living room. She had, in a way, collected him as he had collected her.

Now there was nothing, only an assortment of objects, and she would let it all go. Letters, bills, phone calls. *Forget them all,* she thought. *This house and all its holes and all its creaking noises.* She had never wanted the ugly house to begin with. Job had simply presented it to her as her own, as he had done with every single aspect of her life, beginning with his first lie. Now it would go to the dogs. It would crumble to the ground before all of them. And Ifi would watch it.

Trilling birds outside. A brutal sun. A thud from the newspaper boy delivering the paper. Ifi stretched out on the living room couch, staring at the gaping hole in the wall, taking in the exhausting heat through her nostrils until her head swam and she drifted to sleep.

As she slept, she saw the house from the outside—a chipped door, gray windows. Nothing more than a large mouth full of rotting teeth. This mouth was hungry and consuming. It chewed what was inside and swallowed. *We're all just meat,* she mused. Job, Ifi, and Victor. They were nothing more than meat. This house, it spat the bones outside and left them for the wind to scatter.

❖

A small brown face glared through the window. Ifi bolted up. The eyes, the nose, the mouth. Her fingers came to her face. They covered her lips. Her heart pumped loudly in her chest. She rushed to the window and pressed her face against the glass. She struggled to lift the window. It was stuck. Another problem with this stupid house. A hard yank and it opened. Ifi pried off the screen. She reached out and grasped the face with her hands.

"Victor."

"Let me go!"

"Let him go!"

She pulled the face in to her. A brief struggle. Ifi lunging this way, the face that way.

"Free him!"

He was free.

Gladys toppled backwards and landed hard on her rear, her legs splayed open like used scissors. Her tote bag was on its side. Loose change was dumped everywhere. A cascade of braided ringlets flopped to one side on her head. Short tufts of her hair peeked from under the wig. She readjusted it. One sandal remained on her foot. The other, who knew where?

Ifi was not done. She flung open the front door. "Victor," she said, breathless. "Victor." In one wide step, she took the broken porch stairs, trampling through the hydrangeas along the side of the house. She pushed past Gladys, who was already at the door. "Victor," she said again. She was too fast for Gladys.

He took a step back.

Ifi halted. "You are not my Victor."

"*You* are not well."

Hands were on Ifi's back. She was rising. *Have I fallen?* she thought.

Gladys propped Ifi against her doughy side and walked her around the porch and up the stairs into the house. "Get the mail," she instructed the boy. Gladys sat her down on the couch like a lumpy package. A moment later, Ifi heard the boy's footsteps following them into the house.

"You are not well, my dear," Gladys said again. "Why didn't you call your friends and tell us what happened? If I had not glanced at the newspaper this morning, sef, I would not have known. If I had not seen your husband's car in the street, I would not have stopped. If my boy had not looked in your window and seen you, we would have gone."

Gladys was a blur. There were sounds, the clunk of water hitting the pot, the whisper of flames on the range.

"Boy, get away from the glass." With a broom, Gladys pushed the pieces into a dustpan. A sound like wind chimes as the pieces collected in a heap at the bottom of the rubbish bin. "Look at this floor. Paper everywhere. What have you people done to this table? This kitchen. A hole large enough for a cat in your wall. I tell you, this place is not fit for a human. It smells." She sifted through the papers scattered about the floor. "I will help you, my dear."

A warm cup. Ifi's hands closed around the mug. Her lips parted and the hot, bitter liquid drained into the back of her throat. Her eyes opened. Gladys sat next to Ifi on the couch. Dressed in blue from head to toe, she had a patch of dirt and leaves stuck to her rear. Her headscarf was partially unraveled, and the free ends of her braided ringlets drooped to one side.

Ifi's eyes took her in, and in one fell swoop Gladys's lips twisted into a frowning smile. A large tote bag was draped over one arm. She set it down, and the gold bangles at her wrists jingled. "Had Emeka not said, 'Gladys, my dear, look at this newspaper' this morning, I would never have known."

The boy. His name was Michael. When Gladys admonished him for playing among the broken pieces of glass, Michael sighed in exasperation and cut his eyes at his mother. *No, Victor would never do that,* Ifi thought. Victor would smile that dull smile of his just before trotting away.

"You people have been hiding from us, but I say, we are Igbos in this America."

Yes, the lips were the right size. The nose the same. The belly the same. The legs, just a shortened version. Still, Ifi thought, *He is not my Victor.*

"We are brothers and sisters. We are family," Gladys continued. "We must care for one another."

Michael tilted his face into the hole in the wall. His fingers found a piece of loose plaster, and he placed the pieces in his mouth. He tasted, balked, and spat the moist chunks back into the darkness. He made a sound. "Blech."

Gladys forced her fingers into his mouth and plucked out the remaining pieces caught in his teeth. She raised her nose into the air and pinched it closed with her fingers. "This place smells." Then, "This is unsafe, my dear. One day a big rat will come to your house." Sifting through her purse, she retrieved a phone and dialed a number. As Ifi watched in silence, Gladys arranged for someone to come and fix the wall.

"Mama, what's that smell?" Michael asked.

"Shut up," she said to him.

"Mama, I think you have something on you. Is that doggy doo?"

"This room smells," Gladys said again. She sniffed and glanced around the room, finding the smell on herself. "*Nshi!*" It was from the neighbor's dog. In a flurry she disappeared to the kitchen, her sandal backs clicking as they met the hardwood floors. Water. She returned with a damp spot on the back of her blue wrapper dress.

"My dear," Gladys said on her return, her nose raised, clutching a bag of waste. "You are not taking care of yourself. Take this rubbish." She sent the boy out with the trash.

Ifi chuckled. Gladys was pretending that the smell came from the bag instead of from her.

"You are not well, oh. Why has your husband left you alone? Why did he not take you with him to bury the child? What kind of husband is it that leaves his wife alone when she is not well?"

The thickness in Ifi's head thinned until just a bit of vapor fogged her head. More liquid and her mouth opened up too. In a clear voice, she responded, "Because he is with other women."

Silence. Gladys's hands trembled. The mug in her hand shook. Brown liquid seeped onto the floor. "I am tired," she said for explanation. She found a rag in the kitchen and began to wipe. "Emeka works all day, and the boy runs me around the house all night. You see how skinny I am? Like I don't eat. Because of the boy." But she was far from skinny. In fact, she had grown rather large and lumpy, her face covered in blemishes.

"My Victor kept me too. He was a noisy baby and a noisy child."

"He doesn't allow me sleep. Even now. *Ah ah!* The boy is four years." Gladys had an anxious look to her. "I have six daughters. Why must my last-born give me so much trouble, heh?"

"It is something." Ifi's eyes fixed on Michael. The eyes. The lips. The nose.

His feet thudded along the hardwood floors. Now at the window, he glared out at the sun. He picked at his navel—an outie—placed his finger in his ear, tasted it, mixed it with the snot in his nose.

Disgusting. Ifi cringed.

Just the same, she reminded herself, *He has the eyes, the lips, the nose.* "As if my Victor is walking," she said to Gladys.

"No," Gladys said softly, "not at all."

"The old people would call him ogbanje."

"Nonsense," Gladys said.

"My Victor's spirit cannot rest. My boy's spirit remains in that boy."

"You are not a believer of such foolishness," Gladys said. Still, an unmistakable tremor rippled across Gladys's face. Ifi knew that Gladys had always been a believer, paying native doctors for years in hopes that she would conceive a son. Like Ifi, they had all heard the stories—from their grandparents and great-grandparents, from their superstitious second cousins or aunts—about the children who refused to remain dead.

"My boy's spirit does not rest. He was not ready to go. He is a special child." Ifi frowned. "How long will he live among us this time?"

"Blasphemy," Gladys said, her hands reaching out to the boy. They closed around his wrist protectively.

"Ow!" he said.

Gladys turned on him. "Shut up! Don't talk back to your mother."

He let out a fiendish wail that escalated into a dog's snarl.

"No, not like my Victor at all," Ifi said softly. "Victor does not walk with malice." But then she wondered, *Has he changed so much?* A descent into another world and back. An unjust end. *Perhaps he has learned jealousy,* she thought.

"It is my boy, Victor, born again in Michael. It must be. It has to be him," she pronounced. Then frowning, she added, "My Victor could not leave me without saying good-bye. He has gone a long way only to come back to his mother. Gladys, dear, you can see it. Can't you see it?"

A wave of tenderness washed over Ifi. She reached out to Gladys in concern. "I am afraid for you, my friend." *This boy is in danger,* she thought. His body was slight. He would need to be fed well at the proper intervals. The food must be prepared properly. Because he was blessed and also cursed, his sisters surely despised him. Therefore, it only made sense that they should not drink from the same glasses anymore. And never, never must the boy ride a bicycle. *This time,* Ifi decided, *I will protect my Victor.*

She stared at the peculiar expression on Gladys's face. Why had they not kept in touch for so long? Six years had passed since the two families' last outing together. Just like that, Gladys and Emeka had disappeared from their lives. It had all started with that first birthday party that Gladys and Emeka had failed to attend. After that, Job refused to speak to them, and since Ifi didn't exactly miss them, she considered it an undisguised blessing. Well, she would remedy that. She recalled Gladys withering under hospital sheets after her own son died. They had even donated their baby's crib to her. "My sister," Ifi said, "I will help you watch over him. I will protect him. Ogbanje never stay long with us. But this will be another story. As you say, we are fellow Igbos."

Gladys's words were a sudden explosion. "Shut up!" she protested. "Shut your foolish mouth! He is not some spirit, some ghost. He is a boy, a boy I tell you!" But she stammered the words out. And now her legs were moving her out the door. Too fast. She was gone. But Ifi knew she would be back.

In two weeks' time, Ifi had already paid several visits to Gladys's home, sometimes three to four times a day. Each time, Gladys would grudgingly open the door to her. Each time, she would watch hungrily as Ifi tapped her way into the room and performed her absolutions and prayers. Following this, Ifi would grasp Michael in her arms and thoroughly examine each aspect of his body. If she found a nick or cut on the boy's elbow or knee, she thoroughly chastised Gladys as she did now.

"You will kill him, eh?

"Just like that, you will put the boy in harm's way?

"Is that what you are trying to do, kill *our* only son? Is that right?"

Gladys crumpled on the couch. Tears made their way down her face. Crocodile tears. With one finger, Ifi shoved her hard in her chest, and the tears stopped as immediately as they had started. Emeka calmly watched the scene from the arched doorway leading into the kitchen. His palms hugged an empty mug. Television roared in the background, a football game just breaking for halftime. Two commentators chuckled over the mishaps of the game, one calm and avuncular, the other younger, with a raw spot on his head where the sun struck.

Dinnertime. Gladys led the way into the formal dining hall. A line of portraits documenting the growth of the family hung in the corridor. In the earliest portraits, Emeka and Gladys were young—the expression of youth in matching native prints. These were followed by portraits displaying the succession of daughters, growing in count with each picture. In the last, Gladys and Emeka, surrounded by their six daughters, frowned at the camera. In their lap was Michael, a fat and surly infant. Like Victor.

A large oak table filled the dining room. A drooping chandelier shone rippling shadows and lights against the papered walls. One of the daughters set the table, counting the matching tumblers, forks, and spoons in their places as she made her way around. At nine, she was the closest in age to Michael. There was something about the way she moved, cocking one skinny leg in front of the other, balancing her large belly crookedly, arms akimbo. *She's a sly one,* Ifi thought, remembering her from all those years ago, forcing her finger up her dead brother's nose while her mother lay in agony. *She was trouble then,* Ifi thought. *She is trouble now.*

One dish left. Before the girl had a chance to react, Ifi flung the dish from her. When it struck the ceramic tile, it crumbled.

With wide, frightened eyes, the girl gazed at Ifi. "What did *I* do?"

"I see you," Ifi whispered.

"I didn't do nothing!" the girl howled.

Gladys rushed across the room. "Shush your mouth!" She popped her girl on the back of the head. Her braids shook forward, and the beads in her hair clinked.

She wailed at her mother, "I hate you!"

"Shut your mouth!" Gladys shouted. "You are spoiled, oh!"

Through it all—the wailing, the girl's shrieks, and Michael's sudden banging and tapping of the dishes on the table—Ifi's voice cut in calmly. "He will not eat from any of these dishes."

Gladys agreed.

"That's not fair!" A bellow rose from the little girl. "Why's *he* so special? I'm smarter than him. I'm faster than him. He's *nothing.*"

Just then, Emeka stepped into the room clutching his mug, staring about his home like a floundering fish.

"Go buy dishes for the boy," Gladys said to him. "Biko."

He inspected the damage of the broken dish in a heap on the floor. "What happened here?"

"He needs his own dishes. These are not good."

"What is wrong with these?" He sighed, a long, tired sigh drawn deeply through his nostrils. His eyes met Ifi, who was stooped over Michael as he continued his ruckus. "Hasn't this gone far enough?" he asked, a whine in his voice.

"Do you want something to happen to the boy?" Gladys asked. "Is that what you want? Our only son whom God has finally blessed us with? I only want him to be well."

A thought suddenly occurred to Ifi. She remembered Victor's plastic cups and plates, his toys. "He will need dishes from my home."

"I agree with you of only one thing," Emeka said on the ride home. He cocked the window down and allowed the ashes from his cigarette to scatter into the gusts of hot air. He blew the smoke out the window too. He was trying to keep the smell from staining the car. Ifi already imagined the howling row that Gladys would make of it the next time she rode in the car.

Ifi waited. When he didn't immediately reply, she pressed, "Of what?"

"The girl," Emeka said. "She is jealous. Her whole life she has fought with her sisters for everything. For the last jelly bean, for the last scoop in the peanut butter jar, and because of it, we have given her everything she wants. Why should she stop now? When we bring these dishes for her brother, she will be the first to rush and fill his plate with rice. She will pour juice in his cup, and then she will spit in it. She will mix her mucous with his rice." He chuckled. "But what of it? She is my favorite, you know? Her mother was just like her. And that is how she stole my heart."

Ifi thought this over carefully, remembering the flicker of rebelliousness. "Like my Victor."

Emeka turned a strange glance in her direction. "Yes, I suppose. But you see, my Michael is not like that at all. Michael is simple. He has no conniver in him. I have always liked my youngest child best until another comes along. But this time it is different. My boy will go to the best schools. He will have the best clothes. Even if I starve, I will make sure of that. But, you see, no matter what, the boy will only perform adequately. He has no imagination."

Why is Emeka sharing this with me? she wondered. *Why is he insulting his only son?* It was not right. But remembering the boy with the chunks of the wall in his mouth, his mother raking the pieces out, she hesitated as she responded. "Give him some time. Push him. It will come." Nonetheless, she could feel herself wavering in her doubt. Michael had her Victor's looks, but that was all, nothing more. An answer, any answer, would do for now, she decided. "His journey from the spirit world has filled him with jealousy. Among us on this earth, the light will return."

Emeka tossed up his hands. "You and my wife are competing for the crazy award."

Ifi glared at him. "You are so certain, are you?" Years ago, Job had huffed and laughed over Gladys's attempts to secure a boy child through native doctors. Now she wondered aloud, "You are so certain that your juju didn't interfere with my boy, take him from me, and send him to your home in that simple boy's body? We don't understand how native medicine works in this America. If it had not been for you and your wife, my boy would still be here."

"I thought so at first," Emeka said. "All those years sending money away, coming home to find chicken bones collected by the door, semen collected in condoms, hair collected in Ziploc bags. Then one day the boy comes. Just like that. No explanation. We went and looked at the ultrasound, and there it was, the image of my son. Even at her age, after nine months, she gave birth to a live, healthy boy. Just like that, I began to believe it all. Maybe my wife has been right all these years, you know?

"But now, no uh, I have had enough of juju, ogbanje, spirits, and native doctors." He glared into her eyes intensely. "But what am I to do? I have been losing my wife inch by inch all these years. And now it has come to this. You see, I am here driving you to bring your boy's dishes only because that is what will please my wife. That is all. I am only the messenger." Again, he paused, his face imploring. "Come now, you cannot believe all of this. You're a woman like her. She listens to you. Talk to her. Tell her to stop this nonsense."

"And what if we are right?" Ifi asked. "You have it all figured out, eh? But what if we are right about this boy? He is special," she said. "He belongs to us all, and it is my duty to protect him."

Shaking his head, Emeka blew out the window. "Right," he said. He smiled at her kindly. "Go home. Rest. Take care of yourself." They pulled up in front of the house. From inside, a forgotten light glowed. Probably the light in the kitchen over the stove. It had likely been on for days. Now Ifi wondered if the bathroom faucet still ran. *Has it been running the entire time I have been away?* By now, the floor would be high with water. It would leak through the tiles and pass into the crawl space. *Well, let it go.* She said to herself. *Let it all go.*

Emeka still smiled a half frown, like he was stiff with a thought. Perhaps he still needed proof. *Why do I feel the need to convince him?* she wondered. Deep down, she knew why. She needed to say something so that he believed. *After all, where am I without hope?* she asked herself. "He is the image of my Victor. Just look at him. How can you deny that?"

"Yes. That I cannot deny." Emeka stared at her for a long moment. Finally, he asked, "What of Job?"

She stiffened. "He's fine."

"He is in Nigeria burying the boy?"

"Yes."

"And you are here?"

She didn't answer.

"When will he return?"

"Tomorrow."

"When he comes home, what will you do? Will you continue with your potions and prayers?"

When he comes home? Ifi thought. There was no home. There was nothing. For the first time, it occurred to her that she had no plan. Surely she could not stay in the house with Job when he returned. It could not be just the two of them and the empty spaces that Victor used to fill.

"The dishes," Ifi said back to him. "Come tomorrow evening, and I will be ready."

❖

The knock came an hour earlier than expected. All the light of the day was gone. In its place was the artificial orange from the porch bulbs along the block. Just the same, Ifi was ready. Everything she would ever need, everything that mattered to her, fit in two small suitcases: In one bag, Victor's dishes, his Spider-Man cup, his blanket, his sneakers, his toys. In the other, her toothbrush, hair grease, and a few changes of clothes. She would leave the keys in the mailbox for Job. She would never need to see his face again.

When she opened the door, Ifi immediately glimpsed the cornrowed hair fringed with thick knots of flyaways and knew that it was not Emeka. When he observed her examining his hair so intently, Jamal raked a finger through the space between each braid and nodded almost apologetically. He had, Ifi discovered almost immediately, the look and movements of a man who was used to being watched.

"Gotta get them redone," he said. He held his steel box of tools.

Standing there, she thought of the time many months ago that she and Job had stood in the doorway watching Jamal drive away, the shock of seeing the thirteen-year-old boy suddenly a man. Today, there was no shock. There was only Jamal, aged to eighteen years, standing in front of her with his steel box.

Had he seen the newspaper? Had he come, like Gladys and other figments of her past, to pay his respects? Ifi searched for the answer in his face, the sleepy eyes, the gaunt frame, the barrel shoulders. Looking at him, she suddenly recalled that day, panting at the bottom of the stairs, the cold outside, and this boy—now a man—holding her up with his slender wrists and big hands.

"You were there the day he was born," she said.

His face softened.

"And now he is gone."

"The kid?"

"My son, my Victor," she started again, thinking of Job, thinking of Jamal walking away that day. "My husband would be very angry if my Victor wore his hair like yours." *Would my Victor have grown to be like this man, with his cornrows and low-hanging pants?* she wondered. *Would he wear his hair low like his father? Or would he attempt to slide his fingers through his hair like the American white boys?*

"I see," he said with the remnants of a frown on his face.

In that instant, she knew that he knew about Victor, that in spite of the way they had turned Jamal away, he had come to pay his respects. Knowing this, she explained anyway. "My son," she said, "a car hit him. He was just playing. But everything is okay now."

Jamal nodded. "I'm sorry." What else could be said? "Sorry about that." There was a pause, then Jamal widened his stance. Ifi was blocking the door, preventing him from entering.

"I have found my Victor again."

"Okay," he said.

"I do not need any condolence."

"Okay. I'll just fix your wall and then go."

Ifi nodded.

Lifting the metallic toolbox easily, he strolled past her into the entryway. Hardwood flooring, ugly with scars, creaked as he made his way in. "You can do something about that," he said, pausing. His heel connected with the floor-ing, the raised rubber of his work boots thudding hollowly. "A little lubricant."

Ifi pushed past him into the living room. Old boxes of takeout, tin cans, and dirty plates had accumulated over the past few weeks. Ifi rushed about the room shifting and reshifting the items until the clutter, rather than dis-appearing, was merely displaced. In each of her movements, she could feel the weight of his gaze.

"Damn," Jamal said, "how you do that?" Cold air breathed through the gaping sore in the wall.

Ifi shifted the weight at her feet. The table, broken into three pieces, remained underneath the hole. Jamal knelt alongside her, clearing the debris.

"The first time was my Victor. An accident."

"A tough kid."

"Yes, like you say, a tough kid. He was always bouncing his head on everything, but nothing could break him."

Jamal nodded. "Oh yeah. Got two of my own. Girls."

Ifi's eyes widened in shock. "You? But that's impossible." *What happened to the thirteen-year-old boy?* she thought.

"Yeah. They with they mother now. I take these jobs on the side to get ahead of the bills."

Something about the way he said this, "got two of my own," stayed with her. Girls with floppy braids wrapped in clips and streamers, pretty girls with their father's sleepy eyes, their mother's lips, their father's broad shoulders. Ifi smiled to herself, thinking of the strangeness.

Away, hidden from sight like a dirty magazine, Ifi had stowed the mangled Big Wheel in a box. While Jamal waited, she climbed the stairs to the small storage closet and retrieved the box. She set it down in front of him.

Nothing but a sharp intake of breath revealed that he even saw it.

"His father is too easy with him," Ifi said.

Jamal turned away, knelt at the floor, and produced some measuring tape.

"How can a boy play all the time?" she implored.

"Shouldn't take too long," he said. "Sheetrock, spackle. Not as bad as it looks."

"It is not fun and games every time," she insisted.

"No," Jamal said, turning to her, "but it should be, right?" He grinned a smile that was so generous that it spilled across his face.

The dare was to answer that smile with a glare. Ifi succeeded. "My son would still be alive if his father behaved like a father."

Jamal's smile fell away like broken glass. Now he was ugly, very ugly. His was a face meant only for smiling. Somehow, he must have known this. Immediately, the edges of the smile broadened his face once more. Without it weakening, he said, "We get some sheetrock, cut it around, put some backing in there, and it be fixed."

"A father should behave like a father, *eh*?" Ifi asked, refusing to let it die.

A zipping sound as the measuring tape retracted. Jamal placed it back in the metallic box. "I can come back later."

"No." Various metal tools clinked against one another. Ifi's fingers closed over the tape measure. She could not be alone now in this house without her Victor, even without Job. "Please, I will leave you. Just fix it." Tears spilled down her face. She rolled forward on her haunches. "We must fix the hole, or this house will fall."

Jamal hooked a finger into a belt loop. His eyes rested on the hole. He couldn't look at her. "Come on," he said gently. "It won't fall. It's just a little hole." He picked at a spot on his face, the smile returning uneasily.

"I did this," Ifi said. "I should've watched him more closely."

Still staring into the hole, he talked to himself. "These holes are easy to fix. Just spackle, paint, a cutout of sheetrock just the right size." A pause. "Where is he anyway?" Jamal asked. "Your man."

"Nigeria." And suddenly she was seeing Job, his potbelly, the thick eyebrows, his perplexed smile. She had already considered the ways that she had seduced him. But how had *he* seduced *her*? Yes, there must have been seduction somewhere. After all, he was ugly to her then. Now, his face was neither ugly nor handsome. She had seen his eyes encrusted with flakes, the skin around his face marked from the nicks of a shave. But none of this had deterred the familiarity of his closeness as they lay in bed.

His seduction, she decided, began with the first stories Aunty had told her, the promises of a future. Nearly thirty and unmarried. Practically unheard of on her road. Before Job, Ifi had been wasting with age. She cooked, cleaned, rinsed the feces, and wiped the noses of each of her cousins as they came into the world. And then she went to bed and did it all over again the next day. Each night, she prayed that her actions, her labor without complaint, would unburden Aunty, secretly knowing that her hard work would never be enough. At first, Ifi realized, Job had seduced her through the dreams he made possible.

Still, in his face, she thought, even in her anger or sadness, she would always see her son, his large face, soft lips, and the roundness of his features. *This is why,* Ifi realized just then, *I will not leave Job.* She could not leave Job. She could not leave this house. To leave him would be to leave Victor, and then there would truly be nothing.

The phone rang.

Ifi answered it.

An articulate puff of breath, a forced exhalation of air.

"Job," Ifi said in response, "come home." She hung up without another word.

Tears began to quake her shoulders. "I did this," she said again.

Jamal looked away. He waited until this second round of tears had subsided. "It'll be fixed in no time." He unfurled the tape measure again and handed one end of it to Ifi. Firmly, he said, "Take this."

Tears made their way past her eyelids. Gradually, she straightened up. With the other end, he measured out the length and width of the hole and wrote down some numbers on a scrap of paper. Carefully, he cut out a pattern on a block of cardboard paper. He pointed out a sheetrock saw and a glue gun to Ifi, and she obliged, lifting each object out of the toolbox and handing them to him. He instructed her on the necessity of taking precise measurements and cutting even lines.

Together they worked, squatting low in front of the hole, their backs to the empty room. Together they paused to the scrape of the saw biting through the drywall. They worked with such intensity, such intimacy, that when the phone rang, the sound was merely an embodied whisper in the room.

CHAPTER 20

"PLAY SOMETHING FROM AFRICA." CHERYL BENT BEFORE THE RECORD player—a treasure from one of Job's garage sale expeditions. In fact, she saw it first. She asked the owner to plug it in and show them how it worked. Now, in one hand, she gripped a can of Budweiser. In the other, she clasped a record, yet another yard sale find. It wobbled and rippled under her shaky hand. She was drunk, or maybe pretending. Job wouldn't put it past her. *There are worse things she's done,* he thought. *She's a bad pretender, like me.* A Catholic schoolgirl with parents in the grave, a deaf-mute criminal brother. *What will she be tomorrow?* he wondered.

When Job and Ifi said nothing, stood there instead, clutching the empty suitcases that Job had returned with after sharing his shirts and shoes with his various relatives, Cheryl shrugged her shoulders and placed the record on the player.

Fela. "Zombie." Perfect. First the racing bass line with the low hum of the drums and then the horns. She didn't know how to move to it. She tried anyway, a stiff, forced jerking right then left. She rocked forward and back-wards on her toes. Snapping her fingers was difficult with the beer in her hand, so she set it down. Can sweat left a wet print on the edge of the player. Job resisted the impulse to rush to the kitchen, find a coaster, and place it beneath the beer. At the garage sale, the man had said the record player was one of a kind. *They don't make 'em like this anymore. It's got the real sound. Not that fake digital shit.*

Not that fake digital shit. That's what he had said to Ifi when he brought it home, when he moved the eight-track player, another find, to make room for it on the table. All the while Ifi had stood with her arms crossed in front of her chest. When the Fela record came, she gave in. He could hear her playing the record in the morning, in the evening while Victor wailed for hours. As soon as he woke, Victor began the wail with the horns. After a while, they couldn't tell if he was crying or simply singing along.

A long song. Ten minutes, maybe twelve. *Will she tire before the song has ended? Or will someone intervene?* Someone had to. He looked to Ifi, but there was nothing but a pitying expression on her face, the same look she had when he first walked through the glassy doors at Eppley Airfield. He had been looking for the shuttle, his eyes squinting out past the median dividing the cabs from the cars coming and going. He hadn't expected to see her there, twirling the car keys. She rarely drove—only to work, the grocery store, and the hardware store. And when she did, she came and went straight to her destination, no stops along the way. Every day in America she had complained about driving. It would've been easier for a doctor's wife in Nigeria, she always said, where she could find some boy to drive her places. Still, there she was, looking thinner, ashier, in a printed skirt that came to her ankles like a wrapper, dangling the car keys. Her hair was neat, the flyaways in her plaits brushed from her face. She had put herself together. For him.

He felt pleased. Then he remembered the phone call, his father and his sisters all looking in on him with hard, confident glares as they dropped him off at the Port Harcourt airport. *"Docta,"* the driver had said, taking his bags from him. And no one had corrected the boy. No one, not even Job—at first. They were all okay with it, the pretending. But Job couldn't do it anymore. He couldn't do the dance anymore, not for them, not for anyone. Maybe that was why Ifi had revealed his secret to his father.

As the boy had set his bags on the curb, Job leaned in and whispered to the boy so only he could hear. There was one bag left, the short, black briefcase containing the stethoscope. Job pushed it into the boy's arms. "I am no doctor," he had said. It sounded right in his ears. He was finally owning up, doing what the Americans on the talk shows Ifi craved did, spilling their guts to the world with no shame. He said it all. He confessed. "I am a nurse's aide, and I am a meatpacker. I am no more a father. I am not even a first son."

The boy's face had squeezed up in confusion, then protest. He forced the bag forward, back into Job's arms. There wasn't enough English in him to piece together the meaning of Job's words. Or it was merely his disbelief.

The boy tried harder. He clutched at Job's other bags. He rearranged them. He wiped away the dust that had settled on them. Instead of merely setting them at the curb, he raced ahead to the airport entrance, lugging all the bags, including the briefcase, with difficulty. He believed he had done something wrong, that he was being scolded.

Job handed the briefcase back to the boy. Before the boy could force it back into his arms, he held it there, reached into his pocket, and pulled out a wad of Naira. He paid the boy a hefty tip—even bigger than anything the boy would've expected from a doctor—and from the car, his father looked on in approval. The boy said, "Thankee, Docta." A low bow.

A sick joke, Job thought then as he did now. He couldn't go along with it. He couldn't. Not anymore. Once again, he had reached out to the boy. He grasped him around his collar and shouted into his ear, "No doctor! No doctor!" Twice. Just like that, so the boy could understand.

Still, the boy had arranged his face into a smile. He clutched the notes close to his body, protecting them from Job, bowing as he backed away. "Thankee, Docta."

He could promise them all, like he had promised Ifi, that he would become a doctor, that he would build their hospital, that it was only a matter of time. They just needed to give him time. But they wouldn't hear any of it. Would they?

No, they would hear it, he thought. That was the problem. They would believe it. No protest. No questions. They would go along with it. His father would even sell his car, release the driver, so that he could fund the expense one more time. All Job needed to do was say that the imaginary clinic needed another financial backer. He could make up a story about the stock market in America. He could tell them any lie, and his father and mother would willingly oblige. Because they had to. Because they must go on believing in him.

But Job was tired. Only then did he know that he couldn't come back to Nigeria again. That was what Ifi had said after her aunty died. *I can't go back.* Then he understood. Then he understood what it meant for her to fix the house, to make the boy hamburgers and tater tots. She was trying to make America home.

On the ride through the Nebraska highways and streets, he had begun to forgive her. *We are in the same place, aren't we?* Two who no longer belonged there, but would never fully belong here: foreign Americans.

But they could have more children. Their offspring would grow up to speak unaccented American English. They would never know of police road-blocks, poor water, or power outages. Their children would marry well and wire funds to their family in Nigeria. He had to make this work. They could pay the mortgage, sell the house, and move somewhere brand new, maybe California. They would buy another house with the profits. They could be housekeepers, nurse's aides, meatpackers, fruit pickers, whatever the world needed, just to make things work, to leave a piece of space behind for their progeny, to send money to the village for their retirement. And their children would have it better. And they'd take care of Job and Ifi in their old age. And these would be the stories he and Ifi would keep to themselves, of how they had scraped and groveled to build their own palace. But they would never lie.

In spite of his grand plans, there was a problem: Cheryl. She had worked herself up into a sweat. Complexion raw, the freckles seemed to bounce from her face to her arms and back in her jagged movements. Whatever he did now would matter. It would affect the course of everything.

At Eppley, Ifi had handed him the keys. At first she had said nothing but "Welcome." Then she began with a list of household entreaties: the utilities, the maintenance, and the cable. That was it, as if nothing had changed between them.

He had almost expected her to start in on the boy.

Do you know what your son has done today?

What is it?

Let me tell you what that boy has done today.

Tell me now.

Satan has visited that boy . . .

But he said nothing in return, and it was like old times. Sitting there in the car with Ifi, Job felt, for once, that everything would be okay, that they could start over. He took her hand in his. Flat, empty fields spun by as they split off of Interstate 480 onto 80. They could have another child, a girl even. They would hang Victor's picture on the wall, and his rambunctious eyes would light up every room. They would tell the rest of their children stories about their brother. He would be their Samuel.

If they didn't do well in school: *Victor, your brother, he excelled in his studies.*

After soccer practice: *Victor, your brother, he could've played for the Super Eagles.*

When it came time for university: *Victor, your brother, he would have been a doctor.*

But now, how to put things on the right course? What would Emeka do? What would Samuel do? What would his father do? *It's supposed to be easier here,* he thought. *In this America. Everything is supposed to fall into place. Opportunity is a ripe melon swinging from a tree.* Wasn't that what they had always told him when he was growing up—his father, the boys at school, his mother? A knock on the tree, and opportunity would fall into your hands and split open. No effort. You would take its seeds, its juice, its marrow, and eat as you pleased. Not this.

He must set things right. He must walk over, turn off the music, and tell Cheryl to leave. *That is what Ifi is waiting for,* he thought. She was waiting for him to be the man and handle this. He did that. He walked over and pulled the plug on the player. The music halted. Cheryl stopped dancing, arms midswing.

"You bastard," she said. Purpler than he'd ever seen her, even at the height of climax, she was out of breath. Cheryl took his record player, *not that fake digital shit,* and slammed it to the floor. The translucent lid popped off and cracked in three places. Fela rolled out to the middle of the floor and whirred before landing flatly. The rest of the player—the handle, the needle, all of it—split into pieces all across the floor. It was an ugly, heavy sound. His record player, broken to pieces. Fela scratched.

In three steps, Job was on her. She glared into his face, ready, but not really. He picked her up by the shoulders.

Ifi gasped. "Job!" she said.

There wasn't time enough for Cheryl to react before he'd pushed her out the door and onto the stoop. All he heard was her sopping-wet cry as he bolted the door. Three locks.

A pause. A breath.

He reached for Ifi's hand. His hand lingered for a moment before she accepted it. They could move forward as one.

Each of the locks came undone. Three locks.

Cheryl stood there, the keys shaking in her trembling fingers. She kicked the door open, placed her hands on her hips, and glared at Job. "Excuse me," she said, her voice wavering. "I'm not going anywhere, okay? This is my house too. This is mine."

"Go before we call the police." Ifi rose to the center of the room. She stood face to face with Cheryl with the tough, stubborn look Job had grown used to seeing on his mother, his sisters, his aunts. He remained behind her and allowed them to have it out. "You get out of here, you crazy woman. Out of my house," Ifi said.

Cheryl stammered. Her voice trembled and warbled. "B-but, that ain't fair!" Her gaze implored, full of tears. For a moment, it was almost as if she was begging Ifi. "What he's doing, it ain't fair. It ain't fair." Composure finally came to her. "I ain't going anywhere. This is my house too. I own it. Job owns it. We both own it." She cut through the room and picked up a worn leather handbag next to the dining room table. Sure enough, there was the deed to the house. She held it up triumphantly.

For the second time that day, Ifi looked at Job with that look, a look that said, *What have you done?*

"You can't kick *me* out of *my* house," Cheryl said. "I'm your ex-wife. This is *our* house." She glared at Ifi, the look of a child who has stolen bubble-gum. "Did you know that? Your ol' man here. Me and him were married. Before you were ever even in the picture. And you wouldn't be here. And him neither. If it wasn't for me." She looked to Job. "Don't think for a second that I still love you," she said. "It's business. It's all business. It's papers." There was a familiar ring to it, like the day they met.

"You refuse to go?" Ifi seemed truly confused.

But Cheryl didn't look at Ifi. Instead, she forced her glare on him, a plaintive expression that said, *Don't make me.* "Job, you fight me on this, I'll call the cops. They'll come get *you.* You know it."

It was true. They'd see his color, they'd hear his accent, and they'd take him away and lock him in a cell. *They'll beat me,* he thought. *They'll search my body.* A ring began in Job's ears as the flashing camera bulbs blinked in his eyes. Heat filled his face. She'd take him to court, and she'd win everything.

She was crying again. "You take this house away, I have nothing." There was penance in her tone, but it couldn't erase what they'd all acknowledged. All of what she said was true. They would take him away. They would leave her, the woman, the white American, the house.

"I'll have nothing. Can't you see?" She was sorry. Very sorry. She must have known she had done it all wrong. Job hated her. He could tell that she saw it on his face. She pressed harder. "I'll have nothing. Nothing." Actually, she was begging. "No home. No Luther," she said. "No Victor."

At the sound of Victor's name, something in Ifi broke. Job could see it happening before his eyes. Her face moved, just a piece. The rest of it was still. And then he knew he'd lost her, completely this time. It was over now. He felt sure of it. Suddenly, he hated Cheryl. She had ruined everything. She had ruined his chances at a future. How could he and Ifi grow together? How could they rebuild their future? Victor was never Cheryl's. She bought him a teddy bear, candy, ice cream. She fixed him apple slices with peanut butter. That was it. The boy didn't even like the apple slices. He always spat them out when she wasn't looking. He buried the seeds, said he wanted an apple tree to grow. That was it. *That's not a mother,* he thought.

He advanced on her.

"Job. No," Ifi said. A wrinkle rested on her brow as she thought. All of a sudden, she was all action. A roll of electrical tape was on the floor, near the back wall.

For the first time, Job noticed that the hole in their living room wall was no more. He gawked in surprise. Even the room was tidy, everything put away. From his place by the door, he could see that the dishes were washed and stored in the cabinets. It was as if in his absence their life had been lifted up and set almost right. Almost. *Until this,* he thought.

In awe, Job and Cheryl watched as Ifi ran a thick, jagged line of electrical tape down the middle of the hardwood floor, from the front door through the dining room and the kitchen. Solomon's judgment.

"It's all business," she said.

He saw his life as Solomon dictated: On one side, a couch, half the cracked television, half the dining room table, half the kitchen; Cheryl on one side, Ifi on the other; Cheryl crouched to the floor, nothing but a soggy towel; Ifi with a hard look on her face, a look so hard that Job knew he'd never be able to penetrate it. Maybe they'd divorce. Maybe they wouldn't, not in the courts anyway. Instead, Ifi would continue on at the motel and make her half of the mortgage payments. She'd send money home to her cousins. Cheryl would make the other half of the mortgage payments, but she'd always be a little late. Ifi would cook jollof rice and egusi soup on her half of the stove, and Cheryl would boil hot dogs and drink Slim-Fast shakes on the other side. Over one half of the sink, Ifi would straighten her hair with a pressing comb; over the other half, Cheryl would suds hers with strawberry-scented shampoo. A neat stack of cookbooks and newspapers would rest on one side of the dining room table. On the other, a messy stack of detective novels, romance novels, books about traveling the world.

His face felt hot. His ears were thick. Suddenly, he couldn't tell the two women apart. He'd reversed their faces and bodies, Cheryl's bleached face on Ifi's ashy brown legs. Ifi's plaited hair wisping around Cheryl's freckled forehead. *This will be my world,* he thought in horror. *It can't work. It can't possibly work.*

"Nonsense," Job said. All he needed was to undo this, reach over and undo this. The Great Wall of China. The Berlin Wall. It would come down. It must. He began to unstick the tape. But it wouldn't come up. Not easily, anyway. He marched over the line. *A silly line, just tape,* he told himself. In the kitchen, he shifted through drawers, looking for a knife, any knife. A butter knife. Peeling at the tape did no good. It was fixed, hard and fast. On his hands and knees, he worked himself up into a sweat, scraping at the tape, peeling with the bits of his fingernails. Dirt and dust trapped in the floorboards itched his nose, his face leered that closely. He glanced up. It was a long line. *I'll never remove it all.* Yet he couldn't stop.

A knock. The door. Three sudden sharp pings of the doorbell.

Through the screen, they all could see him standing there, his round gut set on two spindly legs. Never in his life had Job been so glad to see his dear friend. Emeka.

October advanced, yet it still felt hot and humid. Out in the bush, it stank of cow dung. Emeka and Job sat in his SUV riding 75. Job had bragged over beers—made it sound more like a silly anecdote, something to laugh over, made it sound like once the night was over, he could go home—and Emeka ate it up. "Crazy women," Job said, "A-mer-eeka. Nigeria. *Alaska*. They are all crazy."

They were filled with beers and the sight of strippers with bruised thighs. They both had liked one the best, shiny blond hair, lithe movements. Twenty-two at most. Only he couldn't remember if it was him who liked her or if it was Emeka who liked her. Emeka had a thing for blondes. Said she was Swedish in a laughable mixture of Irish and Australian syllables. Like the rest of the dancers, she was some girl from Seward or North Platte. None of that mattered, though. All he could remember was her look when Emeka introduced them both, an engineer and a doctor. They were sweating. She hung on to them all night, until close. They just kept paying up, charging the night to their MasterCards. At the end of her song, she even slipped them her number. She told them she would blow job their brains in.

Now she'd gone, and they were singing and laughing out the window, talking about the way her breasts jiggled, taking in the hot night air. Emeka held up the scrap of paper with her number on it. Just about to flick it out the window, Job snatched it from him and stuffed it in his pocket. "No, uh," he said.

"She was an ugly elephant with a stinky ass," Emeka said.

He's only angry because she gave me her phone number, Job thought. No way was he letting this go. She had a choice. "She gave it to me," he said aloud.

A black sky overhead freckled with stars. Ifi and Cheryl. Job groaned. Would they go on spoiling his night by intruding on his thoughts? What were they doing now, erecting a wall with poles, wrestling, or baking lasagna filled with goat meat and American cheese? He shuddered. No matter what, it looked bad to him. He couldn't go home. He would go anywhere Emeka took him.

Emeka had the tight look on his face Job had seen many times before. He was thinking. As he drove, Emeka reached behind his seat and slipped his hand into the back pocket. He pulled out a handkerchief and mopped up the streaks on his face. He tasted something bad and spat out the window.

Emeka chuckled. "So your two wives have come to you, eh? Your chickens have come home to roost."

Job laughed uncomfortably.

"Think about it, my friend. This is perfect. In Nigeria, I tell you, no one would punish you for this. Only in America. A man can have two wives, split the house equally. And everyone will be happy. Today you service one. Tomorrow you service the other. Equal. They are both happy." He placed a slippery palm on Job's shoulder. "You know, this divorce business is only in America. Cheryl is senior wife. Ifi is junior wife. Ifi knows. She is only a traditional woman. You should praise her for agreeing to share." Again, he laughed hard.

But that wasn't what Ifi had in mind when she drew the line on the floor. *Was it?* he wondered. In a strange way it *was* funny. Wasn't it? He could almost imagine it, his obi, a room at the center just for him, the husband, and his two wives in their bedrooms with their children. His parents hadn't done it that way, but *their* parents had and their parents before that. *Strange how things come full circle,* he thought. He couldn't help but laugh.

"You are laughing, my friend, but what will you do? Have you learned to please one woman, sef?" Emeka asked.

"I have taken three at once." They both knew it was a lie.

"Oh yes? When was this?"

"In 1970. After the war. They were traveling dancers for Fela. I was just a boy, yet I was already a man."

They pitched forward into the black night, choking with laughter. A fly crushed its wings on the windshield. Emeka squirted water from the wipers. Bits of fly washed away in the water. Emeka chuckled. *It is impossible,* Job thought. *Three women at once? Just a boy?* Maybe he'd gone too far with that justification. Still, no matter. They'd been at it all night, laughing, reminiscing over things that had never happened rather than the things that did.

Job: *I wrestled five men at once, beat them all in. They were akatta basketball players, tall as giants.*

Emeka: *Donald Trump, that man is asking me to work for him, but me, I have no time for this. I told him, me, I will think it over.*

"And what of you?" Job was still laughing.

Emeka was not laughing. "What of me?"

"What would you do?" He was asking about Emeka's life, and Emeka knew it. What would he have done in such a situation? Job needed a blueprint, though he couldn't admit it, not to Emeka, not even to himself.

Emeka's face grew serious, almost somber. "Whatever makes her happy."

"You liar!" Job shouted.

"It's true," Emeka said halfheartedly.

Job stewed with rage. Emeka always said one thing and did another. He was always on a quest to make a fool of Job so that he could sit around with his family, with Gladys, and laugh at him one more time, so they could all talk about silly Job in his house with two women ruling over him.

"I know what you would do: You would go to Nigeria and marry another wife. You would forget this nonsense and start over."

Emeka laughed again. "You are right, my friend. You know me too well." He laughed again and dabbed at the corners of his eyes.

Headlights glowed on the other side of the road, something big, a truck maybe. It blared a horn. They'd crossed over the line. They swerved back over. Emeka had had too much to drink. They both had. Still, Job should probably take over. He laughed. They'd battled this way many times: *My friend, you drive like a woman,* Job would say one day. On another, Emeka taunted, *Come now, my grandmother has faster legs.*

"Pull over," Job said. "Let me drive before you kill us."

Emeka's laughter caught up to Job's. He didn't make any indication that he'd even heard him. His eyes were tight again. Only his lips moved. "Job, my friend. You know, I felt sorry for you only until a day ago."

Now Job was not laughing; Emeka was. "I felt sorry for the man who failed at everything he tried. I felt sorry for his simpleness. 'What a simpleton,' I have said to myself many times. 'His plastic bag. His white coat.'" Another laugh, deep and throaty.

But Job was silent.

"Come now. This is funny, no?" A glare crossed Emeka's face, but he still chuckled. His eyes were thin, drunken slits. He was sweating too much for the heat.

"No." Job crossed his arms over his chest. "You are not funny. You are drunk and silly. Let me drive before you kill us both." He'd get Emeka home, then he'd go to a motel for the night. That would be the plan. He could piece everything together tomorrow morning after a night of rest.

Job waited for the fight, but there was none. Emeka threw up his hands. "Okay. You are right. I'll pull over." He drove up ahead and began to pull over onto the shoulder. Another car, another Nebraska truck, streaked past them as they slowed. Another horn blared. The sound rattled the engine. The driver flashed his lights this time.

Emeka's brights were on. "Your lights," Job said.

"I'm coming, I'm coming." Emeka didn't understand, or he refused to pay attention, or he was too drunk for it all. But at least he was finally pulling over.

He didn't cut the engine off completely. He didn't get up from his seat. Instead, Emeka left the keys in the ignition. He leaned back, took a deep breath, and chuckled softly to himself. He sang a little: "*Zombie o, zombie.*" He had a good voice. He could sing backup for King Sunny Adé or Femi. Like Samuel, Emeka was good at everything.

"And she was playing Fela," Emeka said with a giggle. "The white woman was dancing to Fela. Why was I not there to witness this? A-mer-eeka!" He glanced at Job through half-closed eyes wet with tears. "But could she dance? That is the question. Did she have the rhythm?"

"Sadly, no." Job laughed with Emeka. It felt normal again. *It's early,* he reminded himself. There was a saying. How did it go? *It's five o'clock somewhere.* He took the long descent down the running board and into the night. He felt smooth. Over his shoulder, he shouted up to Emeka. "Let's go to your house, my man, and drink whiskey."

"You know, my simple friend," Emeka bellowed out the door to him, still laughing, "I felt sorry for my simpleton friend until I saw his simpleness in my simpleton boy. And then . . ." he looked at Job. His face was suddenly long and still; he almost looked sorry. "And then I looked at my son, my Michael, and I put two and two together." He'd reached the punchline. He laughed, a hard, guttural sound.

Job didn't understand. Not right away. All he saw were the blinding lights of the SUV swerving at him, the passenger door flapping. Job pitched over the side of the shoulder into an embankment. His heart raced. Blood pumped in his ears. *It's impossible,* he thought in astonishment. *Is this a joke?* Like the two of them wrestling in the snow that day. So he laughed with Emeka.

The truck slid down the embankment toward Job. As he scrambled away from it, all he could hear was the grumble of the engine, the traction of the tires on the dirt. *This is a joke,* he told himself again. Still laughing, a laughter like a rattle, bound up in his nerves and fear, Job blindly crawled and backpedaled.

"I knew, my friend," Emeka shouted out the window. "From the beginning, *I had a feeling*," he sang, pushing the tires through the dirt. "Me, I was okay with it. My wife needed a son." He paused. "But now, I am not okay with it."

A deafening blare of the horn cut the calm night air. Job clamped his hands over his ears until the blare stopped. He could see nothing but the glare of the lights. "You're talking silly. Too much to drink," he called back. He remembered that day with Gladys. *Just one time. It only happened one time. It was a mistake,* he thought. "What are you saying?" he called to Emeka. "You are drunk."

"*I had a feeling.*" Drunk with laughter, drunk with pain, Emeka sang in his beautiful, husky voice.

The truck skidded.

Out of breath. Nothing but plains for miles. Job's heart ached. He had nowhere to hide. No trees. No brush. No scrubs. Nothing. Surrounded by fence posts and wire, Job was in a pen of sorts, and the headlights of Emeka's truck formed the barrel of a cocked pistol. Bile filled his throat as he thought of that goat and the three shots it had taken to extinguish its life. He chuckled. *Will I die such a pitiful death today?* Soon he was falling to his knees, laughing and choking and spewing the bile from his mouth. The bile of Emeka, and Gladys, and Cheryl, and Samuel, and America, and Mr. Doctor.

His face was shiny and slick with his tears, because suddenly, all he could think of were the good things, like Victor crashing his Big Wheel into walls, and his father clasping his shoulder in pride, and Ifi. And the curl of her lips in a smile, and the way she moved her hips to Fela. And his breath. And because of this, he wept and gasped for air. Because of this, he thought of that house and decided that Emeka was right. *Whatever makes her happy.* And because of this, a sudden sense of gratitude overwhelmed him. Samuel, Emeka, America—all of it had brought him to Ifi, and that was all that mattered.

Emeka blared the horn and revved the engine.

The truck lurched forward but suddenly jammed in the embankment.

As Job watched in astonishment, Emeka put the truck in reverse, then forward, rocking it, but the tires only dug deeper. Finally, he laughed out the window at Job. "You are right, my friend. I am silly and drunk, no?" Emeka's wheels spun. "Come, my friend. Let us stop playing our games. Help me free my vehicle." As he stepped out of the SUV, he laughed again, but the laughter was without the vigor of pain. "Come, my man. We are both Igbos." Emeka shrugged and reached out his hand.

Job hesitated. Black sky wavered under the glare of the lights. He gazed up and down the long stretch of empty highway. He felt gratitude. *I am alive,* he thought. *Ifi is alive.* He took the hand and warily shook off the dirt that had gathered around his good slacks, his tie, and his good shirt. They worked together, rocking the truck with their backs and teeth and sweat, until it was free. All the while, Emeka's beautiful voice sang, *"Zombie o, zombie."*

CHAPTER 21

JOB HELD OUT A DAMP, CRUMPLED BOUQUET OF FLOWERS. "FOR YOU."
His dark suit was covered in dirt and twigs. Scrapes stained his anxious smile. He smelled strongly of liquor.

Ifi snatched the flowers from him, looking anxiously about the room at the burgundy curtains that ended with a simple golden tassel, just the flourish a low-budget motel lobby could furnish. "Why are you here?" She looked again, but the front desk was still empty. The night manager had stepped away, and Ifi could breathe for just a moment. "You must go before someone sees you."

"We need to talk," Job said. He hesitated. "I want to talk."

Having stepped away from his desk for just a moment, the night manager, an elderly man with a slight limp, returned. He considered the two. "Hello, sir," he said. "Ifi." His eyes fell on the flowers in her hand.

Ifi quickly threw the flowers on the one round table propped in front of the chairs. "He is going."

"We must talk," Job said.

"What are you thinking, coming here?" she asked as she made her way to the sliding glass doors. "You need to go."

Job's brows furrowed, but he didn't follow. Without taking his eyes off her, he strode past Ifi to the night manager, slipped a credit card across the counter, and booked a room for the night. He swiveled his whole body to face her, his lips a tease, a sad tilt to his eyes. "I am a paying customer. I have as much right to be here as you." Only once did he break her gaze to look at the manager. "Is that not right?"

"Looks like your fellow got you there." The night manager chuckled and smiled encouragingly at Ifi and then Job.

Room 123. Ifi snatched the keys from Job and pushed past him up the worn carpeted floors to the room. She couldn't risk any further disgrace. It was the farthest room on the floor. Once inside, she pushed the door shut behind her. Her heart raced, and she experienced, for the first time, something like a plea. *This is all I have left,* she thought. *The motel. The steady pay-check.* There was no home, no family, nothing to return to. So this must do. This must do until she could sort it all. "You cannot come here," she said. "This is my workplace."

"Ndo, sorry. I did not come for trouble. I beg of you, listen to me." Job took out a slip of paper from his pocket. He cleared his throat.

Before he could read from it, Ifi snatched the letter. She read the first line to herself. *I have come to ask for your hand in marriage.* She crumpled it into a ball and threw it as hard as she could at the wastebasket in the rear of the room. She made it. "Ngwa, go."

"I have come," he said anyway, "to say the things I should have said when I met you."

He stepped toward her, but all she could smell was the liquor. It angered her. "This is not Nigeria," she said, remembering the fancy Presidential Hotel honeymoon suite. She recalled the elegant walls, the stylish drapery. Now, as she looked around the room, she could just make out the yellowed stains on the sheets that she would replace at the end of her shift, the frayed edges of the landscape portraits on each wall. How far they had fallen. "This is not Nigeria. And we are not young."

"I have come to tell you about my life in America," he began. "In plain English. And if you are happy with my life in America, then come and be my wife."

"I do not care about your life in America."

Instead of the lies he courted her with, he began to speak the truth. "I live a simple life in America. I am not a big doctor. I am not a big man. I am not a big man, but I will care for you." His voice faltered. "I am not a big man. I am a humble man, but I will buy you a fur coat to keep you warm in winter. I will paint your walls, I will buy you a big-screen TV, and I will buy you your first home."

Ifi swallowed. Yes, she recalled the paint on the walls and in his hair on the snowy day of her arrival. She remembered the fur coat of false pines. She remembered the big-screen TV with the crooked line splitting the rainy pictures. With a shiver, she even thought of the house. But it only angered her. In a way, he had usurped all of her dreams. An elegant coat, a large TV, a beautiful home. These were the things she had always hoped for. But Job had taken her dreams hostage and ransomed her future. "You lied," she said.

"Biko," please, he said softly. "If you wanted a doctor, I would be a doctor. If you wanted a home, I would build you a home. If you wanted a family," his eyes rested on hers, "I would build you a family."

Ifi tried to hold on to the anger, but tears swelled behind her lids. She closed her eyes and turned away. If she looked at Job, she would see Victor, and she could not have Victor clouding her judgment.

"Ifi, darling, anything you want I will do for you whatever way I know how. Is that not true?"

It is true, she thought. Like the wilted clump of twigs and petals that were waiting for Ifi on the table in the lobby, these were his attempts at romance. She glanced uncomfortably at her uniform, at the look of her name stitched on the right pocket, at the slacks that were a little too tight at her hips and the too-long linen shirt, ironed into creases. She allowed her mind to fall away. All she could think was that before her shift ended, she would need to return to this very room to replace the damp, yellowing sheets with bleach-scented ones. She would need to fold triangles into the toilet paper roll and empty the waste receptacle of that single sheet of lined notebook paper with his words.

"Whatever you like. I will build your new dreams for you," Job said. "I will always do for you the best way I know how."

Ifi took a deep breath. "What happened?" she asked. Finally, she asked the question that had been on her mind since he stood in the glass doors, his suit covered in dirt and twigs.

Job looked up with a start. He knew that she was not only asking about tonight, she was asking about it all. She was asking about their beginning. She was asking about their middle. She was asking about their ending.

"Job," she said softly. "What happened to us? I was once a girl who wanted to be a doctor's nurse. I wanted to open a clinic in Nigeria for my mother's memory. That was all I wanted. But instead, I am here cleaning sheets and emptying rubbish. Will this be the rest of my life?" Ifi thought back to that first night and all of its possibility and hope as Job, her new husband, stood before her in a white lab coat, a stethoscope protruding from his pocket. Everything but the darkness of his skin had been muted by the whiteness of the snow as it came down around his world. In those moments, the snow had been beautiful, magical, and she had believed anything was possible. *When did this feeling leave us?* she wondered.

Job had been in America so long; why had he gone on pretending without going after his dreams? Now, more than ever, Ifi understood the need for lies, for the embellishments that cemented the difficulties of each day together. But why hadn't he gone after his dream anyway, in secret at least? Why weren't there journals, like her interior design magazines, something to show for his hopes?

And then she understood. It came quietly as she followed the line of his slacks, perfectly creased in spite of the smudges and dirt. "Was there not something you wanted?" she asked.

"I wanted to be a—"

"You did not want to be a doctor," Ifi said. "No more lies." She met his eyes, finding their momentary confusion. "Your father sent you to America to become *his* doctor. You did not fail, Job."

He bristled. He frowned and backed away slowly.

"You did not become a doctor because it was not *your* dream." Ifi came toward him and clasped his hands.

He stilled.

As she said the words, she felt the weight of their certainty and the gentle touch of his pain. "Job, I was not *your* dream. You must not go on pretending." Tears soaked her lashes. "You were not *my* dream. You were Aunty's dream, and so I married you. And so I followed you to America. And then I had a boy, and I wanted him to be an American. And now he is gone. And now there is nothing left to build new dreams with." Her voice was a whisper. "So I must find my way back to my old dreams." Job's hand trembled in hers, but she couldn't stop herself. "And you must find your way to yours."

CHAPTER 22

THROUGH THE TINY GAPS IN THE DRAPES OF ROOM 123, JOB OGBONNAYA could make out the edge of a flaming orange sun just appearing from behind the purple haze of dawn. He rolled over, instinctively feeling the other side of the bed, now suddenly cold and empty, a rumpled mass of sheets. He took a second to inhale the scent of Avon's Chantilly Lace in the pillows and sighed deeply, allowing the vapor to rise through his body.

A tiny shuffling and a click sounded, drawing his attention to the door. For a moment, he thought it would be Ifi. He begged for it to be her. If it was her, like their first night together in the Presidential Hotel, he'd find out what she needed and he'd be it. That was all he had ever wanted, wasn't it?

Through the nearsighted blur of his eyes, he could just make out a lone figure stooped in the doorway. Job slipped his plastic-framed glasses over his eyes. The door suddenly swung open, filling the room with remnants of the hot night air and a dangerous sun just beginning to crest.

She paused in the doorway, her shiny blond wig sparkling against the light. The red lipstick, wet and dripping like watermelon, that had been so captivating the night before now smudged across her face, the weariness of a long night showing as she adjusted the collar of her jacket. She gave him a dubious expression and began to shrug her shoulders, but midshrug she seemed to change her mind before lunging for the day.

"Wait." Job leaned forward, searching through tangles of sheets for his trousers. "I have more. Just wait."

She rolled her eyes in exasperation. But she remained standing.

He couldn't be alone. Not now. "More beer is in the fridge." He pointed to the stackable refrigerator in the corner of the room, already surrounded by a ring of smashed cans. He gave her a smile that he thought looked innocent enough, as if she were just a friend dropping over for a beer. "Help yourself."

For a second, she seemed to think it over. "Listen, I gotta go," her mangled attempt at a Swedish accent forgotten. "I got places to be."

"I know, just wait." His fingers snagged one of the belt loops in his trousers as he burrowed his hands into the pockets. He finally came up with a wad of cash, extracted from the ATM when their night began. He waved it at her now, suddenly relieved.

She rolled her eyes again, but with less vigor as she swung the door shut behind her and sat on the edge of the bed.

Job smiled, a crooked smile laced with an overdue buzz—the buzz he had been unable to commit himself to after all of those beers. He pulled himself close to her. He gazed into her eyes, remembering the warmth of her skin and the smell of her perfume, the scent of a woman.

He stood up and pulled the tiny chain around the lightbulb, allowing the artificial light to spew over the two of them, the scattered orange deflected by dying flies. Her blond hair, although a wig, was suddenly captivating once more as the strings of synthetic hair caught the light. She was overweight, with flat, saddlebag breasts and varicose veins that shone like purple webs through her ghostly skin. Not at all the twenty-two that the whiskey had convinced Job and Emeka of just the night before. Yet under the orange glow, she was sultry and exotic. He struggled to remind himself of the Swedish girl who had stared down into his face at the bar as she danced, as Emeka introduced them to her one after another, two professional men, an engineer and a doctor, two professionals getting into a little trouble for the night. Job's lips formed into an uneasy smile. He struggled to remember her face as she handed him her number. Him. The doctor, a man she could respect. A man she could admire. A man she could love and believe in. He smiled again, the smile one gives a patient. "You know," he said, "the triple bypass surgery is a very complex procedure."

ACKNOWLEDGMENTS

Thank you to my family for their continued faith in me, especially my mother, who helped me write my first query letter to a publisher at age eight and provided me a steady supply of typewriters each time one ran out of ink.

I would not have completed this book without the encouragement and feedback of the faculty at the University of Nebraska–Lincoln, especially Jonis Agee, the late Gerald Shapiro, Judith Slater, Amelia Montes, and Margaret Jacobs. Thank you to Tim O'Brien and my friends in his 2008 residency, whose initial questions urged me to continue writing beyond the first chapter. Thank you to David Mura and the folks in the VONA/Voices Workshop for their community. A warm thanks to Susan Hubbard, whose character sketch assignment led to the earliest incarnation of Job Ogbonnaya over a decade ago.

A big thanks to the estates of Louise VanSickle, Wilbur and Elizabeth Gaffney, the University of Nebraska Office of Graduate Studies and the Presidential Fellowship committee, the faculty and staff at the University of Dayton, and the esteemed Herbert Woodward Martin, for whom the Herbert W. Martin Postgraduate fellowship is named. Your generous support enabled me to steal away the hours to write.

And a very special thanks to Anitra Budd and Lisa Kopel, who always believed in the vision of the book and whose insights were invaluable.

Excerpts have appeared in the *Kenyon Review,* the *Tampa Review,* and *Passages North.*

COFFEE HOUSE PRESS

The mission of Coffee House Press is to publish exciting, vital, and enduring authors of our time; to delight and inspire readers; to contribute to the cultural life of our community; and to enrich our literary heritage. By building on the best traditions of publishing and the book arts, we produce books that celebrate imagination, innovation in the craft of writing, and the many authentic voices of the American experience.

Visit us at coffeehousepress.org.

FUNDER ACKNOWLEDGMENTS

Coffee House Press is an independent, nonprofit literary publisher. All of our books, including the one in your hands, are made possible through the generous support of grants and donations from corporate giving programs, state and federal support, family foundations, and the many individuals that believe in the transformational power of literature. We receive major operating support from Amazon, the Bush Foundation, the McKnight Foundation, and Target. This activity is made possible by the voters of Minnesota through a Minnesota State Arts Board Operating Support grant, thanks to a legislative appropriation from the arts and cultural heritage fund. Our publishing program is also supported in part by the Jerome Foundation and an award from the National Endowment for the Arts. To find out more about how NEA grants impact individuals and communities, visit www.arts.gov.

Coffee House Press receives additional support from many anonymous donors; the Alexander Family Fund; the Archer Bondarenko Munificence Fund; the Elmer L. & Eleanor J. Andersen Foundation; the David & Mary Anderson Family Foundation; the E. Thomas Binger & Rebecca Rand Fund of the Minneapolis Foundation; the Patrick & Aimee Butler Family Foundation; the Buuck Family Foundation; the Carolyn Foundation; Dorsey & Whitney Foundation; Fredrikson & Byron, P.A.; the Lenfestey Family Foundation; the Mead Witter Foundation; the Schwab Charitable Fund; Schwegman, Lundberg & Woessner, P.A.; Penguin Group; the Private Client Reserve of US Bank; VSA Minnesota for the Metropolitan Regional Arts Council; the Archie D. & Bertha H. Walker Foundation; the Wells Fargo Foundation of Minnesota; and the Woessner Freeman Family Foundation.

THE PUBLISHER'S CIRCLE OF COFFEE HOUSE PRESS

Publisher's Circle members make significant contributions to Coffee House Press's annual giving campaign. Understanding that a strong financial base is necessary for the press to meet the challenges and opportunities that arise each year, this group plays a crucial part in the success of our mission.

PUBLISHER'S CIRCLE MEMBERS INCLUDE:

Many anonymous donors, Mr. & Mrs. Rand L. Alexander, Suzanne Allen, Patricia Beithon, Bill Berkson & Connie Lewallen, Robert & Gail Buuck, Claire Casey, Louise Copeland, Jane Dalrymple-Hollo, Mary Ebert & Paul Stembler, Chris Fischbach & Katie Dublinski, Katharine Freeman, Sally French, Jocelyn Hale & Glenn Miller, Jeffrey Hom, Kenneth & Susan Kahn, Kenneth Koch Literary Estate, Stephen & Isabel Keating, Allan & Cinda Kornblum, Leslie Larson Maheras, Jim & Susan Lenfestey, Sarah Lutman & Rob Rudolph, Carol & Aaron Mack, George Mack, Joshua Mack, Gillian McCain, Mary & Malcolm McDermid, Sjur Midness & Briar Andresen, Peter Nelson & Jennifer Swenson, Marc Porter & James Hennessy, E. Thomas Binger & Rebecca Rand Fund of the Minneapolis Foundation, the Rehael Fund-Roger Hale & Nor Hall of the Minneapolis Foundation, Jeffrey Sugerman & Sarah Schultz, Nan Swid, Patricia Tilton, Stu Wilson & Melissa Barker, Warren D. Woessner & Iris C. Freeman, and Margaret & Angus Wurtele.

For more information about the Publisher's Circle and other ways to support Coffee House Press books, authors, and activities, please visit www.coffeehousepress.org/support or contact us at: info@coffeehousepress.org.

ALLAN KORNBLUM, 1949–2014

Vision is about looking at the world and seeing not what it is,
but what it could be. Allan Kornblum's vision and leadership created
Coffee House Press. To celebrate his legacy, every book we
publish in 2015 will be in his memory.

Mr. and Mrs. Doctor was designed at Coffee House Press, in the historic Grain Belt Brewery's Bottling House near downtown Minneapolis. The text is set in Garamond with Century Gothic used as display.

LITERATURE
is not the same thing as
PUBLISHING

Julie Iromuanya's work has appeared in *Tampa Review, Passages North,* the *Kenyon Review,* and *Cream City Review,* among other publications. She earned her PhD from the University of Nebraska–Lincoln and is currently an assistant professor at Northeastern Illinois University, where she teaches creative writing and Africana literature. *Mr. and Mrs. Doctor* is her first novel.